Take the Donut

Also by Annie Hansen

Kelly Clark Mystery Series

GIVE ME CHOCOLATE

BEAN IN LOVE

Take the Donut

Annie Hansen

HF
Publishing

Take the Donut copyright © 2016 by Annie Hansen.
Published by HF Publishing
Cover design by Cristen Leifheit
Becky's Cinnamon Chip Scones recipe © 2016 by Rebecca Wit.
Reprinted by permission of Rebecca Wit

ISBN: 978-0692778098 (soft cover)

Dedication

In loving memory of Thomas Edward McCarter (Dad)

November 15, 1943-September 2, 2015

Chapter 1

"So, I'll see you back in Chicago?" Jack asked, looking over at me from the passenger seat.

His killer green eyes rested on me for what I knew would be our last quiet moment for some time. The way he was looking at me made me want to drop all of my plans, grab his hand in mine and beg him not to go home yet. He knew. I could just tell. Was he going to let it go and wait for me to say something, or confront me?

"I'll be home as soon as I can," I finally managed, my voice shaky and weak. "I just want to make sure Dad is settled. This was so much more than I thought it would be."

My eyes fell from his and started searching the console like I was looking for something. I was. I was looking for time. Time to make up a better lie than the one I planned to use. But in the confines of the tiny car, with all of the pressure that comes with the airport departures lane closing in on me, I was unable to find more. It was time for Jack to go and for me to do what I needed to do. Alone.

As if on cue, a horn behind me sounded, reminding us both that there was no time to second guess.

"He's doing great. Everything is going to be okay, Kelly," Jack said, pulling my hand into his giant ones. He put his lips to my hand, making me want to crawl into his lap.

"Hey, baby, look at me," he said quietly.

I met his eyes, trying to soak in all of his features one last time before he stepped out of the car. His dark hair had grown a bit longer in the three weeks we'd spent in Florida. I loved the way the color contrasted with his light eyes, making them shimmer with a sexy spark. The long hairs near his neck curled a bit, making him appear more playful, but I knew it bothered him. It didn't fit the role he played in his non-vacation life as an attorney for a Chicago law firm. It was time to let go of laid back, Florida Jack and go back to Corporate Jack. Too bad. Even in the midst of my dad's health crisis, we'd managed to take some breaks for fun time. I'd miss our surfing, running, and chilling on the beach. Going back home meant going back to a lot of responsibilities.

"We went at just the right time. The surgery opened up the blockage and now he's taking his health much more seriously. He's going to be fine."

My dad's heart surgery had been a surprise to all of us. But in a way, we were all expecting it. My mom had been commenting more and more on his shortness of breath, fatigue, and crabbiness. It took Jack and me coming down to Florida to finally make him go to the doctor and have the surgery.

Though my sisters wanted to be here, I was the obvious choice to stay for the recovery since my life was a little more flexible. Being a writer allowed me a certain level of freedom, but these last three weeks I'd gotten nothing accomplished as far as my writing. But that didn't matter. My parent's health trumped all. There would always be time for me to write.

"I don't know what I would have done without you here," I sighed, trying my best to give him a confident smile.

My goal was to get him on the plane feeling confident about our relationship without a doubt that I loved him and was committed to our future. I was committed, but there were still a few doors that needed to be closed. I had a plan, and in order to accomplish what I hoped, that meant going behind his back. Going behind everyone's back. Everyone I loved would have to be kept in the dark. There was just no other way.

"We're a great team," he said, leaning over to pull my face closer to his.

His breath had a slight hint of citrus to it, probably left over from the oranges we'd eaten for breakfast in my parent's condo before heading to the airport. I breathed it in and closed my eyes moving closer to him.

"Always," I said, connecting my lips to his. He kissed me back, softly at first, just barely running his lips over mine, then with a little more passion. "I love you," I whispered, when we were done with our kiss, keeping my face close to his and running my hand along his strong jawline.

"I love you, too, temptress," he smiled back at me, using his favorite pet name for me. "Come home soon. It will be empty without you. I hate the thought of it," Jack whispered in my ear.

The home he was referring to was the condo we shared in Geneva, a suburb forty minutes west of the city of Chicago. It made me sad to think of him there alone for too long. I would have to be quick.

"I will," I promised.

Goodbye, Jack. Please don't be mad at me.

* * * * *

"Mom, I'm home," I called, closing the front door behind me after the ride back from the airport. Traffic had picked up after dropping Jack off, making me later than I had planned. Miami traffic could be unpredictable in that way. Mom and I were planning on shopping this afternoon. We still had plenty of time, but needless to say, Mom would be stressed by my late arrival.

"In here, honey. We're talking to Nikki," she called from the master bedroom. "Come here. She wants to say hello to you."

I dropped my purse and keys onto the kitchen table, off to the left of the foyer. Making my way further into the condo, I stopped briefly to stare out at the aquamarine color of the ocean visible through the balcony off the living room. It never ceased to amaze me what a gorgeous view of the Atlantic Ocean my parents had. No wonder they didn't want to come back to Chicago.

"Kelly?" I heard my dad call. His weak voice snapped me back to reality.

"Coming," I called, heading quickly down the hallway leading to the master bedroom. On the way, I passed the large guest bedroom I had shared with Jack. The bed would be so lonely without him. Already, my body ached to have him next to me again.

I tapped open the grand double doors leading to my parent's master suite and spotted them on the king bed, the phone in between them. Normally, it felt awkward walking into my parent's intimate space. As kids, we were taught to give them privacy and knock before entering their room. But the last couple of weeks had changed so much. All the walls were down. My dad had been so sick and helpless. He needed me and I was happy to be there for him during that time. I had been everything to him. His nurse, his hygienist, his companion. There was always a strong bond with my parents, but now there was a new level of comfort and intimacy. Illness broke down walls and changed dynamics in the blink of an eye. As horrible as it was to face those dark times with them, I was happy to be a part of it all. They deserved to have help, and especially from me. They'd sacrificed and given so much for me to get to a better place when my life went down the tubes.

The guilt I had been feeling since I arrived in Miami once again punched me in the gut. Had I caused this? Was it the stress of dealing with what had happened to me that sent my dad to this place?

I did this to them.

"Everything okay?" I asked, shaking my head slightly to rid the evil voices.

Dad waved me over to the bed to sit down. "She's heading to the doctor. She only has a few minutes."

He flashed me a radiant smile and leaned back down on his pillow, visibly relaxing. Everything seemed to have a heightened sense of panic nowadays when it came to my dad. He was rushing us in everything and everyway. The doctors said this anxiety and impulsivity would be normal after the surgery. Eventually, he would settle down. I worried though how Mom would handle it and when he would re-set.

"Here you go, honey," she said, handing me the phone. I couldn't help but notice she was watching me like a hawk. What was going on?

"Hey, Nikki" I said, trying to keep the mood light. Dad's head drooped back on the pillow and his eyelids shut for a few seconds.

"Can I talk to you alone?" Nikki asked.

"No, we're all here," I said, keeping a smile plastered on my face.

"Get alone. Now."

"Should I put you on speaker?" I asked, trying to make Nikki understand how impossible her request was.

Dad was now watching me through hooded eyes, and Mom was practically sitting on my lap. Who was I kidding? There was no reason to even try and hide from Mom. She knew all of her daughters so well; she seemed to be able to project herself into our minds at any time. She probably already knew what Nikki was going to say, whatever it was.

"Go outside and call me back on your cell phone. Quick."

"You gotta go in now? Ok. That's great that the doctor is on time. They're never on time. Remember the time I waited two hours to see the dermatologist and then he rescheduled?" I laughed uneasily, rambling on. "Ok, talk to you soon."

I reached over and hung up the phone on the handset on my parent's dresser.

"The doctor just walked in the room. She had to go."

"I thought she said she was at home and had to leave for the doctor?" Dad said. His brows furrowed down on his forehead and his lips formed an upside down U.

"No, honey, she was at the doctor," my mom said, confirming my story. "We're going to let you get some rest now. You look tired."

My dad laid his head back on his pillow and let out a sigh. He looked ancient right now and that broke my heart. The surgery was supposed to have helped him, not age him fifty years. What if it had been a big mistake? What if I could never leave them?

"We'll check on you in an hour. Just relax."

We walked from the room both glancing back at Dad before leaving. From the way his breathing flowed at a steady pace, he looked as though he was already dozing or well on his way. We both turned to look at each other with raised eyebrows, asking a million questions without saying a word.

"He's so tired," I commented.

"He's okay, honey. He just needs a nap. He didn't sleep well last night. Don't worry, Dad always looks so much worse when he needs a nap. He'll be better when he wakes. You'll see. The doctor said he would be very tired and then bounce. I can already see huge improvements."

We stood for a moment in silence.

"I'm going to head out for a run," I said, unable to shake Nikki's anxious request to call her back without an audience.

"How are Bob's travels going with his parents?" I asked

casually, referring to Nikki's in-law's annual three week trip to Italy. They always returned just in time for Christmas. This year her husband, Bob, had chosen to go with them, seeing this might be his last chance to go before the baby came. Could her news be in regards to them?

"They're doing great," Mom said, taking my hand in hers. "You just got back, honey. Let's talk for a second before you go. I just want to have a plan for dinner before you go at least. And what about shopping?"

"We can still go. I'll be back quick. But, let's go talk about dinner first," I said, wrapping my arm around her and pulling her down the hall away from the master bedroom. She snuggled into me and wrapped an arm around my waist. I wasn't ready for this. She still needed to be the parent. Not the other way around. I wouldn't be good at this.

Please, God. Not yet. At least let them see me land. Let them see a solid landing after the fall.

"Fish?"

"Yes," I agreed. My mouth opened to say more but I stopped. Whatever she wanted was fine.

"Viola will come over to sit with him while we go shop," she said, referring to their neighbor. "Let's just stay close. I can't leave him for long."

"Yeah, let's stick local. It's not worth going far. We'll be too stressed," I agreed.

Earlier in the day, we had talked about visiting a specialty grocery store my mom was excited to introduce me to, but as the day marched on and the reality of the effort it would take to get there set in, it seemed better to stay close to home.

"Give me an hour. I'll be showered and ready," I promised.

"Okay, go call Nikki back," Mom said, raising an eyebrow at me. She turned to head back to their bedroom.

"What?" she said when she turned once more to look at me. "You honestly think I don't know when something is wrong? Go, quick. Get the story. And don't spare me any details. I can handle a lot. But I can't handle you girls lying to me, Kelly."

With that, she headed down the hall, leaving me standing alone just outside the kitchen. There were no secrets in this family. As hard as I tried, it always came out. Should I just tell Nikki where I was going? Was that what this was about? Had she found out about my plan? Or could it be the baby? Please God, no. Please spare the baby. Nikki deserved a healthy baby. She'd been through so much already with the morning sickness. And I needed to keep making progress. I'd been on such a good track lately.

Please allow the light into this dark place, God. Continue to walk me out of the tunnel.

"Out of the tunnel?" a strange voice echoed.

"Ahhhh," I screamed, pulling my hands up in front of my mouth.

A short woman in front of me dropped the little platter of donuts she'd been holding, causing a cloud of powdered sugar to sprinkle our feet with a small "poof." Her donuts rolled in every direction like little wheels. I watched her watching them roll away and immediately felt remorse.

"I'm so sorry," she began.

"I," I stammered, watching this unfamiliar woman express herself with her short, plump arms.

"The door was open. I didn't mean to scare you. I was just dropping these treats. It's from us. I mean, the condo board." She spoke in a heavy New York accent and let out a long breath as though deflating.

In the weird part of my brain that registers odd details, I noted that because the floors here in Miami were all tiled, unlike the carpeted entrance area in my condo in Geneva, the donuts were not going to be difficult to clean up. And, who was I kidding; I would still be happy to eat them. The pleaser in me wanted to pick one up right now and eat one to show her they wouldn't be wasted.

"Julie?" Mom came from around the corner.

"Barbara, how are you? I'm so sorry to scare Kelly. Especially at a time like this," Julie said, reaching out and hugging my mom.

I relaxed a bit seeing my mom's obvious recognition and acceptance of Julie's presence. I bent to gather the donuts, and Julie pulled up the Mumu style dress she was wearing to assist me. It gave me a second to really check her out and take her in. Her hair, dyed an unnatural shade of black, was teased, sticking out in all directions from her head. Her bright, dramatic make-up was heavily applied. Everything about this woman screamed party. Colors and cheer and vibrancy. She fit right in with the Miami crowd I'd observed. The people, especially the women, really embraced the vibrancy of the city and dressed the part.

"Thank you so much for coming," my mom said, beckoning Julie in.

The phone began to ring in the kitchen, giving me the perfect opportunity to excuse myself and grab my cell phone from my purse in the kitchen. I'd missed three calls from Nikki and she was calling again.

"I'm just going to step out and take this call, Mom. It's Nikki," I said, trying to angle myself around this friendly, yet consuming woman. I wasn't in the mood to make small talk while Nikki so clearly needed to talk. And by the look on Mom's face, she was excited to have the company. And possibly the donuts.

"Wait, you can't go out there," Julie said. She reached out and grabbed my arm a little tighter than what I thought was appropriate. I stopped breathing. What was happening here?

"Don't you know? Hasn't anyone told you yet?" It wasn't until she said those words that I finally noticed the lines of panic around her eyes. And it wasn't about the donuts.

"What is it, Julie?" Mom said, stepping closer to us so that we formed a huddle near the front door. Julie's body blocked the door, keeping me locked in the condo.

"He's out. Your ex-husband, Steve, is out of prison."

Chapter 2

"He's what?" I screeched like a wild animal.

No. Impossible. They said this wouldn't happen. I would be called. They would give me time. He's supposed to be in jail for seven more years for attempted murder. He can't be out yet.

Things shifted into slow motion. I saw Mom's arm reach past me, and the sound of the door bolt settling into the hinge seemed to vibrate through the room for a full minute. It should have been comforting, but it only offered a sense of frailty to the situation. Really? That was all we had? A deadbolt? It wasn't going to be nearly enough.

Julie and Mom simply stared at me, waiting for what, I didn't know. Perhaps there had been a huge mistake. Of course. A mistake.

Their eyebrows raised, they continued to stare.

Wait, the phone. That's why they were staring at me that way. The phone I was holding was ringing in my hand. Julie actually held up her pinky finger and thumb to her face, mimicking the actions of answering the phone. Little beads on the sleeves of her shirt jingled as she shook her pretend phone near her face.

It took a second to come back to reality. I began to register the sounds all around me-the waves of the ocean tumbling into the sand, the jingling of Julie's colorful shirt, the shrill ringing of the telephone, and the absence of Mom's voice or breath.

"Perhaps, you should answer?" Julie said softly.

Mom stood as still as a statue, an unnatural gray color spreading on her face. She looked as though she were turning into granite right before my eyes.

"Barbara, what's the matter?" I heard Dad call from the back bedroom.

Mom's look of pure panic set me into motion.

"Hello?" I managed.

"Don't panic. We don't know for sure yet."

Nikki's tone made my heart sink. Whenever things were really bad, Nikki went into a calm, serene mode. Like a General taking charge of battle.

"They just let him go?" I asked, baffled by the reasoning behind that choice.

He tried to kill his pregnant mistress. He was a monster. How could they let my ex-husband out? Didn't they know how dangerous he was and what this would do to my life?

"No, nothing like that. It's his prison. There's been a jailbreak. A guard was killed."

"But they didn't call me."

"No, they called here. Remember, that's how we set it up."

"No, it isn't."

"We decided on the land line for the store, remember?"

"No, we didn't. I wouldn't have said that," I insisted, arguing a moot point. What did it matter where they called?

"Kelly," Nikki said sharply, pulling me back. "What does it matter now?"

They called. This was real. She was right. I was splitting hairs.

Dad called out again from the back bedroom and the sound of the sheets rustling alerted me that he was getting out of bed.

I pointed at Mom, and then threw my finger in the direction of the bedroom. Her eyes flipped to the ringing phone in the kitchen, which stopped abruptly on the second ring. Either Dad had answered or the person had given up. Mom shook her head frantically as though we both figured out what had happened at the same time. She turned and ran to the back bedroom. We had to keep him out of this.

"What did they say?" I asked.

Poor Julie just stood there staring at me, as though waiting for direction. Again, the weird place in my mind that took in small details at odd times couldn't help but notice her lavender eyeshadow matched the vibrant colors of her dress. There were even multiple variances of the lavender, leading me to believe she'd intricately applied numerous eyeshadows, not just one. Who had time for that? And why was my brain focused on that right now?

"How do we know it's him? I don't understand," I demanded, turning away from Julie, frustrated by her ability to distract me at a time like this.

It made me feel crazy. Crazier than crazy. My mind was filled with a million questions. A million scenarios. And the key. Would he want it? Is that what he was after? Would he come here? Would he go after his mistress, Mandy, the poor woman who ended up having his child, not realizing he'd been married to me when they'd conceived a baby? What was his plan? It hit me then what Nikki had said-he'd killed a guard. He'd killed again. I couldn't believe it. Years after it happened, it was still unbelievable to me that the man I had once loved and committed my life to had the capacity to attempt to kill someone. And now he'd attempted again, but this time he'd succeeded.

"There was some sort of malfunction with the computer systems in the jail. They think the security system was hacked, and they can't account for some of the prisoners. A guard was killed and his uniform and weapon were taken."

"They can't account for them? What does that mean, Nikki? Why do they think Steve is one of the ones missing?"

"They're not sure. They wouldn't give me a clear answer.

Something about identification numbers being messed up because of the computers being hacked."

"Julie, how did you know?" I asked, turning back to her.

Julie's eyes widened a bit and her mouth formed a small O. I noticed a blush fill her cheeks that made the color she applied on her own glow an unnatural pink.

"Your mom told me about what you went through, Kelly. We play cards together on Fridays. I'm so sorry."

"No, not about me, or my past. I mean the fact that he's out of jail."

"Oh," Julie said, the high pink on her cheeks lightning up. "It's on the news. It's on CNN. We knew what jail Steve was in and they're covering it. Here, let me show you."

With the phone still to my ear, I followed Julie into the living room.

"Shall I?" she said, picking up the television remote and pointing it to my parent's large flat screen.

I nodded my head yes. At the same time someone else knocked on my parent's front door. Julie and I both froze and locked eyes.

"I'll get that," I heard Mom say in a hurried voice.

"What's happening?" Nikki questioned.

"Someone is at the front door and Julie is turning on CNN. Apparently, there is some kind of coverage of the jail."

"Don't answer the door," Nikki said.

"Nikki, he can't be here already if this just happened."

"Kelly, don't answer it. What if this escape has set his game in play?"

The fact that Nikki thought of this made me freeze in place. Her voice still held that cold, commanding tone.

"Mom, don't answer it," I said, feeling a cold, sickening feeling rush through me.

"It's okay. It's just Tony, the doorman. I asked him to come up here," she said. "Oh, and honey, pick up the landline in the kitchen when it rings. Detective Pavlik from Geneva is going to call in one minute."

"Oh, thank God. Wait, did Dad hear? Does he know?"

"Sort of," she said, moving toward the door.

Mom swished her hand in the air, not committing to an answer. I knew she would have to tell him something. It would be worse if he was left guessing. Hopefully, she spared him a little bit.

"I just spoke to Detective Pavlik. He's in on everything," Nikki interjected in my ear. I'll let you go so you can talk to him. What about Jack? Should I text him? What if he sees some live coverage of this somehow?

"Yes, text him right now. He should be mid-flight by now, but just in case he can receive a text, that's a good idea. I will do the same shortly. Let me just take this call. Wait, you talked to Detective Pavlik already? What did he say?"

"He's going to be your middle man with the Department of Corrections in California. Kelly, I'm so glad you are not here. I'm in Chocolate Love now and people are coming in asking about you. I think you should stay in Miami for a bit and let this cool down regardless of if this is Steve or not. I'm up in your apartment for some privacy. Wait, someone is at the door," Nikki said, cutting off.

I imagined Nikki pacing the top floor of the beautiful Victorian home she owned with her husband on Third Street, the main commercial area in the Historic District of Geneva. She ran her hugely successful specialty dessert shop, Chocolate Love, out of the main floor of the home.

"It's Miquel. He said there are reporters downstairs looking for you. Kelly, can I call you back? I have to handle the crap storm that's developing downstairs. Let me call you back. Are you okay?" Nikki asked.

A thousand scenes ran through my head. How to best explain the way I was feeling? Steve was out. I thought I had more time, more minutes, hours, weeks, and years to figure out what I would do should I have to see Steve again and come face-to-face with that smirk. That gorgeous, deceitful smirk that ruined my life.

Scenes from that terrible night I found out he was having an affair and planned to kill his pregnant mistress played out in my head. Luckily, I'd managed to make it to the police just in time to stop it from happening and put him away for ten years. Now I spent nearly every minute of every day wondering what kind of revenge he would take on me for turning him in. I thought I had seven more years to worry about it, but apparently he couldn't wait.

I thought about the key in my bag. The one I'd found in a jacket back in Geneva last month. Steve was not only cheating on me, he was cheating on our finances. Only after I began the divorce proceedings did I find out just how much debt he had left us in under my name. I was making headway paying down the credit cards and other debts, but there was still a ways to go. The key I'd found, plus the woman he'd sent to kill me last summer were both signs that I'd just hit the tip of the iceberg. Steve was definitely hiding more, and I was determined to find out everything. I knew that I would never be free from him until I did.

You want the key, come and get it.

"I'm okay," I said to Nikki in response to her question.

Squaring my shoulders back, I lifted my chin and pursed my lips together. Enough. I'd had enough of living in fear. It was time to fight back. I was sick of being scared.

"Okay, I'll call you back in a couple minutes."

My parent's phone in the kitchen was ringing. Mom was busy at the front door talking to Tony Avila, a long, lanky man with a clean shave, a slight paunch, and a dark suit he wore as the uniform for head of security at my parent's high rise. His graying temples made me estimate his age to be somewhere in his late-forties, but the way his lips quivered at me in an attempted smile forced me to knock a few years off. All of a sudden I wished I would have looked into the security for the building a little better. I knew there was always someone posted at the front desk, but what did that mean exactly? How closely were they watching who came in and out of the building?

My mind raced to the back entrance to the building from the public beach. The building was separated from the beach by large black iron gates that you needed to be buzzed through by entering a code. Were there cameras there as well? I couldn't remember. Just a few hours ago, Jack and I had casually strolled on that beach and walked through those gates after our last morning walk, blissfully unaware that my safety was about to be compromised once again.

"Hello?" I said, nodding briefly back at Tony while taking the call.

Tony watched me closely, so much so that I felt a bit uncomfortable speaking in front of him. I walked further into the kitchen, shutting the small, wooden, louvered doors that separated the kitchen from the entrance hall, so I could have some privacy. The doors reminded me of large plantation shutters, so as far as privacy went, they might block the view, but sound was still going to be very audible.

"Kelly, this is Detective Pavlik."

I nodded my head, trying for words.

"From the Geneva Police Department?"

"Yes, of course, hello, thank you for calling," I said, cringing slightly.

Hearing his voice reminded me of the fiasco we'd been involved in a few short months ago solving a murder together at the Geneva History Museum. Nikki had roped me into hunting down a killer and Detective Pavlik had helped. Thank God he was the proverbial "good cop." I liked working with him. He was courteous, open to talking with us, and most of all, calming. He had the same effect on me now. It was nice to hear a familiar, steady voice in the midst of this crisis.

"Are you okay, kiddo?"

Detective Pavlik was a few years younger than my parents and was nuts about Nikki's chocolate store. Our shared love of chocolate was one of the things that we bonded over when we first met. He religiously came into her store, claiming he was buying treats for his grandkids and adult daughters, but Nikki caught him a number of times diving into the treat bags on his way out of the store. I swear those magical chocolates had afforded us much needed leniency when it came to our amateur sleuthing adventures in Geneva. Nikki and I both knew we needed to keep him on our side, so she continued to satisfy his craving for sweets.

"I'm okay," I sighed. "Can you tell me anything? Did you talk to someone from the jail?"

"I've only spoken with the Department of Corrections. They've confirmed that there's been a breach in security at your husband's prison, but for some reason they're having a hard time identifying which inmate or inmates have escaped. Something about the computers being infiltrated. I've already contacted them to try and get more information. They're doing headcount and reviewing tapes. I know for sure one of the guards was killed, and it was from your ex-husband's section. They're just being precautious and calling all of the families of high risk cases from the area where there was a breach, like yourself. It's hitting the media pretty fast. God knows how they get their info."

"That's so horrible," I sighed. "How did this happen? I don't understand. I just can't believe this kind of thing can happen at a maximum security prison?"

"It's awful," Detective Pavlik said. "This is definitely not the norm but think about it. You're talking about desperate people locked up in a desperate situation. One little slip up of protocol and something can go wrong. They just need to catch whoever it was fast and end this. There's going to be a lot of people like you out there waiting to hear if they are in jeopardy. And the press is going to have a field day with this. You'll need to watch yourself and just stay on lockdown for a bit. Don't talk to any press. Can you imagine the poor family of that guard that was killed?"

I nodded silently thinking of Mandy, Steve's mistress he tried to kill, or "Mandy the Mistress," as Nikki liked to call her, and baby Caroline somewhere out there. Was someone contacting them? Was she scared like me?

"I've just placed another call there and am waiting to hear back."

Detective Pavlik kept speaking, but I zoned him out. The last I had heard from Mandy, she was still living in California. She was only a few hours from his prison. Could Steve get to her? But why would he even try? The only reason he had planned to murder her was to keep his secret. And it was all out now.

"And best to stay put, of course," Detective Pavlik was saying.

"What?"

"I said you should stay put where you are for now. Don't go out anywhere. Your story was too big in the media. You might have a little bit of media frenzy over the next day or so until this dies down and Steve is captured or killed."

I gasped slightly.

"Or whoever this is," he said quickly.

A cold shiver ran through me, making me wrap my arms around my body. I sat down at my parent's small kitchen table, scissoring my legs together.

"So, you're confident he will be captured and returned to prison?"

The sound of a click distracted me. Dad. He had been listening on the other phone in the bedroom. I closed my eyes and let out a sigh.

"Kelly?" Detective Pavlik said. "Can you hear me okay?"

"Yes. Sorry. What were you saying?"

"I've got to go. I have a call coming in. Can I call you back?"

"Please. As soon as you hear something."

"Sit tight, kiddo. You'll be okay."

An unnatural silence settled in on the condo.

"No news," I called out to Tony, Julie, and Mom, who I assumed were out there listening to every word I'd said. The cell phone in my hand started to ring. Caller ID notified me that Nikki was calling once again.

"Hello?" I said.

"Kelly, it's me," my older sister, Adelle, said. "Are you okay?"

"Yes, I'm just waiting for more news." I said, putting my head down on the kitchen table. When the louvered doors to the kitchen were closed like they were right now, it gave the room a warm, cocoon-like feel. My parents had chosen to refinish the room with dark cabinets and canned lighting, which made it resemble the kitchen they had in our old home back in Geneva growing up. I tried my best to imagine being back in that place in my childhood when all was safe, and I wasn't associated with a sociopath.

"I'm here at Chocolate Love. It's a mob scene. Your picture is on the news, Kelly. The news hounds have sniffed you out, I hate to tell you."

"Wonderful," I countered.

"How are Mom and Dad?" Adelle asked.

I let out another sigh. Here I was again, dragging my poor parents and sisters through a round of drama. It was like subjecting them to boxing rounds. Come one, come all! Watch Kelly Clark's family get beaten to a pulp!

My parents didn't need this right now. My dad was recovering. I needed to tell Mom that Dad had overheard my conversation with

Detective Pavlik, but I just didn't have the heart to do it yet.

"They're coping," I said, knowing that Mom probably had her ear pressed up to the door.

"You're in the right place, Kelly," Adelle said. "You really shouldn't be here right now.

"Tell me what's happening there."

"I'm in the back office of Chocolate Love. Nikki is outside dealing with reporters. She's going to close the store for the day until this all calms down."

Groaning to myself, I thought of my poor sister losing business because of my maniac ex-husband's genius idea to escape a maximum level security prison. If it was indeed him.

"Are you with the kids?" I squeaked out, imagining my niece and nephews huddled around Adelle, somehow dressed to perfection even in this whirlwind. The kids were probably taking this all in and forming judgments in their little minds about me.

"Why is Aunt Kelly always in trouble?"

"No, they are home with Mike. I couldn't bring them here. It's too much. There's," Adelle broke off.

"What?" I demanded.

"Well, there are cameras and news people here on Third Street. It's," Adelle stopped when I started groaning again.

"It will die down, Kelly. I'm sure they'll capture whoever broke out and this will all be over in a couple of hours. You know how the news is. On to the next. There's just too much going on in the world to stay focused on one thing."

"I know. But what if they don't get him, Adelle? What if he just vanishes into the world, and now I have to carry on with my life, waiting for him to ring my doorbell or crawl in my window one day? I was doing so well, and now I'm right back to that horrible place. At least when he was in jail, I knew where he was. This is awful," I said, lifting my head up.

"Okay, but think about it this way. This could be a good thing. If he did break out and they capture him, his sentence will be extended for life. What was he thinking? This is so stupid of him to do. This is going to sound crazy, but he's too smart to attempt something like this. My bet is he's not even out. He's probably sitting comfortably in his cell right now," Adelle said.

Thinking of ways to kill me, I wanted to add.

I let out another long sigh as my mind raced to Jack. I imagined him on the plane, his phone flooded with texts that were undeliverable until he landed. What would he do? Would he get right back on and return to Florida? Knowing Jack, that was exactly what he would do.

I was distracted from my call by more knocking at the front door and hushed speaking. I heard Mom greeting more people, who I assumed to be her friends in the building. Over the past couple of weeks while staying here, I'd met a number of her friends. She and Dad appeared to be quite popular in this high-rise. It wasn't technically a retirement community, but most of the residents were around their age and had formed tight bonds and social groups.

"Honey, Viola is here," Mom said, peeking her head into the kitchen.

I glanced out and saw Tony, Julie, and Viola staring curiously into the kitchen behind my mother. Beyond them, a few other faces that were familiar to me watched me with great interest.

I waved my mom into the kitchen, motioning her to close the little wooden door behind her so that we could have some privacy.

"Mom, you have to get everyone out of here," I said in a hushed tone. "This is a three ring circus. It's going to stress Dad out," I said, still keeping Adelle tucked into my ear.

"Well, they're here to offer assistance. They're my friends," Mom said defensively, putting her hands on her hips and sticking out her lower lip a bit. Although she was taking a defensive stance,

I could see she was on the verge of tears. Her tiny frame seemed to fold into itself, and the little hump that I worried about on her upper back looked more pronounced.

"Can we just tell them we'll call once we have a better grip on this? I feel like a circus freak right now with them all staring at me," I said, trying to remain calm.

My parents didn't have any other family down here. Between the dinners and gifts dropped off and the assistance offered over the past few weeks for my dad, I was beginning to see how much of a family they had created in this group of people. It wasn't my intention to insult them. I just needed some space to wrap my brain around what was going on.

Mom stood in a stunned silence staring at me. This look had become familiar to me over the last couple of weeks and was so alien on my mother's face. She had been such a decision maker and captain of our ship in Geneva raising the Clark girls. Who was this deer in the headlights? Where was my mom?

"Let's get Tony in here," I said, pointing to the door.

Mom clicked back suddenly and came to life.

"Okay, but you're not going to like what he has to say," she said, turning on her heel and pushing one of the small wooden doors open.

Chapter 3

"Adelle, can I call you back?" I asked.

"What's going on?" Adelle asked.

"I have to talk to Mom's security guard, or front doorman, or, I don't know. Tony, you know, the gentlemen at the front?"

"Wait, why is he there?"

"I don't know. Why is Mom allowing twenty people to crowd into the condo right now? Maybe she's trying to form a human shield around me or something. I have to go," I snapped.

"You sound irritated," Adelle said, stating the obvious. "You need to give Mom a break. She's dealing with a lot right now."

"I am irritated. I'm just so sick of this. It's embarrassing. Can you imagine dealing with this, Adelle? I feel like a comic book character being stalked by the evil villain or something. This isn't a life; it's a front page story. It's no way to live."

"Kelly, you need to calm down. A lot of people are dealing with a lot of things, including our own mother. In a few hours, this will all be over and Steve will still be in jail, so chill out, get yourself together, and deal with this. Call me back," Adelle said, disconnecting abruptly.

Whoa. That was much more biting than Adelle normally was. Her words stung, putting me in my place.

A lot of people are dealing with a lot of things.

What had she meant by that? Adelle had just gone through a major downsizing in her life after her husband's business took a turn for the worst. But I thought she was through that? Things had seemed so good between her and Mike over the past few months. Had I missed something?

I hung up the phone feeling rightfully chastised, irritated, and concerned at the same time. But, not scared. How lovely. Not scared. I was starting to feel a sense of irritation and anger that was new, and yet, refreshing.

"Kelly, why are you smiling like that? Did they find him? Have you heard something?" Mom asked. She entered the kitchen, pulling in Tony behind her. I heard a low laughter from the crowd gathered in the hallway, as though someone had just told a joke. Perfect. Perhaps I should pass a tray of appetizers for this impromptu party being held.

"No, they didn't. Is Dad okay?"

"Viola is sitting with him. I'll send everyone out in a minute. I just wanted you to talk with Tony. He thinks we should hire a personal bodyguard."

"Not yet. I just wanted to let you know that we're going to call in more of the staff until we hear more. You know, in case the media catches wind of this. I mean, obviously, they have already, but if they put it together that you're here and Steve is connected to you. But you don't have to worry, Kelly. You're safe here. I just wanted you to know that," Tony said, reaching out his hand to shake mine in a formal gesture that didn't fit the situation. I clasped his hand in both of mine and smiled at him to try and assure him that I was okay. That I wasn't going to freak out at him. He dropped his tense shoulders and smiled back.

"We can even have Matthew come sit up here and guard the door for the rest of the night, if that is what you would like. It would be our pleasure to assist you."

"No, that's not necessary," I replied quickly, releasing his hand. The thought of a guard slumped into an uncomfortable chair outside my parent's door seemed so ridiculous. Or was it? I'd been getting comfortable in my new life with my violent ex-husband behind bars. All this time, that's what I had been striving for. But perhaps, that was making me weak. That was exactly what Steve would want.

"This is all your fault," Steve's mother had hissed at me outside of the courtroom once it was clear things were not going to go well for him. "You're behind all of this. You're not fooling anyone. I always knew you were trouble."

She spat at me so aggressively that drops of spittle landed on the front of her elegant, navy blue suit. My reproach was to say nothing because my attorney pulled me quickly away. I'd never seen hatred that alive and ready to strike. She reminded me of a wild cobra. As angry as she was, my immediate thought was one of sympathy. I wanted to say, "He really did a number on you, too, huh?"

There was also a bit of me that saw for the first time how someone like Steve came to be. I knew I had to cut ties entirely from every member of his monstrous clan.

My mom must have sensed my hesitation because she said, "Well, what if we just see how things progress over the next hour. Can you have someone on call if we deem this necessary?"

"They're giving an update on the news. You should come in here and see this," Julie said, swinging the doors open from the other side of the kitchen that led to the living room.

One side of her spiked hairdo looked deflated, as though she had been nervously playing with it while stationed in front of the television, and her Mumu hung over her left shoulder exposing her bra strap. Just a few minutes inside the Clark home and she was a nervous wreck. That's how much stress I brought into this environment. Seeing her like this made me worry for my father.

I decided at that point to head to him. If he had any sense of what was going on, which I was sure now he did, I needed to be with him.

It was best to just let him see my face and be with me. He was still my dad. The absence of me was probably much worse than me being with him right now.

"Excuse me," I said, turning and moving swiftly to the kitchen doors in the other direction of Julie.

The crowd of people in the hall stopped speaking as a whole and stared at me in a collective shocked silence. I imagined they were too polite to rush into my mother's living room to see the news, yet too curious to keep their open mouth stares from my face.

"Excuse me," I mumbled, avoiding eye contact. An aisle was formed for me to pass and someone touched my arm as I passed.

"Whatever you need, Kelly. We're here for you and your parents," a woman I did not know said. The kindness in her voice made me change my attitude. All at once, I was glad to have them here. These people were my parent's support system, just like my mom had said. I would be here only for a short time, but their friends would be here long after I went back to Chicago. And clearly, they knew my scandalous, embarrassing past and didn't hold that against my parents or ostracize them. These were true friends.

I stopped briefly and turned toward her. She had white, close cut hair and eyes the color of the ocean.

"Thank you," I said sincerely, reaching out to briefly squeeze her outstretched hand before turning back down the hall.

A quick knock on Dad's bedroom door and I was in. His eyes connected with mine as though I were a large glass of water after a dry spell in a desert.

"I'm okay, Dad," I said immediately. Amazingly, he looked twenty years younger than when I had left him a few minutes ago.

"It's not him," he said.

"What?" I asked, feeling a release.

He pointed to the flat screen mounted on the wall opposite the bed. The photo of a middle aged man with facial tattoos leered at me from the screen. A name flashed across the bottom of the screen, and the voice of a reporter rambled on about a man I didn't recognize. I glanced over at Viola who stared at me with wide eyes from the far corner of the room. Viola was a petite woman who reminded me of my mom in many ways. She was always impeccably dressed, easy to be around, and a good solid friend that respected and honored their privacy, which was why my parents often went to her when they needed assistance with my dad.

"I hope it's okay I turned the television on," Viola's shoulders lifted up, almost touching her ears. Her light brown eyes were apologetic.

"It's okay, Viola," I said, rushing over to sit next to Dad on the bed.

"I'm so glad it's not him, Kelly," she said, releasing her shoulders. The corners of her lips turned up, and she looked over at my dad.

"Me, too," I smiled back at her, feeling a great rush of relief fill me.

Allowing my dad's arms to encircle me, I rested my head down on his shoulder and let a single tear escape, thinking of the broad smile I saw on his face just before closing my eyes. This. This was the way it was supposed to be. He was the parent and my protector. My world functioned better this way and apparently, so did his. Just for a little longer. And then I would step up. Just not yet.

"Are you relieved?" he asked softly, placing his cheek on the top of my head.

"Yes and no," I said honestly.

What if it had been him on the run? The odds of him traveling across the country and actually getting to me were probably slim. He wasn't some slick Navy Seal experienced at diverting the authorities. He would have a target on his back with limited means to travel or do anything else for that matter. It would have been so dumb. And he would have been caught and possibly kept longer, just like Adelle had said. But time after time, I'd painfully learned my lesson. Steve was not dumb. No, he was a very intelligent criminal. Except for the one time he was caught. By me.

"Me, too," he said.

We remained silent for a few minutes, frozen in place. Dad's smell, his favorite aftershave, though I was sure he hadn't put any on this morning, was comforting. He'd worn it for so long it seemed as though his sweat glands knew how to produce the scent on their own.

"You're okay, honey?" Mom said from behind me.

I pulled away from Dad slowly and turned to my mom. She had entered the room and Viola had slipped out without my notice. Now, that was stealth.

"I'm okay," I said, nodding my head and reaching over to take her hand. Mom was smiling ear to ear, probably relieved for the quick resolution.

My phone rang in my pocket at the same time the house phone started to ring. A glance at my phone showed Chocolate Love's number in Geneva.

"It says Geneva Police Department," my dad said, looking down at his phone.

"Mom, will you talk to Nikki or Adelle, whoever this is," I said handing her my cell phone. "I'll go talk to Detective Pavlik in the kitchen."

"No," my parents said simultaneously.

"Everyone is still out there. Stay in here for some privacy. And your dad can help you if you need him," Mom said.

Dad tilted his head to the phone.

"Pick it up. Maybe they have more information for you. Hopefully, he was part of the whole thing, and they killed the miserable excuse for a man."

"Dad!" I laughed, matching his light tone.

I couldn't help but delight in the fact that Dad seemed to be having a good time with this now that we were in the clear. Perhaps he needed to be needed. Necessity was the mother of invention and quite possibly the push one needed to heal oneself.

"Hello," I said into the receiver.

"Kelly, you heard?" Detective Pavlik said loudly into the phone.

"Yes, well, just what I saw on television."

"I was able to reach someone in the prison. Sounds like you're in the clear. They've confirmed that there's only one prisoner who managed to escape. Steve is accounted for."

"Were there any other prisoners involved?" I asked, turning away from Dad.

"I'm sorry, what did you say? The office is nuts today. Sorry to have to tell you this, Kelly, but this news has caused quite a ruckus here in town. We're getting calls from the media for information. Your little fiasco is big news here in our quiet little town."

"Ugh," I groaned. "I was just wondering if you heard anything about the details of the jail break. Something more about the security breach?"

"No, nothing. They're tight lipped right now. This is all pretty humiliating for them to have something like this happen. All I really know is the name of the prisoner, but that's about it."

"Who was it?"

"Franklin Ford. He's in for double murder. Does that name mean anything to you?" he asked. "I'll be with you in one second," I heard him say quietly.

My dad tapped me on the shoulder drawing my attention away from the phone. His eyes wrinkled and his finger pointed to the television.

"That's him," my dad said.

Across the screen, the name Franklin Ford flashed in bold white writing with the words ESCAPED PRISONER. God, I hated the media. They made everything seem like a party.

"No, I don't know him. Doesn't sound familiar to me at all," I said into the phone, shaking my head.

My thoughts raced to the poor family members of whoever it was he killed and what they were going through right now. I pictured them huddled together in a bedroom just like we were now, trying to decide what to do next. They were probably desperate to gain some level of control in this downward spiral of a nightmare.

"Good. Then put it out of your head, hang out with your family, and try your best to put this whole thing behind you," Detective Pavlik said with a little laugh at the end.

"Yeah, right," I said, the side of my lip pulling into a smirk.

"Oh, and don't come home," he said gravely.

"What?"

"I mean, right now. Don't come home over the next few days. Let this die down. Something else crazy will happen to take over all this, and you'll be in the clear. But for now, if you want peace and quiet, I suggest you hang low in Miami," he said.

"What now?" I heard him ask, sounding uncharacteristically annoyed.

"Everything okay?" I asked.

"Yeah, it's the media. It's my Achilles' heel. I can't stand when they beat us to all this information. How do they know this stuff so fast? Our media relations manager is out today, and I've called him in. He can't get here fast enough. This is getting out of control."

"Oh, don't tell me that," I groaned again.

"No, Kelly, it's okay. You're just talking to the wrong person. These guys make me so crabby. Let me go take care of this and I'll check in with you later. Everything will be fine here."

"I'm sorry this happened, Detective Pavlik."

"This isn't your fault. Don't worry about it. Gotta go," he said, disconnecting.

Sure, this wasn't my fault, but coming home to Geneva after my divorce in California had brought so much drama back to my small town. That wasn't my intention, but it sure was happening. Drama followed me like a shadow.

I hung up the phone and turned to look at Mom. She'd disconnected from Nikki and was sitting next to me on the bed, waiting for me to hang up.

"Well, that's that then. Don't worry, your sister is sending over a boatload of those chocolates Detective Pavlik likes to thank him for his help today. All's well that ends well," she said, standing up and pulling down her white cotton shirt over her pink Capri pants. "I'll just go ask everyone for a little privacy. See, Kelly, everything is okay. She handed the phone back to me and turned quickly to the door, stumbling a bit as she turned.

"What else did Nikki say?" I asked, raising an eyebrow.

Sometimes my life felt like watching a horror movie set to a soundtrack. After the traumatic scene we just had, the music should be dying down now, but for some reason, I still sensed the frantic violins squeaking away in the background. This was too easy. It was all over now? Steve was locked up? I was safe? False alarm? Chocolates being distributed?

Mom straightened herself by the door and raised her eyes up to the ceiling as she spoke.

"I spoke with Adelle. All is fine. She said Nikki closed the store for the afternoon and is just trying to keep things quiet. It's all dying down."

"Uh huh," I said, watching my mom's lips shake a bit when she attempted a smile. I would have called her out right then and there if it weren't for my dad in the room.

My parent's phone began to ring. This phone would be ringing non-stop now for the next couple of days as this news spread like a virus to family and friends. My dad needed rest.

Leaning forward together, Dad and I looked over at the caller ID then at each other. Our eyes locked in shared recognition of the number.

This couldn't be happening. Not her. The woman that tormented me for years was back.

Chapter 4

"Who is it?" Mom asked.

Unable to speak, I pointed to the phone.

"No," she said in a caged whisper when she leaned over to look at the caller ID. "But how did she know?"

"She called Chocolate Love, didn't she? She spoke to Nikki," I asked.

Mom's staunch refusal to meet my eyes confirmed my suspicions.

"We were hoping because the number isn't listed, she wouldn't try calling here. How in the world did she find us? That woman is like the CIA/FBI/Scotland Yard combined into one evil force," Mom said, slamming her fists down on her legs.

"We don't know it's her," my father offered, leaning back on his pillow.

Diane Nosely. A fitting name for the nosiest person I have ever encountered in my life. Her press badge gave her permission to make a living off of being, ironically, nosy. Like a blood hound, she'd followed my case from day one back when Steve was arrested. For whatever reason, she was absolutely obsessed with the story and pursued me like I was the key to her Pulitzer Prize.

After the forth ring, the phone stopped and we all took a breath.

"I can paint you in a good light, Kelly. Not everyone feels you were the hero in this story. Some people are rather suspicious of you. When Steve goes to trial, this isn't going to be a slam dunk.

Especially with the angle his mother has been preaching to the press. It's really your word against his," Diane said in a cocky, know-it-all tone.

"What are you talking about, Diane? They caught him red-handed messing with her car. You don't know what you're talking about."

"His family is saying you told him to kill her because you didn't want his mistress and their love child around to haunt you. He says you agreed to take him back if he did that."

"That's insane. I never. There's no proof of that."

"No proof? See, Kelly, now you sound guilty of conspiracy. I can help you. I can coach you to speak the right way to the press. A way that will paint you in the best light. Give me an exclusive. I'll help you, Kelly. I promise. I believe your story. I believe you," Diane had cooed.

Diane was young, blond, attractive, and intelligent with well-respected political parents that gave her instant credibility. Her network gave her a lot of high publicity stories because she seemed to excel at drawing an audience and growing a following. But behind the scenes, Diane had a terrifying, soul sucking gaze that burned into you. She was like a ruthless animal when it came to trying to get the story out of you. I barely ever watched the news anymore, mainly because of my experience with Diane. Everything I watched now seemed like a hoax. I saw firsthand how the media could twist and bend the truth in order to draw more viewers by upping the drama.

"I'm getting everyone out of here. We need to focus on," Mom stopped when the ringing of the phone picked back up.

All three of us leaned in and simultaneously took in the number on the screen. Diane, the soul sucker, was calling again.

"Go, get everyone out. I'll take her call in the kitchen after everyone leaves. She's not going to stop," I said.

"Take it in here," Dad said quickly.

"All I'm going to do is tell her I'm not interested. She needs to hear me say that. You rest, Dad. This has been one hell of a morning. We all need to rest."

I leaned over and pressed the button on his phone that would mute the calls. I thought we had done that yesterday, but for some reason, it had been deactivated. I was pretty sure I knew how.

"Oh, alright. I am losing steam and could use a nap. But promise me if there's anything else that happens, anymore news, you'll wake me," he said, pulling the white duvet up to his chin and turning to his right side. "I'm so glad everything is okay, Kelly," Dad said, eyes already shut. "Still though, why don't you stay with us a little longer? Let this all die down back home. It will be good for your mom to have you here."

"Of course, Dad," I said with a smile. "I'll be here as long as you like. You just rest now."

Pulling the covers to help tuck him in, I leaned in and kissed his head, noting that his thick head of hair was in need of a good wash. Perhaps when he woke up we could use some of the dry shampoo the neighbor brought over. He could use a full shower, but I hated pressing him to do that. There would always be time for that. Right now he needed to rest.

Mom slipped out the double doors of their bedroom suite to go talk to her friends, and I made my way into the bathroom that was connected to the master suite.

I closed the door quietly and made eye contact with myself in the mirror. My long, brown hair hung in waves down around my shoulders, making me look much more glamourous than I felt at this moment. The ocean air had been good for me. My hair looked healthy and full. My complexion shone a nice bronze, and my eyes glimmered back, the whites of them alert, bright, and alive.

Yes, Miami had been good for me. Life had been good. All was moving forward except for this slight set-back this morning. I wondered how this news would change my path. California was certainly on hold for now. My sleuthing would have to take a backseat until I was able to regain my ambiguity.

Moving closer to the mirror, I turned my head from left to right, examining the small diamond earrings Jack had presented me as an early Christmas gift. They seemed a little out of place with my fitted yoga pants and sleeveless, hot pink running top, but I'd barely taken them off since I got them. Besides, this was Miami. There was a lot of bling here, so I fit right in.

Another diamond gift from Jack was approaching. I could feel me getting to the point of being able to accept it with an open heart. No more hesitation on my part. I really wanted California to be over and done with before saying yes, but now things might be changing. I'd just have to see what the fallout was from this morning's events. My past was not done with me. Especially if Diane Nosely was back in the picture. But Jack knew that. He accepted that the past was always going to be a part of my story, no matter how hard I tried to close that door. He had a past. I accepted his. Right?

"Kelly?" Mom called from the other side of the bathroom door.

I stepped back, pulling my eyes from my reflection.

"Come on in, Mom," I called out.

"Are you okay?" she asked, her eyes sweeping over me.

"Yes. Just taking a moment. Everyone gone?"

Mom stepped into the large room and sat on the side of the white marble Jacuzzi tub. She looked more relaxed than I'd seen her in weeks here in her large, spa-like bathroom with all the amenities-double sinks, bidet, floor to ceiling mirrors, and heated floor. This was my favorite room in the condo and knew it to be hers as well. It was a little sanctuary.

"Yep. They're anxious to help in any way they can. You look thin, Kelly. We should go have something to eat. Are you stressed?"

"Mom, I'm okay. Don't worry about me. I'm supposed to be

helping you guys. I feel like I've just brought more trouble."

"No, it's wonderful having you here, honey. You have no idea how nice it is for your father and me to see you happy. And with Jack. And the books. It's so good."

"Well, it was until this morning," I laughed, running my hands through my hair and sitting down next to Mom on the tub.

"Let's just be glad it turned out the way it did. It could have been much worse, right?" Mom said, reaching out and grabbing my hand.

"I'm just sorry Dad had to go through this in the midst of his recovery."

"Did you see his face?" Mom said, tilting her head back and laughing. Her hair fell gently back from her face fully exposing her gleaming smile. "That was the most alert I've seen him in the last two weeks. This sounds crazy, but I think this morning's incidents did him good. It's a reminder that his girls still need him."

"Ain't that the truth," I laughed, squeezing my mom's hand.

"Oh, Kelly, for the first time, I feel like everything is going to be okay. Dad is going to recover, you're going to be okay, and who knows, maybe in a few months we'll be flying to Geneva for a special event," Mom said, bouncing her eyebrows up and down.

"Special event?" I laughed.

She stood and pulled me over to face the mirror over the double sinks.

"Just imagine," she said, winding her arms around me and squeezing. "Another wedding in the family. How exciting."

My face flushed and my eyes dropped to the floor. When they rose back up, I saw myself in the white, simple gown I would pick, my hair flowing down in waves just as it was now, the way Jack liked it. I saw myself running up to meet him at the altar, skipping this time, knowing I was with my soulmate, the true mate this time, no mistakes. No suspicion. No darkness. White. Right.

"It is exciting," I said, smiling down and meeting my mom's

eyes, her height reaching just below my shoulders.

"So exciting," I said.

Ten minutes later, I readied myself to call Diane back. I had to face the inevitable. She was going to keep calling and calling and that was the last thing we needed. This was supposed to be a place of peace and tranquility for my parents, not a trauma call center.

"Kelly," Diane said, in her fake, soothing phone voice.

"Diane," I shot back with a bite.

"It's so good to hear from you, my friend," she cooed.

I pictured her sitting in her home office with the fluffy, well-crafted throws over the inviting, soft leather couch that smelled really expensive. She was probably snuggled up next to a cup of coffee, the steam from the cup wafting up in the air while candles burned all around her, calling you to relax and open up. I imagined her perfectly bobbed, blond highlights accentuating her gentle, friendly smile. She'd probably have on a casual cashmere sweater that screamed, "Be comfortable, be relaxed, come snuggle with me, tell me your inner thoughts, let's be besties!" That was how I remembered her. That was the trap I'd fallen into.

I'd managed to hold her off until after the trial, but then the negative press really revved up. Somehow in my darkest moment, I'd let my insecurities get to me and accepted her invitation to her home in New York for a non-televised interview. I'd been determined to quiet the relentless Steve supporters that raged on. In my naiveté, it seemed possible for me to break this incorrect viewpoint. I'd spent countless hours brainstorming with my family and my editor on how to do that and move on with my good name still intact. I needed my name. It was everything in the industry I worked in. After serious consideration on changing over to a pen name, we'd decided against that because it would halt any forward movement we'd made on building the Kelly Clark name in the literary world.

But what I'd been told would be a private conversation turned very public when Diane put together an hour long special featuring me as the misunderstood, yet mysterious ex-wife of a felon who tried to kill his girlfriend and unborn child. Her show blasted into homes during primetime hours, drawing millions of viewers. When I'd told her I was confused by Steve's actions, that was turned into, "I was questioning why Steve chose his girlfriend over me, so I was angry and looking to get revenge on her." '

That couldn't have been further from the truth, but Diane seemed to know how to twist my words just enough to get the most amount of viewers and leave unopened questions that sparked doubt. She'd misquoted me, misinterpreted me, and used me for her own advancement. I could still picture her pretty face, filled with fake concern:

"Why is Kelly so confused by her husband's actions? Why did Kelly wait so long to confront her husband about his affair? Had she known and waited till the right opportunity to make it all go away? Kelly is the author of a well-known mystery series, so why wasn't she able to solve her own mystery? This is a smart, intelligent woman who missed the mystery unraveling under her own roof. Follow me tonight at seven as we piece together the clues of 'The Kelly Clark Mystery-A scorned woman turned accomplice or an innocent victim?' Tonight at seven."

The whole story was polished and manipulated into a captivating, scandalous, evening soap opera by the time Diane was done with it. I felt cheap, used, and humiliated. And to top it off, she included clips from interviews featuring Steve's family members who were all too happy to trash my name, his mother leading the pack.

In hindsight, it was foolish to even attempt to convince doubters that I was innocent in any wrong doing. There would always be people out there that questioned my story. But the truth was on my side, and so was the law.

But the few that had doubts, well, the interview didn't do me any good there. I never should have accepted the interview with Diane. She seemed like the kind of person who would at least try to air on the side of justice when we'd been sitting together in her Manhattan apartment in her snugly little office. She'd been a staple on the morning shows for years and had always come across so perky and friendly. Looking back now, it was clear she was a bad pick. Unbeknownst to me, she was gunning for a more lucrative role on a "serious" evening slot pursuing "serious" stories, and I was her ticket to that venue.

Because of that experience, I vowed I'd never buy a leather couch. Leather couches would always remind me of Diane-inviting at first glance, yet slippery and cold when you got close, leaving you vulnerable to a fall.

"Diane, I don't know how you got this number, but you need to stop calling me. I will not talk to you and I will not have you harassing my parents. My father is recovering from surgery and we need peace here," I said, happy with how strong my voice sounded. I'd been practicing in the mirror for the last ten minutes.

"Oh, no," she said, her voice dropping with concern. "What happened? Is he okay? Your dad seemed so well the last time I saw him."

My stomach dropped, and for a second I faltered. I'd forgotten Dad had accompanied me to Diane's home in Manhattan for the interview. Things were still such a blur from that time in my life. My parents and Nikki had insisted on flying to New York with me. Nikki tried very hard to make the trip a bit of fun with plans to shop on 5th Avenue and see Times Square. But the interview aired so quickly that I refused to leave the hotel room. I'd already been a marked woman at that point with the media coverage of Steve's trial. Diane's interview made things a thousand times worse. I couldn't go anywhere without being recognized.

Refusing to fall into her obvious attempt to buddy up with me about Dad, I marched on.

"Did you hear me, Diane? I'm calling the police if you continue to harass me."

"I just want to know that you are okay, Kelly. I'm so concerned about you. Did you worry that Steve was the one that escaped when you heard the news there was a break at his prison? His mom was worried. I talked to her this morning. Do you know anything about Franklin Ford? I've done some research on him if you want me to give you some of the details. I'm just wondering if these two could be affiliated in any way. We both know how cunning and smart Steve is."

I cut her off before she could say anything else. This was exactly how Diane was years ago in our interview. She was going to "help" me. She was on "my" side. She was dropping little pieces of crumbs, hoping that I'd pick them up and ask for more, like the mention of Steve's mom.

"Leave us alone, Diane. This is your final warning," I said before hanging up. Standing alone in the kitchen, I closed my eyes already regretting what I'd just said. She'd twist those words around somehow, I just knew it.

Chapter 5

Three days later, my mom and I snuck out to the beach for sunrise yoga with an instructor/friend that Mom knew from the building. She was at least ten years older than Mom but had more energy than my sister, Nikki, which I hadn't thought possible.

"After this, let's go get a coffee," Mom whispered to me from her downward dog pose next to me.

She winked and broke out into a big smile. She'd been in a great mood the last couple of days and I knew why. Dad was on the road to a major comeback, and we all knew it. He'd been agreeable, easy, willing to work with the physical therapist, and in general, happy, which made Mom very happy. My little incident seemed to have turned the tide in the Miami Clark home. Mom said that Dad actually seemed better than he had in years. The doctor said that things would progress for Dad after the surgery, but no one seemed to predict it would be this good.

"Okay," I whispered back. "Where?"

"That little place just north up the beach. At the bottom of the hotel you love," Mom said. She could have been referring to one of many hotels. I found Miami's buildings fascinating, the way the pastel colors and art deco styles lined up along the beautiful beaches. It felt like living in Candy Land.

"Coco's?" I asked.

"Yes!" she whispered back.

"Let's head into shavasana now by lying back on our mats or

towels, and laying our arms out to our sides. Open your hands, palms up to the sky, and take in full breaths of air, tongue away from the roof your mouth. Listen to the sound of the waves and be in this place and only this place for the next few minutes. Quiet the mind. Quiet the mind," mom's friend said in a soothing tone. I couldn't remember her name despite the fact that I had met her a dozen times during my stay here.

The problem was, I had met so many people. My parent's network in Miami was unbelievable. They were so well supported and so well taken care of by friends that clearly enjoyed being close to them. I'd begun to feel a bit foolish for rushing here prior to surgery like I was going to save the day. The truth was, they didn't need me as much as I had thought they would, though they seemed to prefer me most when it came to company. Thank goodness.

This trip felt like it was as much for me as it was them. If anything, it made me solid in my decision. Jack was a wonderful man. He was my man. Forever. I was ready. Our relationship reminded me of what my parents had– solid and right. Perhaps I should be the one to propose? Since I turned down his proposal a few months ago, asking for more time, maybe he was waiting for me to put the engagement back on the table? And I would. As soon as I returned home and the opportunity presented itself. I wanted to do something nice. Something that would wow him. I'd never forget the way he rushed to Miami and spent weeks here when I needed him. How could I let him slip away from me?

The man next to me chose that moment to let a burp escape, which turned my focus to suppressing a giggle. From my experience, body gas, though shunned in the outside world, was ever present in yoga. You were supposed to kindly ignore it in the form of burps or farts because they were natural, considering you were twisting and turning your inner digestive system. But how could you? How did you stay in a peaceful state of mind when the person next to you was releasing toxic gas from their behind?

Finally refocusing, I struggled to keep my mind "at present." It kept running back over the past days' events and into the near future. As Detective Pavlik suggested, I had remained tucked away in Miami to allow things to die down, which as he had predicted, happened. The calls from Diane stopped. The news had switched almost immediately to other more pressing matters, even though the escaped inmate, Franklin Ford, remained at large. Even the questions from Mom and Dad's friends had stopped. Everyone seemed to have gone back to their quiet, safe lives here in this euphoric, retired community in Miami.

"Remember, clear the mind. Be in the present only," the instructor called out. "Palms up to the sky, releasing anything that is in your heart, in your mind, anything heavy, allow it to evaporate from your palms into the air. It floats up into the air and is carried away by the breeze coming off of the ocean. Listen to the waves pull it away from the air and out to sea. Your troubles leaving you. Out to sea."

Yes, out to sea. How nice would that be? I imagined Steve's face, materializing out from my palms and being pulled out to the sea, floating away, far away. See you, punk. I saw his face disintegrate into a million pieces as he screamed, trying to keep it together, but then realizing it was hopeless. He was being pulled away and apart by something stronger than him. The fight was useless.

Wow. What if he had escaped? Been killed during his re-capture? How nice would that have been? All of my problems, gone in an instant. All of my worry, gone. Out to sea. No more stress about the future and what he had planned for me. No more guessing about his hatred for me and if he carried a grudge for helping put him away for attempted murder. No more fear about him coming for me. Hunting me down.

"Kelly?" I heard my mom say, touching my shoulder lightly.

My eyes popped open and I quickly realized that something was wrong.

"What?"

"We're done, honey. Didn't you hear Meghan?"

"What? No, I didn't," I said, turning over on my side and using my hands to push my body into a seated position. The other people in the class were already rolling up their mats or walking away down the beach, anxious to start their day.

"I must have dozed off a little bit there."

"You're okay though?" Mom asked.

I squinted up at her face, blocked now by the rising sun.

"Oh, yeah, Mom. I think I just relaxed too much. Following Meghan's instructions," I laughed, standing up and brushing off some sand from my bare legs.

The shorts I'd worn to yoga class were riding up, so I pulled them down and straightened them out. They were shorter than what I would normally wear back in Chicago, but I'd figured out quickly here in Miami, if you can't beat em, join em. Short shorts were the in thing here in Miami. Everything was shorter, glitzier, and skimpier than the styles in Chicago. Considering the soaring temperatures, it all seemed appropriate, so I was happy to go along with the fashion norm.

"I feel great. Let's go get that coffee if you're still up for it," I said, rolling up my mat. "How long is Viola willing to stay?"

"She said take your time. They're playing chess and watching the morning news," Mom said. "I'm not worried. Your father knew I would be gone when he woke up. We talked about it last night. He said we should enjoy the morning. Let's go."

A few minutes later, we were breezing into the open air coffee shop that serviced Miami Beach. The tables were packed, so we decided to take our cups to go for a little walk on the beach. The beach was filling up with early morning surfers, parasailers, and toddlers playing in the sand.

"Have you heard from Detective Pavlik?" Mom asked as we strolled on the sand. A gentleman passed to the right of us at a fast clip calling out, "Excuse me" as he passed. How people ran in the sand, I did not know. Walking was strenuous enough for me.

"Not a peep," I said. "No news is good news, right?" I smiled.

"Agreed," Mom said, slipping her arm around my waist. "Should we head back? We should head back."

I noticed this was how it was for Mom. One minute, she could appear completely relaxed, and the next minute, she was in a panic to get back to Dad.

"Yes, let's head back," I agreed, reaching my arm around her shoulder. "This was so nice, but Dad's probably getting anxious. You know how he loves to hear all the gossip from yoga."

Mom laughed and her skin twinkled in the sunlight bouncing off the water, making her look twenty years younger than her true age. I loved Miami. It was like the fountain of youth for my parents. I couldn't wait to return home to Geneva to report in to my sisters just how well my parents were here. We all knew it, but to stay here for an extended period of time and see it first hand was so nice.

Back in their high rise, Tony waved to us from behind the front desk enthusiastically.

"Morning," he called out, while sorting mail. "You're looking well this morning."

"Hi, Tony," Mom called.

"All's quiet, Kelly. I think you dodged a bullet," Tony said, his hands moving frantically over the piles of mail in front of him on the desk. He stopped suddenly and looked up at me, his hands freezing over the mail. "I mean," he balked.

I laughed to try and calm him, knowing he meant no harm.

"I'm happy. We're all good. You're right. That could have been bad."

"I'm sorry, Ms. Clark, I don't mean to make light. I can't imagine what this whole experience has been like for you. I'm just glad you don't have any more trouble coming your way."

"Me, too," I said, pressing the button to call the elevator.

"Have a great day, Tony," Mom called, stepping into the elevator to head up to the thirteenth floor. "We'll see you later."

Once inside, Mom turned to me and spoke in a low voice even though there was no one else in the elevator with us.

"You know, everyone really does seem to be over the incident here, Kelly. All of my friends were calling to check in on us after they heard the news, and now it's not even brought up. They're all focused on the news about Janet and Peter's divorce."

"The woman I met at the grocery store? She's getting divorced?"

"After 45 years together. Can you believe it? She's the one pushing for it. Met a younger man," Mom said, bouncing her eyebrows up and down.

"A younger man, huh?" I said, leaning in closer to my mom even though there was no need for secrecy in our solitude.

"In a café on Miami Beach. She's just up and left him. Can you imagine?"

"No, that's horrible."

"It happens," Mom said, shaking her head. "You'd be surprised how often it happens."

The doors opened and we were out on the floor heading toward my parent's front door.

"I was actually thinking of inviting Peter to dinner. And Viola. She's lonely. She would like a gentleman's company."

"But Mom, they're not even divorced yet, right? They just made the announcement?"

"Yesterday."

"Mom, that's way too soon."

"You're right. That was a crazy thought. I would just love for Viola to meet someone. She's such a catch," Mom said, sliding her key in and pushing the heavy, front door open.

Viola and Dad were not in the living room playing chess, as I assumed they would be. I could hear quiet voices coming from my parent's back bedroom. Something about the way the voices were speaking in low, quiet tones raised my attention.

Mom must have picked up the same energy because when our eyes met briefly, her furrowed brows read concern.

She turned on her heel to head to the bedroom, and after a moment of hesitation, I followed.

"Viola? Everything okay?"

Mom pushed open the double doors leading to the suite.

"What's wrong? What's going on?" Mom said, her voice sounding strained.

"Mom, what is it?" I asked from behind her. Instead of explaining, she merely stepped forward, allowing me in.

The first person I noticed was Viola in her favorite chair by the window. She had her light brown eyes trained on Dad in the bed, like she normally did when she stayed with him, but her lips were pursed in a tight line, and she wouldn't meet our gaze.

"It's Jack. There's been some kind of car accident in Geneva," Dad said quickly with the phone to his ear.

"What?" I shrieked, instantly in a panic. "Is he okay?"

"Jack is fine. He's the one calling. It's Mike," he said, referring to Adelle's husband. "He's been in a car accident."

"What?" I said, moving quickly to the bed. "Is he okay?"

Dad nodded his head, yes.

"Were the kids in the car?" I asked frantically, thinking of my five-year-old niece, Cindy, and how scared she must be right now.

Please, please. Not the kids.

Another nod.

If Mike was okay and the kids were okay, I couldn't understand the lines of anxiety on my dad's face. He seemed to be holding his breath. I could tell that the worst of the story had not yet dropped.

"He's okay. He was alone. He's in the hospital getting x-rays. The woman he hit was hurt pretty bad."

My mom and I both sucked in air at the same time.

"Oh, no. That's horrible. When? How?" I asked, still searching my dad's face, looking for clues.

"Let me talk to Jack," Mom said, reaching for the phone.

"Kelly, the woman he struck," my dad started, his mouth twisting into a grimace.

"What?" I demanded.

"It was the reporter, Diane Nosely."

Chapter 6

"What?" Mom and I both shrieked at the same time. We made a beeline for the phone Dad was holding, and like two forces completely unaware of each other, both tried to snatch it out of his hand.

Both of our hands gripped the receiver until our eyes met, registering the struggle.

"Sorry," Mom said. "Take it, honey. Find out the rest of the story."

She released her death grip on the phone and went around to the other side of the bed to sit next to Dad. I sat as well, noting that this was the second time in less than a week that I was sitting on what was supposed to be his place of rest and healing, taking in very stressful news.

"Jack?"

"Hi, babe. Are you okay?" Jack said in his warm, calm voice.

"Yes, please just tell me what happened," I demanded in a shrill, unfamiliar voice.

"There was a really bad snowstorm last night. Mike lost control of the car this morning on Third Street and hit Diane Nosely right in front of Chocolate Love. We're waiting for an update on her condition."

"No," I groaned. "How awful."

Although I hated her, I would never wish something this terrible to happen to her.

"I know," Jack said. "Mike is very lucky. His air bag went off and he was wearing a seatbelt. It could have been much worse for him."

"Adelle?" I asked.

"She's okay. I'm here at their house with the kids. Nikki went with her to the hospital. They'll be bringing him home soon. As far as I know, he'll be bruised up pretty good, but no breaks or other injuries. We're waiting to hear an update on Diane."

"Who's with your mom?" I asked, micromanaging the situation from a thousand miles away.

"She's with Mari," Jack said, referring to his sister.

"What was Diane doing there?" I asked, addressing the real question that popped into my head when I'd heard what happened. "What time did this happen?"

Jack let out a breath, and I imagined him shaking his head no as he often did when he didn't have an answer for me.

"Good question. It happened at five in the morning. Mike was on his way to the gym and Diane was crossing the street. I guess she wasn't crossing at a crosswalk, so she surprised him. He hit the brakes but started to slide because the streets weren't quite plowed yet. The good news is that he wasn't going that fast. And they took her to Delnor Hospital here in Geneva. As far as I know she's still there. Wouldn't they have air-lifted her to a higher level trauma center if it was more serious? " he asked.

"I have no idea," I replied.

"I'm sorry to sound cold, but I wonder will Mike be in trouble because of this? I mean, I know he wasn't at fault, but will the police see it that way?" I asked, worried about the fallout Mike would face.

"The good news is that there were witnesses that saw her dart out on the street."

"Who?" I asked.

"There were a few chocolatiers in Chocolate Love working in

the front room that saw the whole thing. There was also a delivery man dropping off supplies. You know Nikki. She's already got everybody lined up to speak on Mike's behalf. It'll be okay for Mike."

"I don't get it. Why was Diane there? What was she doing at Chocolate Love at five in the morning? She knows I'm here."

"I have no idea. That woman is nuts, babe. Don't make yourself crazy trying to understand crazy," Jack said.

A scream in the background, followed by a high pitched giggle interrupted our conversation. The kids.

"Hey guys, I'm on the phone. Can you wait for me to start?" Jack called out to them.

"What are you guys playing?" I asked, a little jealous that I wasn't there with the crew.

"Harry Potter on Xbox," Jack said with excitement.

"I wish I was there," I said.

"So do I. Why don't you come home? It sounds like your dad is doing well? Come home."

The sound of his voice made me want to race to the airport. I wanted to feel his strong arms around me, snuggle up to him in bed and smell the Jack smell I loved so much. It had only been a few days since he'd left Miami, but the drama that had been dropping like bombs made me miss being by his side. I missed my partner. He'd offered to come back to Miami when he heard about the jailbreak, but I'd told him to sit tight when we found out it wasn't Steve.

"But, what about this new development? Surely once this hits the news about Diane, the media will make a big deal out of how close it happened to my place of residence. That must be why she was there," I said, trying to be logical.

"Stay here, Kelly. They'll be all over you," Dad said next to me.

His brain must have been thinking the same way mine was. I'd told her to leave me alone and that I wasn't taking interviews. That had been a few days ago. I'd spoken to her live from Miami. She knew I was here, so why had she gone to Geneva?

"Yeah, I guess, you're right. There's nothing out yet, but once this hits, they'll probably trace it back to you. Just sit tight," Jack said reluctantly. "I just miss you."

"I miss you, too, Jack," I said, feeling defeated. Although I was enjoying my time with my parents, my anxiety to get back to my home turf had been building ever since the false alarm on Steve's jailbreak. Now, it would be delayed even further.

"Wait, this just happened a few hours ago? Tell me how you figured out it was Diane? Was she conscious?" I asked, still trying to put it all together.

"Nikki was in the store and heard the accident. She immediately called 911, and then realized it was Mike's car. She's the one that recognized Diane. I guess true to form, she was an absolute bear on the scene. Screaming at the EMTs and trying to run the whole show from her stretcher. Nikki said the last thing she heard her yell before the ambulance door closed was, "Pain meds now, you idiots!"

I closed my eyes and moaned, worried about the aftermath. If Diane was well enough to demand pain meds on the scene, she was most likely going to be okay. There was a small part of me that found myself, for the second time this week, wishing things had ended more tragically for my enemy. It would put me in the clear.

I shook my head to clear these terrible thoughts. What was wrong with me?

Poor Nikki. She was well into her pregnancy. I pictured her and her bump racing out the front steps of Chocolate Love and slipping and sliding to try and get to Mike.

"Is Nikki okay?" I begged.

"She's fine, Kelly. You know Nikki. She's unbreakable," Jack said in a confident tone.

"But," I stopped, not wanting to press him in front of my parents. I'd talk to Nikki later when I was alone. They didn't need more stress right now.

"Okay, sounds like everything is under control."

"Kelly, I have to go. I'm sorry. I'm supposed to be watching these kids and they're waiting for me. I'm doing a bad job. Let me call you back in a little bit. Okay?"

"Of course. Go play Harry Potter. Call me later."

"I think I should come back to Miami, Kelly. You might be there a little longer now."

"I," I paused, trying to figure out what to say.

Yes, I wanted to see Jack, but I'd been planning on seeing him home in Geneva. My desire to be home in his condo, really our condo now, was growing stronger. But I didn't want my parents to see that. There was no telling when I'd be able to jump on a plane now. The fact that a reporter from one of the nation's major news networks was injured basically on my doorstep was not going to go unnoticed. Like it or not, her being in Geneva was going to bring media focus back to me.

"Yeah," I said finally.

"We'll talk about this later, okay?" Jack suggested, probably picking up on my inability to talk.

"Okay," I said, feeling Mom and Dad's eyes on me.

After we hung up, Mom had plenty of questions. Between the two of us, we were able to answer most of them except for the biggest one. What was Diane Nosely doing in Geneva? Steve had not been the fugitive on the run, nor had he had anything to do with the jailbreak, so what was she pursuing? Seems to me that the hot lead to pursue right now was the man on the run, Franklin Ford. If I were her, I'd be chasing down that family and the back story there. Wouldn't her network be sending her there?

"Should we turn on the television and see if anything is on yet?"

Mom asked.

I shrugged my shoulders in a non-response. I wasn't sure if I really wanted to watch this storm develop on the news.

It hit me then that I'd been looking at this whole thing from such a selfish angle. What if Diane was severely hurt? What if Diane had a family? I'd never even considered that, never thought of her as a multi-dimensional person. What if she had kids and wouldn't be able to take care of them? I knew nothing of her personal life because I refused to spend any time getting to know her. I didn't want to know her. She was terrible to me. But I still had empathy for her.

"I'm going to take a shower," I said, patting my dad's hand and standing up. "I just need a moment to clear my head."

"Take your time. I'll make us some lunch," Mom said, standing and stomping her foot. "Let's get focused and back on track."

"I'm glad Mike hit her," Dad said in a light tone. "She was a rotten, little wench."

"Don't say that!" Mom said, visibly trying to hold back a laugh.

"What?" my dad said defensively. "She is a horrible person."

The phone rang distracting all of us.

"It's Adelle's cell phone," my dad said, looking up at me.

I winced and contemplated bolting for the shower.

"Do you want to take it, or should I?" Dad asked, looking to me for an answer.

Of course I wanted to talk to Adelle. The truth was, I was just a bit scared to talk to her.

Chapter 7

I pointed to him, thinking it best he pick up. She probably didn't want to speak to me anyway.

"Hello?" Dad said. By the way his blue eyes moved around the room making eye contact with anything but me, I knew where this was heading. I could only guess what Adelle was saying on the other end of the line. My Dad, forever maintaining his status as a neutral party when it came to his daughters, simply nodded his head.

"No," he said.

I could hear Adelle's voice squawking on the other end of the line but couldn't make out anything she was saying.

"Do you want to talk to her? She's right here," he said hopefully.

Mom, I noticed, was extremely quiet, but leaning over close to my father as though trying to listen in. Mom and Dad stood on very different grounds when it came to how they handled being caught in the middle of their daughters. It was a bone of contention in our family that Mom historically took her eldest daughter's side when stuff hit the fan. It often caused Nikki and me to develop hurt feelings, and in the end, turn on Adelle, whether she deserved it or not. Mom, of course, denied doing this. Yet time and time again, she'd taken Adelle's side, even when she was clearly in the wrong.

This only got more and more hurtful as we grew up and our issues were no longer centered around silly things like who took the best Barbie outfit from the stash. As we got older, our problems and issues with each other got bigger. This was a perfect example. I didn't know what she was saying, but my gut told me she was blaming me for Mike's accident this morning.

The worst part was, she was right. Diane Nosely never would have been in town if it wasn't for me and my past. And now because of me, Mike was in the hospital and they were dealing with the aftermath of the accident. Could there be a lawsuit? Would the fact that Diane was clearly in the wrong as far as crossing in an unmarked crosswalk keep Mike from getting sued? Or was he going to have to be wrapped up in court over this? Would they have to pay for her medical expenses? If I was thinking this already, I was sure Adelle and Mike were worried as well. Diane was no shrinking violet. She was probably going to be a monster to deal with. A monster they did not need. Adelle and Mike had enough problems already.

Dad shook his head, no, signaling that she did not want to talk to me. His eyes crinkled in that same stressed way I'd seen over the years when the three of us fought in front of him. It was like the more he crinkled up his eyes, the better he blocked our nastiness from infecting him.

"I'm going to take a shower," I told my mom, dropping my shoulders and schlepping over to my bedroom to collect my robe.

Did you take a look outside yet?" Steve asked, his face aglow with excitement.

"No, why? What are you up to?" I asked with a mixture of excitement and fear. He'd been spending money way too recklessly. Things weren't matching up for me, but I couldn't deny how nice it was to be on the receiving end of his generosity.

I moved to our bedroom window and gazed out. Another perfect day in sunny California. Being the Chicago transplant that I was, asking someone to check outside normally meant, "Go look at the ten inches of snow that fell."

Gazing down from the second story, it finally caught my attention. A shiny luxury car, the color of sapphires, glistened up at me.

"No," I said simply. This couldn't be. My mind raced to all of the treatments we'd just completed. We couldn't possibly afford this now. What had he been thinking?

"Steve, no. What about the IVF? We can't do this now," I panicked.

"Kelly, calm down. I thought you would be happy," he said, going immediately into angry, defensive mode. He switched so fast. Faster and faster these days.

"No, Steve. I can't take all of this spending. What is happening with you?"

The fight that followed was one of many that escalated for a few months, before . . .

"Kelly?" my dad asked from behind me. He stood in my bedroom doorway, holding onto the door frame and leaning in.

"Dad? What are you doing out of bed? Come sit down," I said, beckoning him into the room to take a seat in the rocker they kept in the guest bedroom.

"I'm just coming to check on you. Are you okay?" he asked, taking a second to lower himself gingerly onto the chair. I reached forward to help him steady himself in the chair, and he waved my hand away.

"I'm fine," he said, playfully slapping my hand away.

I sat down on the bed and folded my legs together. For a second, my eyes connected with Dad's, taking me to a place I desperately longed to be. It would have been so easy to just unload on him, like I'd done so many times in the past, but could I? Should I right now?

He reached his hand over and grabbed mine in encouragement. He must have sensed the window opening.

"Don't let Adelle's anger bother you. She gets emotional. Especially when her family is involved," he said in a clear, strong voice.

Perhaps it was true what the doctors were telling us. Dad was going to be stronger, physically and mentally, now that the blockage was gone. The strain on his system had been taken care of and now he could be better. Super Dad.

But not yet.

"I won't. I'm just tired from the early morning wake up and then this news. I just need a shower and a coffee. Possibly even a nap."

Dad's steely blue eyes searched my face. Surely the mask I'd put on was visible to him, but he allowed me to maintain my charade.

"Okay, sweetheart, go shower. I just wanted to make sure you were okay."

"I'm fine, Dad. I'm sad about this news. I didn't like Diane, none of us did, but it does make me feel sad for her. And I'm upset for Mike. This is the last thing this family needs, especially after the year they've had," I said, referring to Mike's struggling business and the recent downsizing the family had to go through.

"They will be fine. I never worry about Adelle. She always seems to come out of these things just fine," Dad said, raising his eyebrows.

You on the other hand, Kelly, can't seem to find your way out of trouble, I imagined him thinking.

"Yes, she does, doesn't she," I agreed, feeling just a tinge of jealousy for my beautiful, blond, wealthy sister with the statuesque, traffic-stopping figure and seemingly, bottomless bank account. Even her "downsized" house was still ten times the size of the condo I shared with Jack, which he owned. I hadn't contributed a penny. I didn't HAVE a penny to contribute, considering I was still financially broke and paying down all the debt I'd been left with after divorcing Steve.

"Alright then, you go shower. I'm going to go scrounge around for those donuts someone brought over earlier in the week," Dad said, slapping my knee and standing up slowly from the rocking chair.

"Dad! You're not supposed to be eating those," I said in a nagging voice.

"I'm just kidding. Your mother would be furious. But I could really go for something sweet.

I smiled in agreement.

"You should see the donuts Nikki's been serving at Bean in Love. She's got a double chocolate cake donut to die for," I cooed, dreaming of her display case at the front of her newly opened café.

And that wasn't all she served. Seven layer chocolate cake, cinnamon crumb cake, scones, and pies. All the things you'd like to tuck into while sipping coffee, curled up next to the blazing fire she kept going in the main room of Bean in Love. It had opened in the fall and was doing amazingly well, considering she was running both Bean in Love and Chocolate Love, her specialty chocolate shop two doors down, while pregnant with her first child. She'd taken on some help, which was uncharacteristic for Nikki since she liked to do everything herself, but this was the new Nikki. Ready for some help in order to expand. And because she did accept help, she was feeling better in her pregnancy and her stores were flourishing. They were getting more attention now than ever. She'd recently been recognized by The Chicago Tribune, The Hungry Hound, Check Please, and Chicago's Best. She was kicking butt.

"I plan to see them. And I plan on eating them. Your mom and I talked last night. I'm heading to Chicago as soon as the doctor gives the thumbs up," he said proudly. "I hated not being there for the opening of Bean in Love. I didn't realize how bad I'd been feeling. I know I have some recovery time ahead of me, but if I can, I'd love to be there for the parade."

"Nikki's parade? The Christmas parade?" I asked, astounded by this proclamation. Every year in early December, Nikki was part of a small parade on Third Street to kick off the Christmas season. The first candy cane of the season was presented to the mayor, and Santa officially came to town. The parade had grown so popular over the last few years; it was featured on the major news stations. The community loved it.

"Yeah, that's what I was hoping for," he said.

"But Dad, the doctor said six weeks recovery time. At least. It's only been a few weeks. Nikki's parade is, what, less than two weeks away? Isn't that a little too soon to travel? And what about your cardiac rehab?"

I couldn't believe Mom had agreed to this. Yes, Dad was doing great, but there was no way he could travel right now.

Dad just kind of waved me away with a smile.

"I'm Superman now. Didn't you hear? On that note, I'm going to take my nap. All of this planning is wearing me out. Go take your shower. You'll feel better."

I watched Dad turn the corner down the hall back into his room. Had my parents lost their minds? A three hour flight a few weeks after surgery? There was no way he'd be able to handle that. And to take him into the frigid temperatures experienced in Chicago during the month of December rather than allow him to heal in sunny Miami? Why?

I shook my head and gathered my things for my shower. Just this morning, yoga on the beach had me imagining my problems, my stress disintegrating into nothing. Now I could feel my neck tightening up, all of my stress re-entering my body and settling into tight balls at the base of my neck.

Time for that shower. Perhaps the warm water would beat away my anxiety. I couldn't take anymore crazy surprises.

Chapter 8

That evening, the three of us lounged in the living room and watched the sunset while listening to various reports about Diane Nosely on the news. It was confirmed that she had indeed been injured in a car accident, but it sounded like she was going to make a full recovery. In fact, true to form, Diane herself made a statement to the press thanking all of her well-wishers and posting various snapshots of herself smiling from her hospital bed. Apparently, both of her legs and an arm had been broken in the accident, leaving her bound to the hospital while she recovered from minor surgery. In the pictures, she smiled, waving from the bed, somehow looking elegant and relaxed in full hair and make-up. Her legs were elevated slightly in slings, and her arm cast already appeared to have signatures on it.

I was glad to see that her story was quick and light, no mention of why she was in Geneva or if she had been on assignment. So far, there was no talk of lawsuits or mention of my brother-in-law's name. Thank goodness. Her incident had been labeled a freak accident due to the winter storm in Chicago. However, much to my dismay, she promised she'd be reporting in on a "big story she was working on" by the end of the week live from her hospital bed! Oh, joy! She didn't reveal any details, making me worried that her arrival in Geneva could still be centered around me. Why else would she be there?

The main focus of the evening news was on the escaped convict,

Franklin Ford, who, surprisingly, remained at large. Even though it wasn't connected to me, it stressed me out to know he was still out there.

When a knock sounded on the front door, the three of us all looked at each other and gave a collective shrug.

"Have you heard anything from Tony?" I asked.

"He said he got a few calls from reporters, but he sticks with his story–he's not allowed to reveal the name of the residents of the high rise."

"Well, well," I laughed. "Sounds very hoity toity," I joked, standing up to go take a look through the peek hole.

It was probably just a friend of my parents. They'd been stopping in throughout the day to check on how we were doing.

"I bet we're getting another casserole. We're going to have to start figuring something out. We don't have any more room left in the freezer for . . ." I stopped mid-sentence.

"What the?" I said, trying to make out the hazy image on the other side of the door. It looked like I was staring into a cup of dark coffee. Whatever it was started moving. It took a second to realize another eye was pressed up to the peek hole on the other side of the door.

"Who is it?" Mom called to me from the living room.

"Let me in," I heard Nikki say from the other side of the door. "I'm being followed."

I pulled the door open quickly and stood back watching a belly first Nikki cross the threshold.

"What are you doing here?" I squealed, unable to contain myself.

Nikki was one of my favorite people in the world. She made every situation brighter, funnier, better.

"And what do you mean you're being followed?"

She'd cut her hair into a pixie cut since the last time I saw her.

It suited her growing, round face. This style had been trending lately in Hollywood, so it didn't really surprise me to see Nikki follow suit. She was always on point when it came to figuring out what was hot.

"Some lady spotted me in the hallway and has been hot on my heels since I got here."

"Nikki!" both of my parents squealed in delight.

I leaned out to take a peek at who she was referring to when Nikki pulled me back in.

"No, don't do it. I lost her when I rounded the corner. I don't want her to spot me again."

She pulled me away from the door and locked it, raising an eyebrow.

"It's probably just one of Mom and Dad's friends. They're cool. Everyone has been stopping in and dropping off casseroles since Dad's surgery and, well, you know," I said.

Mom rushed over to Nikki, and Dad rose from the couch with some effort.

"No! Stay there, Dad. I'm coming to you. Sit down," Nikki ordered in her usually spunky way.

"Nikki is in the house!" she sang out. "I heard there's a recovery party going on, and you know me. I never miss a party!"

Mom engulfed her in a big hug and rocked her from side to side. Mom and Nikki were about the same height and resembled each other in so many ways. Now with Nikki's hair cut short, the resemblance was uncanny. I couldn't help but join in, rushing to be a part of the group hug and smiling ear to ear. There was no mistaking what Nikki brought with her. Even here in sunny Florida, Nikki was the brightest source of light. As though she were the sun, we circled around her, soaking in her enthusiasm.

"What about the shop?" I asked, always worrying about the details.

"Oh, no worries. I'm a delegator now, remember?" she said,

releasing us and making a beeline for Dad. He was back to a seated position on the edge of the couch, waiting for her with extended arms. She folded into them, allowing her tiny body and growing belly to be taken in by Dad's large frame.

"You look great, Dad. How are you feeling?" she asked.

"Great. How about you?" he asked.

"A little tired here and there, but for the most part the second trimester has been a breeze. So much better than the first. No more nausea, thank goodness. That was nuts."

"I'm so glad. Why didn't you tell us you were coming? You know you really shouldn't risk surprising me," he said, leaning back with a big smile on his face.

"Really?" Nikki asked, her eyes widening.

"No!" Dad laughed. "Relax! I'm just messing with you." He reached out and punched her lightly on the arm.

Mom and I sat on the other couch opposite Dad and Nikki, enjoying this little reunion.

"Well, I saw a window to jump on a plane and I thought, why not? I'm feeling good and things were slow at home. Pretty soon I won't be able to travel, so why not get away? Besides it's snowing in Chicago and I needed some sunshine. This is the life!" she said, standing up and twirling around. "You guys really did it right. Sun, energy," she said, shaking her hips and dancing a bit. "God, I love Miami. I feel so hip when I come here. The food, the people, the music, the food. Oh, I said food twice, didn't I?"

"But what about Adelle and Mike? Are they okay with everything that's happened with Diane? And what about the parade?" Mom asked.

"Don't worry about the parade, Mom. Got it all under control. And as far as Diane, ugh, I just wish she would have died. Mike should have done a better job of running her over."

"Nikki!" Mom said. "Don't say that!"

"Well, I'm sorry, Mom, but it's true. Diane Nosely put Kelly through hell. Don't you remember the call-in show she put together? 'Kelly Clark– Innocent or Guilty?' She wasn't even the one on trial. She made a mockery out of what happened to her!"

"Oooh, I totally forgot about that," Mom said, looking over at me.

So had I. When I'd refused to cooperate with Diane, she'd hosted an hour long program where she allowed people to call in and voice their opinions on whether or not I had been a part of Steve's evil scheme to kill off his mistress and unborn child. I'd refused to watch it but had been in total shock when the results came in. It had been a seventy-thirty split, in my favor, which was nice, but also showed how many people doubted my story.

"Can we not talk about that?" I said, widening my eyes at Nikki and jerking my head in Dad's direction.

"Yes, we can definitely not talk about that. Let's talk about anything else, but Geneva. I'm away from the drama for a reason. Tell me everything that is going on here."

"Let's get you comfortable first, honey. Can I get you something to eat or drink? You must be starving. We have wine or, well, wait. You obviously can't have wine now, dear," Mom said, rising up from the couch, ready to serve as hostess.

Dad sighed openly at the mention of wine.

"I want wine," he smiled at Mom. She smiled back at him and shook her head no.

"I would love a glass of water. You know how those flights can dehydrate you. I feel like a dried up prune being pregnant."

"Why don't you and Kelly unload your bags in the guest bedroom, and I'll put together something for you to snack on. Get situated and we'll lounge on the terrace and watch the sunset. This is so exciting having us all under one roof again. If only Adelle were here, it would be just like old times," Mom called excitedly on the way into the kitchen. She shook her hips back and forth and spun in a little circle before pushing the small wooden doors open.

Nikki looked over at me and smiled her radiant, familiar smile. Her pixie cut accentuated her expressions now that there was no hair to distract from her mischievous, playful brown eyes.

On our way to the bedroom, she spoke quietly to me under her breath.

"Yes, come with me in the bedroom. I have to talk to you. What exactly are you up to, Kelly? Did you honestly think I wouldn't find out?"

Chapter 9

"What?" I asked, frozen in shock by Nikki's words. Nikki stopped rolling her giant, hot pink suitcase down the hall and shot me a look between squinted eyes.

"Uh, huh," was all she said, while twisting her neck to look back down the hall behind me. I assumed she was checking to make sure our parents were out of earshot.

"Did you really think I wouldn't find out? It's me!" she said, thumbing her two thumbs to her chest. "Why would you hide this from me?" She demanded, plopping her hands on her hips.

I reached out and grabbed Nikki by the sleeve, pulling her all the way into the guest bedroom. I motioned with my head for her to close the door behind her, which she did. The last thing I needed was for Mom and Dad to overhear any of my crazy plan.

"But how could you know about California? I haven't even booked the ticket yet." I whispered close to Nikki's face, despite the fact that we were definitely out of ear shot now.

"California?" Nikki said, her eyes widening and her hand covering her mouth. "You're really going back there? But why?"

"Wait, you didn't know? I thought," I stopped, realizing I'd been bamboozled by Nikki.

Judging by the color draining quickly from her face, I could tell I'd shocked her. She sat down on the bed slowly, her hands spreading out to ease her body into a comfortable position. It made me feel bad and angry at the same time. She wasn't supposed to be involved. I'd purposely kept my well-meaning, but sometimes overly zealous, sister out of this recent adventure because I wanted to keep her pregnancy stress-free. Too late now.

"I was just guessing. But why are you going back there now? I don't understand?" she implored as though I'd betrayed her. Her large, cocoa eyes stared at me, searching my face.

"You tricked me!" I said with an indignant air. "You had no idea I was up to something."

"Well, now I do, so you have to tell me why," she said, changing direction.

She no longer looked scared, just her normal determined self. And I had to admit, I liked this better.

"What could possibly lead you back to California? I knew something was up when you sent Jack back to Chicago and decided to stay here. I've talked to Mom. I know that Dad is progressing just fine. You could have come home."

"What are you talking about? Look at him. He's still very weak. There's no reason for me to come home yet. And Mom! Look at her. Can't you see how scared she looks? How could I possibly leave now? I was just waiting for a window when they were in a better place," I said in much too high an octave.

"But, you just said you were going to California," Nikki said, reaching up for my hand, which she immediately used to pull me down on the bed to sit next to her.

"I'm not going to California. I didn't say I was going," I said, tripping over her suitcase and landing next to her on the bed at an awkward angle.

I righted myself and avoided meeting her eyes, choosing instead to look out the window and catch a glimpse of the high-rise just north of my parent's place. Miami's real estate had been on a boom in recent years, so much so that they were tearing down a lot of older buildings to build new ones, especially along the ocean where my parents were. The building I was gazing at now was due for demolition any day now. The timing couldn't have been worse for my dad, considering he needed peace and quiet, not constant construction.

"Hey, eyes on me, my friend," Nikki said.

She was beginning to sound like one of those television show detectives trying to get a perp to confess. "Tell me what's going on. Why are you hiding this from me? Let me help you, Kelly. Like I always do."

Like she always did. I couldn't help but let out a little giggle thinking back to our adventures in Geneva as both children and now adults when Nikki was "helping" me or someone else. To be around Nikki was to be wrapped up in an adventure or mystery of some sort. She was an inevitable magnet for trouble. But, she always did end up getting to the bottom of things.

"Fine, yes, I was thinking about it. Are you satisfied?" I said, a little relieved that the jig was up.

It was too hard to hide things from Nikki when she was on my case. She was like a little pitbull going after me when she thought I was hiding something from her. But Nikki was my best friend, and truth be told, I wanted her input. Things were at a standstill with California ever since the jailbreak and Diane Nosely's accident. I didn't know what to do. I was scared to travel until I knew the media wouldn't be watching me.

"I can't believe you were going to go without me," Nikki said.

"You would have stopped me," I said, meeting her shocked gaze.

"No, I wouldn't have. Surely, if you're going back, you must have a good reason. Tell me what's going on," she said, reaching out her hand to take mine in hers.

"It's stupid, really. It's about something I found. It's probably not worth me going back there, but it's been bothering me. I found this key and, well, I want to look into it."

"What kind of key?"

"I'm not that sure. My guess is that it might be to a safety deposit box."

"Why do you think that?"

"I showed William when he was in town. He has a safety deposit box and thought this key looked like his," I explained, referring to the man we helped last Halloween. His twin brother had died under suspicious circumstances, and Nikki and I had teamed up to help look into the death.

"Wait, you showed William the key and not me?" Nikki said, pulling her hand up to her chest.

"No. I mean, yes. I didn't tell him the context to which I was showing him. It just happened. Anyway," I said, trying to redirect the conversation.

"Wait, have you been speaking with William?" she asked, raising an eyebrow.

"Of course not, Nikki! You're getting off topic. I don't talk to William. When he was in town, we discussed the key, that's it," I said, rolling my eyes.

"But does he call you? Is he still kind of flirty with you?" she asked, not letting it go.

The truth was he did call. I didn't call him back. I'd shoot him a short text back just to say hi, but I didn't want to lead him on. I had no interest in William in a romantic way. It was nice to know he thought of me, but Jack was my man.

I looked up to the ceiling and stopped talking to show how annoyed I was by the direction this conversation had taken. Or rather, the direction Nikki had taken.

"Okay, have you called the bank to see if you have an account there?" Nikki asked, crossing her legs and letting my hand go.

"Not yet. I don't even know which bank to call. I'm still putting together my plan" I said.

"You think it's for the bank in California where you shared an account with Steve? That would be the logical place to start. What do you think is in that box?"

"I have no idea. As you can see, I really haven't thought this out that much. I've just felt that getting the answer to what this key is for is going to close some loops for me. Remember last summer when Sharon broke into Chocolate Love? I can't get rid of the feeling that Steve sent her to look for something. Maybe it was this key. Maybe if I close this up, I'll be able to put my past more in the past and move on. If I get rid of whatever it is Steve is sending his ladies to get from me, maybe it will stop. I don't want to have anything of value to him. I want this all to stop for good."

Nikki uncrossed her legs and broke eye contact with me.

"Hmmm, well, let me tell you what I know about safety deposit boxes. You need to pay a maintenance fee every year in order to keep them up, so that's the first thing we should check on. If you did have your name on an account, you would be getting billed. Do you still have an open account with them?"

"No, not that I know of," I said, feeling sick to my stomach at the thought of once again sharing or blending accounts with Steve.

"Does Steve?" Nikki asked, raising an eyebrow.

"How would I know? We are completely disconnected in that sense. There's no more mingling of finances. I think all of his accounts were frozen once he was sent to prison, but to be honest, I'm not completely sure what his story is."

"We need to find out if that box exists before we fly out there. There's no reason to waste our time if that's a dead end."

"We?" I asked with a little smirk.

This is why I didn't tell her. I knew the second she sniffed out an adventure, she would be all over it. She didn't have time for this. She was now running two businesses, while trying to keep herself and her unborn child well rested and healthy. To ask her to come along with me on this was too much. But there was a big part of me that was grateful she was showing interest. All of a sudden, the thought of flying out to California on my own, especially with all of this crazy media action going on, seemed daunting and just plain stupid.

"Well, come on, do you seriously think I would let you do this on your own? Are you nuts, Kelly?" Nikki stood up and started pacing the room.

"The news hounds are just waiting to take you down right now. They're waiting like vultures outside of Chocolate Love. It's just a matter of time before they track you down here."

My hands flew to my mouth.

"Wait, it's that bad at home?"

"We live in small town, USA, Kelly. The story about Diane's accident is huge right now in Geneva. Plus, the Franklin Ford jailbreak, which everyone knows stems from Steve's jail."

"But, it wasn't Steve. It had nothing to do with me!" I rebuked.

"I know that, but you know how people think. He killed a guard. People are terrified. And then the fact that this huge news anchor was in town at the same time. It's got people freaked out. You need to let this die down. They'll catch Franklin Ford and this will all go away. The media will relax. How long could a fugitive be on the run with no money and everyone in the country looking for him?"

I cringed at the thought of a violent, desperate man out there somewhere roaming the countryside.

"We haven't told you how bad it is because we're just trying to keep things in perspective. This will pass. The world will hand us something else that will take the place of this story, but we need to let things die down a little bit. Keep you under wraps until something else big breaks in the news and the press gets distracted. It's just the wrong time to be jumping on a plane. Diane Nosely is a big freaking deal. Yesterday when I left, there were news trucks all up and down the street."

"Oh, no. Is Jack being hounded? Now I feel like he's sheltering me, too," I said.

"He's been staying downtown close to work, so he's kind of keeping out of the scene."

"He has? Where downtown? He didn't tell me that," I said, feeling a bit stung by Nikki knowing more about Jack's whereabouts than me. Why didn't he tell me he wasn't staying at home? I guess two could play the secret keeping game. Being on the receiving end of it didn't feel so good. Perhaps I needed to re-think my strategy of hiding my trip to California from him.

"I'm not sure. I thought you knew," Nikki said, looking a little dumbfounded. "Anyway, let's get on this key thing tomorrow. We could make calls from here and at least get to the bottom of tracking this down. It will be fun. Like solving another mystery," Nikki said, clearly trying to redirect my attention. "You know me and my mysteries," Nikki said, with a gleam in her eye.

Watching a smile spread across her face made me a little worried. Actually, a lot worried.

Chapter 10

"Call me back if you get a chance. I need to talk to you," I said, trying to think of some kind of witty closing remark that would make light of the situation at hand. Pulling my lips back over my teeth, I held my breath. Now this was just silly. Too much time had passed. If I said something more, it would only confirm the awkward moment of silence.

"What are you doing?" Nikki asked, walking into the room with a towel wrapped around her head like an Arabian queen.

"Shhhh!" I said, slamming my eyebrows down over my eyes after I hit the "End" button on my cell phone.

"It looked like you were going to take a bite out of your phone or something. Who were you calling?"

Nikki sashayed into the room and proceeded to disrobe and dress as though I weren't there. I couldn't help but stare openly at her pregnant belly. She quickly pulled on undergarments, but her blossoming stomach remained exposed for me to see.

"Kelly?"

"What?" I said, unable to take my eyes off of her stretched skin. It looked like she had swallowed a tiny beach ball. She was absolutely, breathtakingly beautiful.

"Who were you talking to? And quit staring at me like that. What's the big deal? Haven't you ever seen a pregnant woman before?"

"Yes, but not you," I chuckled.

"Isn't it crazy? Look at this belly," she laughed. "I didn't mean to frighten you."

"You look adorable. I just can't get over it. You're really having a baby, Nikki."

"You're going to be an aunt again."

"I can't wait," I said, genuinely happy for Nikki.

Staring up at her, I felt like my heart would burst with joy for my sister. She was getting everything she wanted in life. Her life was so full, beyond capacity in my opinion, but she handled it all with grace.

"Can I?" I asked, holding my hand out.

"Sure. Just don't make fun of my stretch marks," Nikki laughed, waddling over to me on the bed.

"Oh, please. Don't get all bashful on me now," I laughed, laying my hand on her warm belly. She was still rather small in my opinion, but on her petite frame, any weight gain was visible. Considering how much trouble she had putting on weight and getting through the nausea at the start of the pregnancy, I was sure Nikki didn't give a hoot about the pounds.

"You're still feeling well?" I asked, constantly paranoid.

"Yes. I feel glorious. Compared to the first trimester, this one has been a breeze. I feel invincible compared to a few months ago. I feel like Dad feels. Like Superman," Nikki said with a smile. She stepped away and pulled a sundress on over her growing body.

"Like Superman, huh? Can you use your powers to deflate my situation?" I asked.

"Not needed. The universe has done that for you already," Nikki said, reaching into her suitcase and pulling out a pair of red flip-flops that matched the pattern of red flowers on her dress. That couldn't have been by chance.

"Franklin Ford was caught?" I guessed, sitting upright on the bed.

"Better," Nikki said.

"What do you mean?"

"A huge college football sex scandal just broke. Just in time for all of the holiday football bowls coming up. They're accusing the schools of hiring prostitutes for the players and blah, blah, blah. Tons of players are coming forward. It's all over the news this morning. Huge scandal."

"And," she said, holding up her pointer finger, "wait for it."

I smiled, feeling bad that someone had taken on the weight of the media spotlight from me, yet hopeful that my troubles might be lifting.

"Two Chicago area schools are being investigated in the sex scandal. They think the coaches in Chicago were the ringleaders. Maybe that was why Diane was in town."

I breathed out, feeling a gush of relief pour over my body.

"Really?" I asked, smiling from ear to ear. "Maybe it was never about me? It all makes sense; she would have been all over that kind of story. And while she's in town, why not pop in to torment me at Chocolate Love? Or if I wasn't home yet, find someone to talk to in order to try and get dirt on me."

"Yep," Nikki said, walking over to the mirror hanging on the wall next to the window.

"I love my hair like this. I should have done this a long time ago," she said, swinging her head to get a look at all angles.

"These accusations might lead to some of the schools being taken out of the bowls and that would cause a ripple effect for people who bet on these games, fantasy football, and all that stuff. It's huge. Do you have any idea what a huge industry fantasy football has become?"

"No, can't say I do," I said, leaning back on the bed and crossing my arms.

"It's huge. Anyway, the bottom line is you're back to being a ghost. Just as you like it. Well, at least on a national scale. Geneva might be another story. Who are we kidding? You will probably always be front page news in Geneva. I mean, it's Geneva."

"So, can I go home now?" I asked, craving to be near Jack.

"I think so. We should probably wait a couple days. Make sure this is as big a deal as I think it's going to be. Figure out your California deal. Hang out with Mom and Dad. Have some fun."

The word fun caused me to raise my brows.

"Did you have something in mind?" I asked.

Nikki just smiled her megawatt smile and raised her hands up in the air.

"Food Truck Tuesday!" Nikki called out in a drawn out voice, mimicking our favorite media personality, Oprah Winfrey.

"As in tonight?" I asked.

A knock on the bedroom door interrupted us.

"Come in," I called.

"Girls? Are you going to have breakfast?" Mom asked from the doorway.

She held a spatula in her right hand like a wand, and her hair and make-up looked perfectly applied. She must have risen with Nikki to watch the early morning news. For a second, a wave of guilt ripped through me, imagining my mom and Nikki up at the crack of dawn pouring over the television newscasts to see if my name popped up at all. I'd been fast asleep, dreaming of sugar plums and fairies while they fretted.

"I'm serving pancakes to celebrate," Mom said, her face lit up with a smile. "Thank goodness for sex scandals and football. Looks like we're in the clear for now."

Nikki and I both burst out laughing at Mom's irreverent joy.

"I'm in," I said. "Let me help you, Mom. I feel like a bum. Look how productive you two have been this morning. I'm still in my pajamas."

"Let me finish getting dressed and I'll meet you in there. Where's Dad?" Nikki asked.

"He's still sleeping. I want to leave him be. He heard about the news early this morning and has been sleeping since. He needed this. He's been so worried."

Another wave of guilt ripped through me.

"Yes, it's all going to be okay now. I just know it," Nikki said triumphantly, spreading moisturizer on her face.

I closed the door behind me, leaving Nikki humming to herself in our room. It was nice to see her and Mom so happy. Nikki always seemed to do this. Every time she stepped into the picture, problems were solved. Could she have done something to get this sex scandal exposed? I wouldn't put it past her. It was like she snapped her fingers and things changed for the better.

Mom went back to the stove where she flipped over two sizzling, heart-shaped pancakes. She began to hum, and if I wasn't imagining it, it sounded like the same tune Nikki was just humming.

"Are you humming the tune to that commercial for the travel website?" I asked.

"Yes, how did you know?" Mom said, turning with a smile to face me.

"I think Nikki was just humming the same thing," I laughed.

"I can't help it. It plays constantly. I can't imagine the budget that company spends on advertising."

"Just how late did you two stay up last night? I swear, it's like you guys spent the night hatching up a plan to make my problems go away," I joked, still half believing it could be true.

"I wish we could take the credit for this," Mom laughed, turning back to poke at the pancakes on the stove. "Nope, sorry, honey. This one was given to us by the heavens. Oh, and maybe good old-fashioned lust had something to do with it. You should write a thank you letter to those college football teams. Thanks to their pursuit of female company, you're off the map."

"Mom! So vulgar," I laughed.

"Now if only we could do something to fix Adelle's problems," Mom sighed, her shoulders slumping.

"What do you mean?" I asked, stepping closer to Mom.

From this close, I couldn't help but notice how bloodshot her eyes were.

"Oh, nothing, nothing," she said, dismissing me. "These are ready. Let's eat while they're hot."

Chapter 11

"Mom, come on," I pushed. "Now you have to tell me. What's going on with Adelle? I've been calling her, and she's not calling me back. What's up? What's going on?"

"Well, I really don't want to get in the middle of this, Kelly," Mom said.

"You brought it up," I pointed out.

"You girls need to work this out," Mom said. "I just can't get in the middle."

Middle? Since when have you been in the middle? You always take Adelle's side.

Refusing to take the bait, I kept quiet and busied myself with getting out plates from the cabinets, humming the tune I'd picked up from Nikki and Mom. This was not the time or place to get into family drama. We were supposed to be celebrating the fact that a bunch of naughty football players had wiped my story from the news.

"Why are you making light of this? This isn't funny. Your sister is really hurt," Mom said, spinning around with the spatula held in her hand like a weapon.

"Whoa. What are you talking about?" I asked, genuinely dumbfounded as to what she was referring to.

The last I'd heard from Adelle, Mike was okay after the accident and no charges were being pressed. She was prepping for the holidays, happily shopping away, and decorating her rental home.

Since the jailbreak and Diane Nosely's accident in Geneva, we hadn't really said more than a few words to each other on the telephone. If there had been other breaking news in Adelle's life, I was completely unaware of it. She hadn't shared anything with me.

"She hasn't told you anything?" Mom asked, raising her eyebrow at me.

I shrugged my shoulders, a little fed up with this cloak and dagger guessing game. Enough already. Just tell me.

"Maybe I shouldn't then," Mom said.

"Alright," I concurred, setting the plates down on the counter. Nothing got Mom's attention more than feigning disinterest in her precious Adelle.

"The ladies in her Junior League Club have iced her out. She's been asked to step down from her role in the Christmas parade," she said, whispering conspiratorially to me.

"What?" I said, drawing up my lip in a sneer. I couldn't help it. This wasn't what I was expecting.

"Kelly, don't be insensitive. That club was important to Adelle. It *is* important to Adelle."

"Mom, a few days ago, I thought my violent ex-husband may have been involved in a jailbreak from a maximum security prison. Oh, and then a reporter who was obsessed with me was run over by my brother-in-law in front of my pregnant sister's store." I stopped to take a breath. "I don't really care about a Junior League Club right now."

"Well, Adelle does. She has a respected role in that community that she works hard for. You need to think about those things. You need to think about how your actions affect the rest of the family," Mom threw at me. Her tone sounded freakishly close to Adelle's when she'd said basically the same thing to me on the phone the other day.

"My actions? What exactly have I done that has led to Adelle's downfall? I don't quite understand," I said. "You guys need to dumb this down for me because obviously you and Adelle have discussed something about something I have done. You're both saying the same thing to me, yet I'm just not quite grasping what it is you're saying."

I was rambling, not making much sense, but I was aggravated. I was willing to take responsibility for something, because God knew I'd brought trouble to this family. I owned that. But these vague accusations were infuriating.

Mom's lips pursed together and her eyes turned from me. "Oh, I don't know."

"Come on, Mom, you have something to say, go ahead and say it," I said, really angry now. "I've caused all of the problems in this family, right? I've brought so much stress on Dad, he had to have surgery. And my ugly, scandalous past has cost Adelle her volunteer job with the Junior League Club," I said, sticking on the word volunteer as though it were a dirty one. "And, now Nikki is here, risking her health, because Steve caused ruckus in the media and you're going crazy living in this apartment with me because I'm like a circus animal that needs to be locked up."

Like a grand finale, my frantic outburst drew Nikki into the room just in time to see me accidentally drop a plate on the floor. White shards of glass ran to all corners of the room like they were scared of me as well.

"I'm sorry," I squeaked out, immediately feeling remorse. "I didn't mean to do that. It slipped."

Mom stood, staring at me as though I'd gone mad, which at the moment, I felt could have been possible. Once again, Steve had managed to figure out a way to crawl back into my life and wreak havoc on any sense of normalcy I'd established. Again and again, this happened. It would have been so much better if he would just disappear forever. Dad was right. If he would have just died in the jailbreak, things would have been so much better.

"What the hell is happening in here?" Nikki demanded.

I looked to Mom for her to explain, but she remained frozen like a statue at her place by the stove.

"I have to get out of here," I said to Nikki. "Now."

"But," Nikki began.

"I need some fresh air. I have to get out for a bit," I said, cutting her off.

"Okay, okay, give me a minute to figure this out. Mom and I came up with a plan last night. We'll get you out of here, Kelly. You're right. You need some fresh air," Nikki said.

* * * * *

That afternoon, we stood in the guest bathroom, applying the finishing touches to our make-up.

"You sure about this? I don't know if this is overkill or not enough. What do you think?" I asked, reaching up and playing with the blond, bob wig Nikki found for me.

One of mom's friends in the building had battled cancer last year and kept the wig she had to wear while she was going through chemo. It was a perfect cover for me. I looked nothing like my normal self. My naturally wavy, long, brown hair was tucked in a bun under the wig, and the make-up I wore, much more than the natural tones I normally sported, made me unrecognizable. At least, I hoped so.

"I think it is overkill. No one is even thinking of Kelly Clark right now. Trust me. The focus is football and Franklin Ford. And Tony said the calls have stopped, no visitors, nothing suspicious," Nikki said, whipping her fake, long, dark tresses over her shoulder.

Fortunately, Mom also had a friend in the building that liked to dress as a woman on Friday nights for his weekly visits to the South

Beach clubs. Hey, it was South Beach. I didn't judge. I was grateful for our disguises.

"I look hot," Nikki said, puckering her lips out in the mirror. "I'm totally going to get some digits tonight," she said, rubbing her hands over her burgeoning belly to make the statement even more ridiculous.

"Shut up," I laughed, sitting down on the counter. "Yeah, we're going to pick up for sure at Food Truck Tuesday. That's all I need in my life. More men."

"Hey, don't knock it. Food trucks are super-hot right now. Technically, this could be deemed a research trip for my business. I'm getting one going back home."

"Are you serious, Nikki?" I said. "Don't you have enough going on?"

"Kelly, you would be so proud of me. I've turned a new leaf. We're expanding, but I'm farming out the responsibilities. I'm delegating, baby. The food truck responsibilities are not going to fall on me. Don't worry. I really am becoming less of a control freak with my businesses. I can't take the stress right now. The baby needs me to be less stressed."

"Good," I said, my voice filled with doubt.

"Wait till you see all the hype that comes with these food truck events. And just wait till you see the crowds that show up. People post things all over social media, plus the event itself has its own Facebook page. These food trucks are big business," Nikki said, giving her hair one last fluff in the mirror.

"So, change of subject, what did you mean, that's all I need, more men? Is everything okay with you and Jack?" Nikki asked.

"I thought so. He's been so quiet over the past couple of days. This Adelle thing has me all freaked out. I just feel like everything I touch turns bad. Jack's probably going to get fired or something from his job because he's got me as a girlfriend."

"No, he's not. Don't overreact. I'm sure he's just super busy trying to get back to work after being gone for so long."

"He is. And to make matters worse, I know he was put right on a big case when he got home. He wanted to come straight back to Miami after the news of the jailbreak, but when we found out it wasn't Steve, I told him to stay put. Besides, it looks like I might be heading home soon. But, he never said anything about staying downtown and sleeping near the office. That's news to me," I said, my voice trailing off.

Not knowing where Jack was staying was just one more thing adding to my stress. It didn't sit well that he was keeping his whereabouts secret from me. Or perhaps I was being overly paranoid.

"Kelly, Jack is crazy about you. Haven't you figured that out yet? If there's one thing you don't have to worry about, it's his commitment to you. He's probably just really busy with work. Like you said, he missed a lot while he was here and is probably working double time to try and make up for that. Believe me, Jack is smitten like a kitten," Nikki said, turning back to the mirror to apply yet another coat of mascara.

Nikki's words made me feel better. She always made me feel better. And she was right. I had no reason to doubt Jack. Going out tonight was going to make me feel so much better. Jack probably was just busy with work.

"What about Adelle?" I asked, hoping she could pour her magic on that problem as well.

"Adelle will be okay. This thing with the Junior League Club has been coming for quite some time. Mom is making a mountain out of a molehill. If you ask me, Adelle is better off," Nikki said.

"You mean better off now that she's been kicked out of the Junior League?"

"She wasn't kicked out. That's not how it works. You know how women work. They're much too vicious to do something like that to your face. They strategically make you feel like you are not wanted in little ways until you have no choice but to quit. Then you have to deal with not only the fact that you were shunned but also now feel guilty that you may have been reading the situation wrong and left your committee friends with all the work," Nikki said, blinking violently all of a sudden. "Oooh, I think that was too much mascara."

"Can you tell me exactly what happened?"

"As far as I know, like I said, this has been coming. Ever since Mike's company took a downturn and they lost the house, some of the Junior Leagers, have had it out for her. And not all of them. On a whole they're really a nice group. I partner up with them all the time for events at Chocolate Love. It's really just two of the ladies that have taken on positions of power. Kim Lakes and Brandy Morgan. They're kind of the mean girls of the group. And unfortunately, they've somehow weaseled their way into leadership roles, as mean girls tend to do. They've made it their life's mission to go after Adelle, probably because she's an easy target right now," Nikki said, turning to me. "I know this all seems kind of silly to you right now."

"No," I said, anxious to hear more. I was finally getting the details of the story. This was exactly what I wished Mom would have been able to verbalize this morning. "Tell me more. Who the hell do these women think they are, going after Adelle? Especially when she's going through a hard time. Now I see why Mom was so upset."

I couldn't help but think of Adelle and Mike's kids. Had these women somehow managed to sneak their poison into the school system and work against my niece and nephews? Like Nikki had said, that was how vile women worked. When they were upset, they went after your reputation, your children, and your family's good name.

"So, this past week, when Mike got in the accident, this Kim and Brandy suggested Adelle hand over her role in the Christmas parade so she could look after Mike," Nikki said, throwing quotes around the word "suggested."

"That was the last draw for Adelle. They'd been doing this for a couple of months now. 'Oh, don't take on the back to school fundraiser. You need to focus on moving into your new rental home. Don't worry about Halloween decorations for the kid's party. You're busy selling your cars.' You know, things like that," Nikki said, using her best snotty girl voice to imitate them.

I could just imagine Adelle trying to weave her way through their passive aggressive comments and digs. It must have been exhausting.

"What jerks," I said, forming my hands into fists. "They can't get away with that. What can we do?"

"Well, too late. They did get away with it. She quit," Nikki said.

"No!"

"Yep."

"Where were the rest of Adelle's friends? Why didn't they knock these girls off their high horses?"

"Adelle said plenty of the women served it right back to them. Like I said, they're a good bunch. But you know how mean girls get. People get scared to stand up to them. They don't want to be the next one on their list to be bullied."

"This is so horrible. It sounds like high school."

"It does. And like I said, if you ask me, she's better off. It's just a shame. The Junior League always does so much good for the community. I served on it for a year with Adelle. Don't know if you remember that or not. You were living in California at the time. Eventually, I had to leave the organization because it was just too much extra responsibility while I was in the midst of taking over Chocolate Love. I loved it while I was on it though," Nikki said, rubbing at her stomach while she gazed at something on the wall. It looked like she was taking a trip down memory lane. She smiled and I imagined she was remembering a time in her life when there were fewer responsibilities on her plate.

"Did you know these two women, Kim and Brandy?" I asked.

Nikki's eyes refocused on mine with a new flicker of passion.

"No. They weren't in the club when I was there. I think that's kind of the kicker. These are fairly young girls, new blood, as the existing members sometimes jokingly call them. Both girls are new to the area and looking to flaunt their new "Mrs." titles and newly acquired money. Oh, and they're both looking to oust the existing women in seats of power for their own advancement, so they can become the new queen bees."

"And it sounds like they're not afraid to play dirty in order to do it," I said with heavy resentment. Adelle was so fragile right now with all of the financial changes going on in her life. These mean girls were the last thing she needed.

"Yes, but they're forgetting one thing," Nikki said, turning back and fluffing her ridiculously long, black wig.

"What?" I asked, sitting up, awoken by the hopeful suggestion in Nikki's tone.

"One, they're forgetting just how fabulous Adelle is. She's going to put all of her energy now into launching her new pastry business. We're going to use the parade as her launch party for the business."

"Wait, what? How did I miss this?" I said, feeling totally out of it. "I thought Adelle was just into making a couple of pies for Bean in Love?"

"No, no, she's going bigger. I'm pushing her to go bigger," Nikki said, that signature Nikki gleam in her eye taking over.

"Does she know this?" I laughed.

Ignoring my question, she soldiered on.

"And two, I'm in the Chamber of Commerce and guess who is in charge of the parade this year?" Nikki said, dancing her eyebrows up and down.

"Oh my God, Nikki, what are you up to?" I said, a smile forming on my face.

"You'll see," Nikki said, laughing a maniacal laugh. "Don't worry, I have no intention of hurting the Junior League Club, they're awesome as a whole. But I do intend to serve a little trouble back to Kim and Brandy. It's not right what they did to Adelle. She's a nice person. And, they shouldn't have treated my sister that way. But enough about this, we have to go. It's getting late. It's Food Truck Tuesday!"

Chapter 12

"Ladies," Tony said by way of greeting as we stepped off the elevator onto the marble floor of the lobby. The lights, shining down from the ceiling, accentuated the beauty of the immaculate marble floor and freshly vacuumed entryway mat. The lobby always smelled of fresh hibiscus thanks to the well-kept plants that lined the windows.

At first, Tony gave us only a sideways glance then returned to his papers in front of him. Suddenly his head snapped back up, and his hands spread over the security desk like webs, balancing his upper body as he leaned over to get a better look.

"What in the world? Kelly? Is that you?" he asked, his mouth dropping open. His red tie fell forward onto the desk and his dark, brown eyes nearly popped out of his head.

Nikki and I took a second to turn and examine each other. At the last second, I'd decided to stuff one of the throw pillows from the couch under my shirt. It gave me a decent bump, suggesting I was well into my fake pregnancy. I didn't want to admit to myself how much of a thrill I got from sporting a bump, nor did I want to get too emotional about it. It was just a disguise. And a really good one at that. If the world was still looking for Kelly Clark, they would be looking for a thin brunette on the tall side, not a pregnant woman with a blond bob. I'd been pretty proud of my disguise until seeing Tony's reaction.

"Do we look that bad?" Nikki asked.

She reached over and straightened my shirt over my bump and smoothed the back of my hair with her hand. As she was doing that, I reached out and fluffed the bangs on her dark, long wig.

"Wait a minute, is that Henry's wig, I mean, Margo?" he asked, referring to Mom's friend who loaned us the wig.

"Well, um," Nikki said, stalling. Apparently, it was no secret Mom's friend was a cross-dresser, but Nikki seemed a bit hesitant to confirm and possibly out him.

"It's okay, we all know about Henry. It's no secret. He's loud and proud," Tony laughed.

"He asked me to go with him once. I mean, she did. Margo, I mean. Or Henry dressed as Margo, or whatever. We're all cool with it. I'm seriously thinking of taking him up on the offer just to check it all out. I mean, I'm straight and all, but hell, it's South Beach. When in Rome, right?"

"Agreed," Nikki laughed, moving closer to the desk. "Are you from this area, Tony?"

"Oh no, originally from Chicago, like you guys," Tony said, a large grin spreading across his face. His brown eyes sparkled a bit and his Midwestern accent got more distinct when he talked about his hometown.

"That's right, Chi-Town. Or Chi-Raq, as they refer to it now. The shootings there are out of control. I mean the violence, my lord. It's not right. I moved here over fifteen years ago to work for the Miami police, so I've seen my share of violence and crazy, but it's nothing like what my friends tell me about Chicago now. But, of course, you ladies are from your nice little hometown, Geneva. No trouble makers or violence there." Tony stopped speaking abruptly and looked at me.

"I mean, it's a nice place and," Tony's large hands moved frantically in the air like he was physically trying to reach out and grab a hold of something to say.

"Wow, I didn't realize you were on the police force for that long," Nikki said, filling in the gap for him. "You were a policeman in Chicago as well?"

"Yes, that's right," he said, refusing to make eye-contact with me. "I got sick of the cold, so I accepted a job here. Then after twenty years on the Miami force, I decided I had seen enough and it was time to retire. I was eligible for a pension, and it was time to take that donut and swim for shore."

"Take the donut?" I laughed.

"Yeah, you know, that pension was like having a life tube thrown out to me. I was drowning in violence. Felt like I was starting to get PTSD after that many years on the force. Couldn't take anymore. The idea of a pension and a job with less stress was like someone throwing me a blow up raft, you know, one of those air donuts. A buddy of mine was connected to this building and the rest is history." Tony turned back to me and smiled.

"So, we're heading to Food Truck Tuesday," Nikki said, changing the subject. "Are we dressed okay?"

Nikki had on a long, blue and white, maternity sundress with spaghetti straps. I thought she looked adorable. I had on one of her maternity tops in light blue, over a pair of maternity jeans I'd snagged from her suitcase.

"Absolutely. You're going to love it. Looks like Kelly's eating for two now, as well, huh?" Tony laughed. His pointer finger extended in the direction of my fake bump.

"I thought it would help my disguise," I laughed. "You know, just in case any reporters are trailing me."

"It's a great idea," Tony laughed. "Though, I think you're in the clear. No calls or visitors for a while now."

"It is kind of freaky that this Franklin Ford is still on the loose though, don't you think, Tony?" Nikki asked.

"I can't believe he hasn't been caught," Tony said, shaking his head.

"How can that be?" I asked, leaning against the counter. "All of those people after him, you would think he wouldn't be able to get anywhere. His picture is all over the news."

"I agree," Tony said. "I don't know much about his past, haven't really had time to watch all the reports or read up on him, but in my opinion, I think he's getting a lot of help."

"What do you mean?" Nikki asked.

"Well, someone is setting him up with food, shelter, and money. He must have had people set up to help him. It makes me think this was not just a freak jailbreak. This was an elaborate scheme."

"Tony, did the mail come? Oh, hello, ladies. Sorry to interrupt," a man said, coming around the corner.

"Hi, Mr. Banks," Tony said. "Yes, the mail has arrived. Better late than never."

The gentleman gave us a once over, and we both nodded a hello. Mr. Banks turned and headed into the mailroom, looking completely unfazed by our get-up.

"Anyway, forget about Franklin Ford, right?" Tony said, changing the subject. "You don't have to worry about it and you deserve a night out."

I let out a breath, realizing I'd been holding mine while he was theorizing about Franklin Ford.

"You were asking about Food Truck Tuesday. The one in Haulover Park, right? It's about ten minutes from here, right down Collins Avenue. You'll see the kites and trucks as soon as you cross the bridge. Great lobster rolls. Go to the lobster truck first thing."

"So, you really think it's okay for me to go out, Tony?" I asked, leaning closer to him.

Now that I knew Tony was from Chicago, I felt more of a kinship to him. There was a kind, Midwestern vibe about him that I liked and connected with. I felt like he would tell me the truth.

"I do, Kelly. Franklin Ford has nothing to do with you. The media is refocused on this football sex scandal. I heard about the big name reporter that was injured in your town. She's not even talking about you. If she had a story on you, don't you think she would have used the spotlight that's been put on her to promote it?"

"What about heading back home? Do you think I could do that yet?" I asked, not even trying to hide the desperation in my voice.

Over the last couple of days, a deep yearning to return home had taken over. I missed Jack. I wanted to see him, hold him, and be in the same bed with him again. I missed Chocolate Love and Bean in Love and the little family I'd come to know and love there. And all the talk about Adelle made me ache to return home and try to make things right for her again. I wanted to hunt down those mean girls, dethrone them from the posts they had unfairly gained and were unworthy of, and return Adelle to her rightful seat as queen of the Junior League Club. If that was what she wanted.

"Return home to Geneva right now?" Tony said. "Well, I think so."

"You don't seem too sure about that," I said, watching him closely.

"Let's just say, you're no longer front page news nationwide, but in small town Geneva, you're probably used to this by now, you're always going to be the talk of the town," Tony said, laying out the reluctant truth.

"I know," I said, letting out a sigh. "The news about Steve's jail and Diane Nosely's accident kind of blew up any anonymity I'd established there."

"Well," Tony said, starting to laugh. "you always have the wig and fake bump as an option."

Chapter 13

While Nikki parked the car at Haulover Park, I caught myself actually grinding my teeth together. Tony's words about Geneva were haunting me.

"Look at the kites! There's a man selling kites over there. So cute. They're all fishes. Look at the scuba diver kite! I get it. He's swimming with the fish. That is so cute," Nikki jabbered on and on, completely oblivious to my pain. "Wow! Look at all of these trucks. There must be over twenty-five trucks here. Geneva needs something like this. Third Street would be a perfect place to host a food truck event. I am going to take a boatload of pictures tonight and bring them to my next Chamber of Commerce meeting. Oh, wait, what do you think of this? See! I need a food truck for Chocolate Love and Bean in Love. I could drive all around the Tri-Cities selling my chocolates, coffee, muffins, all of Adelle's pastries. This is going to be so cool," Nikki said.

"Kelly! What is wrong?" she said, finally picking up on my unresponsiveness.

"Nothing," I managed.

My stomach had begun to hurt, and I wondered if I had any appetite for this event Nikki was clearly excited for. I'd been so anxious to get out, but at the moment, I just wanted to turn the car around and go back to my parent's condo.

"Your face looks so tight. Oh no, was I annoying you?" Nikki asked, looking genuinely concerned. "I was babbling on and on, wasn't I? I just get so excited to talk about new business ideas. You know how I get. I'm sorry."

"No, it's not you, Nikki. All of a sudden, I'm just getting really anxious to get home, and after what Tony said, I'm more worried than ever that I'm going to be a big spectacle. Or that I'm causing you and Adelle harm by being back in the area. Maybe it's not the best thing that I'm associated with you two. You're both high profile people in the community to begin with. I'm just throwing shade on your hard earned reputations."

"Oh shut up, Kelly. That couldn't be any further from the truth," Nikki said, playfully punching my arm. "We're so proud of you."

"But, Adelle," I began.

"You can't blame yourself for Adelle's bad blood with the Junior League. Really, it's just bad blood with Adelle and those two nasty women. You're blowing this out of proportion. And Mike hitting Diane Nosely was a freak accident. It was a horrible snow storm, and she was in the wrong place at the wrong time. And quite frankly, I don't feel bad for that woman. The universe is just paying her back for being so nosy," Nicky laughed.

"Nikki, don't talk that way," I said.

"I know you're right. It's wrong to take any joy from someone's pain, but I still say that is one wicked woman. She terrorized you. And if she did it to you, I'm sure you're not the first. I bet there are a lot of people out there that feel the same way I do."

I closed my eyes and let out a long sigh, allowing Nikki's words to sink in.

"Let's not worry about Geneva tonight, okay?" Nikki pleaded, nudging my shoulder gently.

"We are going to have some fun tonight as these alter egos we've created, eat some good food, and then I promise tomorrow we'll get serious. We'll make a ton of calls about the banking stuff in California, so we can figure out where that key leads us. Dad's got an appointment with the doctor tomorrow, so we'll know an update on his health. And then, once we know all of that, we'll be able to make some plans to get us both back home. One step at a time. Sound good?" Nikki asked, pulling a little bit at my cheek to make me smile.

I couldn't help but laugh. When I turned to look at Nikki, I noticed her wig was askew. Here I was again, wrapped up in another one of Nikki's crazy adventures. I was wearing a wig, with a fake bump, in the middle of a park in Miami about to eat a bunch of food from trucks. How did I always end up in these crazy moments with my sister?

"Okay," I said with confidence.

As nuts as she seemed to me sometimes, Nikki always came through for me. Being around her and hanging out with her always ended well for me one way or another. That was the thing with Nikki. As nuts as she came across sometimes, she was a winner. She always came out on top.

"Alright, let's go do this Food Truck Tuesday. I'm just as curious as you are. Tony has me all fired up about the lobster rolls," I admitted.

Walking into the park, the combination of the night air, the music blasting from the deejay, and the energy coming from the enthusiastic crowd made me glad we came. All around us, people smiled and laughed while bending their heads down to mysterious and enticing looking bundles of food. Just seeing everyone chewing away happily made my stomach growl.

All of a sudden the possibilities seemed endless. Would I choose the lobster roll? Or perhaps the fish tacos I saw advertised everywhere were the better pick. Wait! Was that a cupcake truck? A cupcake truck here in the middle of an open field. What a delightful idea. Why couldn't I have them all? Why choose? The little bundles the people were holding looked small enough to allow a nice sampling from a few of the trucks.

Being holed up in the condo made me long to be around other human beings. It had been wonderful to have so much one-on-one time with my parents, but I had been yearning to be able to walk free among the public. And so far so good, no one was staring or pointing at me like I worried they would. Perhaps, Nikki was right. I was old news. The latest scandal had taken over, and I'd been pushed aside. Thank goodness. It felt freeing and exhilarating.

"Wow! This is amazing. I just can't get over it," Nikki said, clicking away on her cell phone camera. "I'm sending these pictures to Bob. I was so right about the food truck frenzy."

I just nodded my head manically, pointing. "Yes, take a picture of the burger truck. You know how your husband loves burgers. Bob will totally be on board for the food truck idea when he sees that."

Nikki clicked away.

"Take a picture of that one, no, that one. Wait, the purple one. Look, that one has mini grilled cheese sandwiches. Grilled cheese sandwiches!" I shrieked.

"Should we go there first? Or wait, what about the lobster rolls? That's got to be the truck for the lobster rolls. Look at the line. Just like Tony talked about. Let's go there first. Oh, my God, Kelly. That truck is selling donuts."

Nikki took off like a rocket in the direction of the donut truck. I worried that she was walking so fast her unstable wig would fall off. That would draw a little bit of attention her way. A pregnant woman speed walking so fast her wig falls off.

"Nikki, wait for me," I called out, chasing behind her and worrying that my fake pillow bump would plummet out of my shirt. I couldn't help but giggle, waddling up next to her to line up for a donut. All of a sudden I could envision this as real. Nikki and I both pregnant, growing our own families, having adventures back in Geneva together. Taking our kids on outings like this and building memories, not only with each other but with our kids. I felt light and airy and joyful. Every time I thought my life was falling apart, spending time with Nikki, even just a few minutes, turned things around for me. I thought of what Tony talked about earlier. The way you could be drowning in life, and then suddenly something comes into your path or an idea for a new way to live pops up, allowing you to begin again or start down a new path entirely.

I was there. I'd been there for a while now. Dad was going to get better, Adelle would forge ahead with a new business while Mike's business recovered, Nikki was going to grow her family, and I was going to move full speed ahead. Together, Nikki and I were going to figure out that key, Steve would remain in jail, and Jack and I would continue our progress forward as a couple. In fact, the way I was feeling tonight, it occurred to me that perhaps it was time for me to propose to him. He tried a few months ago and I'd asked him to wait. Well, the waiting was over. It was time.

It registered then that Nikki had put something directly in front of my face. The heavenly smell told me what it was before my eyes could focus properly.

"Here, take it, Kelly. Take the donut," Nikki said.

Chapter 14

In typical Nikki fashion, she managed to talk me into exploring Miami after Food Truck Tuesday. We somehow ended the night at a club right in the heart of downtown South Beach dancing like fools as our alternate identities. I'm sure we made quite a spectacle of ourselves, two pregnant ladies dancing the night away, looking as though we had not a care in the world.

As Nikki pointed out a number of times, we'd gone completely unnoticed and unharmed. There were so many other things for one to take notice of from the cars, the clothes, and the overall party atmosphere of Miami. We were literally able to hide in plain sight.

"Well, that's that. We've contacted every bank within a twenty mile radius of your home in San Francisco. Man, aren't you glad you didn't go out there?" Nikki said the next afternoon. She'd awoken bright and early ready to get to work. I, on the other hand, was still a bit hazy from the late night.

"Yeah," I said, sitting back against the headboard in my parent's guest room.

Used coffee cups and plates were scattered, left abandoned on various posts throughout the room. We'd spent the day calling banks near the home I'd shared with Steve. Each one of them had been a dead end. There was a part of me that felt that being there in person would have been better because we would have had the ability to sweet talk some unsuspecting teller into giving us more information. But the ones we had been able to sweet talk over the phone kept telling us the same thing. If there was a box in my name, I would have had to be paying a yearly fee in order to maintain it. And although it was a nominal fee, I watched my accounts so closely now, I would have noticed it. It would have been coming out of my account by automatic withdrawal, or I would have been issued a yearly bill. And if there was anything I knew for sure it was this– I was not getting this bill, and I did not have any accounts set up in California anymore. The measly accounts I had were set up at a bank in Geneva, and I watched those like a hawk.

One of the tellers told us that even if I showed up with the key to one of Steve's accounts, which they couldn't verify if there was one or not in his name, I would have to be on the account as well, and my name was not showing up in the system at all. So, bottom line, it would have been a wasted trip if I had gone out there. Still.

"Girls, we're leaving in thirty minutes. Will you be ready?" Mom asked, knocking on the door.

We'd told her that we were going to spend the morning researching food trucks, which wasn't a complete lie. We'd scanned a few online websites to look into costs for trucks, but it had not been our true focus this morning. I just didn't want to get her involved. She had enough on her plate with trying to get Dad back on the road to recovery.

"We'll be ready, Mom," I said, feeling like we were teenagers again the way Mom's eyes bounced around to each dirty cup and dish scattered about the room.

"And we'll clean up, Mom. Don't worry," Nikki said.

Mom and I had reached a peace since yesterday's outburst. I'd come to a better understanding about why she was worried about Adelle, and she'd backed off on using me as a scapegoat for Adelle's problems.

She was right in a way. My drama had not helped Adelle's situation, but it certainly wasn't the root of it. Either way, when

Mom pulled me in for a hug last night whispering, "I'm sorry," I'd accepted the white flag and offered my own apology. That's how the Clark women rolled. No time for grudges. We needed to press on. Dad needed us.

"Okay, I really want to leave in twenty. Dad's dressed and ready. You know how anxious he can get. Maybe the doctor will see us earlier if we get there sooner than the scheduled time. You'll just love him, Nikki. Kelly's already met him. He's always on time and is straight to the point. No dilly-dallying. Just like Dad likes it," Mom said, reaching into the room and grabbing a discarded cup within her reach.

"Nikki, you're not drinking all this coffee, are you?" Mom asked, peering into the cup and taking a sniff.

"Oh, no, Mom. Strictly decaf for me after my first regular cup in the morning. Kelly's the one who's been hitting the caffeine too hard," Nikki said, pointing a finger at me. "Can't you tell?"

My eyes moved instantly to the mirror above the dresser and caught my own reflection. My hair looked as though it had never met a brush, and my over-caffeinated eyes were red and bug like.

"You're right. I have to get out of this room," I said, unsuccessfully trying to pat down my hair.

"All of this just for food truck research? Is it really that stressful? Perhaps this is too much to put on your plate right now, Nikki," Mom said.

"Kelly, you go jump in the shower, and I'll clean up," Nikki suggested, ignoring Mom's words. "Mom, how is Dad's mood? Is he okay with going to the doctor?"

"Oh, yes, he's like a changed man in the last week. He's determined to get some good news and possibly the green flag to head to Geneva for the parade."

"But Mom, that's insane. The doctor said six weeks of recovery. We're not there yet. Do you really think this is a good idea?" I asked.

"Of course not," Mom laughed. "But you know your father. Once he gets something in his head, there's no stopping him. He's not going to listen to me, Kelly. He needs to hear it from the doctor. And even that might not be enough for him. He doesn't want you heading back to Geneva alone. And now that he's got wind of this Adelle story and Mike's accident, he is absolutely determined to go back to Geneva to spend some time there. And as far as the parade, Nikki said-" My mom stopped when Nikki walked over and grabbed her arm.

"Oh, never you mind what Nikki said. We don't have time for that now," Nikki said, snapping her fingers in a hurry up motion. "Kelly, let's go, you've got to jump in the shower or we'll be late. And for the love of God, wash that hair, will you? It's stinky from the wig."

At the mention of the wigs, Nikki and I looked at each other.

"Are you going to wear it again?"

"Are you? Do you think it's necessary?" I asked.

"Not really. But maybe back at home. It could be useful."

"Are you girls serious? You're getting a little looney with this wig business. You are enjoying it just a bit too much if you ask me," Mom said, shaking her head, her voice carrying a hint of humor. "Honest to God, you girls could find fun sitting in a cardboard box."

"Mom, Tony thought it was a good idea. We didn't run into any trouble last night, and most importantly, Kelly was comfortable. It allowed her to walk around in public without any worries about being recognized."

"Oh, I suppose you're right. Fine, keep the wig thing going. Though I still maintain that we're safe now. The college football sex scandal has grown even bigger than when it first broke. It's all over the news this morning. Apparently, even the President made a comment about it on air yesterday. We're in the clear, Kelly. I would never have let you go out last night to Food Truck Tuesday if I didn't think so, wig or no wig. Diane Nosely was in town to help expose the scandal. I think she just decided to pop in on you since she was so close to Geneva and her plans were foiled. She was probably just going to try and get you to comment on how you felt about the jailbreak at Steve's prison, but it didn't pan out for her."

"I know, but she knew I was here," I said, thinking back to her calling me, and Dad sitting next to me.

"Maybe she thought you'd gone home. Or maybe she figured since she was in the area, she'd check in on the off chance you were home. Or, maybe she was there to try and get a comment from me. That makes the most sense. The bottom line is, who cares? She didn't get to any of us. She got hammered by Mike," Nikki said.

"Nikki!" Mom said, chastising her for her blunt description.

"I just wish they would catch this Franklin Ford," I said, bringing up the one thing none of us seemed to want to address over the last couple of days since the jailbreak.

"They will eventually. You don't escape from a maximum security prison and just walk the streets freely for the rest of your life," Nikki said, shaking her head and scrunching her eyebrows together. "Anyway, the point is, we're just borrowing trouble. Franklin Ford has nothing to do with you, Kelly. You're in the clear. He's on the run, but trust me, he's not thinking of you. If he's going after anyone, it's not going to be you."

"Wait, what do you mean?" I'd been rummaging through my closet picking out clothes to wear for the doctor appointment. Nikki's words made me stop what I was doing and whip my head in her direction.

"Just, you know, he's probably got his mind on his own drama. You know his story," she said, the color draining from her face.

"No, I don't," I said, my stomach dropping.

"Oh, I assumed you would have googled him when this all broke," she said quietly. "Or heard it on the news."

"Well, I know that he was in jail for murder."

Mom remained silent next to Nikki, alerting me to the fact that she knew the story as well.

"You know what, don't tell me," I said, returning to my task at hand. "It's not going to do any good except scare me. What's the point of that? I'm already scared enough. We have an appointment to get to. We're going to collect our good news that I'm sure we're going to get and then come home to celebrate. End of story. Okay?" I said.

Mom and Nikki both nodded their heads together in silence. Now I was scared.

"I'll be quick," I said, pulling out my undergarments from the dresser while simultaneously managing to slip my cell phone under the pile of clothes I had in my hand.

As soon as I was behind the closed door of the guest bathroom, I leaned into the all glass shower and turned on the water but did not go in. Instead, I sat on the marble sink and searched the name Franklin Ford, feeling foolish that I hadn't done this already. The words "double murder, pregnant wife, mistress, gruesome scene, and witness account" caught my attention. The haunting similarities to Steve's case were what hit me first. Franklin's story was a bit different though in that he killed both his wife and his mistress, unlike Steve who had just gone after his pregnant mistress unsuccessfully.

Shivers ran through me at the thought of this violent man still out there, roaming the streets somewhere, perhaps stalking his next victim. The similarities to my own story left me feeling scared and angry for the family of Franklin's victims that probably went through hell making sure he was properly tried for his crimes. Now all of that was in vain if he was free to roam about. I didn't want to think of how frightened I would be every second of every day if Steve had been the one to escape.

Finally, I stepped into the hot steam of the shower, hoping it would warm me up from the frigid chill I couldn't shake after reading Franklin's story. I longed to have Jack's strong arms around me while listening to his confident voice telling me everything was going to be alright. I needed that. Needed him. It was great to be here in the little cocoon Miami had been for me. But it was time to go back to the life I had put together in Geneva and forge ahead, regardless of my fears.

It was time to go home.

Chapter 15

"But the doctor said it was okay," Nikki insisted, leaning over the aisle for the umpteenth time to catch a glance of Mom and Dad buckled safely into their seats for our plane ride home to Geneva.

"The doctor said he wanted four to six weeks. We're just hitting three weeks, Nikki," I said, keeping my voice low so they wouldn't be able to hear us. "Careful, you just hit my wig. And my belly! You're smashing it. Sit back please!" I hissed, half serious, half joking.

"Oh, come on, I didn't hurt you," Nikki laughed.

Mom's friends had sent us home with the wigs, thrilled to be a part of our little scheme to get back to Chicago incognito. Like Mom said, it was probably overkill, but I just wanted to maintain my privacy while traveling.

"But you heard the doctor. He was thrilled with Dad's progress and told us to make him happy. This is what's going to make him happy. He wants to go back to Geneva and spend the holiday season there. I guess you can take the man out of Geneva, but you can't take Geneva out of the man. Even though they've been gone now for years, it's still their home. Maybe they'll move back. I think this little health scare really made them think about the future," Nikki said, playing with her long, dark wig. She didn't want to miss out on the fun, so she'd worn hers as well.

"I know," I sighed. "I would love for them to move back home, but they've done so well in Miami. They moved away so they could enjoy better weather in their retirement. They're not supposed to be moving back to the cold as they get older. They're supposed to be moving away from it."

"Yeah, I agree, but we're not there. Look what happened when something bad happened with their health. They didn't have anyone there to help take care of them. We had to go there."

"They have their friends," I offered, still wary of the idea of my parents giving up Miami entirely.

"It's not the same," Nikki said.

Glancing over at them, I saw Dad reach his hand out and fold over Mom's on the seat tray. His eyes caught mine, and he shot me a huge grin. He still looked thin, but there was no denying he had turned a corner. This morning, he'd pulled out a wool sweater that I'd bought for him two years ago as a Christmas present, which at the time seemed silly to me because they were already living in Miami. But even then, they'd been traveling home so much that I thought it would be appropriate. The blue and red combination reminded me of the outside coloring of Chocolate Love. The shoulders hung on him now, making him look a little deflated.

This morning, he'd gotten into a bit of a snit with my mom over the pants he'd chosen to wear. He wanted to wear his favorite corduroys that went well with the sweater. Mom thought the pants looked silly on him because of all the weight he'd lost. She had been right, of course, but not wanting to make him anymore self-conscious, she'd finally let it go, promising him a shopping trip once he'd felt up to it. The promise of Brooks Brothers always made Dad light up.

I smiled back at my dad, returning the thumbs up sign he flashed me and let my head rest against the back of the seat.

"I know," I said. "I really want them with us. We're all together again back in Geneva. The sisters, I mean. Who would have known that would happen. They should be there with us. The fun is just beginning."

"Totally," Nikki said. "I couldn't agree more. The grandkids, you and Jack back together, Chocolate Love and Bean in Love, all the adventures. There's just so much for them to be a part of. There is so much for them in Geneva. They'd be back right in the middle of it all."

"That's exactly what I'm afraid of," I sighed. "I feel like we're bringing them right into the lion's den."

"Nonsense," Nikki said, waving her hand. "You remember what the doctor said. Keep him happy, keep him motivated, and give him a purpose. We've got a great referral for a doctor in Geneva, he's signed up for cardiac rehab at Delnor Hospital, and he's with his girls. He'll be happy. He definitely won't be bored, I can tell you that. And now with all the excitement surrounding the upcoming parade next week? Whoooo!" Nikki said, letting out a little whoop. "This is going to be cray cray!"

I raised my eyebrow and blew on the blond bangs that kept falling over my eyes and blocking my ability to look directly at Nikki. "Like I said, that is exactly what I'm afraid of."

A few hours later, the four of us positioned ourselves in baggage claim to wait for our luggage to arrive. Dad sat comfortably in the wheelchair we'd negotiated for him. He'd agreed to the chair if we promised to let him walk after we left the airport. Considering the doctor had cleared him for walking, we all agreed. We'd been anxious though, to put him through the airport scene without a wheelchair. Travel had become so hectic between the security checkpoint and the gate changes. We wanted to keep it as simple and non-stressful for him as possible.

We ended up landing around seven at night, which was a great time for Jack to be able to pick us up after work. I scanned the crowd anxiously, looking for his tall form. His extreme height normally made it pretty easy to spot him. I couldn't wait to jump into his arms, smell his heavenly Jack smell and feel his excitement to see me. We'd finally had a chance to speak live last night. Over the past couple of days, it had been one thing after another interrupting our chance to talk. He'd been assigned to a high profile case downtown, and I'd been busy with my family in Miami. It worked out well for him to stay downtown in one of the corporate suites his firm had available for their employees.

The timing could not have been better considering he was trying to avoid the Geneva scene while my story circled the headlines and talk of Diane Nosely's accident was front page news. Things had certainly died down, but there was no way around it, I would be a target of major gossip for quite some time in Geneva, which in turn would make Jack face the same scrutiny. The truth was though that regardless of the jailbreak and Diane Nosely, I already had been the talk of the town, so what really changed? I was beginning to accept this more and more. It was just the way it was.

"Temptress," I heard Jack's deep voice say from behind me. Somehow he'd been able to sneak up on me.

"Jack!" I cried out, turning and diving straight into his open arms. I buried my face into his chest, allowing him to engulf me into his bear-like hug. He still had on his suit from work under his long trench coat. I purposely turned my face away so as not to get my lip gloss onto his white button down shirt.

"I dig the hair. You look like a secret agent," Jack said, pulling me back closer into him when I started to pull back to get a look at him. "You smell so good. I've missed you."

"I missed you, too," I said, breathing him in.

"Is there something you need to tell me?" he laughed, putting his hand on my fake belly.

I laughed in response, "I wish."

"Me, too," he whispered in my ear.

When he leaned down to kiss me, for a few magical seconds, it was like the whole world faded away around us. This was how it had always been with us. I just didn't care what was happening in the outer world when we were together. I enjoyed his company and his energy so much that I just wanted to focus on him. Nothing else around us mattered at this moment.

"Hi, guys," Jack said, finally pulling from our kiss to address the rest of my family that stood a few feet away from us. I'd forgotten them.

Trying to pull myself together, I released my hold of Jack and let my hands fall back down to my side.

Get a grip, Kelly, I thought.

My mom beamed in our direction, gripping her phone in her hand like she was going to take our picture. She looked so happy. My dad, though he shared the same look of approval, couldn't quite hide the glare every father lays upon a gentleman courting his beloved daughter. I imagined on the tip of his tongue were the words: You better marry my daughter and make an honest woman out of her.

It made me laugh a little thinking of Jack down on bended knee a few months ago. I'd asked him to wait till I was ready but agreed to move in with him. I'd only shared with my parents that I was moving in with Jack, not the story about the ring. I wanted to share that when it was right and both sides were ready to move forward.

"Thank you so much for picking us up, Jack," Mom said, moving closer to him. Jack extended his hand down to my dad but was cut off by Nikki coming in for a hug.

"It's good to see you, Jack," Nikki said, jokingly pushing me out of the way to hug Jack. Jack's eyes had widened to saucers until Nikki spoke.

"Oh, you're both wearing wigs," Jack said laughing. "For a second, I thought I was being assaulted by a random stranger."

Jack laughed and hugged Nikki before releasing her to shake my dad's hand.

"They talked you into one, huh?" Jack said, pumping my dad's hand.

"Can you believe it?" Dad said, his voice going down a few octaves to play tough man for his likely future son-in-law. "I don't need this stupid chair. But you know how these Clark women can be. Best to just go along with what they say. They'll give you hell if you don't let them boss you around."

"Oh, I know," Jack said, shooting a smile back in Dad's direction.

At that moment, a bell went off. The suitcases from our flight started to float down the magical turn style that delivered suitcases from some mysterious cavern underground. Jack and I moved forward to retrieve our belongings. He chose that moment to whisper into my ear, "And God knows I can't wait for you to boss me around in the bedroom tonight."

* * * * *

After dropping everyone off, Jack and I had the chance to finally reconnect. We made-out like teenagers all the way up the stairs to his condo. Once inside, Jack had to break away from our heated embrace to lock the front door of his condo that we had foolishly left open because we'd been so caught up in the moment. After bossing him around for a couple of unforgettable, glorious hours, we lounged on his couch with a bottle of wine.

"Jack, what do you think? Do you think they'll be okay there?" I asked, playing with the sash of my silk robe.

"I do," he said simply, reaching over to pour more Cabernet into my empty wine glass. "You saw the look on their faces when they saw the room Adelle put together for them."

"I know but the kids. They're going to be around all three kids all the time," I said, referring to Adelle and Mike's young children.

"Frank and Cindy are in school during the day, so it's really just Craig they'll see most of the time. And Adelle's got a good handle on him. She'll keep him occupied so your dad can rest. Besides, she's got them in the study. They can lock the door if they want."

Even Adelle and Mike's "downsized" rental home was a palace compared to the small condo I shared with Jack. Besides the fact that Adelle practically demanded they stay there, it was the obvious choice for Mom and Dad. It had a first floor study with an attached bathroom that could be closed off for privacy. And besides that, Adelle was home all day every day, willing and able to be there for them should they need anything.

The other options were to go to Nikki and Bob's, which was much too small on the main floor for them to set up a bed, and then Jack's place required a hike up three flights of stairs. Depending how long they stayed, there was always the open apartment above Chocolate Love that I had left fully furnished when I'd moved into Jack's place a few months ago. Once Dad got more comfortable with stairs, they always had the option to go there. Nikki would love that, having them there all day long to go up and visit whenever she wanted. Our parents would really enjoy the hustle and bustle of the store's activities. It would also allow for their old friends from the area to come and visit whenever they pleased without feeling like they were intruding on Adelle.

I also wanted to be able to visit Mom and Dad freely without the stress of worrying about going out in public. For me to visit Chocolate Love right now would be very stressful for not only myself, but perhaps for my parents too if they were there. It would be so much better for me to just go see them at Adelle's.

"It's late," Jack said, pulling me out of my thoughts. "Should we turn in? I've got an early morning."

"That's right. I forgot about that."

"Kelly, as much as I hate to do this, I think it's best I stay downtown tomorrow night. I have a late dinner with a client, and then I'm set to interview a witness," Jack said. He rubbed at his eyes and gave me a weary sigh.

"What time is your interview?" I asked, trying to sound sympathetic but feeling extremely disappointed.

"Ten. It's kind of shady. This witness keeps blowing us off, but we really need his testimony for this case to be a slam dunk. He keeps giving us off hours to meet with him. I feel like he's trying to break us. Like he's hoping we get so annoyed with him that we'll decide we don't need him."

This didn't mesh well with the decision I'd reached in Miami. I half thought of popping the question tonight, but it didn't feel right to just throw it out there without a special dinner or some kind of effort put into it.

Perhaps with him gone all day tomorrow, there would be opportunity for me to put together something special just for us. A surprise of some sort that carried a special meaning. When Jack had popped the question this past fall, he'd filled the bedroom with flowers. It was beautiful, perfect. I wanted something just as nice.

I thought of Jack's love of food. I needed something big, a grand gesture like he'd done.

"What are you giggling about?" Jack asked, pulling me from my daydream of filling the condo with bacon, hamburgers, pizzas, pastas, and all of his other favorites.

"Nothing," I said.

"Sure," Jack said, raising an eyebrow. "I know that laugh. What are you up to?" he pushed.

"Nothing, I promise," I said, unable to hide my guilty laughter.

He pulled me closer, his large arms encircling my body.

"Tell me," he growled, snuggling closer to me and nibbling at the weak spot on my neck. I laughed and tried to squirm away.

"You'll just have to wait and see," I said finally, giving into the fact that I wasn't going to play this off. Jack knew me too well.

"Fine," Jack said, "but whatever you're up to, it better not be dangerous. I've had enough worry over the past couple of weeks. Does it involve Nikki?" he asked, pulling away and giving me a look.

"Why do you say it like that?" I asked, smirking and knowing perfectly well why he asked that question. Nikki and I were known for getting into a bit of trouble together.

"Oh, man, it does," he said, shaking his head no and closing his eyes.

Truth be told, my idea did involve Nikki, but probably not in the way he was thinking.

"It will be wonderful, my love. I promise," I whispered in a soft voice near his ear, making him sit up in attention.

"Time for bed. Let's go, temptress. I'm going to attempt to wear you out tonight so that you don't have enough energy to go through with this evil plan you are concocting," he said, rising instantly from the couch and pulling me with him.

He succeeded in one thing that night, he wore me out. But if anything, my time with him made me more determined than ever to go ahead with my "evil plan."

Chapter 16

"Nikki," I whispered, sticking my head in through the back door of Chocolate Love. Normally this door was locked, but I'd managed to grab it when one of her employees, Ivy, walked out of it. At first she'd smiled and started on down the steps, but then her head whipped back in my direction, doing a double take.

"Hi," she'd said quickly. She then proceeded to perform the awkward dance of pretending not to watch me while walking down the stairs with a cardboard box in her hand. The way she'd looked at me made me think back to what Tony had said. About how the world would quickly forget me, but to the small town of Geneva, I was still going to be big gossip.

Before stepping all the way in, I contemplated if it had been a mistake to come here. I'd been okay in my car this morning, thinking I'd made way too big of a deal on the way home protecting my identity. No one had given me a second glance. The wig had been overkill. Life had moved on and my story was old news.

Even Diane Nosely had been wiped clean from the headlines she lived her life trying to make. I had a new conspiracy theory floating around my head. Could she have actually thrown herself in front of Mike's car to get publicity for her story? He'd said she popped out of nowhere. Impossible. Even for Diane Nosely, that was over the top.

Standing in the doorway of Chocolate Love, I decided I'd been foolish to attempt to slip back into society in small town Geneva. It was too soon. Before I could turn and make a run for it, I heard a familiar voice call out, "Hey, Kelly! What are you doing here?"

"Shhh!" I said to Miguel.

He stopped abruptly, and the large tray he was carrying of chocolate covered Oreos with tiny Santas on top threatened to tumble to the ground.

Miguel took a moment to rebalance the tray. "Whoa, that was a close one," he said in his heavy Spanish accent. He set the tray down with a clang on the counter and reached up to straighten his hairnet.

I stepped all the way in, allowing the door to close behind me.

"Are you okay, Miguel? What was that noise?" Nikki asked, stepping up next to him and touching the tray on the counter. She followed his gaze to me, and a big smile formed on her face before it turned down into a frown.

"Wait, what are you doing here? I thought you were heading to Adelle's first thing to see Mom and Dad. What's wrong?" she asked, locking me in her laser-like stare.

She was dressed this morning in baking attire, black and white checked pants with her stained, yet well loved, Chocolate Love shirt that she refused to give up though she'd long ago changed the logo. It barely made it now over her growing bump. Her hair was wrapped up in a hairnet, and even from this distance, I could tell from the lines by her eyes she'd been up early. Her skin had a slight sheen to it as though she'd been sweating.

"I just came to talk to you quick. Are you busy?" I asked. "I'm sorry for scaring you, Miguel. All of a sudden I changed my mind about coming here and was going to duck out before getting anyone's attention."

"It's okay, Kelly. Nobody's really here yet. This is a good time to be here. The crowd is over at Bean in Love this early in the morning. We don't open till eleven here on Wednesdays," Miguel explained, turning back to his work. "These good, Nikki?"

"Yeah, look good to me. Can you bring them over to Delnor?" Nikki asked. "Oh, wait; you're not on deliveries today, are you?"

"It's not me. I'll check the schedules," he said. "Shoot, I left them in front. I'll be right back," he said. "Glad you're back safe and sound, Kelly. It's been a little nutty here."

Miguel left to head to the front of the store without saying anything more. It's what I loved most about him. He always seemed to sense when Nikki and I needed our privacy and would make himself scarce.

"So, what's up?" Nikki asked, pulling out a chair at the little table where her employees always took their breaks.

"I have to ask a favor. Do you remember that private chef you hired last year to cook in your home for Valentine's Day?" I asked, sitting at the table next to her.

"Yeah," Nikki said, lighting up at the mention of the chef.

"You really liked him, right?" I asked.

"Yeah," Nikki said again, rubbing her hands together.

"Can I get his info? I want to put together a special dinner for Jack at his place tomorrow night."

"Wow, what's the occasion?" Nikki asked, bouncing her perfectly arched eyebrows up and down.

"It's just, he's done so much over the past month with helping Dad and now this big case he's in the middle of. I'd really like to do something nice for him, and you know how Jack is about food. I thought putting together a really nice dinner would be a great way to show how much I appreciate him."

Nikki leaned forward in her chair, leaving her face blank from expression. I knew what she was doing. Hoping I would fill the silence.

Finally, she caved. "Coffee?" she asked.

"Of course."

Nikki stood up to brew us a cup from the machine she kept in the back for her employees.

"How are you doing with coffee these days?" I asked, always on alert for signs that Nikki's health was suffering. Because she'd suffered so much with nausea, headaches, and weight loss in her first trimester, I was always scared she was going to fall back into that rut.

"Great. I'm still using it in small dosages, but it sits just fine with me. In fact, I don't really need it all that much. I've got lots of energy. I'll tell you what, Kelly, once you've experienced bad health, you really appreciate good health. I don't take anything for granted. Just being able to get up out of bed and not feel like vomiting means it's going to be a great day," Nikki said, shooting me a radiant smile. "Life is pretty darn good right now."

"It is," I smiled back.

"Okay, let me find my phone, so I can get the number for you," Nikki said, gliding past me in the direction of the little office she kept just off the kitchen. She patted at her apron, mumbling something incoherently. It sounded like she was saying something about "to do" lists, but I couldn't be sure.

"Lobster, that's what he made. It was so delicious," she called out from the office. "I couldn't remember what he made for us. What was his name again?" Nikki picked up something from her desk and flashed it at me. "It'll be on my phone, I'm sure of it. But it might be hard to book him for tomorrow night. I remember he was in high demand."

I cringed, realizing for the first time that my little plan was probably not going to work. God forbid something be easy. Of course the chef would be booked.

"Chef James! That was his name. Maybe if I call him and talk to him he'll make an exception. Want me to try that?" she asked.

I nodded, thinking now would be the time to say something about the engagement if I was going to. Maybe the chef would make an exception and fit me into his tight schedule if he knew how important this night was going to be.

When I opened my mouth to tell Nikki, she held up her finger for silence.

"Yes, hello, Chef James, this is Nikki Connors. My sister is looking to plan a special night for her boyfriend tomorrow night, and I was hoping you would be able to help her out. If, by chance, you have any availability for tomorrow night, would you give me a call back so we could set something up? Thank you!"

Nikki tapped the phone to disconnect and smiled back at mine in triumph.

"Okay, let's just see what he has to say. I'll let you know the second he calls back. Time for some coffee," she said, placing the phone back on her desk and gliding back to the coffee maker. "This has been a good day so far. You're back in town, we've already got a lot done for the store, parade planning is almost complete, Christmas is coming, and you're going to ask Jack to marry you."

"How did you know that?" I stammered.

"Kelly, come on," she said. "I can read you like a book. It's me, remember? You can't hide anything from me."

Nikki started a little dance that could only be described as a jig. She hummed to herself and pumped her arms, looking down at her feet.

"Balloons. We need balloons," she said, changing her dance to a march and pointing up at the ceiling. "Let's make balloons drop from Jack's ceiling. We can time it so that it drops when he says yes. Adelle and I can be hiding in the room, and we'll pull the string to make them drop. Then all the kids will come out from the back bedroom with Mom and Dad."

I groaned and put my head down on my hands, watching my dream of a quiet, intimate dinner waft away up into the air, just like the steam drifting up from the coffee Nikki placed in front of me.

Chapter 17

I lifted my head at the sound of the back door opening. The cold air from outside slapped me in the face, making me long for the warm Miami climate I'd just left.

"What are you doing here?" Adelle asked, balancing some kind of tray in her left arm.

When she turned to close the door, I pulled a finger up to my lips in a shushing motion to indicate to Nikki to not talk about the engagement dinner. Right now I just wanted things between us.

Normally, Adelle glowed like a fairytale princess– perfect clothes, hair, and makeup all while running a household with three busy kids. Today, however, she looked a little worse for wear. Her luminous skin was still aglow, but there was something off about her normally perfect makeup this morning. Even from this far away, I could see a line along her jaw where she'd failed to blend the foundation she wore.

It struck me then how odd it was to see her here at this hour. If she was here, who was watching her kids? And who was helping Mom and Dad?

Nikki walked over to her and carefully slid the tray out from under Adelle's arm. Her head bent over the tray, and she took in a dramatic sniff.

"Aunt Becky's Cinnamon Chip Scones?" she asked.

"Yep, let me know what you think. I think this batch turned out really good. I'm just looking for another clincher to add to the pies and donuts. I think this is it. They're a twist on the ones that Aunt Becky used to make us. More heavy cream though, which is always a good thing," she said, pulling off her purple snow cap to allow her long, golden hair to fall luxuriously around her shoulders.

"Oh, I love it! Remember how we used to fight over the last one?" Nikki said, biting into one. "Oh my," Nikki hummed. "They have that soft consistency just like Aunt Becky makes them. Good job."

Adelle hung up her coat on the hook near the door and moved closer to the table to give me a hug. She smelled of cinnamon. I'd seen her briefly when we dropped off Mom and Dad after our flight home from Miami, but not since then.

"It's so nice to walk in and see you, Kelly. Glad you're home. You're still coming over this morning, right?"

"I'm just catching up with Nikki, and then I was going to head over to your house to visit with you and Mom and Dad. I'm picking up the donuts. Didn't Mom tell you?" I asked.

My body was here in Chocolate Love, but my mind was already there at Adelle's house, looking around to see where my parents were and if they were taking care of the three kids. Surely, Adelle wouldn't have done that. She wouldn't have left the kids for my parents to babysit while Dad was still on the mend from heart surgery. It worried me that she wasn't quite meeting my eyes.

"Are the kids home alone with Mom and Dad?" I asked, unable to keep the accusatory tone from my voice.

Adelle and I had our struggles in the past when it came to our relationship. I sometimes found Adelle to be self-absorbed and self-focused, but we'd made great strides over the past few months. The turning point for me had been when Adelle had literally thrown herself in the path of danger to save my life last summer after one of Steve's girlfriends came to kill me. It was tough to still view her as self-absorbed when she'd chosen to put her own life on the line to save mine.

I'd come to understand that Adelle was heroic, laser-focused, and yes, somewhat self-absorbed, but in a good way. She needed to be to maintain her well-run family. Especially when they were going through the financial hardships they'd faced.

"No, they're in school, silly. Craig is home napping, but I have a sitter there for a few hours, so I can do my errands," she said, meeting my eyes with a questioning look.

"Oh, I'm sorry," I stumbled, feeling instantly guilty and upset with myself. Hoping to make some kind of amends, I stood, pulling out a chair for her.

"Let me get you some coffee," I said, making a motion for her to sit. "How's Dad today?"

"He seems really good. Mom said he slept well. You know we moved that queen mattress down to their room from the guest room. They seem to love that one. I suggested to Mom that she go out for a bit once you get there this morning. Is that okay with you, Kelly?" she asked.

She plopped down on the tall, ornate iron chair that reminded me of something that would be found in a café in Paris. Hanging out in Nikki's back kitchens of Chocolate Love was by far my favorite place to be, besides the condo I shared with Jack, of course. After Mom and Dad sold our childhood home, the kitchen of Chocolate Love had become the new home base for the Clark sisters. It was warm, cozy, and always flowing with activity and energy just as Mom and Dad's kitchen had been. And even though Nikki owned the place, it always felt like somewhat of a neutral ground for us since it wasn't one of our homes.

"Of course," I said, though I felt a bit disappointed. I'd been looking forward to spending some time with Mom this morning and catching up.

I'd really been spoiled getting all that one-on-one time with both of my parents in Miami. Now that we were back in Geneva, they were going to be pulled in a million different directions by their kids and grandkids. But it was important that Mom get out and not be caretaker 24/7. That wasn't healthy for her.

"What does everyone have planned for dinner tonight?" I asked, struck by an idea.

Nikki and Adelle shook their heads simultaneously.

"Why don't we do a family dinner tonight? Jack is going to be gone because he's working, but I'm sure he wouldn't mind if I hosted at our place," I said.

"That sounds lovely, but Mom and Dad have been on the go so much. Why don't we keep them situated in one place? I'm happy to host," Adelle said.

"Are you sure?" I asked. "You've got so much on your plate right now managing the kids and now taking on Mom and Dad."

"And launching a new business," Nikki said proudly. "What do you think of the sign, by the way? Did you pick the logo? The truck is ordered, the launch is happening. What did you decide? Come on!"

"I'm still thinking Adelle's Pastries in red rather than pink. What do you think? The truck has a deep fryer, right?"

"Yup," Nikki said.

"Wait, you're getting a food truck for this? When?" I asked.

"For the parade!" Nikki and Adelle said in unison.

"What? You're launching your business at the parade? As in the parade that's in a few days?" I shrieked, feeling stressed for them.

"We've got plenty of time. This is a soft launch anyway. We'll have a proper party once we get feedback about her products. The parade is just such a great opportunity to expose her product to a lot of people. We're going to park the truck right in front of Chocolate Love, where the parade starts, and BAM! The world will know Adelle's Pastries. Pies, donuts, scones and wait, that's it so far, right?" Nikki asked, looking over to Adelle.

"I think it's best to stick to that for now. Those are my specialties," Adelle said. "I could always grow more, but I want to stick with my best ones to start."

"And to rub it in their faces," Nikki said, with a little laugh.

"Nikki, stop. We said we weren't going to talk about them anymore. I don't want my success or my failure to have anything to do with them. This is just me and you teaming up to launch a good product."

"Oh, you're going to succeed. You bet your butt you're going to succeed," Nikki said, forming a fist with her right hand and pumping it in the air while starting her march again.

"Anyway, back to tonight. Honestly, it's easier for me to host. The thought of taking Mom and Dad out in the cold and packing up the three kids is much more daunting than hosting. Besides, I've already got dessert ready," Adelle smiled.

I contemplated then pointing out her make-up line but held back. I felt like a jerk doing it even though I was truly only wanting to help.

"How is Mike?" I asked, feeling like I needed to address the accident again.

"He's good," Adelle said, not missing a beat. "I mean, he's still horrified by what happened, of course. The roads were so slick that day. I just wish he hadn't gone out in the first place. We feel bad about Diane."

Nikki let out a little bit of a snort.

"She shouldn't have been here. Kelly spoke with her directly and told her no interviews. She was being Nosely and sticking her nose where it didn't belong."

"Nikki, no one hated her more than me, but it's still sad what happened to her," I said.

Nikki rolled her eyes and shook her head, "Yeah, yeah, I know.

I'm awful for saying it. But come on, Kelly. She's not a good person. And she's going to be fine. It's just a few broken bones."

Appalled by Nikki's coldness, I bit my lip and held off on saying anything more.

"The good thing is, the whole thing is behind us now. Mike was clearly not at fault, and he's trying to move on. In fact, he's been so busy, we haven't had much time to talk. He's been gone a lot lately working on new projects."

"If this isn't a good time for Adelle's Pastries, I totally understand. We could pick it up at another time. I've been pushing you because I just want you to be happy and successful. If you want to put it off till spring, we can totally make that work, too," Nikki offered, finally sitting down next to us at the table. She'd been flitting around with paperwork behind us this whole time.

"Are you kidding? Adelle's Pastries is what's keeping me going," Adelle said, a huge grin lighting up her face.

"What's going on here? You have to blend your make-up in better," Nikki said, reaching over with her thumb and running it across Adelle's jaw.

Typical for Nikki to get right to the heart of the matter without any hesitation. To my surprise, Adelle just laughed and stood up to pull out a small compact from her purse.

"Oh my goodness, the light in this room is unforgiving," Adelle said, referring to the morning sun pouring in from the large glass windows Nikki made sure to keep sparkling clean. "I lent Mom my normal make-up mirror, so I applied mine in bad lighting this morning. I'll have to go home and fix this."

"Okay, back to the pies and donuts. And scones! How did this come about? Tell me more," I said fixated on these plans that I'd been unaware of.

"Well, I've been looking to grow the product line for my two stores, and I just happen to know a very talented baker. Bean in Love is looking for more things to serve to the late afternoon crowd or book club meetings for evening discussions. Pies and donuts are the perfect fit," Nikki said.

"Adelle, how in the world are you going to have time to take this on? You have so much going on in your life," I said.

"I know. But the kids are not going to be little forever. They're not going to need me as much in the coming years. It's hard to imagine that right now, but it's true. I'll eventually be able to go back to work and this is something I would love to be doing," Adelle said. "It's kind of depressing to think of them growing up and not needing me. This project is exactly what I need. It's my next baby."

"Mike is cool with it all?" I asked.

"Mike is cool," Adelle said, not meeting my eyes. She kept her eyes focused on her compact, rubbing at her jaw line.

"Good," I said, feeling unsatisfied with her answer.

As usual, I felt locked out of Adelle's full story. She gave surface details of her plans but not enough to make me feel like I knew what was really going on. What was she hiding this time? And why didn't she trust me enough to tell me?

Chapter 18

"Wait, who's this now?" Nikki said, pulling her cell phone from her back pocket. "Hold on one second. I have to take this."

Nikki walked out of the room with a little smile on her face.

"So, really, Adelle, how are things at home? Are you sure you can handle all of this? I can help with Mom and Dad anytime," I said, taking advantage of the quiet moment.

Adelle nodded her head.

"Mom and Dad are good," she said in a high-pitched voice. Her eyes were up at the ceiling, in her coffee cup, glancing over her manicure. Anywhere but on me.

"Really?" I probed. "I feel like you're not telling me everything. Adelle, I know you're upset with me for bringing so much trouble for you. We should talk about this. I don't want things between us to be strained."

Adelle fell silent and looked down at the table. I'd gone straight to the problem at hand and that didn't normally fly with Adelle. She seemed to prefer to keep things light and positive.

"Adelle, I didn't mean for any of this to happen. I'm very sorry Mike was involved in that accident. And I'm sorry that I brought Steve into our lives and that you're being affected by it all. This is not what I wanted," I said, imploring her to look at me by placing my hand on her arm.

When I did, it was like I'd shocked her with an electric bolt. She pulled away and scooted back further in her chair.

"Kelly, I don't want to get into this right now. I have things I have to do," she snapped, practically snarling at me.

"But how come you have time to vent to Mom and Dad about me behind my back?" I bit back.

I couldn't help it. Her stance made me automatically defensive. I did my best to beat down my aggression and remain cool.

"Please, come to me. Tell me. Haven't we gotten to a place where we can communicate better?" I asked.

"Kelly, it just seems like you bring a black cloud everywhere you go. You come back in town, and now we're all dealing with the scandals you've brought back with you. The trial, then the press, and now this recent possible jailbreak and Diane Nosely. It's never ending. When is it going to stop? It's just too much," Adelle snapped at me, a nasty edge to her that wasn't there a few seconds ago.

I sat back in my chair feeling like Adelle had shot me with a gun. The words she'd spoken were what I'd feared my family had been thinking but wouldn't say aloud.

"Mom and Dad are getting older, Kelly. They need this to calm down. This," Adelle said, waving her arms as if to indicate the air space around me. "It needs to stop," she said, in a tone indicating that I'd been purposefully crafting up the trouble that followed me around. "Clean up your mess, Kelly," she said, giving her final death blow.

"I am not the root of all your problems, Adelle. It feels like you're blaming me for Mike's business taking a hit. My divorce did not make the economy sink. Kelly Clark did not cause the housing bubble or the recession."

"Yes, but you certainly put a black mark on the Clark name and that didn't help Mike's business. You can't tell me that the way people look at me now isn't tied to you. You must be somewhat aware that your actions have tarnished the Clark name in this area."

"You can't blame me for what Steve did. How can you blame me for that?"

Nikki chose that moment to come marching into the room all jumpy and excited, completely oblivious to what was happening.

"He can do it, he can do it," she sang joyfully, sounding like an out of tune opera singer. She held the phone out to me and bounced her eyebrows up and down. Her pixie cut was tussled in a way that told me she must have been picking at it while she was on the phone. "Talk to him!"

Adelle shook her head and started to collect her things, apparently done with her chastising. I didn't move to take the phone from Nikki. It felt like my body was on high alert, heart pumping erratically and head buzzing.

"What just happened? What did I miss?" Nikki asked, turning to look at Adelle.

"I have to go," Adelle said, throwing her coat over her arm and turning to leave.

"But," Nikki said, "the parade?"

"We'll talk later," Adelle said, slamming the door behind her.

It was her unmasked anger that hurt the most. The words that were clearly kept under the surface all this time, waiting to be unleashed, had finally been spoken. I imagined her and Mike at home, sneering at my name over a bottle of wine. I could only imagine the conversations they must have had about me on a daily basis.

"Kelly is always causing trouble for this family. When is she going to learn? When is she going to take responsibility for her mess? She's a wreck."

She was ashamed of me. She felt I'd brought shame upon the family name in Geneva. The worst thing was she was right. Adelle was only stating the obvious.

"What just happened?" Nikki asked, putting her hand over the phone to try and keep our conversation private.

I just shook my head, unable to speak coherent words. Closing my eyes, I fought to keep tears from escaping.

"Would it be possible for Kelly to call you back?" I heard Nikki say into the phone.

When I opened my eyes, Nikki was sitting down at the break table next to me.

"Seriously, I was gone for under two minutes, what the heck just happened?" Nikki begged, searching my face with her cocoa eyes.

"Adelle," I began to speak, anger leading the way, but then I hit a wall almost immediately and started to cry. "Oh my God, she's right," I managed to get out before breaking into tears.

* * * * *

An hour later, I finally made it to Adelle's house. I knocked hesitantly at first, feeling like I didn't have the strength to make it through the rest of the day. A big part of me wanted to crawl back in bed and let the day go on without me. But Mom needed me and Dad was expecting me. They would worry if I didn't show up.

The gargantuan wooden door creaked open and a young woman I did not know stood on the other side, peering out at me.

"You must be Kelly," she said, motioning for me to come inside. "I'm Katrina."

Katrina stood just less than five feet and looked to be about sixteen years old. Her long, black hair hung almost all the way to her waist, and her almond eyes smiled up at me.

"Hi, Katrina," I said. "Nice to meet you."

I reached out to shake her extended hand, making me think my initial estimate was off by a few years. Sixteen-year-olds were generally not confident enough to offer a handshake and such solid eye contact.

"Adelle should be home shortly. She told me you might be coming. Your mom and dad are waiting for you in the kitchen."

The sound of a large boom made both of us turn and look up the staircase to the second floor. I half expected to see Craig there, but when he didn't appear, Katrina dashed toward the stairs.

"I think I better go check on Craig. He's supposed to be napping, but, well, you know," she said, shrugging. "He's Craig."

I smiled at her and lifted the little brown bag I was holding.

"I'll just go ahead into the kitchen," I said.

"Okay," Katrina called over her shoulder, her small frame already at the top of the stairs.

Taking in a long breath, I kicked my shoes off and hung up my coat in the front hall closet.

"Kelly, is that you?" I heard my mom's voice call out from the kitchen.

"Coming," I called, feeling bad I was so late. I hadn't intended on staying so long at Chocolate Love, but it had taken awhile for me to get myself together. Adelle's words had really rocked me to the core.

"We're waiting for our donuts," Mom sang out.

Plastering a huge smile on my face to overcompensate for the real way I was feeling, I held up the brown bag over my head.

"Here they are!" I sang out cheerfully.

Mom's face fell as soon as her eyes connected with mine.

"Where have you been?" Dad asked, his eyes locked on the bag and a huge smile on his face. "We've been waiting forever."

"Dad, did you come back to Geneva to be with us or was it all about the donuts?" I laughed, grabbing a plate from one of the large cabinets.

Mom stood up and made quick work of arranging the donuts on plates. I'd grabbed a few of the double chocolate cake donuts that I knew were Dad's favorite.

"Now, remember, this is a very special treat. We are not going to eat like this on a normal basis anymore. We're just testing out Adelle's new donuts, and then we're back to our healthy eating like the doctor said, right?" Mom nagged. She moved over to the table and set down the dish in front of my dad who watched her every move.

"Mmmph," Dad said, stuffing his face with a donut the minute it was set down in front of him. He nodded his head in agreement, but I could tell he was just appeasing her. He gave us a thumbs-up and closed his eyes while he swayed back and forth.

"Kelly, we need more coffee cups. We used them all this morning. I think Adelle has a few extras stashed in the dining room. Will you come with me to check?" Mom said, motioning me with her head to accompany her into the other room.

"Be right back, Dad," I said, slapping playfully at his hand that was reaching across the table for Mom's donut.

He laughed, spitting a few crumbs of donut out onto the table. Before I left the room, I gave one quick glance back in his direction and noticed he was picking the crumbs up and sticking them in his mouth.

"Whoa," I said, nearly running into Mom standing just on the other side of the doorway at the entrance to the dining room.

"What's wrong?" she demanded. Her eyes blazed into mine like she was shining a flashlight into my very soul.

"Nothing," I said, breathing in to try and catch my breath. "Let's get those cups."

I tried to move around Mom, but she blocked my way and held her ground.

"No, I can tell you've been crying. What's wrong? Adelle told you, didn't she?"

What?

My heart stopped beating at the way Mom said those words.

What did she mean by that?

"Mom," I creaked out, feeling a little frightened now. "What do you mean? What are you talking about?"

"Oh no," Mom said simply.

At that moment, I heard the back door open and Adelle call out, "I'm home!"

Chapter 19

"Where is everyone?" I heard Adelle ask Dad.

"We're in here," I called out, keeping my eyes on Mom. I watched her face tighten and her lips form into a tense line

"Mama!" Craig yelled out joyously from Katrina's arms. She carried him down the hallway toward the kitchen.

Adelle walked out into the hallway to meet him, spotting us in the dining room.

"Oh, hi guys," she said, nodding to us while simultaneously scooping up Craig from Katrina's arms. He snuggled into her, nestling his nose into her neck.

"Mama's home," she said, snuggling him back.

Adelle snuck a peek back in our direction. I was sure from the way her eyes scrunched up, studying us, she could tell there was tension in the air. Mom looked as though she'd just swallowed a canary, and I was sure I didn't look much better.

"Did the donuts go over okay?" she asked, trying to peer around Craig's face. He was sticking it in front of hers and holding her head in both of his tiny hands, as though trying to demand all of her attention.

"Great," I said, nodding my head and holding onto the back of one of the dining room chairs just to have something to do with my hands.

"Kelly, can I talk to you for a second?" Adelle asked.

She was a completely different person than the one I'd

encountered an hour ago. For one thing, she was meeting my eyes this time when she spoke.

"I'm going to head out," Katrina said. "Don't worry about paying me today, Adelle. I'm coming back tomorrow, remember?"

"Are you sure, Katrina? Let me just grab my purse," Adelle said.

"No, no. Square me tomorrow. Bye," she said, turning to head out the front door.

"Craig, let's go play that game you wanted to play earlier with Grandpa. The video game," Mom said enthusiastically.

"Okay!" Craig called out, jumping into Grandma's arms.

Adelle released him and motioned for us to head into the living room, so we could have some privacy. I was glad she'd picked this room to talk. From the second they moved into this rental home, this room appealed to me the most. It was painted a light, soothing gray color and the elegant floor to ceiling cream, silk drapes allowed a ton of light in, creating an almost ethereal feeling to the room. I was hoping the gentility of the room would influence the way our conversation went.

"Kelly, I just want to start by saying I'm sorry," Adelle said, surprising me. She pulled me down next to her on the couch that was lined with overstuffed throw pillows.

"I shouldn't have snapped that way at you. That was all wrong. I handled that whole thing so poorly," Adelle said. "It's no excuse, but I'm under so much stress. I'm taking it out on you. I don't know what's wrong with me."

Adelle wasn't one for apologies. Normally, it took a long time for her to say she was sorry, if she did at all. Most of the time, she waited for you to apologize and then maybe you got her to own some of where she was in the wrong. But I had to stop expecting what I knew of Adelle in the past to be the Adelle of the present. Adelle was grown up now. So was I. Things were different.

That was the thing about moving back home and being with your siblings again. I was constantly trying to live with the person I'd known from the past. But we were all different people now.

I let out a sigh.

"No, you were right, Adelle. I've brought so much trouble to this family. I need to own that and figure out a way to make it stop."

"No, Kelly. I'm expressing myself incorrectly." Adelle sighed, leaning back on the throw pillows. "That's what my counseling sessions with Mike have taught me. So much of the time, I'm upset about one thing, but I take it out on the wrong person."

I frowned, taking a more relaxed stance, just like Adelle by leaning back on the pillows along with her. We were going to have a real conversation here, I could tell.

"As you know, things have been stressful here since," Adelle waved her arms above her head, I assumed to indicate her surroundings. "We're doing okay, but all of the changes: the home, the drive to rebuild the business, everything. It's all taking a toll. I'm just tired. I'm so tired," Adelle said, closing her eyes for a second.

"And the car accident didn't help the situation," I said, referring to Mike's car hitting Diane Nosely.

Adelle just nodded her head.

"I'm sorry, Adelle. I'm really sorry," I said, able to give a genuine apology now that her anger was gone, and I was no longer feeling defensive.

Adelle just reached over and took my hand in hers but kept her eyes squeezed shut. A single tear, elegant and shiny, just like my sister, slid down the side of her face. The sight of it made my heart rip to pieces. My strong, beautiful sister was carrying too much weight as she normally did, but now it was breaking her, right in front of my eyes. Watching it seemed so similar to watching my dad get sick; like a powerful giant being taken down. It was too much.

"Adelle, please, let Mom and Dad live with me while they are here. It's too much to have them here. Not while your family is going through all of these changes. It's too much for you," I said.

Adelle wiped her cheek and shook her head no. She pulled herself back to a seated position and took a deep breath.

"No, it's really okay having them here. I love having them here. Besides, if we move them into your place, then Dad will struggle with all of the stairs. No, we've gone over this. It's best for them here. They'll be okay," she said. "I'm okay, really. I'm just having a weak, hormonal moment. That's okay, right?"

"Of course it is. You're always so strong, Adelle. You don't have to be. And I'm really sorry about Diane Nosely. That was awful. She was here because of me, I know that. I own that and I'm really, really sorry."

"Thank you, Kelly. I just, I don't know. I'm not trying to drop more blame or guilt on you. You go through enough, I know you do. I just wish the fallout from Steve would stop. For you, and for us. It just keeps going and it's awful," Adelle said. Her tone was not accusatory like it was this morning, just more like an observation.

"You and me both, sister," I said, feeling like I wanted to cry now. "It's like a nightmare that I can't get out of. Sometimes, I replay the day we were married in my head, searching for some moment where I could pinpoint an inner voice or some warning to not go through with it. I want to be able to say, 'See! You should have listened to your inner voice telling you not to do it!' But, Adelle, that is what scares me the most. I have no recollection of feeling hesitant, or scared, or even a feeling of doubt. I completely bought in. And look where I am now. I chose this."

Adelle shook her head.

"No, you didn't choose this, Kelly. You survived this. This is not what you wanted. And we all approved of Steve."

"You know what I mean. Of course, I didn't want Steve the sociopath, but shouldn't I have seen something? Felt some hesitation? Picked up on a flaw in his character?"

"That's not how sociopaths work. That's the science behind the sociopath. They are so good they fool people," Adelle said.

"I know. I probably sound just like every other person who's been a victim. I just want to stop being a victim, like you said. I want the fallout to stop."

Adelle nodded. "Yeah, I get it."

"Adelle, are you sure this is the right time to kick off your business? With all you have going on? How are you going to have time to bake all of this stuff?"

"Well, actually, I've got some good news. Now that I've perfected the recipes, I've actually hired someone to bake part-time at a small commercial kitchen in Geneva, The Party Kitchen. That way I won't be in Nikki's way in the stores, and I won't have to figure out how to do it here. And I won't have to get up so early."

"Wait, you've been baking early in the morning? I've heard of The Party Kitchen. I've been there for a cooking party. It's awesome!"

"I've been getting up at three to make my samples. It's the only time I can do it without the kids in the way."

"Oh, my gosh, Adelle. No wonder you're so crabby." I cringed. "Sorry."

"No, you're right. I'm on edge. I mean more on edge than normal," Adelle said, laughing a bit. "But things are about to get much more streamlined once my bakers are trained."

"Can't your stuff just be made at Bean in Love or Chocolate Love?" I asked.

"It could. But there's already so much product made there. The amount I need to make is just too much. I'd be hogging all the ovens. And I really want to expand this and be baking closer to five or six mornings a week. I've hired a PR firm, and they're stirring up some interest in some of the larger chain stores. And besides, Nikki does not have the deep fryers and all the equipment I need to produce the donuts.

"Wow, I'm impressed. I'm so proud of you," I said, smiling.

"Thanks," Adelle said, smiling back at me.

"I want to tell you something. Change of topic, but I'd like your input," I said after a pause in our conversation.

"What?" Adelle asked, leaning back on the pillows again, allowing a smile to take shape on her face. "Tell me."

I hesitated for a second, wondering if I should dive right in or work up to what I wanted to tell her.

"What are you up to, Kelly Clark?" Adelle teased.

"It's good," I laughed, pulling my feet up onto the couch and twisting my legs together like we were two school girls getting together to gossip.

"Oh, I can see that," Adelle said, turning to face me. She pulled her legs up to mirror mine and whipped her long, blond hair behind her back.

"Have you ever hired Chef James?" I asked, choosing to go in for a soft landing rather than just blurt out what I was doing.

"Nikki's personal chef that she uses for special occasions?" Adelle guessed correctly.

"Yes," I confirmed.

"Yes, he's great. Why?" she asked, raising a brow and puckering out her luscious lips.

"I think I'm going to hire him for tomorrow night to make dinner for Jack," I said, blushing a bit just at the mention of my plans. Now that I'd said it aloud to Adelle, it all felt very real.

"Okay," Adelle said, pulling her shoulders up to her ears. "And?"

"And I'm going to propose to him," I said, pushing my chest out. "It's time."

Along with Adelle's shoulders dropping, her face fell, ever so slightly. For someone who didn't know Adelle, it would have been completely unrecognizable, but for me, she might as well have screamed, "What are you thinking?" She quickly recovered and her face blossomed into a smile.

"Great," she said.

Chapter 20

"Girls, Dad is asking for you," Mom said, floating into the room at the worst moment.

I was still in shock from Adelle's reaction to my news. Did she think it was a bad idea? I was confused. My family had been so supportive of my relationship with Jack thus far. Why did she look so freaked out by the suggestion of what I assumed everyone else was expecting?

"What time is it?" Adelle asked, jumping up from the couch.

She scooped up Craig when he ran into the room, released from Mom's hold. He started screaming and laughing with joy in his mother's arms and hitting her head with his hands. I could hear my father calling out from the kitchen.

"Girls?"

"Oh no, I'm late to pick up Cindy. I have to leave right now. She gets upset if I'm not standing in my usual spot on the front lawn. I'll be right back. Craig, get your shoes on quick," Adelle ordered him.

Craig continued to pound on her head and laugh. His face was covered with crumbs, and even from this distance, I could see his fingers were laced with a sticky substance, presumably frosting from the donut my parents had just fed him.

"Leave him here," I offered, reaching my arms out to extract him from his tight grip on Adelle. When I made eye contact with him, he gave up his grip and jumped into my arms. I snuggled him to me, trying my best to hold his hands away from my sweater in order to avoid getting sugar all over it.

"I'll be right back," Adelle said, bolting from the room, out the front door.

"Girls," Dad called impatiently again from the kitchen.

"Just a sec," Mom called back.

"Let's go wash this guy up," I said, taking a firm hold of Craig's wandering hands. It was a battle to keep them out of my hair. He giggled and laughed as he tried to touch my face.

"Look at this bugger. He knows what he's doing," I laughed. "Look at that mischievous grin!"

"So, you and Adelle talked? All is well?" Mom asked, leaning in toward me and smiling.

I nodded my head, unsure how to answer her.

"Mom, what were you talking about in the dining room before Adelle got home? You asked me if Adelle had told me something. What were you talking about specifically?"

"Oh," Mom said, clearly trying to buy some time. Her hands went to her waist and her eyes moved away from mine. "Well, I don't remember now."

Craig took that moment to sneak his left hand out of mine and dig it into my hair. When his eyes met mine, his lips formed a soft O, and his face turned to a panic. Although he intended to tease me with his sugared hands, he probably didn't think he would actually succeed. As frustrated as I felt, I did my best to comfort him and stay calm.

"It's okay, Craigy. We'll fix it," I cooed.

It was clear Mom wasn't going to divulge anything, so rather than get frustrated with her, I let it go and walked into the kitchen, carrying Craig in my arms. After washing him up, I threw my hair into a ponytail, knowing it was useless to try and wash out the stickiness here. I would just have to jump in the shower once I got home.

"What were you guys talking about in there?" Dad asked, still seated at the table, paging happily through the newspaper like he used to do when we were kids.

"Nothing. Just catching up."

I motioned with my hand for him to wipe the crumbs off of his cheek and he reached up.

"Oh, let that one slip by," he laughed. "Come see this, Kelly. There's a big article in here about your sister's parade coming up."

He waved me over to the table enthusiastically. Drying off Craig's hands, I set him down on the floor. He immediately took off in the direction of a small red truck in the corner of the kitchen.

At the table, Dad passed over a section of the paper and pointed.

"See. It's promoting the parade. And right here they mention Chocolate Love and Nikki's involvement. I'm so proud of you girls. You're really leaving your mark here in Geneva," Dad said.

I smirked a bit with a hint of sarcasm.

Oh yeah, I'm leaving a mark alright.

"Stop," Mom said, hitting my arm, shooting me a knowing smile. Our eyes met for a brief second over the table, connecting us. I wondered if she could hear what my inner voices were saying. Probably.

Tell me what's going on, Mom. I know you're holding out on me. Something is happening, and you're not telling me.

Just then, my cell phone began to vibrate in my pocket.

"Hello?" I said.

"Hey, Kelly. It's me," Adelle said.

From her clipped tone, I could tell right away that something was wrong.

"What's wrong?"

"I was supposed to go with Mom and Dad to a cardiac appointment this afternoon, and I totally forgot that Cindy has a dance rehearsal for her recital. We were all going to go to lunch afterwards."

"I can take them," I offered.

"What's wrong?" Mom quipped.

"Really? Are you sure?" Adelle asked, sounding relieved. "I would skip it, but she needs the practice for the recital. It's a huge deal."

"I understand. Really, I'm happy to do it," I said, meaning it. Adelle had been doing so much for Mom and Dad while they were in town. I was happy to do my part.

"I don't have plans today. There's really nothing I need to get done, and Jack is out tonight, remember?" I said, purposefully sliding Jack into the conversation. I glanced over at Mom to see how she would react to his name but didn't see anything obvious.

"What's wrong?" she mouthed again.

"Hold on, Adelle," I said. "Mom, I'm going to go with you and Dad to the doctor. Adelle has a dance recital practice for Craig, I mean, Cindy. Seriously, Adelle," I said, getting back on the phone. "How do you keep it all straight?" I laughed, my head spinning.

"Okay, I'm on my way home to pick up Cindy's costume, and then I'll give you all the logistics."

"I don't have to go to the doctor," my Dad said, waving his hand in the air.

"Yes, you do," Mom and I said in unison.

"Yes, you do!" Craig copied us while pushing himself along the floor on his truck.

"I'll be home in a few," Adelle said, disconnecting.

I placed the phone down on the table and looked at Mom.

"So, who's the doctor?" I asked.

"He's actually a friend of Mike's," Mom said.

"And, he knows Dr. Rowen in Florida. Dr. Rowen recommended him before Adelle mentioned his name. That worked out, didn't it?" Dad said.

"That's perfect. So, this is just a check-up?" I asked.

"Yeah," Dad sighed, dropping his shoulders a bit.

"What?" I asked.

"I'm so sick of these doctor appointments. When does it end? I have to go to cardiac rehab tomorrow, right?" he asked my mom.

"Yes, you do. And you're doing great so stop complaining. Do you know how many people have it much worse than you?" Mom said.

"We'll make it fun, Dad. We'll head to lunch somewhere afterwards. What time is the appointment?" I asked.

"Noon," Mom said.

"I'm going to go get ready for our date," Dad said, standing up from the table and using the air quotes around the word date. He pulled up his sagging pants and let out a "humph."

"Think about where you want to go for lunch. We need to fatten you up, Dad," I joked.

"Let's stop at Bean in Love and get some more donuts," he said, allowing his bouncing eyebrows to purvey his excitement.

"No!" Mom and I both said in unison.

"No! No! No!" Craig began to chant from the truck.

Dad smirked at our reaction, but then he visually perked up a bit and raised a finger in the air.

"Gaetano's in Batavia for lunch? Or what about Swordfish on Randall? There's always Town House Books, you know I love that place. Wait! I know, Stockholm's. That's where we're going. Stockholm's for burgers." His voice got quieter and quieter as he walked down the hall, continuing to call out local restaurants.

"He reminds me of Jack with his obsession with food," I laughed, shaking my head at my mom. "But look how well he walks now."

"He's completely regained his mobility. I'm just happy he's back to his normal self. He wasn't excited about eating when he wasn't feeling good. Look how much weight he's lost," Mom commented.

"It'll come back. I already see him perking up so much."

Mom nodded in agreement. "Thank God."

* * * * *

That night, after an exhausting day of doctors, lunch, and then our family dinner, I stretched out on the bed I shared with Jack and finally opened my laptop. Dressed in my favorite flannel pajamas, I rolled my ankles and wrists until they cracked, smiling at the obnoxious sounds they made. Cradling a steaming cup of herbal tea, I scrolled through my emails, trying to catch up after the busy day I'd had.

Dad's check-up had gone well, so I was happy, but was still on information overload. The new doctor had been great, but he had been intent on giving us as much information as possible on cardiac recovery. Mom and I both scratched down notes, but he'd been a fast talker. Being at that doctor appointment with my mom made me think more and more how much I believed it was best for Mom and Dad to move home and be closer to their kids if they were about to face health challenges. Who would be there to help Mom if things got worse with Dad? Or what if she got sick? I couldn't imagine Dad having to take care of Mom. He'd been a great provider, husband, and father, but he'd have a tough time being a caretaker. That was always Mom's role.

My phone beeped alerting me that a new text had just come in.

What happened with Chef James?

Crap! Seeing Nikki's text message reminded me that I'd never caught up with Chef James. The day had turned into such a whirlwind of activities that I'd missed his call. Plus, I'd been with my parents or Adelle's family the entire day. I wanted to be alone when I talked to him because I'd been a little freaked out by Adelle's reaction to my news that I was going to ask Jack to marry me. What was up with that?

I'd never had an opportunity to feel her out. I guess the bottom line was it didn't really matter. Her opinion was clearly important to me, or I wouldn't still be thinking about it, but the only one that really mattered was mine. And I was sure. Jack was the one for me.

I nodded my head and leaned back on the big fluffy pillows Jack insisted we keep stocked in the bedroom. He only actually slept with one pillow under his head, but he was adamant about having at least ten pillows on his large king bed.

"I need them," he always insisted when I'd suggested we cut down.

"For what? You don't sleep on them?" I'd made the mistake of asking him once.

"For this," he'd said, picking up one of the pillows with his long, muscular arms and playfully whacking me in the head.

I laughed and found myself desperately wishing Jack could have come home tonight instead of staying in the city for work. I was proud of how hard he worked, but being here without him was making me lonely. I missed his voice, his interest in my life, and his companionship. We were so well connected as friends and lovers, my life felt empty without him. Jack brought a great energy to my life. The thought of his sweet, sexy smile and his ability to make me feel like the most important woman in the world was everything to me. Jack had brought me back to life after my horrific divorce. I needed him and wanted him all the time. Forever.

I leaned over and reached for my phone I had placed on the nightstand. It was late, but I needed to make a call. Hopefully, he'd still take calls this late at night.

Chapter 21

By six the next morning, I'd completed my three mile run and was doing a quick stretch on the sidewalk leading up to Jack's condo building. It had snowed lightly overnight. The cars in the parking lot looked as though they were dusted with a thin layer of sugar. I thought of Nikki's upcoming parade and wondered how the weather would affect the turnout. It was supposed to warm up through the week, but in Chicago, things could turn on a dime. I thought of the famous saying here: If you don't like the weather in Chicago, wait five minutes.

I stood up tall, pulling my legs up one by one to stretch my hamstrings. It was still dark, the sun refusing to wake up yet. Still, sun or not, I needed and loved my morning routine. It was the only way I was able to get my mind in the right place to write. It shut any demons away so that my mind could play.

Speaking of demons, as much as I wanted to forget it, the key I'd found still weighed heavy in my thoughts. That darn key. If only I'd never found it in the first place. It hung on me, pulling me down like a weight. Every time I started to move on, that key wrestled me back down.

It tied me to Steve somehow. Or maybe not. What if it had nothing to do with Steve, and I was the one making up the whole thing in my head? I thought that the key was what Steve's new girlfriend, Sharon, had come looking for last summer, but she'd never specifically mentioned a key. Maybe Sharon was just as crazy as she had appeared.

God, that would be nice. If in reality, all my ties to Steve had been cut. He wouldn't come looking for me. His accomplices, if there were any more left, would leave me alone, and life would be great. But when Sharon had come that horrible night last summer to try and kill me, she'd specifically said, "The biggest thing we're worried about is you finding out more."

I was able to expose her for skimming money off of the charity she was running for hospitals, but she'd implied that she and Steve were involved in some kind of scam that was much bigger than that. She'd never turned him in, but perhaps it was just a matter of time before she did. Currently, she was rotting away at a women's prison downstate. That was my greatest hope. If Sharon turned on Steve, there would be more charges against him on top of the attempted murder charge he was currently serving. That would prolong his sentence, making me a safer, happier person.

If only I could convince Sharon to turn on Steve. But the thought of trying to have a reasonable conversation with that lunatic was almost worse than the thought of coming face to face with Steve again. Her petite frame and blond hair had probably made her a target in prison. Or perhaps, her time in prison had only sharpened her criminal skills, the little devil.

Shivering slightly, I wrapped my arms around myself, suddenly anxious to get inside. All of a sudden, I didn't feel as safe and secure being out here alone with all of the dark shadows of the early morning. I wanted to be back in the safety of Jack's cozy condo. The thought of a hot cup of coffee and a warm shower made me leap toward the door.

Just as I was almost to the door, my eye caught the shape of something on the hood of my car under the light dusting of snow. My first thought was that I must have gotten a ticket by the way the paper was tucked under my windshield wiper. But why? I had a valid pass for parking in this spot. This was going to be a pain to call the police and justify my right to park here. I would probably have to go into the station and present the form I'd been given by Jack's building manager. That was the last thing I needed to do today.

I made my way over to my car and snatched the piece of paper from the windshield, a little put out that the police had been out last night giving tickets.

"Well, at least I can feel safe here," I said to myself, glancing around to see if anyone else had received tickets. A little uncomfortable feeling began to scratch at my skin, just lightly at first, like when the tag on a shirt bothers you a bit, then a little more, then a little more, until you can't ignore it and you end up ripping it off. I glanced down at the piece of paper in my hand and saw it was actually a small envelope. It looked like an ordinary white, business envelope, nothing special or official about it.

Panic set in. I bolted for the front door, keeping a firm grasp of the envelope in my hand. This wasn't going to be a ticket from the police; it was more likely a personal note. Someone had come up to my car in the middle of the night and left a note. I would be damned if I was going to open it alone outside in the dark.

Punching my key code in, I was in the lobby in a flash. My legs took the three flights of stairs as though my life depended on it, and within a few seconds, I was locked behind the condo door, leaning back against it. My chest rose and fell a few times while I worked to catch my breath and pull myself together. I glanced down at the envelope I clutched in my right hand, willing myself to open it and deal with whatever it was.

It was probably nothing. I was being silly; paranoid even. The fact that I was listening to the little voices in my head telling me something was wrong made me crazy. I needed to calm down.

But remember when you listened to the voices in your head telling you to be paranoid about your husband's late nights?

"Oh, man," I said, stepping away from the door and heading straight for the bathroom. I locked the door, turned on the shower as hot as it could go, and allowed the room to steam.

"Wait a minute," I laughed suddenly to myself, a wave of relief rushing through me like a cooling breeze.

The dinner cards from Chef James. That's what was in the envelope. When we'd spoken last night, he'd mentioned something about little place cards he liked to put out for his dinners. He knew I was planning on going all out and setting a big romantic scene, so he was giving me all the cards before his arrival. I'd carried on and on last night about color schemes and table cloths when I'd finally gotten a hold of him.

My phone beeped, alerting me to a new text message. My heart leapt at the sight of Jack's name.

Good morning, temptress. I miss you like crazy. Can't wait to see you. Looking forward to our dinner tonight.

I shot back a quick text.

Love you. Don't be late. Have something special planned. You're going to love it.

When I'd last spoken to Jack last night, I'd told him I had a dinner planned, but kept it casual because I didn't want to ruin the surprise or have him start snooping around.

Ooh, sounds good. What are you up to?

I laughed, picturing Jack with his early morning hair tousled every which way and sleepy eyes reading my texts. He was only about an hour's distance, but when he stayed away, it felt like he was a gazillion miles away. I yearned for him to be back home with me in our bed, not some strange corporate suite. My body ached to have him snuggle me back into bed the way he sometimes did after I'd returned from my early morning runs.

You'll see, I texted back.

Placing the phone back on the bathroom sink, I glanced up at my reflection in the mirror and smiled. My "Jack glow," as Nikki called it, was apparent on my face, my cheeks aglow and my eyes lit with excitement. It was good to be in love. It was good to have a partner again in life. Someone who you trusted to be by your side no matter what. This proposal tonight was going to solidify all that I'd been working for over the past three years after Steve's betrayal. I was getting my life back together.

After showering and throwing on jeans and a long-sleeve tee-shirt, I set to work cleaning the condo in preparation for our big night. Chef James wasn't due until a little after four, so I had plenty of time, but I wanted to make sure everything was perfect. Plus, if I could get it done early enough, I might be able to get a little writing done and still have time to swing by and see my parents today.

By ten o'clock, the condo was spick and span and the table was set. I'd ended up going with a red and green theme in honor of the approaching holidays, per the suggestion of Chef James. As he'd said, "What could be more romantic than a Christmas engagement? The lights, the music, the built in celebration. It's perfect."

He was right. I went ahead and set up Jack's traditional Christmas garland and his artificial tree. We were going to be setting it up very soon anyway, so why not have it for tonight? The tree shone in the middle of the living room, illuminating the small table I'd placed next to it for our romantic dinner. Now all we needed was the food; and how nice that I didn't have to cook any of it. Chef James was planning on making a homemade risotto with shrimp and crab, arugula salad, one of Jack's favorites, followed by a homemade Tiramisu and walnut brownie dessert. Two desserts. Jack was going to flip out.

I scanned the room quickly, amazed by how much I'd accomplished in so little time. Things had gone so easy that I began to worry I'd missed something.

"The place cards!" I said aloud, remembering at that moment

that I'd left the envelope from Chef James on the bathroom sink. I raced into the bathroom and snatched them up just at the same time the buzzer for the front door rang. Holding the envelope in my hand, I went over to Jack's front door and hit the button on the intercom.

"Hello?" I called out.

"Kelly, it's Chef James," he said in his heavy Italian accent.

"Oh, yes, hello, come on in," I said, buzzing him in. I unlocked the door and pulled it open, watching Chef James's tiny frame climb the stairs two at a time. He called out to me as he approached.

"Good morning, my lady," he sang. Although he was a tiny man, standing only 5 feet and 5 inches high, his energetic persona made him a giant. Nikki warned me he would always be singing, sometimes in English, sometimes in Italian, to himself as he walked or cooked. If he wasn't so talented and well respected as a chef in the area, he'd have quite a reputation just from his inability to stop singing. Even now, he hummed and sang as he climbed closer and closer to me. Once he reached the top, he stopped, held out both arms to me still singing.

"That's amore!" he bellowed.

"Hush," I laughed, afraid we'd upset Jack's neighbors.

"Come in," I said, waving him inside.

"No, no, I cannot stay," Chef James said. "Much to do. I just, oooh, what is that I see? You take the Chef James advice, no?" he said, peering inside the condo.

"Yes, yes, please come in and see," I begged. "It's totally decked out for Christmas, per your suggestion."

Unable to contain my excitement, I pulled him inside, determined to make him see what I'd been working on all morning.

"Oh, Miss Kelly. The tree, the lights, the garland. It's so beautiful," he said, clasping his hands together and swaying back and forth. "I'm in the mood for love!" he sang out, drawing out the word love. "This is going to be so good. So good."

He walked quickly over to the table, examining my work.

"Yes, yes, and here the plates, correct. No, no, this fork, over here, this better," he said, making quick work of his hands and rearranging what I had set up. "Oh, and wait! The most important! The place cards!"

He reached into his back pocket, pulling out a large envelope. My mouth dropped as I watched him pull place cards from the envelope and lovingly place them all around the table.

"This one says the menu, this one says the name, and this one says the date. You keep these for your memory book. You can look back on this day and remember the dinner Chef James lovingly prepared for your engagement, no?" he said, popping his head up for my reaction. His hands waved over the table. "Voila!"

"Kelly, what is wrong with your face? You look at me like I just killed your cat or something. What's wrong, my dear? You don't like? We change it, my dear. No worries," he said.

His arms dropped to his side and his mouth pulled down in worry. Chef James, who was constantly in movement, either singing or swaying, stood perfectly still, staring back at me.

He was nearly invisible to me at that moment. My mind was stuck on one thing and one thing only. If he was here right now to give me the place cards he promised, then who had approached my car in the middle of the night and put some kind of mystery envelope on it? And better yet, what was in it?

Chapter 22

"Kelly? Hello?" Chef James' voice called to me from the end of a tunnel. It wasn't until his hand connected with my arm that it hit me there was still a person in front of me.

"Kelly, are you okay? Should you sit down? Come," he said, pulling me by the arm over to the couch. "You need to sit down. You have gone so white. Like ghost. You know, spooky, Halloween ghost. Sit down. I'm going to get you water."

Chef James bolted in the direction of the kitchen. In slow, purposeful movements, I ripped open the envelope that I was still holding in my hand and pulled out a single piece of paper. I read the words on the paper, feeling nothing at first.

Meet me at Big Rock Library today at 2:00PM.

~A Friend

I nodded my head, yes, staring at the blinking lights on the tree. On. Off. On. Off. A memory from the past flashed before my eyes. I saw Adelle, myself, and Nikki singing and laughing around the tree, awaiting Santa's arrival. My parents loved Christmas time. It was a huge deal in our house growing up. Mom would go all out to make it special for all of us. If my parents were still in town for Christmas here in Geneva, it could be really nice, just like it was when we were kids. All of us together again.

Or.

I looked down at the envelope in my hand.

It could be totally psychotic and crazy because I was involved and nothing seemed to go well when I was involved. I could be drawing more psychopaths into town, just like I'd done in the past, and we could all be in danger. Again.

Who was this friend? And why did they want to see me? And *why* did they choose Big Rock Library? I knew of it, but by chance alone. My parents had taken us there as kids on one of our adventures. Even back then, I'd been a big reader and they thought I would enjoy seeing this off the beaten path little gem of a library. Big Rock Library was an old, restored Victorian home in the middle of a cornfield in the very small farming town of Big Rock, about thirty minutes west of Geneva. It was nearly impossible to find because it was so isolated and extremely private. Why meet me there? And how did my "friend" know about this place?

"Kelly," Chef James stood in front of me, waving his right hand in front of my face. When my eyes connected to his, he sat down next to me, handing me water. "Kelly, you're really scaring me. It's like you don't even see me. What is happening?"

"I'm not sure," I said simply.

"Do you still want to do the dinner? Should I telephone someone from the family? Should I call Nikki? You don't seem well. You seem sick or something," Chef James said, reaching out and holding his hand up to my forehead.

"No, no," I said, shaking my head. "I'm not sick. I'm okay."

My mind raced to my fight with Adelle this morning and what she'd said about it needing to stop. How I needed to stop involving the family in the drama that was my life.

"I'm fine, really. I think I just tried to do too much this morning. I had too much coffee and not enough to eat."

The weight of the water glass he'd given me finally registered in my hand. I pulled it up to my mouth and drank the water, trying to buy time to put together a plan.

Figure it out. Don't tell anyone. Solve the problem. Have the dinner.

"So, we were talking about times and place cards, right? What time should we aim to start serving the dinner?" I asked, trying my best to smile. Despite the fact that I'd just downed a full glass of water, my lips cracked when I smiled and seemed incapable of moving over my dry gums to form a smile. Instead, I cleared my throat.

"Kelly, do you want to answer that phone? It's been ringing non-stop." Chef James raised an eyebrow and pointed to the front door. He sat back a little on the couch.

I didn't blame him if he was a bit frightened by my slightly erratic behavior. I would be if I were in his shoes. He was probably thinking something along the lines of, "Why did I take this referral? I thought I could trust Nikki. What was I thinking? Her sister is clearly a lunatic."

Sure enough, he was right. I could hear my cell phone ringing from the small table where I normally kept keys, glasses, and phones at the entrance to our condo.

"Excuse me," I said, pushing myself up from the couch.

Once up on my feet, my legs felt weak and jiggly. I stumbled against the coffee table in front of the couch, hitting it with my leg.

I cursed quietly, grabbing at my shin.

"Are you okay?" Chef James said.

"Yes, yes, one second," I said, walking gingerly to the phone.

Glancing at the screen, I noticed three missed calls. All from Nikki.

Three missed calls? How had I missed these?

While I was holding the phone in my hand, it started ringing again.

"Oh, my God, what's wrong? Is Dad okay?" I cried into the phone.

"Hello?" I demanded when no one spoke up.

"Wait, one second, Kelly," Nikki said into the phone. I could hear her talking to someone else, but it was muffled. I tried desperately to make out the words. I managed to get, "So, it's been confirmed. You're sure. He's dead?"

My hand flew up to my mouth, and my eyes instantly filled with tears. It felt like someone punched me in the gut and kicked me in the head at the same time. No, no, no, this can't be happening. Dad was doing so good. I just saw him yesterday. The cardiologist said he'd been making amazing strides in his recovery. This wasn't real. This couldn't be real.

"Nikki," I croaked out. "He's gone?"

"Hello," Nikki said, finally directing her attention to me. "Sorry about that, Kelly. I was just trying to get more information."

"Dad?" I asked, barely able to form the word.

"No! It's not Dad. Dad is fine. He's fine, Kelly," Nikki said, her normal tone taking over. "Everything is okay. Mom and Dad are fine."

I sat down on the floor next to the front door and closed my eyes. Lying back, I sucked in air and readjusted my body so that I was on my back, looking up at the ceiling. Chef James was standing above me, eyes like saucers, watching me, then turning on his heel and bolting into the kitchen. I could hear Nikki's voice rambling on but wasn't making out what she was saying. Dad was okay. Nikki said everything was okay. So, someone was still dead, but maybe it wasn't in our direct family. I was bargaining and rationalizing like a crazy person, but a wave of happiness and peace coursed through me.

"Kelly? Kelly can you hear me? Hello? Did you hear what I said?" Nikki called out.

"You have to sit up and drink this water," Chef James said. "Here, I pulla you up. Give me the phone. Is this Nikki? Give ita to me. You sit up. Ugh," Chef James grunted as he pulled me up by my arm. "Now take this."

Chef James placed a cup of water in my hands and snatched the phone, which I happily gave up. I wanted desperately for someone else to take charge, so I was glad he felt the need. I was having a little break-down here.

"I don'ta know. She's having a tougha time here. What's a going on?" Chef James said, his Italian accent taking over. He mumbled something in Italian that I couldn't understand. He looked bug eyed and stressed, kneeling down next to me. Perhaps stress made him revert to his roots.

I watched him closely, feeling like a wimp for not hanging onto the phone and talking to Nikki, but also recognizing that my body was shutting down somewhat by the thought of bad news. Taking in a breath, I steeled myself for Nikki's news. The one thing I knew for sure was that something really bad had happened, and I was about to be hit by it.

"Who is this Tony Avila?" Chef James said.

For a second, I thought the same thing. Who is Tony Avila? Tony was dead? I didn't know a Tony. Why was Nikki calling me about this, and why was it such a big deal?

After chugging the glass of water, I waved my hand at Chef James to signal that I was ready to take the phone back.

"I'm okay. Thank you for the water. I'm so sorry about all this," I said, accepting the phone that Chef James held out to me.

"She says that a Tony is dead? He's been shot to death. A guard or something?" he said, raising both eyebrows and making the sign of the cross. "Do you know this Tony?"

My brain finally computed why Nikki was so upset and anxious to talk to me.

"Tony in Miami is dead?" I said roughly into the phone. "Mom and Dad's Tony?"

Chapter 23

"Yes, he was shot to death early this morning," Nikki said. "I've been trying to get a hold of you. Where have you been?"

"Here at Jack's condo. I'm with Chef James. We're getting ready for our dinner. Where are you?" I asked.

"I'm with Mom and Dad at Adelle's right now."

"Kelly, you have to answer your phone. We were worried about you," Nikki said.

"I'm sorry. I was busy and distracted getting stuff ready here. Tell me everything you know. Did you really say he was shot to death?" I asked, still in shock from the news.

It was setting in that poor Tony, the man who left the police force for a more peaceful job, had been killed in a violent act.

"He was working at the front desk and someone came in and shot him. We don't really know any more details yet. I guess the police are still investigating. Remember that the lobby had those video cameras? I'm really hoping they got something on tape."

"Wait, this happened in Mom and Dad's building?" I asked, eyes bulging. "Are you serious?"

"Yes, Kelly, he was shot in the lobby. They had everyone on lock down this morning. They might still be."

"How did you find out about it?" I asked.

"Viola called to tell Mom. They're really upset. Everyone just loved Tony," Nikki said.

"I'm coming over," I said. "Let me just close up here, and I will be over."

"Okay, I'm putting on a pot of coffee," Nikki said. "Be careful."

I ended the call and looked at Chef James. He'd sat down on the floor next to me and folded his legs together like mine. For a few seconds, we just stared at each other in silence. The quiet of the condo around us seemed odd, considering the last couple of minutes had been filled with such high drama.

Finally, Chef James spoke.

"Well, I heard that you and Nikki were some kind of sleuths and that you investigated crimes, but now I believe it. I feel like I'm in the middle of a mystery movie on television or something. What is happening?" he said, a bit too enthusiastically for the circumstances. His Italian accent had definitely settled back down though.

If only I were in the middle of a television movie. That would be nice. I could simply pick up the remote and turn it off. Nope. This was my life.

"A friend of my parents was killed in Miami this morning," I said simply.

"I'm so sorry," he said softly, reaching out and taking my hand in his. "This friend, you and Nikki are gonna find the killer?"

Startled by his words, I simply stared at him and shook my head no. Was he right? Were Nikki and I really building some kind of reputation as amateur sleuths in Geneva because we helped the police solve a few cases in the past?

"I don't know," I stammered. "I don't think so."

"You're gonna go to Nikki's now?" he said, helping me stand up.

"I'm going to head to my other sister's house, Adelle. I want to hang out with them for a little bit and talk to them," I said, steadying myself once I was on my feet.

"What about the dinner? Do you still want to have the

engagement dinner for Jack tonight?" he asked, putting his palms toward the ceiling and holding his arms in the air in show of the little set-up we'd put together. I looked around the room at the extravagant scene we'd set.

Meet me at Big Rock Library today at 2:00PM.
~A Friend

I thought about the note sitting on the windshield of my car this morning and the fight I'd had with Adelle. Pausing for a few seconds to glance around, I came to a decision.

"Yes, dinner is still on. We'll serve at seven if that's okay with you?" I said.

As soon as I wrapped up with Chef James, I made my way over and stood in front of Adelle's. I hated to arrive empty handed, but I didn't have time to pick something up, and we didn't have anything in the house that seemed appropriate. What was one supposed to bring when people were in the throes of grief? Sweets, I imagined. My mind raced back to Mom and Dad's friend, Julie, arriving at their condo with a tray of sweets after the jailbreak at Steve's prison.

Like a car coming to a screeching halt, all the thoughts in my head stopped. Wait a minute. Wait just a stinking minute. Franklin Ford was still on the loose. Could he have been the one that shot Tony? What if he really was connected to Steve, and I'd been living in a fool's paradise? What if Steve had sent Franklin to get me? Yes, that made perfect sense. He'd come to kill me, Tony had gotten in the way, and he'd killed Tony. Yes, that was it. And, that's why Nikki had ended our last phone conversation with "be careful." Her mind had traveled down the same path as mine. That's why she was so anxious to get me on the phone to tell me the news and make sure I was okay.

"Why are you just standing out there? Were you going to ring the bell, or what?" Nikki asked, reaching out and pulling me into Adelle's foyer. Nikki was dressed in her normal baking attire with a

Chocolate Love apron on. I imagined she must have dashed out the door of her shop and come straight here when she'd heard the news.

"Do you think it was Franklin Ford?" I whispered, anxious to hypothesize with her before talking with the rest of the family. If they hadn't talked about this yet, I hoped to keep it between us; no sense getting everyone in a tizzy about this theory. I had to keep reminding myself that Dad needed to be kept out of as much drama and stress as possible. He was still a recovering cardiac patient, albeit a strong one judging from what he'd displayed so far.

"I thought about that," Nikki said, confirming my suspicions and speaking quietly. "We have to get some more information."

"What time did it happen?" I asked.

"Five this morning," she said. "That's all I know so far and even that's a rumor. The police are still interviewing the residents, trying to find witnesses. They still have the lobby taped off."

"How did the residents know it happened?" I asked.

"Julie, their friend, heard the gunshot. And as you can imagine, they went into a panic. They're all over the police trying to get information. We'll hear something soon."

"Do you think Steve sent Franklin Ford after me? This can't just be a coincidence that he's still on the loose and Tony gets killed. He killed one guard in prison already, and now Mom and Dad's doorman is dead. He was in the same area as Steve at the jail. They even have similar backgrounds with going after women they were in relationships with. Maybe Steve bribed him or something. Maybe they were in a cell together, or spent time together in those classes they take, you know, like knitting class and stuff," I said, interlacing my fingers.

"What?" Nikki said, twisting her neck at me.

"You know, how the inmates can take classes to keep busy? Anyway, that's not the point. Maybe they had similar stories, you remember Franklin's background, killed his wife and all those other things. What if Steve managed to coerce him into breaking out and killing me?" I hissed in a whisper.

"Kelly, we're getting ahead of ourselves. I'm glad you're thinking this way, because we want to be careful, but we just can't go there yet. What if this was a random act of violence? We have to remain calm until we know more."

"Nikki, when has anything been a random act when it comes to me? We know better now than to believe in coincidences, right? We have to talk to the police and tell them that I was staying there and that it was possible that someone came looking for me, and, and," I rambled.

"I know, I know," Nikki said, putting her arm around me. "I'm with you. Just, come see Mom and Dad. We have to remain calm."

Nikki guided me into the kitchen where Mom and Dad sat at the large kitchen table, a puzzle laid out in front of them.

"I did it!" Craig boasted, pumping his fists into the air.

"You did it!" Dad cheered back.

Mom sat silently next to Dad, pale as a ghost, a look of pure panic on her face. She seemed to stare right through me, her pale brown eyes out of focus and red rimmed. Her hair fell limp around her face, not in its usual fluffed up way.

"Auntie Kelly, I did the hard puzzle. I'm smart now. I can go to school with Cindy tomorrow?"

Craig crawled down from his chair and raced to me, whacking into my knees. He banged his fists against my legs, his signature move to let me know he wanted to be picked up.

"Yes, soon. Soon you'll go to school with Cindy. You're so smart!" I said, nuzzling him closer to me. "So smart." I kissed his head, smelling the sweet scent of his hair.

In all the years Adelle's kids had been a part of my life, I couldn't think of one time I saw them dirty. They were always impossibly clean, except for a few sugar crumbs perhaps, and sweet smelling.

"Do you want some coffee?" Adelle asked from the kitchen sink.

I could barely meet her eyes. Was she thinking the same thing I was? If Nikki was, surely Adelle was too, and for that matter, Mom and Dad. Who was I kidding? My mother the psychic probably knew of the death before it even happened.

"Yes, I do," I said in response to Adelle's question.

She handed me a cup and in my mind, I imagined her saying something like, *"Good job, Kelly. You did it again. You managed to make a mess of our home. Only this time, it was Mom and Dad's home. Oh, and it was in Miami. Couldn't stand to give them the peace and quiet they deserve. You know, the peace they went all the way to Miami to get? Yeah, you ruined that safe haven, too. Good job, sis."*

But Adelle didn't say any of those things. She simply handed me a cup of coffee with a small smile, which was even more telling and intimidating than anything cruel she could say.

Chapter 24

"So, we need a plan," Nikki said to me under her breath. We were huddled next to Adelle's fridge on the other side of the kitchen while I rummaged through it. I'd made up a quick excuse of how I wanted more milk in my coffee just to escape the hot pressure cooker atmosphere of the kitchen table. My parents looked zombie-like this morning, and the guilt I had for that was choking me. I just needed a few minutes away from the table to regroup.

"Let's call Pavlik. He can speak directly to the Miami police and tell them my story. He'll be able to cut through all the red tape. And, maybe he'll be able to get us a copy of whatever was recorded by the cameras. We can see who it was," I suggested.

"Great thinking," Nikki said, lighting up a bit. She stood up straighter and arched her back, sticking out her burgeoning belly.

"I can't believe I didn't think of that," Nikki said, flashing me a smile. "Of course, those busy bodies in the high rise have probably already told the police about you."

"Maybe. And don't call them busy bodies. Those are Mom and Dad's friends," I scolded.

"I'm just saying. They're probably all talking. And like you said, it's just too much of a coincidence that all of this went down with you having just been there, and now there's a shooting in the building."

"Well, Miami is a violent city," I managed.

"Um, yeah, but not Mom and Dad's Miami. They're in a high rent district. There's virtually no violence in those kinds of places," Nikki said.

"Yeah, Geneva is high rent as well. And look what's happened here," I smirked.

"Ah," Nikki said, "touché."

"We're going to make a quick call in the other room," I called out to the rest of the family.

Adelle had the large, wall mounted flat screen tuned to Sesame Street, and Craig was doing a little dance to the intro song of Elmo's World. Mom and Dad clapped along with the song, seemingly pretending to pay attention, but both were watching me closely.

Adelle nodded at both of us and put her hands on her hips, watching us through squinted eyes.

Stepping into her formal living room, my attention was drawn to the Christmas tree that had suddenly appeared. It towered over me, reaching up toward the vaulted ceiling. Now when did Adelle have time to do this? I leaned in and took a sniff. Real.

"Huh," I said aloud. She couldn't possibly have gone and chopped this down in the last couple of days. Maybe she had done it earlier and was storing it in the garage? Mom and Dad must have helped her put it up. But when? Did she ever sleep?

Shaking my head, I tried my best to clear my thoughts and focus on the matter at hand. The tree was making me think about the one I had just set up in our condo this morning and the upcoming dinner.

Taking my favorite spot on her couch near the window, I pulled out my cell phone and dialed.

"Good morning, Kelly," Detective Pavlik said after only one ring.

His normal cheer was somewhat capped. He'd given me his direct line and sounded as though he were expecting my call.

"Hi, Detective," I said, trying a casual tone.

"I haven't forgotten about you. I'm waiting to hear back from them. I've already explained the background. They're working on getting me the video. I guess the guy that knows how to extract the video is away from the building on vacation, so they're looking for someone else that knows how to run it. I see this a lot. All of this modern technology: cameras, cell phones, you name it. It's all great, but if you can't operate it, it's useless to law enforcement."

I kept silent, trying to figure out what was happening here.

I pointed my finger at Nikki, who had scooted in next to me on the couch and was leaning her head in close to the phone. We locked eyes in mirrored confusion.

"Detective Pavlik, how did you know I wanted to see the video?"

"Your sister Adelle called earlier asking for it. Didn't you know?"

"Oh, yeah, of course," I said, feeling a little bamboozled. Glancing at Nikki, I could tell from her furrowed brow that she was just as shocked as I was. Perhaps Adelle was just being proactive, but still, I wish she would have told us she had done this. I liked it better when we were a united front.

That being said, Nikki and I had not told her what we were doing.

"So, let me call you back in a bit. I'll be able to send the video to you electronically in a bit. Or better yet, why don't you just come here to view it. We can watch it together."

I thought about this and waited for Nikki's reaction to this suggestion. She raised her eyebrows and shrugged as though saying, "Whatever you want."

"I'll come in. Just me," I said quickly.

There was too much going on here. Craig watching Sesame Street, Mom and Dad watching me with those haunted eyes, and Adelle peeling my skin off with those unspoken words I could see floating around in her brain. Just having her near me right now was enough. I could feel the insinuations knifing out at me.

"You ruined our name. You killed Tony. You did this."

I needed to get out of here to a quiet place to watch the video and figure this out. If my past had something to do with Tony's death, I wanted to help. But I needed to do this alone, just me.

"Kelly, are you sure? I can come with you," Nikki stammered.

"I'll call you soon," I said, jumping up from my seat on the couch and cruising to the front door. Grunting, I pulled it open and took a quick second to turn and wave back at Nikki. Mom's bright red sweater was starting to peek into the doorway of the living room from the kitchen. Not wanting to meet her eyes, I jumped through the doorway and fled for my car.

* * * * *

"Alright, here we are," Detective Pavlik said, placing a cup of steaming coffee in front of me. "This one is a vanilla latte as you requested. What did we do before Keurig?" he laughed.

Detective Pavlik was dressed in navy slacks and a white button down shirt. He'd loosened his burgundy tie a bit at the neck and rolled his sleeves up to his elbows, giving him a more relaxed look. We'd been waiting for almost an hour in his office at the Geneva Police Department. I'd spent the time agonizing over asking him to accompany me to Big Rock Library for my 2:00 PM appointment with my "friend." The clock was ticking, and I'd have to leave soon if I was going to make the meeting.

I rechecked the directions on my phone, trying to figure out the exact time I'd have to leave in order to make it there. Having never driven there myself, I wanted some extra padding in case I got lost. I knew so little about Big Rock. The little I did remember was that it was a small farming town, fifty miles west of the city of Chicago, with a teeny tiny population of about 1500 people. It was only about a thirty minute drive from Geneva, but for some reason, it felt like going to another planet.

Why had my "friend" asked me to meet there? Why not somewhere in Geneva? What kind of "friendship" did we have that it had to be so secretive?

"How about just call me?"

"What? Why would I call you? I'm right here," Detective Pavlik asked.

I shook my head, trying to clear my thoughts.

"Kelly, are you okay? Do you want me to call your sister?" Detective Pavlik asked, sitting down across the desk from me.

I shook my head and picked up my coffee so that I would have something to do with my hands.

"No, no, I'm fine. I just didn't sleep well last night. I'll be fine. What were you saying?" I asked, pulling my head out of the clouds.

"Have you got something on your mind you want to talk about? I mean, besides the obvious?" he said, leaning back in his chair.

Releasing a breath, I tried to buy time by taking in my surroundings. Detective Pavlik sat in front of a huge bookcase filled with binders, pictures, books, and other accolades. If I had more time and more brain space, it would be great to feel my way through all of those.

"Is that a picture of you with the mayor?" I asked, pointing out a gold frame on the shelf behind him.

"This one?" he said, reaching up and pulling it down. "Yes, this was taken last year at the Geneva Christmas parade on Third Street. Nikki always presents the mayor with the first candy cane of the year at the end of the parade. It's a big deal. Tons of people come out for it."

"Oh, yes, I remember. It's been a few years, but I was here for," I paused, struck by a memory of me and Steve at the parade right after we first got married.

It was before we moved to California. Nikki had just taken over Chocolate Love from her father-in-law. I remember it being a huge deal that she would be the one giving the candy cane to the town officials, not her father-in-law. It was like a passing of the torch, and she'd been extremely nervous.

"I can't wait to take my grandkids to this someday," Steve's mom, Bernadette, had leaned in and whispered.

Her overtly aggressive comments about procreating were becoming annoying, considering we were just newly married and not looking to expand the family just yet. We were still just enjoying each other and trying to pave out who we were as a married couple. I wanted to tell Bernadette to "back off," but by this point, I'd learned it was best to just smile and say nothing when it came to her comments. She had, to put it nicely, a strong personality. I was getting used to the family allowing her to openly give her opinion on all topics without much of a pushback or a challenge.

"Alright, Mom. Let's just be in the moment," Steve joked, putting his arm around me and pulling me in closer to him. The people marched past, smiling and waving their hands frantically.

I smiled and tucked myself into Steve, happy that he'd defended us. Kind of.

"Well, don't wait too long. You're not getting any younger and Kelly's eggs are only going to decline in viability. I've seen this happen way too many times to my friends," sneered Bernadette.

I cringed at the mention of my eggs like they were her property to discuss.

"Their children get way too obsessed with their careers and their alone time and wham, it's too late and they don't get grandchildren," she hissed at Steve, spewing her unsolicited opinion about our sex life. She waved back at the parade and smiled as though she'd done nothing wrong. In fact, she was helping us, at least in her mind. I could tell by her self-satisfied smile that she was

happy with the way she'd "helped us." Clearly, someone had to.

I stepped away from her and closer to Steve. Bernadette was like this. Sweet as can be one second and then nasty as a snake when she didn't get her way or if you refused to accept her generous and all-knowing point of view. I'd let it slide when we'd started dating, thinking that Steve was too good of a catch to let go. She'd seemed rather harmless. Extremely opinionated, but still, harmless. What did it matter if she spewed her venom? It wasn't like we were going to let it affect us. After we married though, her opinions got stronger and stronger and her hold on Steve tighter. It was like a damn broke. I was worried.

"Mom," Steve said again, a little sharper this time.

"Oh, look, there's Doris!" Bernadette said, changing the topic as she often did once she saw things weren't going her way. "I'll be right back. I've been dying to see her. You know her son was just arrested for stealing a car. Poor thing. Look at her. She looks so stressed. She's gained some weight. I'm sure she's just dying to talk to me. We've been missing each other. She hasn't had time to return my calls I'm sure. I'm just going to run over there and talk to her. See what I can find out. Be right back," she said, darting away from us.

Doris was an old friend of Steve's family. They'd served together on the PTA board years ago. The last I'd heard from Steve, he thought Doris had been avoiding his mom, though she would never pick up on that. In her mind, I was sure she thought she could do no wrong.

I snaked my head away from Steve to watch Bernadette approach Doris. Sure enough, when she tapped her on the shoulder and opened her arms wide to great her, Doris looked horrified. Her lips moved slowly over her teeth, and I could see the hesitation to return the hug. I think everyone could see it except my mother-in-law. Or maybe she didn't care.

"It's here, Kelly," Detective Pavlik said, pulling me back to the present.

"The candy cane?" I asked, still stuck in memories from the past.

"The candy cane? No, silly. The tape from Miami. They emailed it to me. It's here," he said, pointing down at his laptop on his desk. "Here, let's take a look. Let me know what you think."

I took a deep breath in, trying to shake the memory of Bernadette. She'd disappeared into the universe after the trial. The last I'd heard, she and Steve's father had gone incognito and moved away from the area, which was a blessing. Thus far, I'd never been contacted by her or received any threats. My lawyer had made it very clear that we would pursue extreme legal action if they did, considering they'd been so hateful to me during the trial, trying to smear my name.

Thank goodness Steve had been an only child. I didn't need his extended family lurking in the area, ready to pounce when I returned back to town.

"Okay, ready? I'm going to play this. You tell me if you see anything that stands out," Detective Pavlik said, punching a few keys on his computer.

"Okay," I said, kneeling down next to him and placing my face close to the screen.

"Do you want a chair?" he asked as the video began to play.

I shook my head no, entranced by what was playing on the screen in front of me. Like a bad horror movie, a figure in a black cape rushed into the foyer of my parent's high rise, pushed an elevator button, then turned inexplicably and fired a gun at Tony. Everything happened so fast, it felt like I was watching an action movie, not real life.

"Again," I said, a sickening feeling spreading through my body.

Chapter 25

My anxiety rose as I watched the video for a second time. The intruder punched the elevator key and then suddenly, turned and got a clean shot off, killing Tony. What was it about those quick and broken movements of the intruder, like the way a sprinkler spouts out in one direction and then suddenly shifts 180 degrees? It felt familiar to me somehow. Like I'd seen it in a movie before.

I just wish my brain would register where I'd seen that twist before.

"But why did they shoot Tony? It's not like he was trying to stop him. And he's wearing the cape. It's not like Tony could identify him," I said to Detective Pavlik, my nose almost pressing against the laptop to see if I could unravel the mystery.

"There's no audio. For some reason the audio was turned off or malfunctioning. We see this all the time. Cameras are law enforcement's latest and greatest friend, if and only if, they function correctly. Cameras are everywhere now," Detective Pavlik said, letting out a little whistle and shaking his head. "It's really changed the way we can convict felons. But technology continues to be a thorn in our side. If we can't get to the video fast enough, or talk to the person who knows how to work the video fast enough, we're in trouble. A lot of these places with cameras just use the same tape over and over and re-tape over the old footage. It's a race against time to get the footage before it gets deleted. So, like in this case, we have fool proof evidence of the shooting, but the audio would help close the whole story. Maybe we could hear the shooter's voice to help identify him. Or at least hear Tony's input. Maybe he recognized the shooter and called out his name? That's my theory. I wonder if he yelled out his name, the shooter realized he would be identified, and then turned to kill Tony so that he couldn't turn him into the police."

"Could it be Franklin Ford? The escaped convict?" I asked, presenting what had been my assumption from the moment I heard this news. Steve had sent Franklin to kill me, and tie up some loose ends.

"Unfortunately, the only person that can identify him is dead," Detective Pavlik said. "We need to learn more about Franklin Ford and do some comparisons. For example, does Franklin's height match that of the suspect? Hard to tell from the angle of the camera."

"This went violent so fast. What were they after?" I asked.

Detective Pavlik shook his head.

"No one knows. Look how he bolts the second he shoots the gun. It seems like such a waste. Nothing was taken, and he appears to change his mind completely once he shoots Tony. That's the other theory. He was looking for Tony. He came to kill Tony, mission accomplished, job done."

"Like a professional hit? But, why?"

"Don't know. We don't know anything about Tony's past. You said he was a police officer in Chicago and Miami, right? Maybe there was someone who had a grudge against him? Someone he put away? Or maybe he was involved in something we don't know about. That was quite a shot. They were standing at least twenty feet away. He was killed with one shot."

I cringed, thinking about Tony's comments about how he was searching for a life less violent, so he became a security officer. So much for that. He was killed in cold blood. My only hope was that he died instantly with no pain.

"But why not just walk right up to him and shoot him if that's the case? Why walk over to the elevator and shoot, risking a bad shot? If they were after Tony, he was visible at the front desk. Walk up to the front desk and shoot him. Say something like they do in the movies, 'I've been looking for you.' Don't make a beeline for the elevator and then shoot."

"I agree. And then, of course, there's this," he said, reaching down to backtrack the video. He stopped it at a specific point and said, "I thought you would catch this on your own, but it took me a few tries as well."

He hit play and leaned back, "Watch his right hand."

The shooter, sheltered in a black cape and wearing black gloves, reached up and tapped a button on the elevator screen. Detective Pavlik quickly clicked a button and paused the video, pointing his finger to the screen. "There," he said simply.

I squinted to get a better view of what he was referring to. There, on the wall in between the two elevators, I saw that only one number was lit up. The button the shooter hit when he walked up. Number thirteen. My parent's floor.

* * * * *

On my way to Big Rock, my cell phone rang. The screen lit up with Diane Nosely's number. I raised my eyebrow, considering picking it up. I had no idea of her current status. Was she still at our local hospital or had she been sent home? Didn't know. Didn't care.

Or was she "my friend" I was about to meet in Big Rock? Now that would be interesting, considering she had two broken legs. How would she get herself there? And why would she pick that destination?

I let it go to voicemail. The last I'd heard, Diane wasn't pursuing any kind of lawsuit against my brother-in-law for striking her with his car, but I wouldn't put it past her. I half expected that her voicemail would be something along the lines of, "Call me back and give me a story, or I'll sue your brother-in-law."

After a few minutes, the phone beeped, notifying me that she left a message. Unable to contain my curiosity, I dug around in my purse to find my earpiece. Something I should have done before starting my drive to Big Rock, instead of risking taking my attention off of the road.

Sure enough, while digging, I hit a patch of ice on the highway and skidded just enough to make my stomach drop. Small white snowflakes began to pelt the window, causing my anxiety to spike. Shaking my head, I realized I'd completely bypassed checking any weather reports this morning because I was so distracted by the day's events. It was entirely possible I could be heading into a blizzard and had no idea.

"Great," I mumbled to myself. As though I didn't have enough to worry about. Now I was on my way to a secret meeting, in an unfamiliar out of the way place, in the middle of a storm. Just great.

Finally, I was able to attach my earpiece to the phone and play the message. Diane's perky voice called out to me, reminding me why I didn't want to pick up the phone in the first place.

"Hey, girl," she said, as though I were an old friend she was trying to reconnect with. My lips pulled over my teeth at her casualness.

"Just checking in on you. I'm still chilling at the hospital here in Geneva. It's actually been kind of nice to be here relaxing."

She sounded a little too "relaxed" to me. I could picture her putting on an air of tranquility, bending her arms and folding them behind her head as she leaned back in bed. It sounded way too staged. What did she want? Get to it, Nosy Nosely.

"Always so busy," she rambled on.

Just as I was about to hang up, she got to the point.

"Anyway, I heard some interesting information from a source this morning about your ex. I just thought you would want to know. If I were in your situation, I would want to know," she said.

"Information about my ex?" I said aloud, burrowing my brows together. The way she referred to Steve as my "ex" made my stomach hurt. He was so much more than my "ex." He was a psychotic criminal on top of also being my ex. Let's not forget that.

"So, call me. Woman to woman, let's talk. No one has to know you heard it from me. I just think, well, just call me. It might affect your future," she said in a more serious tone. Where did her light façade go?

When she said the word future, my mind switched direction. What would Steve have to do with my future? He was my past. Jack was my future. And technically, Jack could be described as my ex as well since we broke up after college. But now he was no longer my ex. Which ex was she referring to? I was confused.

Chapter 26

When I got into the town of Big Rock, I pulled the car over, took a deep breath, and stared out the window at the snowflakes for a few seconds. My directions on my phone had taken me this far, but I wanted to review them before going any further into unfamiliar territory. The snow was now pelting my windshield at a rapid speed, leaving me feeling tense and distracted. There was a voice inside my head telling me I should just turn around and go home. But it was battling the second voice that was telling me I needed to go find out who "my friend" really was.

After studying my directions for a few minutes, I scratched my jaw, pondering my next move.

"Oh, what the heck. Why not?" I said aloud, hitting the call back button on my cell phone.

Diane answered immediately. She must have known how irresistible the seed she had planted was.

"Hi, Kelly. I'm so glad you called," she said, her voice sang out in a welcoming way. Welcoming like the singing Sirens, luring me to a shipwreck.

"What did you want to tell me, Diane," I said, bypassing all niceties and fake talk.

"Look, I just want to help you. I heard something," Diane said, emphasizing the word heard. "It worried me. I just keep thinking if I was in your shoes, I would want to know."

"Mmmhhmm," I said, pulling down the rearview mirror and

checking my make-up. "Don't you want to tell me in person?" I queried, trying to bait her into telling me if she was "the friend" I was about to meet at the library.

"You want to come to the hospital?" she asked, sounding thrilled.

"No," I said simply.

"Well, you're welcome to if you like. I'm sorry, but I'm just not able to leave yet. I could make it happen soon though," she said, her tone quick and anxious, like she was caught off guard, but more than willing to make provisions.

"I don't want to see you, Diane," I said bluntly.

"But, why did you say?" she cut off. "Well, I'd love to see you. Anyway, what I heard is about Steve," she said.

Hearing that relaxed me a bit. Of course it was about Steve. Did I really think she was going to give me dirt on Jack? What could she possibly have on Jack? It was that weird look from Adelle I got the other day when I mentioned my intention to marry him. That was still bothering me. But, I had to let that go. It was probably just me being paranoid. Adelle would have told me if something was up. Look how freely she'd spoken out about my mistakes in the past.

"What did you hear?" I asked, my voice heavy with irritation.

"Did you know he's getting married?" she asked, her voice laced with a sympathetic tone.

Part of me wanted to say yes. Yes, in fact, I did know. Last summer he'd sent crazy Sharon, and she told me they were to be married. Sharon was now rotting in jail, refusing to give up Steve's connection to the whole thing, and I was waiting for another one of his conquests to show up. So what? Why was any of this big news?

"Are you talking about Sharon?"

"Who's Sharon?" Diane asked.

"The one who's in jail for attempted murder. The one that came after me and my sister last summer," I said, rolling my eyes.

Keep up, the snarky voice in my head suggested saying to Diane. It would only fuel her fire though.

"Of course, that's right. No, this is someone else," she said.

She wasn't doing a good job concealing the excitement in her voice, which only made me more irritated.

Someone else?

I stayed silent, figuring that was the best way to get her to say more. The truth was that this news had me a little on edge, so I needed a few seconds to pull it together before speaking.

"Till death do us part," Steve confirmed with a smile the day we said our vows. Our guests had cheered when we kissed in my sweet little hometown church. The future looked bright, and I couldn't wait to spend my life with him. He took my hand, kissed it ever so gently and led me down the aisle to our reception to dance the night away.

"I love you so much," he'd whispered into my ear as we stepped into the limo.

"I love you, too," I said, fighting back happy tears.

"So, who's the lucky girl this time?" I finally managed. The sarcasm in my voice hid my sadness, my disappointment, and my distress at the thought of another woman stepping into Steve's web of deceit and lies.

"Well, I don't know her name yet. I just know that's the talk of the prison yard right now," Diane said conspiratorially.

"And how in the world are you privy to this prison yard info?" I asked, still keeping my guard up. For all I knew, Diane was making this whole thing up just to keep me on the phone to try and get something from me.

"I'm still investigating the Franklin Ford case, so I've been snooping around there."

"Really," I commented, wondering who her sources in Steve's prison could be.

"You know he hasn't been caught yet, right?" she said. "Is that concerning to you at all considering he was in the same prison as Steve? Practically in the same cell."

Instead of commenting, I sat silently, picking at a piece of lint on the sleeve of my sweater. The image of the cloaked figure in my parent's lobby popped into my head. The hand reaching out to hit the elevator call button.

Say nothing, my inner voice chanted over and over in my head.

"It's just a strange coincidence. Anyway, do you want me to call you back once I find out the name of the woman Steve is marrying?" she asked, changing course.

Pulling the phone away from my ear, I glanced at the screen before hitting the "End Call" button.

Could Steve be her source? Could they actually be in cahoots? I didn't want to give her the satisfaction of asking her. Better to end the call.

After a few seconds, I plugged in my current location on the mapping system on my phone and waited for my new directions. When Diane's call came in again, I sent it straight to voicemail.

Chapter 27

Driving along the gravel road, I was able to easily spot Big Rock Library approaching on my right. The large, white farmhouse in the middle of a field was hard to miss. Also on the property, a huge, spooky looking red barn loomed in the distance. All of the crops were cut back for the winter months, allowing a passerby full view of both buildings.

I barely remembered any of the details of this place from my childhood visit, but from the research I'd done, I learned that the three story library was built as a home for a couple around 1908. It was formerly known as the Michael House before the woman who owned it moved out to remarry after her husband's death.

The building itself appeared very well taken care of despite its age. The shutters and the siding were in mint condition, and the grounds had well-kept landscaping groomed back for the winter months. A red open sign flashed at me from the front window. O...P...E...N! OPEN!

I smiled to myself thinking how out of place that modern light was in such an old architectural beauty. It gave me a good feeling about what the inside would look like. Someone was taking good care of this oldy but goody.

The gravel parking lot that separated the red barn from the library had a few cars in attendance, but for the most part looked fairly empty. I studied each car quickly to see if any of them looked familiar. Nothing struck me. Apparently my "friend" wasn't going to be a close acquaintance, as far as I could tell. A brand new looking luxury SUV called out to me as being a little out of place from the rest of the cars, but still, I wasn't able to trace it to anyone I knew.

Shutting the car off, I turned to get a better view of the spooky barn. A bit larger in size than the home, it sat parallel to the library with the farm fields running behind it. Just like the library, it appeared to be in pristine condition. I couldn't put my finger on what it was about the barn that spooked me. I'd never had a warm fuzzy feeling about barns. Probably due to the scary movies I'd watched with my sisters as a kid. People were always getting killed and thrown in the hay in the horror movies we'd watched.

For the first time, I noticed a sign on the barn that read, "Big Rock Historical Society."

"Interesting," I said quietly to myself. This would be a great find for the series I wrote, The Antique Murder Mysteries. My main character, Mary, would have a field day with finding a mysterious barn that housed historical treasures in the middle of a farm field.

Pushing open my car door, I pulled the hood of my coat over my head and started to make my way over to the barn. Halfway there, I changed my mind and turned to head for the library. The snow was coming down hard now. I knew it was best to get this meeting over with and get home. No time for investigating. Another time.

Gazing up at the library, I was faced with a choice. Walk in through the front door facing the main road, or in through the side door with the little covered porch. Based on the footprints up the stairs to the side door, my guess was this was the obvious choice. I noticed there were a few footprints made by large boots, indicating to me that a man had entered recently. But there were also smaller ones that could have been left by a woman or a smaller man. For the first time, fear replaced the bravado I'd been feeling on my way here. Perhaps this wasn't such a good idea to come here alone. I'd wanted to solve this on my own, but now that I was here, in the middle of nowhere in a snowstorm, this seemed just plain stupid.

I pulled my cell phone out and typed in the words:

At Big Rock Library

The message was intended for Nikki, but instead of sending it, I slipped the phone back in my pocket and made my way up the stairs. Pulling the door open, I was met immediately by a friendly face just to my left. A woman with dark hair streaked with gray sat behind a tall counter that served as a circulation desk. She gasped when I opened the door, as though I were an unexpected visitor. The wind I carried in with me ruffled her hair in all directions. She pushed herself away from the desk, retracting from the wind. I pulled the door shut quickly behind me and tried my best to return her smile.

"Sorry," I said, regretting my decision to use the side door. If I would have come in from the front, I'd have spared her from the windstorm.

"No problem," she said, smiling. "It's gotten a lot chillier out there, hasn't it?"

"Yes," I said, nodding my head and taking a second to look around.

Directly in front of me, a bulletin board announcing upcoming events in the community caught my eye. Smack dab in the middle of it was a promotional picture for my latest book that included a large picture of me. Wow. Very cool.

"Kelly Clark," she said, by way of greeting.

A nervous laugh escaped my lips in response.

"I'm a big fan. We just read your book for my book club," she said, sitting up a little taller in her chair and leaning forward.

"Oh, how nice," I said, feeling slightly awkward. I couldn't shake the feeling that I was intruding on someone's home, since Big Rock Library was just that– someone's home converted into a public place.

"It's so nice you're here. Please come in and make yourself at home. My name is Jennie. Would you like me to show you around the library?" she asked. She started to work her way around the desk.

"I'm actually here to meet someone," I said, stepping further into the library, trying to get a feel for the place. My guess was that this being the back of the house, it must have served as the kitchen at one time. A wall or two was probably knocked down to make this room so big. From the older farm homes I'd visited, I knew this room was too big for the way kitchens were initially built back then.

"Oh," she said in a knowing tone. Her eyes moved skyward, and her finger pointed up to the second floor. Was that to mean my visitor was upstairs?

I wanted to blurt out, "Is it Franklin Ford?" but held back.

Stay cool.

Instead, I took a second to turn my head and continue to take in the rest of the first floor. The first thing that held me was how neat and organized this little farmhouse/library was. There were floor to ceiling bookshelves with DVDs and CDs behind the circulation desk, a small kitchen and bathroom to the right of the shelves, and signs in primary colors clearly marking the basement level as the children's section of the library. The signs did such a good job at drawing my attention in an appealing way that I found myself wanting to take a peek at what they had put together for the kids. I had no recollection of the basement being used in a functional way for the library when I'd last been here as a child.

To my right was the dining room that still held a grand table in the middle of the room for people to work and read.

"This is really nice in here," I told Jennie.

"It's the pride and joy of Big Rock. Along with our history museum out back," she said, tilting her head in the direction of the big red barn.

"Here, come and see your section," she said.

"My section?"

"We have a local author section in here," Jennie said, cruising past me into the dining room. "Since your book was last month's book club selection, we have a little display going."

I followed her through the dining room, noting a small computer room just off to the left with very modern looking technology from what I could tell.

"Wow," I said aloud.

"That's our tech center. Isn't it beautiful? It was all donated to us by an anonymous donor last year. Can you believe it? It was quite a windfall for us," she said, shifting her arms over to the room to try and entice me to check it out.

I peeked in, noting that the six computers sat unused, watching me like eager worker bees, waiting to be put to task. They looked nicer than the computer I had at home, that was for sure.

"How nice," I said, not knowing enough about computers to be able to comment on much. It didn't take a genius though to figure out that these cost someone a pretty penny.

My mind reviewed the outside of the building, trying to remember if there had been any notification of a security system set up for the library. Hopefully, they'd had that in the budget. I personally wouldn't want to leave these babies unguarded at night.

"And, over here we have our local author section," Jennie said proudly, pulling me into the front sitting room that was decked out with shelving units like the ones found in libraries. They weren't quite as tall as what I was used to seeing, which was a good thing. The natural light from the grand front window poured in, allowing the beauty of the room to be kept intact.

If the circumstances were different, I could see myself hanging out here all the time to work, read, and escape my life. The environment was clean, cozy, cheerful, and conducive to productivity. With its isolated location and quiet atmosphere, I could write and work undisturbed for days at a time.

"Wow," I said, taking note of the bookshelf Jennie was pointing at. Sure enough, all of my books in my Antique Murder Mystery Series were on display with a framed headshot of me taken a few years back.

"Look at this," I said, genuinely pleased and honored by what they had put together. "I'm floored."

"Like I said, we're big fans here. Would you mind signing your poster," Jennie asked, smiling from ear to ear.

Whoever was upstairs chose that moment to make a move. The floorboards above us creaked, reminding me we were not alone.

My eyes moved to the wooden staircase to my left leading up to the second floor. The creaking stopped just as quickly as it had started, making me think whoever it was had made just a slight adjustment of their position and was not planning on coming downstairs. Still, I kept my eyes trained on the stairs a few seconds longer just to make sure. The wooden stairs, carved with intricate detail noticeable even from this distance, reminded me of the ones in Chocolate Love. They hugged the front entrance room on the right side and turned after a small landing cut the stairs in two.

"Is everything okay, Kelly?" Jennie asked me.

When I turned to look at her, her hazel eyes watched me with interest.

"Oh, yes, of course," I said, my face reddening.

"He's waiting for you upstairs?" she asked.

He?

"He is," I said, unsure of how to go on.

"Did you recognize him?" I asked, pulling out a pen from my purse. "You know, is he familiar to you?"

My hands shook as I took the poster from Jennie's hands in preparation of autographing their copy. My head turned frantically, looking for a place to properly lay the poster down in order to sign.

"Well, yes. I've seen him on television a few times, that's for sure," Jennie said, motioning me to use the dining room table as a place to sign it.

My stomach dropped at the mention of television, and my mouth gaped open. Jennie was okay with Franklin Ford sitting upstairs waiting for me? A known killer, here on her premises, just lounging upstairs reading library books? Why hadn't she called the police yet?

Chapter 28

"You saw him on television?" I croaked out.

We have to get out of here. We have to get out of here, right now.

My mind raced back to the tape I'd just watched with Detective Pavlik. The way the killer shot Tony in cold blood. Just a quick turn and BAM. Tony was dead. No questions. No negotiations. No "Are you the person I came here to kill?" Just a shot. A deadly one.

I also thought about what I'd learned about Franklin Ford and what led him to prison. He was a ruthless killer. And he was sitting upstairs.

I pictured my husband leaning close to Franklin Ford in the prison yard. Close enough to whisper into his ear what he'd wanted him to do to me. How a woman had ruined his life, just like what happened to him. Whispering lies and stories, and knowing just the right thing to say to motivate Franklin and push him over the edge. I could almost hear the offers and the promises he'd made him.

Kill her for me, and I'll make things right for you. I'll set you up really good. I'll give you whatever you want. Kill her for me, man, just like you did your wife. You had the guts to do it then. You were smart enough to get her out of your life. I should have done what you did. I've got connections. I can set you up for the rest of your life.

"In those commercials he's in," Jennie was saying.

We were standing in the dining room, facing the picture window that gave us a view of the barn across the parking lot. Before the words she'd said registered with me, I took notice of the flakes in front of me, blowing like dust across the window. All at once, I was back in Big Rock, IL, not the California prison yard, overhearing my husband hiss into Franklin's ear.

"The commercial?"

"You asked me if I recognized him. I recognize him from the commercials that run for his company every now and then on the local stations. What's that little jingle that goes along with them? I can't remember now. Something about their phone number," she laughed. "Anyway, I don't remember now. Would you like a cup of coffee? I can make you two cups? I offered him coffee when he arrived, but he wasn't interested. But if you're going to talk for a while, perhaps you would like some?"

Open mouthed, I continued to stare at Jennie, trying desperately to piece together what she'd just told me. Franklin Ford was definitely not in any local commercials promoting his local business. I was pretty sure I was safe from that threat. For now.

I began nodding my head, just to look as though I had some kind of response for her.

"Great! I'll just put those together and bring them up once they're ready."

"Okay," I squeaked out. I bent over and signed my name to the poster, nearly forgetting how to spell it.

"Would you like cream or sugar?" Jennie asked.

"Yes. Both please," I managed.

"Do you know if he would like either?" Jennie asked.

"He likes both as well," I confirmed, sticking with my final guess of who I thought was upstairs.

"Great, I'll meet you up there in a minute," Jennie said, bolting to the kitchen and leaving me alone holding the giant poster of me. I set it down on the table, trying my best to gain my composure so my hands would stop shaking and my autograph would look nice. They went through so much trouble to feature my work here. The least I could do was give them a nice autograph.

Taking a deep breath, I turned to head over to the stairs that would take me to the second floor. I heard the floor creaking again, as though the inhabitant of the second floor was pacing, anxious to see me.

Grabbing onto the solid railing with my left hand, I breathed in again and began my ascent up the stairs. Distracted for a brief second, I turned behind me to glance at the front door. I could see now that it was locked up tight and not really used as an entrance or exit at all. The side door that I'd come in was the only intended entrance to the building. I wondered if the front door behind me was even functional at all. Just in case I needed it to be. Just in case I was wrong. Something about the way it sat locked up tight told me it was a no go.

That was fine. I was pretty sure I wasn't in danger at this point. At least not physical danger.

I heard the sound of the wooden floors creaking once again. He must have seen my car pull up. Maybe this was not as serious as I thought. Maybe he was just meeting me here to plan something good. Why the cloak and dagger though? Why not just call me?

"I'm coming," I called softly.

Once at the top of the stairs, I was momentarily distracted by a seating area to my left roped off by a little string. The seating area contained ancient looking chairs and a secretary with china in it.

Not knowing where to look for him, I chose the room directly in front of me first. My breath caught when I spotted its guest.

"Oh, hello," I said quietly, to a large Native American doll standing just to my left. She grinned back at me by way of greeting. All around me were Native American relics labeled for their various tribes they belonged to. My eyes moved quickly over the glass displays and cases that hung on the wall. In just a quick glance, it was obvious the library had done a fabulous job of meticulously displaying these treasures. In quieter times, I would definitely have to come back and check this out properly.

"In here," a familiar male voice called out from down the hall.

Yep, it was exactly who I'd thought it would be.

"Coming," I called out.

Turning on my heel, I left the room of relics and made my way further down the hall. On the wall, I saw a picture of a woman standing proudly next to a horse. Above her, I caught a quick title, naming her as the original owner of the farm home turned library. If I had more time, I'd read more about her. I could almost feel the ghost of this woman watching me from these second floor rooms. It was hard to distinguish why, but these rooms had a complex energy to them.

Spontaneously, I chose to whip my body around. I crouched down, holding my hands up, half expecting to see the ghost of the previous owner staring back at me from the roped off seating area. Empty. Perhaps if I just stayed a few seconds more her ghost would appear, watching me with a critical eye over tiny glasses. I could almost see her bun, and the long, cotton farming dress draping down as she relaxed in her easy chair with a book after a long day of work.

"What are you doing here in my home, girl," she'd ask me. "I donated this room to be used as a library, not a secret meeting place."

"Kelly," a soft voice called out in the room just to the left of me.

"Oh!" I jumped.

He reached his arm out to me, catching my left arm and pulling me into the sitting room where he'd been waiting for me.

"Are you okay?" he asked.

"Yes," I nodded. "I'm just, sorry, distracted." I didn't dare mention the ghost I'd just been speaking to.

I allowed him to pull me further into the sitting room, observing the quiet blue walls and high back chairs that looked ancient but well taken care of. My eyes took in a small white envelope on the tiny antique couch. Something about the envelope scared me. All at once, I knew, by no uncertain terms that this was not going to be about planning a surprise for Adelle. Between the wrinkled brow Mike was sporting and the way he looked behind me to make sure I was alone, I knew. This wasn't going to be light and cheerful as I'd hoped. Mike was in trouble. And somehow I was involved.

Chapter 29

"Mike, what are you doing here?" I asked, watching him poke his head out the door and look to the left and right.

He was dressed in a full suit and tie, most likely coming straight from work. His black hair was slicked neatly back, not a strand out of place. A long wool coat hung over the back of a chair in the far corner of the room. I couldn't help but notice the lone bead of sweat that ran down the side of his face. He wiped it away quickly and turned back to me.

"Thanks for meeting me. I'll explain everything. I just want to make sure we have some privacy," he said. His right hand reached for the ring finger on his left and played with the band, spinning it briefly on his finger.

"Here, let's sit," he said, gesturing for me to choose first.

The room was small; the focus of it being the large double windows that looked out onto the farm fields that lined the small dirt road I'd driven in on. He must have seen me approach. I could picture him watching me from this window, chewing on his nails or narrowing his eyes as I approached. I didn't like the way he was looking at me. It felt like he was sizing me up. I didn't like the secrecy and the isolation of the place he chose to meet me. This man I'd grown to accept as a brother was suddenly someone I wasn't so sure I wanted to be alone with. It wasn't clear why he needed to see me, but it was clear he wasn't alone. He had some kind of baggage with him, and by the way he was pacing the room and releasing anxious energy, I knew he was about to unload that baggage on me.

"Mike, what is going on? Why are we here? Why do you look like you're going to tell me you just shot a man?" I said, finally giving up and choosing one of the high back chairs instead of the tiny couch. I didn't trust its size or its ability to hold my weight. It appeared as though it really should be more for décor than functional couch. I imagined it looking up at me and saying, "please pick another option" if it could speak.

Mike exhaled and finally let out a little chuckle that gave me a bit of ease. His laugh was one I was familiar with. I'd heard it escape from his mouth countless times over family dinners and parties.

"I'm sorry. This whole thing is, just, crazy," Mike said, finally making the call and walking over to the chair he'd laid his coat over. Apparently, he didn't trust the couch either. He pulled off his suitcoat and threw it over his wool coat before plopping down on the chair and putting his head in his hands.

"Mike, what's wrong? What is it?" I begged, scooting my chair across the floor to get closer to him. I wanted to be more accessible to my brother- in-law during his obvious time of suffering.

"Kelly, I screwed up so bad," he said, shaking his head and not meeting my eyes.

"*Oh my God, he's had an affair,*" was all I could think. My mouth involuntarily sneered up in disgust, and I inched back a bit on the chair.

Another scumbag who couldn't keep his vows. Just like my ex-husband. But this time there was a whole family involved. He was going to ruin his kids' lives. All because he couldn't be faithful to his wife, my sister.

"Who is she?" I managed, sneering at him. Any bit of sympathy I'd felt for his obvious dismay was gone once the image of my niece and nephews popped into my head. I was already thinking about them being schlepped back and forth at holidays and weekends.

Adelle wouldn't be able to spend every day with them anymore. She would be crushed at the thought of her kids being taken away from her. They were her life. She wouldn't make it through this.

"What?" Mike said, his head popping up. His dark eyes focused on mine, and a look of pure confusion registered on his face.

"You," I stumbled, "you're going to tell me you're having an affair? You screwed up?'

"What? No," Mike said, sitting up straight in the chair and recoiling from my assumption. His eyes grew round, and his nostrils flared as though I'd just struck him.

"Oh, I'm sorry," I said, my face flushing.

"Kelly, I would never be unfaithful to my wife. I love Adelle. I love my family," Mike said defensively.

"Of course, I know," I said, pulling my hands together and crossing my legs. "It just came out because you said you made a mistake. It was a stupid assumption. I'm so sorry. I think I just assume when men say they've made a mistake, most of the time they're referring to infidelity. You know, because of my experience. Or maybe I watch too much television. Or books. I don't know. Like I said, it was stupid," I said, emphasizing the word stupid and talking way too much.

I pulled my arms up and lifted my palms to the ceiling in an "I don't know" gesture.

"But please, before my mind goes to more crazy places. Please, tell me what is bothering you, Mike," I laughed nervously, twisting uncomfortably in my chair.

Mike released a long breath before speaking.

"Kelly, I was trying to tell you that I think I've done something terrible that may affect your future," Mike said, stumbling over his words.

I wasn't used to this kind of Mike. Mike had run his family business for years. He built and sold high end homes all over

Chicago to very wealthy people. He was smooth. He was slick and suave. The man in front of me right now was sweating and scary looking in his awkwardness.

"What are you talking about?" I asked, feeling a chill run through my body. There was that word again. Future. So much was always focused on that. What was Kelly's future? What was Kelly's past? How did the two intermingle?

The only thing I knew for sure was my future was Jack.

"Jack?" I probed when Mike didn't speak, thinking back once again to the weird look Adelle had given me when I'd brought up our possible engagement.

Mike simply shook his head in a weird way. Not a no and not a yes.

"Right now I'm specifically talking about Steve," he said. The way he said it, slow and clear, it felt like he was picking his words carefully.

"What about Steve?" I asked, hating the feel of his name on my lips. Again, the flash of him in jail smirking at me from a jail cell leapt through my mind.

"Hi, Kelly. Hey, baby, it's me," Steve cooed before blowing a kiss.

Mike closed his eyes briefly and shook his head, hanging it down under his shoulder blades.

"I made a huge mistake and helped Steve out a few years ago. I was in a tight spot, and Steve was able to get me out of it," Mike said, not able to meet my eyes.

"In what way?" I asked, staring down at his thick head of dark hair.

Mike finally lifted his head up and found my eyes.

"I'm honestly not quite sure, but I'm scared we're going to find out," Mike said.

"What are you talking about?" I asked, feeling very confused and frustrated at the murky waters we were swimming in.

Mike pushed his hands down on his knees and stood up. He walked over to the couch and snatched the envelope up from it before sitting back down on his seat. Overturning the envelope, a small metal object fell from it into his hand. He held it open so that I could get a good look at it.

"No," I said quietly to myself when it registered what it was.

Chapter 30

"The key for the bank," I said, reaching for it.

"You knew about this. I thought you might," Mike said.

"I have a matching key. It's to a safety deposit box, right?" I asked. "But what is it? Why do we both have one? I don't understand."

"It's a safety deposit box, that's right," Mike confirmed. "I'm holding this for Steve."

"What?" I whispered. The fact that Mike was partnering with Steve, still partnering with him, felt like a punch in my gut. How could he after everything that had happened?

"Not purposely, Kelly. It's a long story. Please let me explain," Mike said, raising his eyebrows at me and reaching out with his arm, as though he thought I was going to bolt from the room.

"I've been holding onto this for years. I'm not even sure what it is. I'm not sure why I have it," Mike said softly in apology. "A few years ago, I needed some extra cash while the housing market was falling. I'd taken out some bank loans and was struggling. I was desperate. Steve offered to help me out. He gave me a loan, but he said he needed something from me. He asked me to open a safety deposit box in Geneva. It seemed harmless at the time. Or maybe I was just so desperate I didn't allow myself to think about it too much. He didn't go into detail on what was in there, he just asked me to open it and keep it up to date. I pay a small fee every year to keep it going."

"You do? But why did you keep it going? What if it had something to do with the murder?" I begged.

Mike let out a long sigh and wiped at his brow. Finally he spoke.

"Kelly, I'm not going to make any excuses for myself. What I did was wrong. I kind of justified it by knowing he'd been put away, and whatever was in that box wasn't needed to prove his guilt. And honestly, I'm a little scared to look at what's in there. I don't want to know, especially now that I know what Steve is capable of. I've kind of just been hoping it would go away. Like I said, it was wrong of me, I know. I just can't keep going like this. The guilt is eating me alive," Mike said.

"But, Mike, what if there is something in there about the attempted murders? You could be looked at as an accomplice," I said, standing my ground. There was no denying the anger I had toward Mike for doing this. I thought about all the debt that was sitting still to this day on my credit cards because Steve wanted me to charge our infertility treatments on them. Meanwhile, he was shelling out cash to Mike and playing high roller. Why would Mike have gone to Steve in the first place?

"I honestly don't know what you were thinking asking Steve for money. We were struggling so much during those years with the infertility and our own expenses. Why would you think Steve would be a good source?" I questioned, still unable to feel sorry for the man perspiring in front of me.

"Kelly, I'm so sorry. Like I said, I'm not going to try and justify my actions. It was stupid. I was just so desperate. Adelle was spending and living it up, and my business was sinking. I didn't have it in me to tell her to stop. I needed some cash to float me through what I thought was going to be a bad couple of months. I was close to Steve at the time, and he offered it before I really asked. Now I see how slick he was. He never led on to being in any financial trouble himself. He used me when I was desperate. And then everything blew up. And then, well, the attempted murder. Obviously, I had no idea Steve was who he was. I never would have gotten myself involved with him. The whole thing is," Mike looked down again at his gleaming, polished shoes, "a mess. I've been scared to close the account and scared to keep it open. I just keep paying the fee every year, trying to buy more time to make a decision."

Feeling at a loss for words, I sat up straighter and glanced out the double windows beyond Mike. The snow fell in steady waves behind him, glittering in the little speck of sun that tried to pop out from behind the clouds. This was too much.

"We have to tell the police," I said quietly, almost to myself.

Mike kept his head down and wiped at his eyes with one hand, moaning slightly.

"I'm so screwed," he said. "Will I go to jail? My kids."

There was something that was bothering me about Mike's story. The fact that we both had keys this whole time. I'd been stalked by Steve's new girlfriend last summer presumably for the key, but Mike had been left alone?

"Mike, why are you telling me this now? Why did you wait so long and then decide to tell me now?"

Mike lifted his head and locked eyes with me.

"Adelle said Mom overheard you and Nikki talking about checking out something that involved a key. When I opened the account, they gave me two keys. One I kept and Steve took the other one. I started wondering if perhaps you somehow got the second key when Steve went to jail."

"I did. I mean, I'm not sure if he intended me to have it, but I found a key in one of my old coat pockets, and it looks just like yours, so it must be the duplicate. I think it's what that crazy woman, Sharon, came looking for when she hunted me down last summer. But why didn't she come after you? And does Adelle know about the safety deposit box?" I asked.

"No," Mike said, vehemently shaking his head.

"Why didn't Steve put his own name on the account? Why go through all this trouble?"

"Because whatever is in there is probably very illegal and very incriminating. He was smart to make himself just a bystander in this."

"He's such a dirt bag," I seethed.

"So something Adelle said made you think I had another key and that I was looking into things," I went on.

"I think your mom overheard you and Nikki on the phone in Miami and then she told Adelle, who told me," he said. "You know how that goes."

"Geez," I said, imagining my mom pressing her ear against the door while Nikki and I made calls to California banks in the guest room. There were no secrets in this family.

"I didn't want you going on a wild goose chase. I wanted this over. It needs to be over. I'm guilty of helping out a criminal, and I deserve whatever is coming for me," Mike said, clasping his hands together. His lip quivered slightly before continuing. "I just wanted to meet you face-to-face to tell you how sorry I am, Kelly. I'm humiliated. Like I said, I justified it by knowing Steve was in jail for his crime, and whatever I had wasn't needed to prove his guilt. But now, you're trying to get married and close that chapter, and these people are coming after you for the key, most likely. It's not right. We need to get to the bottom of this and be done with it. I don't want you to get hurt or threatened anymore."

Mike shook his head and wiped at his eyes before looking away. I'd never seen Mike cry, not even at a family funeral. He looked like a man on edge. I believed his regret and his willingness to take on the consequences of his actions. Mike was a brave man, a good man. Perhaps a bit stupid and too willing to do whatever it took to make

Adelle happy, but still a good man. I couldn't exactly stand on principal anyway. I too had been swindled by Steve, The Great Manipulator.

"Coffee?" Jennie said, making me jump in my seat.

I worried how long she'd been standing there and how much she'd heard. All of a sudden Mike's insistence on a quiet, out of the way place for our discussion made a lot of sense.

"Thank you," I finally managed. I'd completely forgotten about her offer to serve us coffee. I also hadn't heard her approach, which was odd because the stairs had squeaked so much when I'd taken them a few minutes earlier.

"I'll just set this down right here," she sang out, placing the tray with our coffee down on the couch. She stood up and smiled down at us expectantly.

"That's very kind of you," I said, wondering what to do next. Did she want me to offer her to take a seat? This was a horrible time for socializing.

"I'm sorry. I don't mean to stare. It's just that we don't get a local celebrity in every day. And you, as well, Mr. Stefano. Your homes are gorgeous. I was browsing through them online while I was waiting for the coffee to brew. I thought I recognized you from your commercials. Have you ever built this far west, near Big Rock?" Jennie asked, making polite conversation.

"Yes, I have actually," Mike said, nodding his head.

To the common person, Mike probably sounded calm and in control, but knowing him as well as I did, I could sense the panicky undertones in his voice. I bet he was thinking the same thing I was: How much had Jennie heard and how come we hadn't heard her approach?

"We'd love to have you come speak at our architectural club. It's a small group, maybe only five to ten members at most, but if you would consider it, we'd love to have you. They meet every other month here at the library," Jennie said.

"I'd be honored," Mike said, reaching into his pocket and pulling out his wallet. He handed her one of his cards. His hand shook slightly on the interchange. "Call me anytime to set it up."

"Great! And you, too, Kelly. Would you consider speaking at our Murder Mystery Club? That group is rather large. There's about thirty of us that meet once a month. You wouldn't believe how many Big Rock citizens we have that are interested in a good mystery. And they love yours!" Jennie said.

"Yes, of course, I'd be delighted." Any other time, I would be thrilled by her offer, but right now I was too distracted by Mike's revelations. I tried my best to smile, but felt my lips shaking in a weird struggle.

"Great, I'll leave you be," Jennie said, turning suddenly and leaving the room.

She turned to the right rather than the left, the way I'd entered our little meeting room. I stood from my seat and tiptoed to the door to watch her go. Sure enough, I watched her exit down a second set of stairs. This one was a carpeted back staircase that absorbed the sound of her footsteps.

Disheartened, I returned to my seat and reached for my coffee.

Mike watched me for a few seconds before whispering, "How much do you think she heard?"

I grimaced and shrugged my shoulders.

"Crap, we should go," he said, first reaching for his cup of coffee and chugging it down. "I thought I had done such a good job of finding a quiet, secret place.

"That's the problem. Secrets don't work. At least in my life. All of my skeletons are determined to come out," I whispered back.

"Mike, there's one thing that's really bothering me," I said, as quietly as I could.

"What?" he said, eyes widening.

"If Steve knows you also have a key, why isn't he sending his lackeys after you? That would be so easy. Or, why not just contact you and demand it? Are the keys different? They're the same, right? What would it matter if it was my key or yours?

Mike shook his head and looked back into his coffee cup.

"You know I've been asking myself the same thing since you girls were attacked last summer by that crazy woman. Why is Steve making this so hard? That scares me the most. He knows I have a key and that he's got something over me. Why not just get it from me? And what if I decided to close it myself? Maybe he knows I won't because I'm scared. It's like he wants me to remain a partner in this whole thing. Why?"

Because maybe you are, I thought.

Chapter 31

"I don't know," I said, trying my best to shake the suspicious voices out of my head. It was silly to think that way. If Steve was hiding something of worth in the safety deposit box and Mike had a key, he could just take it anytime he wanted, especially when he was going through his hard financial times. Mike had just lost his house. If he really wanted what was in the safety deposit box, surely he would have used his key and taken the money, or whatever was in the box when he really needed it.

"What are we going to do, Kelly?" Mike asked. "I'm willing to go to the police right now if you want to."

As much as I wanted to, I was worried about doing that. What about Adelle? What about the kids? How would they handle this news? And what if Mike had to go to jail? What would happen to his business and the welfare of my sister?

I shook my head and released a sigh.

"I don't know what to do. I think we should at least consider . . ." I was interrupted by the ringing of my cell phone in my purse.

"Are you going to answer that?" Mike asked when I made no move to search for it.

"No, not now," I said, shaking my head. Whatever it was, it could wait.

"Which bank, Mike?" I asked.

My phone beeped next to me, letting me know I had a message. Ignoring it, I chugged the last of my coffee, waiting for Mike's answer.

"The one around the corner from Chocolate Love," he said, holding back from saying the name. Was he still worried that Jennie was listening?

My stomach flipped at the notion that whatever it was Steve was involved in was sitting here in Geneva the whole time.

"I was going to go out to California to go hunt this down at my old bank."

"I kind of had a notion that was what you were doing. That's why I was trying to stop you before going on a wild goose chase."

My phone beeped again in my purse and then started to ring. With an impending feeling of dread, I turned and looked at the purse then back at Mike. He nodded his head for me to answer it.

Reaching into my purse, I saw Diane Nosely's number registering on my caller ID. Shaking my head, I sent it to voicemail. Whatever she had to tell me could wait. Seven new text messages popped up on my phone after I'd sent the call to voicemail. My eyes flew open wide when it started to register what they said.

"What?" Mike asked.

Before I could answer him, the clunk, clunk, clunk of someone running up the front stairs of the library made us both freeze.

"High speed chase," Jennie said, running into the room, gasping for air. "On television."

Jennie bent over, taking in deep breaths.

"Your guy, high speed chase near Canada. The police are saying they've been watching a cabin right near the border of Canada," she managed, breathing heavily. "And now, huh," she gasped, "he's on the run."

"Steve?" Mike asked, sounding just as baffled as I was by Jennie's behavior. This mild mannered librarian was absolutely manic right now.

"No, Franklin Ford. The one that was in the same prison as your husband," she said, widening her eyes.

Mike looked at me, and I held up my phone and nodded my head.

"We have to go," Mike said suddenly, pulling at my arm to get me to stand up. "Thank you, Jennie," Mike said.

He pulled me out of the room and toward the front staircase of the house.

"Wait," I protested. "We're not done talking."

"We're done talking here," Mike said quietly. He mumbled something inaudible; the sound of our shoes on the stairs blocked out any possibility of hearing him. Mike stopped at the bottom of the staircase and tried the inoperable front door. He gave up quickly after a futile couple of seconds and pulled me toward the side entrance where I'd initially entered.

We quickly approached the little entrance counter where I'd first met Jennie. I could hear the chatting of voices somewhere near the counter, though no one was visible.

"I said that woman is way too interested in us. This is not the private setting I'd imagined. We have to get out of here."

Jennie suddenly popped out of nowhere, assumedly having taken the back stairs at the same time we'd chosen the front ones.

"You guys be careful now," she breathed heavily, her cheeks flushed a bright red. "I hope they catch him."

The voices I'd heard just a few seconds ago were now easily identifiable. They were coming from the small television Jennie had on behind the counter. For a brief second, I saw the visual of two reporters talking as the mugshot of Franklin Ford sat in the upper right hand corner of the screen.

I nodded in response to Jennie's question, trying to remain polite.

"Goodbye," Mike said gruffly, basically shoving me out the door.

Outside Mike and I stumbled down the wood steps to our cars.

"Okay, I'm finally understanding your frustration with the public's interest in your crazy story. How do you handle it? Let's go to my car for a second and finish our conversation in private," Mike suggested.

"Where are you parked?" I asked, looking around for the BMW I knew he took to work most days.

"Right here. This is my rental till my car is fixed," he said, pointing to the shiny SUV I'd spotted earlier. He scrambled with the keys as snow fell all around us. The snow made me want to be back in Jack's apartment setting up for the dinner. The dinner!

I whacked my hand to my head.

"Mike, as much as I want to talk more, I really have to go. I have a special dinner planned tonight for Jack. I even hired a personal chef for it. Do you think we could continue this later?" I asked.

I was worried about getting home to prep for the dinner, but a bigger part of me just wanted to take a minute to absorb all of this new information and figure out what to do with it.

Mike turned to look at me.

"What? What about the police? I dump this crazy confession on you and you want to go make dinner? Kelly," he said, eyes wrinkled in worry. "You're not going to propose to him tonight, are you?"

I didn't respond. I couldn't. How did he know? And why did he look so opposed to the idea?

"Why? Is that a bad thing?" I asked, not bothering to hide my irritation. Why was everyone so opposed to me doing this? I thought this was what everyone wanted for me?

Mike's mouth formed an unattractive grimace, and he looked away in the direction of the barn.

"We really have to talk more," was all he said.

Chapter 32

"You're really scaring me now," I said, feeling overwhelmed. We'd made it inside of Mike's car. I was rubbing my hands together while waiting for the heat to kick on.

"Listen, I don't want to break dude code, but you're my sister. I don't want you to get your heart broken again," he said, poking at various buttons in the car that I hoped would make heat come faster. I was freezing.

"Okay," I said, feeling my heart sink.

"Jack is a good guy. You might just want to wait a little bit before proposing to him," Mike said.

He was being annoyingly cagey at this point. I wanted him to just come out with it, whatever it was. This wasn't helping me.

"Mike, you need to tell me exactly what you know. We're both ready. Why would I have to wait? That doesn't make any sense," I argued.

"Oh, no," I said, suddenly struck by an idea.

"Is he seeing someone else? He is, isn't he?" I pointed my finger at Mike and demanded his gaze by pressing my finger sharply into his arm. It all made sense. The late nights "working" and spending time at the firm's hotel suite. Our inability to connect over the phone as much as we used to. He was busy. Too busy for me because he was seeing someone else.

All the while we were talking, my phone beeped and buzzed in my purse. I'd ignored it, assuming it was family members hearing about the high speed chase involving Franklin Ford. Now, I wondered if Jack was one of the people calling. I wanted to grab my phone and confront him immediately, but I couldn't take my eyes off of Mike.

"No, Kelly, it's nothing like that. Jack loves you. He just needs to work through some stuff from his past," Mike said.

I couldn't deny the unmistakable sense of relief knowing that there wasn't another woman, but a sense of fear lingered. Why was Mike being so cagey?

"What does that mean?" I pushed. "Mike, COME ON. I can't take it. You have to be straight with me. Tell me everything you know."

"I just overheard Adelle talking to your mom. Seriously, this is all based on a phone call that I overheard. Hearsay. I was giving the kids a bath, and Adelle took a call from your mom. I overheard her say something about Jack's ex-wife still being in the picture," Mike said.

"What?" I gasped, feeling as though I'd been shot. How would Adelle know this, and what did that mean "still in the picture?" As far as I knew, Jack had a restraining order against his ex-wife, Callie. How could she possibly be in the picture?

"I don't know," Mike said. "Like I said, this is all based on a comment I overheard. Not that I was eavesdropping. We had one of the baby monitors on, and I don't think Adelle realized I could hear what she was saying. I felt so weird about the whole situation that I didn't even ask her about it. It's been a weird thing between us. She doesn't seem to even want to talk about you. When I bring up your name, she gets all stressed and annoyed. It's causing a lot of tension in our house," Mike said, rubbing his hands together.

"Mike, does Adelle know about the safety deposit key?" I asked.

"Absolutely not. I told you that already," Mike said adamantly.

"You're one hundred percent sure," I pushed.

"Yes," Mike said, nodding his head. "I'm not proud of the fact that I hid it from her, trust me. There's been a million times I've started to tell her but have always stopped. My business has been in trouble. You know that. This bailout that Steve gave me was just the tip of the iceberg. But things are turning the corner now. I've hidden a lot from my wife in these past few years to make it through this hard financial time. But we're turning a corner now. I can't tell you how much better I feel to have told you this. I'm ready to bring all the truths to light, no matter how much trouble I get in."

I shook my head and looked away, out the window. This was the naiveté Adelle always talked about when it came to Mike. He seldom got down about his circumstances, but rather pushed through. In business, it'd helped him make it through tough times, so that character flaw was actually helpful. But in this case, I didn't think he really knew what he was doing. We didn't even know what was in the safety deposit box. I assumed Steve was probably hiding money, based on the information I had and the things that his girlfriend, Sharon, had told me last summer. There was the possibility though that it could be much worse. In trying to do the right thing, Mike could go to jail for a very long time for a stupid, stupid thing he had done.

We had to at least get him some help before walking him into the police station; hire him a lawyer possibly, to look into what he was facing. I couldn't send him in without at least that prepped. The faces of his three children and my sister kept running through my mind. What would they do without Mike? How would they support themselves?

My phone buzzed again. Needing a distraction, I reached into my purse and pulled it out. The entire screen was filled with text messages. The first one at the top caught my eye.

It's not Franklin Ford that was caught. It's his accomplice. Call me. I can help you.

The text was from Diane Nosely.

"What?" I yelled aloud.

"What's wrong?" Mike asked, patting his pockets. He pulled out his phone. "Adelle is calling me. Shoot. I should take this. Wait. I don't want her to know I'm with you."

My phone started ringing at the same time. It was Nikki. I had to take this call. Both of my sisters were probably freaking out at the news about Franklin Ford and me being nowhere to be found.

"Mike, I have to go. I have to go home. I have to take this call. They're probably terrified."

"But, what are we going to do about the safety deposit key?" Mike asked, his eyes widening. "Don't you want to take it to the police?"

I shook my head and made a decision.

"Mike, you've been in possession of it for years. A couple of days won't hurt us. Let me just think about this for a day. There's too much going on right now to think straight. Please, just hang onto it and chill for a bit."

Mike's lips moved a bit as though he wanted to say something but nothing came out. He just stared at me without breathing.

"Do you want me to take it?" I asked, trying to read his thoughts. I'd stuffed the envelope in my purse when he rushed us out of the library.

He simply nodded his head and broke eye contact. Pulling a hand up to his mouth, he rubbed roughly at his face and looked out the window.

"I'm really sorry, Kelly. I swear, I had no idea what I was doing at the time. Didn't know what Steve was capable of. I just thought," he broke off and swung his eyes back to me. They sagged, a mixture of sadness and guilt. "I didn't think. I thought only of myself and the trouble I was in and the loan he promised me if I did this for him."

"It was a stupid thing to do," I said angrily.

Mike simply nodded and cringed.

"Steve had a way, didn't he?" I said quietly, softening a bit.

Again, Mike nodded in silence.

"God knows I did a lot of stupid things when Steve was a part of my life," I said, holding my purse over my stomach.

The phone stopped ringing and then immediately started up again. This time, I noticed it was Jack calling.

"I have to go, Mike," I said again. Without looking back, I opened the passenger door and stepped out, slamming it behind me.

The window came down immediately.

"Promise you'll call me in the morning. Or as soon as you've made a decision. I'm not going to sleep tonight," Mike said.

I nodded my head quickly and turned to run to my car. The flakes were coming down at a rapid pace, so fast that it was getting tough to see long-distance. This was not going to be an easy ride back to Geneva.

Once inside my car, I fiddled with my keys, all the while listening to my phone ring. When the ringing stopped, it chirped as texts kept pouring in. I pulled for my earpiece and fumbled with the phone. My fingers had numbed to the cold weather, making them difficult to work with. I cursed aloud, struggling to dial the number.

"Where the hell are you?" Nikki screamed into the phone. "You're killing us. Do you know what's going on? Are you okay? Get home NOW!"

"Who did they catch if it's not Franklin Ford?" I demanded. There was no time to look up the news on my phone. I knew Nikki would be in the know.

"What do you mean? It is Franklin Ford. They have the house he ran into surrounded. I'm with Mom and Dad, and we're watching the news right now."

I shook my head and looked back down on my screen. Sure

enough, another text from Diane Nosely popped up.

It read:

Don't believe the media. It's not Franklin Ford. Call me.

Chapter 33

"Nikki, Diane Nosely is telling me it's not Franklin Ford that they caught," I said, reading her the text.

"What are you talking about? We're watching the news right now. They have his picture all over. They're showing pictures of the house he was hiding out in."

As Nikki spoke, a dark shadow fell over me from the driver's side window. I screamed, feeling my lungs burn and turned to the window. My heart stopped then restarted when I saw Jennie's friendly face waving at me from the other side of the glass.

Frozen in place, I stared back at her while Nikki's voice shrieked on the other end of the line.

"What's happening? Why are you screaming? Kelly?" I heard her repeating my name over and over.

"Nikki, let me call you right back. Everything is fine. I'm just leaving the library. I'll be home in a few," I said, disconnecting. Jennie was motioning for me to roll down my window. Her fuzzy gray mittens moved in a circling motion.

"I was just checking to see if you are okay? You've been out here for so long," Jennie said, the wind blowing her hair in every direction.

"I'm okay," I managed.

"Well, you should head home. They're calling for a big storm. I'm closing up the library early and heading home to my farm. I'm not going to get stuck out in this cold today," she said, already starting to walk backwards in the direction of her car.

My mind raced to Nikki's parade. How would it fare in this cold weather? Would she still have a good turn out? And what about Adelle's big launch party? What if it was a bust?

As though she could read my mind, Jennie called out, "This storm will just be a quickie. Supposed to finish up overnight. The rest of the week will be nice. All the snow we get tonight will be gone by noon tomorrow. It's supposed to be high forties by tomorrow afternoon. That's Chicago, right? If you don't like the weather, wait a few minutes and it will all change. I bet you wish you'd stayed in California, right?" Jennie laughed and waved.

"See you in a couple days," she called out before turning and fiddling with her car door.

I wasn't sure what she meant by that but could only assume she meant the parade. Shaking my head and returning a polite laugh in her direction, I turned out of the parking lot to head home.

* * * * *

Back at home, I paced the hallway in Jack's condo in my fuzzy, pink slippers. The snow was coming down in sheets outside, and I was glad to have finally made it home.

"But how did she know?" Nikki demanded for the fifth time. She sat on the little entrance bench she'd plopped herself down on upon her arrival twenty minutes ago.

"I don't know. Stop asking me that. I don't know. Should I call her?" I repeated, probably for the fifth time as well. Nikki and I were in panic mode. Holed up in Jack's condo, it felt like we were trapped.

"Let's just turn the television off. It's not helping us," Nikki said. "My God, Dad's gonna have a heart attack. This is all too much."

"Nikki, don't say that," I said, freezing in my tracks. "You don't think I'm thinking about that every second of the day?" I closed my eyes and smacked my hand to my forehead. "I'm a huge nuisance to this entire family. I need to just disappear. Move to the arctic or something. "

"Like that would help? It would just make things worse. We'd all be heartbroken worrying about you. I shouldn't have said anything," Nikki said. "That was dumb. We need to calm down."

I plopped down next to her on the bench, moving closer and lifting the remote up to shut the television across the room off.

"You girls need a glass of wine is what you need," Chef James said, floating into the room with two full glasses of wine. "Oooo, I forgot baby," he said, pointing to Nikki's bulging stomach. "You cannot. Hold on."

Chef James turned and disappeared back into the kitchen.

"What are you going to do about Jack?" Nikki asked quietly.

Though I was upset by what Mike had told me about Jack, I didn't have the heart to call the dinner off. In fact, I'd moved it up because Jack was planning on coming home a bit earlier now with the storm hitting us.

"I don't know," I said, shaking my head.

"Here you go!" Chef James said, returning with my original glass of wine and another fruity looking concoction for Nikki.

"Sparkling juice for you and wine for Kelly," he dropped the glasses in our waiting hands and stepped back, raising an eyebrow. "Is this what you are wearing for tonight?" he asked, scanning my jeans and turtleneck sweater. "Because," Chef James rolled his one hand in a twirling motion as if to search for an appropriate way to tell me I needed to up my game.

Nikki and I both stayed silent.

"Anyhow, I return to the work," Chef James said, taking the hint. "It's gonna be a sensational dinner," he called behind me, driving his point home. He was right. I needed to spruce it up a bit.

"He's right, Kelly. So what about Franklin Ford still on the run. They caught his accomplice. He's admitted that Franklin was with him at some point. He can't be too far behind. They'll catch up with him in the next couple of hours, I'm sure of it. And they'll catch him in Canada or something. Nowhere near where we are. In the meantime, you have this beautiful night planned. Forget the rest of it."

I hadn't shared with Nikki what Mike had told me. I'd kept everything from our visit today to myself. To be honest, that part wasn't even at the forefront of my mind. I could look into the safety deposit box later. That had been sitting for years; it could sit for a few more days.

"Can you just make sure Mom and Dad get a break from the television tonight?"

"Are you kidding? Done. They're coming over for game night tonight, so we can wait for your call," Nikki said, chugging her sparkling juice and letting out a small burp. "Oh, excuse me. That was delicious."

"What call?" I asked.

"The one telling us you're engaged to that hunk of a man you're living in sin with. Come on, let's go pick out your outfit," she said, slapping my knee and standing up from the bench.

* * * * *

An hour later, I was dressed in a long sleeve, silk, sapphire blue wrap dress I'd purchased specifically for the night I decided to propose to Jack. I'd seen Kate Middleton wear something similar when she announced her engagement to Prince William and fell in love with the look. I had to have it. Or at least something like it. Mine was a knock off but still very chic. Or so I'd thought when I bought it.

Slipping it on tonight, I didn't feel as light and beautiful as I'd pictured I'd feel at this moment. All the stress from the day was wearing me down and was visible in my face. Nikki's comment about telling our parents about the engagement had pushed me over the edge. I didn't need more pressure. Especially after hearing Mike's insinuations about Jack.

Could it be true? Could Jack still be involved with his ex-wife somehow? A huge part of me felt that it had to be some kind of mistake. There was no way Jack would let that woman back in his life. And if he had, there had to be a reasonable explanation for it. I could still see the look of terror on Jack's face last summer when he revealed what had happened in his marriage when they'd lived abroad. Jack had discovered that she'd been stalking random people and videotaping them for no reason. He'd divorced her and tried to move on just like I had from my ex. I couldn't see a reason why he would want to start up any kind of communication with her. Looking down at my phone, I reviewed the text Jack had sent just a few seconds earlier.

See you in twenty!

That meant I had time to call Diane Nosely back if I still wanted to. She'd been shooting me texts all day, begging me to call her.

There was a part of me that just wanted to wait it out and see if she got desperate enough to just text me the juicy piece of information she was holding. But then why would she do that? It would take away any control she had in this situation. She was obviously desperate to speak to me live.

Rubbing my lips together, I made an impulsive decision to find out.

"Kelly, I'm so glad you called," Diane breathed into the phone.

"Are you still in the hospital?" I asked.

Ignoring my question, she went on.

"There's so much I have to tell you. Do you want to meet? I can arrange for that. We really should. I have so much to tell you from my intel," she whispered into the phone.

I couldn't help but roll my eyes. Intel. Please. Like she was running a behind the enemy lines operation in Afghanistan. A voice in my head told me to hang up. I'd made a mistake. No matter what piece of information this woman had, even if it was true, it wasn't worth the mind games she was about to play. She'd proven that she was not to be trusted.

"I can come to you. I have help that can get me wherever you want to meet," she said.

I pictured her being lifted in a large sling up to the third floor of Jack's building, her legs stuck in large, bulky casts.

"Umm, let's just talk over the phone. I don't have much time," I said, trying to be polite but firm.

I thought I heard a flip of pages and imagined her scrolling through her notes to come up with Plan B: Kelly said no in-person meet, move to the hard sell.

"Oh, Kelly, my doctor just came in the room. I've been waiting for him all day and really need to speak with him. Can you come to my rehab facility? I'll give you the address."

Right. And walk into a room filled with cameras for a one-on-one exclusive interview with Diane Nosely to be featured on the late night news.

No, Diane. I don't think so. Been there, done that.

"No," I said simply. Polite but firm.

"Kelly, my intel in the jail is telling me that Steve is getting married, and he's talking about taking you out of the picture before that happens. I'm trying to get more, but I'm really worried that this Franklin Ford thing might be connected to you," Diane said, laying down the bread crumbs.

But I'm already out of the picture? He doesn't need me dead to get married.

"Uh huh," I said, squinting my eyes and catching my reflection in the mirror again over Jack's dresser. I'd spent a good amount of time making sure my rosy cheeks and light pink gloss were applied perfectly for tonight. I took a Kleenex and dabbed at my cheeks lightly, reminding myself to have no reaction to anything Diane said.

"I'm home!" I heard Jack call out from the front room.

My stomach did a little flip at the sound of his voice. I'd planned on meeting him at the door for the big reveal of the Christmas tree and the fancy table set-up. So much for that. Now he was seeing it all without me.

"I have to go, Diane. I don't have time for this," I said. These theories of hers were old news. I'd been worrying about this same thing since the story broke. This call felt like a waste of time.

"You need to hear this, Kelly. You have to put together some kind of plan."

I hung up on Diane without feeling any sense of remorse. She was not to be trusted. I didn't care what kind of "intel" she had. Diane was looking out for number one. And there was a big part of me that was sick of being told I was in danger and needed to be warned of the threat of Steve coming after me. What more could I do? He was coming. No kidding. I knew that. What control did I have over that? None. Apparently Steve was determined to have his revenge on me for ruining his life. I'd accepted that, but that didn't mean I couldn't come up with my own plan to beat him at his game. He'd underestimated me for the last time. Thanks to my meeting with Mike this afternoon, a plan was beginning to take shape that would stop all of this running. I just needed more time to figure out how to carry it out.

That all had to be put to the side though for the moment. Right now, there was Jack.

Chapter 34

"Wow, what a ride," Jack said, brushing snowflakes off his coat. "Wait, what's happening here?" he asked, setting his briefcase down on the bench by the front door and hanging up his overcoat in the closet.

A smile spread across his face as he took it all in. Chef James had insisted on putting the final touches on the table, including some sparkling garland running down the middle for our romantic feast. I had to admit he was right. The little details he added really made the scene.

"I planned something nice for us," I said, moving hesitantly toward Jack and studying his face. His boyish grin captured my attention, making me wonder if Mike had the story all wrong. How could this man possibly lie to me?

"Baby, are you okay?" Jack asked, moving swiftly to me. "Today's news was nuts."

"I know," I said, allowing Jack's huge bear-like form to engulf me in a hug.

"Why don't you go change, and I'll open a bottle of wine," I said, avoiding his eyes when he pulled back to examine me.

"I came home as fast as I could when I heard the news about Franklin Ford. I'm sorry I wasn't here earlier. Traffic was rough with the snow," he said, with a hint of defensiveness in his voice.

"I know," I said, reaching up and caressing his cheek. "It's been a long day."

"Come here," Jack growled, pulling me closer to him.

"Wait, I don't want to mess up your suit," I protested.

"I don't care," he said, pulling me to his chest. "I missed you. I've been worrying about you all day. Are you okay here? Do you feel safe here? We can go away tomorrow if you want," Jack said, rubbing his nose into my hair.

"No, I can't," I said. "I have to stick around for the parade. It's Adelle's big launch for the donuts."

"I'm sure they would understand, considering the circumstances. Come on. We'll go to that romantic little hotel you like in Wisconsin. Just you and me. Let's escape the madness for a few days," Jack whispered into my ear.

As tempting as that sounded, I couldn't leave my sisters on their big day.

"Jack, go get changed. You're missing all the romance right in front of you. I have something special planned for tonight," I laughed, forgetting for a moment that I had to have a serious conversation with Jack about what Mike said. In this moment, the whole idea of Jack cheating on me or seeing his ex-wife behind my back seemed ludicrous. It just couldn't be true.

"Wait a minute, what are you wearing here? This is gorgeous. Why are you so dressed up?" he said, reaching down and playing with the blue sash of my dress. "Are you sure you want me to change? I'll feel underdressed next to you."

I slapped his playful hands away and smiled up at him.

"Just go get a little more comfortable and get your appetite ready. I have a special treat planned for you."

"Oh, you do?" Jack teased, leaning in to kiss me, slowly at first and then with a kick of passion. "I love you," he whispered, before turning to head down the hallway to the master bedroom.

I followed Jack down the hall with my eyes. Finally, I turned and headed into the kitchen to open a bottle of wine.

Jack was back in a few short minutes dressed in a gray wool sweater pulled over the button up shirt he'd worn into work. It felt weird for us to both be so dressed up in our home environment. Normally the minute we walked in the door, we both changed into sweatpants and loungewear. Jack had a pair of flannel pants he jumped into the minute he walked in the door most days.

"You look nice," I commented, sneaking a look back in his direction. He pulled the bottle from my hands after he saw me struggling and took over the job of opening it.

"Why are you using this opener, silly? We like the other one much better," he said, turning his back to me and getting the correct one out of the top drawer near the refrigerator. He was right. I'd been so distracted, I'd grabbed the wrong one.

His sweater rested at his waist, revealing his tight behind in his dress pants. Unable to help myself, I reached over and gave him a quick squeeze.

Jack didn't even turn around.

"Temptress, do you want to eat or not?" I could hear the smile in his voice.

Moving closer to him, I wrapped my arms around him from behind.

"It's been a long day, I said, nuzzling my head into the back of his sweater.

"Tell me about it," Jack said.

The wine opener slipped slightly on the bottle. For a second, I thought the whole thing was going to tip, but Jack easily caught it and continued the task.

"Do you think it was easy for me to be away from you today? Especially with all the Franklin Ford mumbo jumbo going on. Are you sure you don't want to just sneak away for a couple of days? I'm sure they'll catch him fairly soon, especially with finding his accomplice near the Canadian border. He can't be that far behind.

Still, maybe we'd feel safer getting away."

"You think he's really after me?" I asked.

The sound of the cork releasing filled the room.

Jack sighed. "Who knows? Probably not. Why would he be near Canada if they were after you? I just want you to feel safe, honey."

"But the shooting in my parent's building? That's a weird coincidence," I interrupted, shivering slightly at the thought of the tape I'd seen earlier.

"I was leading to that. I don't think it's connected to you because these two idiots are up near the Canadian border. The shooting in your parents building is a weird coincidence, but clearly they're not tied together since they were on complete opposite ends of the country."

That is how Steve would work though. He would distract you, leading you to look one way while he was going after what he really wanted, I thought.

"Are you okay, babe?" Jack asked, turning and handing me a glass of wine.

"Wait," he said, setting the glass down before I took it. "Come here."

Jack pulled me into his arms.

"We can do something here. Like add some extra locks or even talk to the building about adding cameras outside. Whatever would make you feel safe," he said, locking me into his iron chest and kissing the top of my head. "At least until Franklin Ford is caught. And you know it will be very soon now."

Instead of responding, I let Jack nuzzle me to his chest and smiled. This was where I really felt safe. If I could just stay wrapped in Jack's strong arms all the time, everything would be okay.

"Do you want more security?" Jack pressed again. He started to pull me away to gage my reaction, but I held on tight in protest.

"No, I just want to stay here in your arms. Can you be my

security system?"

Jack laughed lightly and held me tighter.

"You know I would love to be. Having you in my arms is what I would love. Every minute of every day. But I have to go to work, and you have to leave the apartment to see family and live your life. It's just not realistic to think I can protect you all the time."

"I know that," I said, leaning back and looking into Jack's green eyes. "I do. If you think more locks on the door are a good idea, let's do it."

Jack raised an eyebrow and the left side of his lip pulled to the side.

"Well, that was easy. Usually you wave away my attempts at more security," he said, studying me closely.

My mind ran back to the video of the intruder at my parent's condo building. The way the hand reached out to hit the button for my parent's floor.

Eventually I would tell Jack the full details of that story, but right now, I wanted to get dinner going. We had big things to discuss.

Chapter 35

A few glasses of wine later, Jack and I laughed together at the dinner table, happy in our little bubble. Our worries about Franklin Ford and the other news of the day were long tucked away in a place we'd revisit when we needed to, but not now. Chef James had delivered on everything he'd promised. The small morsels of food that remained on our plates were a testament to that. I'd held off on bringing up what Mike implied earlier about Jack speaking with his ex-wife. Here in Jack's presence, I knew that Mike had misheard. There was no way Jack was betraying me.

Jack finished telling a story about an obnoxious client yelling at the secretaries in his office and took a final swig from his glass.

"We had to tell him to calm down. That's no way to treat our staff," Jack said, half-laughing, half-disgusted by the day's events. "Well, Kelly, I don't know if this was your master plan, but you certainly have managed to distract me from the stress of the day and get me a little tipsy."

"Don't get too tipsy yet. We still have some business," I laughed, leaning closer to him and kissing him lightly on the lips. We'd re-positioned ourselves so that we were seated next to each other rather than across the table as Chef James had initially set us up. He'd wanted us facing each other so the glistening garland shimmered between us, but in reality, that kept us too far apart. We wanted to be able to hold hands and touch each other throughout the meal.

"Ooh, I think I'll still be up for business," he laughed, bouncing his eyebrows up and down suggestively.

"Not that kind of business," I laughed. His lips fell into an overly exaggerated frown. "At least not yet. I have to clear the decks on something. Just so it doesn't bother me later. I want it totally out of my head because it's stupid. I know it's stupid. I just want to talk to you about something that someone told me, which I'm sure is bad information, but just humor me, will you?"

"Oh, this does sound serious," Jack said, releasing his hold of his wine glass and taking hold of my hand.

"I just want to clear something up, so we can move onto the happy part of the night."

"You mean, there's an even happier part of the night? Because I was pretty happy with that food," Jack laughed.

I could tell that I was possibly choosing the wrong moment to do this. Jack wasn't tipsy. A couple of glasses of wine for someone of Jack's stature were nothing, but he was not in a place to have a serious conversation.

Still. How could I propose to Jack without clearing up what Mike had told me? I needed to have a clean slate.

I decided to just go right at it. Never mind the maneuvers.

"Jack, this is crazy, but someone told me today that you've been in communication with your ex-wife, Callie. I told them that was absurd. You would never."

The expression on Jack's face stopped me from moving any further. Or rather, it was the lack of expression. He'd turned into a wax replica of himself; frozen in one expression of pure shock. Finally, he turned and pulled his eyes away from me to the Christmas tree, a glazed expression settling in.

"Jack, you have or you haven't spoken with her? It's a simple question," I asked, feeling the heat in my cheeks rise. Was I being played a fool here?

I'd planned to do my whole proposal bit during the extravagant dessert Chef James had prepared. Now though, based on Jack's blank expression, I wondered if there would be any proposal. The image of Chef James throwing his arms up in the air and shouting, "My beautiful dinner is ruined!" flashed through my mind.

"Kelly, I," Jack paused and closed his eyes.

"Oh, no," I said, sitting back in my chair. My stomach churned, and for a brief second, true to form, I thought I might throw up the delicious dinner we'd just consumed. My weak stomach never did well in stressful situations, and this was looking as though it was building up to be one.

"Are you seeing her?"

"No," Jack shot back quickly. "Are you serious?" His eyebrows dug down over his eyes and his mouth lay open in shock. Finally, he was making eye contact with me.

"Who told you this?" he asked, leaning forward and placing both hands balled up in fists on the table.

I simply shook my head.

"It doesn't matter," Jack said, shaking his head. "I didn't want to have to tell you like this."

"Go on," I urged.

"First of all, I'm not upset because you found out. I just wanted to tell you myself. It's not what you think," Jack said, reaching out to grab my hand.

"There's been a huge mistake, Kelly. I've been set up. You have to believe me. Please help me," Steve begged when he was being led down the hall by the police the night he was arrested. I'd directed the police to the home of his mistress where they'd caught him in the act of trying to mess with her car. The evidence was so damning that they were able to arrest him on the spot. As they were bringing him into the station, I stepped out of my place of hiding and let him see me. I remember clearly that the patrol officer who'd been assigned to stay with me placed his hand on my arm as though he thought I

was going to try and approach Steve. I just wanted him to see my face.

"Help me, Kelly," *he yelled out, before being led away with his hands behind his back.* "Please get me a lawyer. This is a set-up."

His voice sounded so desperate and scared that for a brief second, I wondered if I'd made a huge mistake. But then I snapped back to reality. The woman he'd attempted to kill, Mandy, sobbed next to me, clutching at her swollen belly, Steve's child growing inside it. The heartless monster was going to kill them both. He'd laid it all out in an email I'd been able to intercept and send to the police. Luckily, the police had her and her unborn child out of the house in time.

"Steve, why?" *she sobbed next to me.*

After that night, he never spoke directly to me again. He only sneered at me from across a courtroom. His parents managed to land him a great lawyer, but in the end, it didn't matter. He was sent away, guilty.

"Kelly? Are you listening?" Jack asked, pulling me back to the present. It was something that Jack had just said that had spun me whirling back to the past. Oh, now I remembered. He'd said the words, "It's not what you think."

Steve had said those words before being caught in the act of cheating. He was always out late with female clients, mainly doctors or nurses who were his customers for all of the pharmaceutical products he sold. When I'd shown any suspicion or raised an eyebrow at how late the client dinners went, that had been his favorite saying. "It's not what you think. Those medical professionals have long work days. They love going out at night to kick off the stress. Even if we are talking about work. Don't doubt me, babe. I'm number one in my district this month."

Don't doubt me, babe. Was I really going to live that again?

"I need some air," I said suddenly, standing up. The glasses on the table clinked together, threatening to topple over. Jack dove for the table to save my wine from spilling. I made a bee-line for the balcony and pulled the door open, feeling foolish and claustrophobic at the same time.

It was freezing and snowing like crazy outside, but I didn't care. My cheeks were on fire.

"Kelly, come back inside," Jack said, joining me on the balcony. "It's freezing out here."

"I was going to propose to you tonight, Jack," I exploded. "You're seeing another woman, and I was going to propose to you."

"Wait a minute, I am not seeing another woman. Please, Kelly, come back inside and let's talk about this. You're acting crazy," Jack said, reaching out and grabbing a hold of my arm. I pulled it from his grasp.

"What would you have said, Jack? If I had proposed, would you have just accepted, knowing the whole time there was still someone else in your life?"

Jack cringed and stepped back a bit as though I had slapped him.

"Answer me. Would you have said yes," I blazed on, feeling a demon take over me. My hair was going to turn into hundreds of small snakes at any moment.

"I couldn't have said yes," he said softly, looking down.

At that admission, my eyes filled with tears and my anger flew away like a balloon releasing air.

Jack held up his pointer finger, indicating that I needed to hear the rest of what he had to say.

"I couldn't say yes because," Jack released a breath. "Because I'm still married."

Chapter 36

"What?" I whispered, feeling like I'd just been punched in the stomach.

"Please, Kelly, just come inside with me. It's freezing out here," Jack said, pulling me inside forcibly.

"This is not the way I wanted this to go," Jack said, shaking his head back and forth. He reached past me to slam the door shut. His anger and annoyance were confusing me. Shouldn't it be the other way around? What right did he have to be angry in this moment?

"Who told you this?" Jack asked, pulling me over to the couch. I let him lead me, too numb and in shock to protest. There was still a small part of me that was asking, "But, the tiramisu and the brownie? Will we still have it?"

"You're still married to her? You've been seeing her?" I asked quietly, ignoring his question. It was almost to quiet my own mind and its quest for the desserts. I needed to understand the gravity of what Jack had said. He was with someone else.

"No. I mean, yes, I'm still married, but no, I'm not seeing Callie, nor have I seen her for years. I found out there was a glitch in my divorce papers when I tried to move something overseas that we once jointly owned. That's it. There's no romance, there's no secret affair. There's just a mix-up in paperwork that is getting resolved. She hasn't contacted me. I haven't spoken with her, though I'd like to. That's a whole other story. I need her signature on something, but Callie refuses to be found, making it impossible for me to go on with my life," Jack growled.

I hadn't seen him this angry since Nikki and I got involved in solving a local mystery last fall, putting our lives in danger. That was really a different kind of anger though. Now a vein in his right temple I'd never noticed before pulsated, threatening to blow at any minute.

"Calm down, Jack," I said, instantly feeling a little relieved. Clearly there was more to this story, in a good way.

I placed a hand on his knee, trying to calm him.

"Kelly, there is no betrayal here. It's a kink in the paperwork. We're going to get this resolved," he said. The lines in his forehead stacked on top of each other, making him look much older than he was. When he placed his hand over mine, I couldn't help but notice it was shaking slightly.

"But why didn't you tell me?" I begged. "We're supposed to be partners."

"I know," Jack sighed. "I've been meeting with my attorney after work late at night, so we could contact her attorney in London and get this settled. It's been a nightmare with the time change. I didn't want to involve you in this. You have enough going on. I thought I could get it settled quickly and be done with it. But it's dragging on."

"This must be killing you," I said, feeling horrible for Jack and still a bit giddy that there was a reasonable explanation. There was a part of me, a very small part that still felt a tinge of suspicion, probably because of my ex-husband's infidelities. But on a whole, I believed Jack.

"It's humiliating. It's embarrassing," he said.

I simply nodded my head.

"I'm an attorney. This divorce, which I thought was complete, is not because a piece of paper wasn't filed that was supposed to be. What kind of an attorney am I if I can't even manage my own divorce correctly?"

"Well, you're not a divorce attorney, first off. And second, the divorce is in the United Kingdom. I'm sure there are a million things that are different."

Jack shook his head. "There's so much to keep track of it's insane. Basically because I'm an American citizen, it makes it such a mess. I'm just so glad we didn't have kids together. I can't even imagine what a mess that would be. I wouldn't let her near my child with her mental state. And if she fought me on it, I would have to basically take the child back and forth. The courts have a lot of leniency for the biological parents maintaining their rights when the child is raised here and abroad. Anyway, why am I even talking about that? It's not an issue," he said, placing his head in his right hand and still clinging onto me with his left one.

"The worst part is, I can't marry you until this is done. And if I can't find Callie, it will make it all the more difficult."

"There's got to be another way," I said, trying to pull myself together for Jack. He was always the strong one. Always the person saying everything would be okay. This was my moment to return that favor.

Jack said nothing. The defeated look on his face was so unnatural on him. This must be what he always saw on my face when I spoke about Steve: a combination of disgust, fear, resentment, and defeat. It wasn't very flattering, but I completely understood it. Jack always had hope in some of the most hopeless situations. But not right now. Right now, he looked deflated and a bit scary. I couldn't blame him though. I understood the way he was feeling.

"But how did you find out? I've only confided in my attorney. I don't understand," Jack said. "Wait a minute; I did take a call when we were at Mike and Adelle's house for a family dinner. Someone must have overheard me. Was it Mike and Adelle?" he asked.

I nodded my head, not wanting to get into details.

"That wasn't right of them. They should have approached me first. Adelle was sticking her nose in where it didn't belong," Jack said, making the incorrect assumption that she was the one that had told me. I didn't correct him, knowing that if I told him it was really Mike, he would ask for more details. That might lead to me having to tell him I'd met with Mike, and that was a whole bag of worms I didn't want to open up.

"She's just looking out for me," I said.

"Yeah, I guess if my sister overheard that you might still be married, she'd come straight to me with the information. Any good sibling would do that," Jack said.

"Jack, we're going to get this figured out," I said again, reaching to put my arms around him.

"Don't propose to me tonight, Kelly," Jack said lightly. "The timing is all wrong."

I couldn't help but laugh as he pulled me into a hug.

"Yes, I see that now," I laughed, still feeling relieved that it was simply a technical issue holding us back, not something bigger.

"What was it you wanted from overseas?" I asked.

"I completely forgot we had a storage locker with a few pieces of furniture in it. Some of it was passed to me from my grandmother. I'd paid for the locker years ago for an extended period of time. When that ran out, the company contacted me to let me know I needed to pick it up. Both of our names are on the unit. That's what started this whole mess. I wasn't able to ship the stuff back to the US without her permission. During the whole process of doing paperwork for this shipping, I discovered that my divorce paperwork wasn't complete. I figured this out all because of a few stupid end tables I had an attachment to. I guess it's better to figure it out now though and not when we're at the altar, right?" Jack said, releasing me and pulling me back to gage my reaction.

"Definitely," I said, leaning in to kiss him. "We'll get our day when it's the right time."

"Wait," I said, pulling away from the kiss. Jack raised his eyebrows.

"I know what will cheer you up," I said enthusiastically.

"That was cheering me up just fine," he smiled.

"Dessert!" I said, pumping a fist in the air.

"Oh," Jack said, forming his lips into a little O. "You are correct. That will cheer me up."

"Come on," I said, pulling him off the couch to head into the kitchen.

I pulled the cake from the fridge as Jack gathered plates and utensils.

"I'm so sorry your night was ruined, Kelly. This was a beautiful dinner. Chef James did a great job. His food was awesome," Jack said. "Maybe we can hire him for a special reception someday?"

I laughed and shook my head. "I don't think we'll be able to afford him. He's quite pricey. But worth every penny, right?"

I turned to look at Jack. The look on his face was as though I'd just slapped him.

"It's okay, Jack. We deserved a special night, even though it didn't turn out as either of us thought it would."

"I'm so sorry to have ruined the night. You know I'll say yes to you the second I can, right?" Jack said, slicing the cake. "In fact, can't we just be engaged to each other now? Does it really matter that I'm still married?"

"I guess if we existed in some trashy day-time talk show world that would be fine," I laughed.

"Kelly!" Jack laughed back. "Okay, you're right. I guess we've waited this long to be together, a few more months isn't going to hurt us."

"A few more months?" I balked.

"Well, I don't know how long it's going to take to find Callie. That woman is a wild card," Jack said, slicing a huge piece for himself and then motioning for me to choose what size I wanted.

I held my pointer finger close to my thumb to indicate that I wanted a much tinier slice.

"You know what's ironic about this whole thing?" I asked.

"What?" Jack asked, putting all his attention into slicing my piece just right.

"Callie was a stalker. You couldn't get her out of your life for a long time. And now that you need to find her, she's nowhere to be found. That's a little scary, isn't it?" I said, watching Jack nod his head.

"It's terrifying," Jack said, standing up and looking at me with a serious look. The lines on his forehead were back, stacking up like little blocks of stress.

"You have no idea, Kelly."

Chapter 37

After running through a million scenarios of where Callie could be, we finally gave up and turned in for the night. Dinner had been a mixed bag. The good news was, I felt closer to Jack because we'd finally cleared the air about what he was dealing with. But now we were both more confused than ever on how to move forward.

"I'm a lawyer, Kelly. I'll get this settled." He cuddled me closer to him and began to fall asleep.

"Of course, I was also a lawyer when I messed up the paperwork to begin with," he said after a few seconds of awkward silence, causing us both to break out in giggles.

"At least we have each other. We're imperfect but we're perfect for each other," I said.

"Agreed," Jack said, yawning and turning off the light. "Let's go to bed. This was quite a night."

Within minutes, the sound of Jack's snoring filled the room. I was happy to see that he was able to rest. Maybe he was relieved that I finally knew what he'd been dealing with.

* * * * *

The next morning, I walked into the backroom of Chocolate Love carrying a huge travel mug of coffee.

"Whoa, breaking out the big guns this morning, huh?" Nikki asked, nodding her head in the direction of my mug.

I rubbed my eyes and let out a yawn. "Yep."

"You didn't call last night," Nikki said, watching me closely from across the room.

"It is or it isn't going to be ready? Just give me a straight answer," Adelle barked at someone from Nikki's small office around the corner. I didn't see her when I first walked in, but now there was no mistaking her presence.

Nikki winced and gave me a "one minute" sign with her pointer finger.

She waddled over to where Adelle was working and put her palms up in the air as though to question, "What's up?"

Adelle put her hand over the receiver and moved closer to Nikki.

"Oh, hi, Kelly," she said, addressing me quickly. "They told me the banner would be ready by tomorrow for the donut launch, and now they're giving me the runaround. What kind of a promotional company is this? I knew we should have gone with a bigger group and not just use one of your friends."

"Calm down, Adelle. Yes, Cassandra is my friend, but she also runs one of the largest promotional businesses in the western suburbs. I'm sure she'll come through. Let me talk to her," Nikki said, gently coaxing the phone out of Adelle's hand.

"She better," Adelle snarled, stepping away from the office area and letting Nikki take charge.

"Are you okay?" I asked, sitting down at the little wrought iron table and chairs with my huge coffee.

Adelle huffed and sat down across from me. She didn't look good. It looked like she hadn't even attempted to hide the dark circles under her eyes, and her hair was frizzy and out of place. Her clothes had little dribbles of caramel colored flecks on it, and on top of that, she had a huge zit forming at the very tip of her nose.

"My launch is almost here and it's a disaster, Kelly. The donut fryers in the truck are not working like I thought they would. I've been practicing all morning and they're not turning out. My sitter quit and now my promotional material is not turning out," Adelle flopped her head down on her arms and moaned.

"Who's watching the kids?" I asked hesitantly, knowing the answer.

"Mom and Dad," Adelle snapped, raising her head up to challenge me.

I said nothing, wondering if Mike had told her about our meeting yesterday. If he did, she was staying mum on the whole thing. My guess was she didn't know. If she did, she would be more worried about Mike going off to jail than her donut launch.

"Hello!" A shrill voice called out. "Sorry, we're late," the voice sang out in a cheery tone that didn't sound apologetic by any means.

Adelle's eyes widened and stayed locked on mine.

"Who is that?" I whispered. Adelle stayed silent and continued to stare at me like a deer caught in the headlights.

Two very well made up ladies, who I guessed to be in their late twenties or early thirties, walked into the back room. The blond had her hair cut in choppy layers that perfectly framed her smooth, fresh face. She didn't have a wrinkle in sight and her full lips puffed out in an attractive, yet borderline unnatural way. The brunette, I noticed, had very long, wavy hair that could only be achieved by extensions. There was just too much of it and it was too perfect. Her tight shirt clung to her curves, and her designer jeans fit her petite figure perfectly. Though the girls were a bit too made up for what I deemed attractive, there was no denying they were hot little numbers.

"Can I help you?" Miguel asked, fumbling on his words. He placed his heavy tray of chocolates on the counter and released a sigh. Taking a second, he once again attempted to be hospitable, which was more than Adelle and I were doing. Adelle stared back at the women, and I stared at her. I couldn't figure out who they were.

"Are you looking for someone?" Miguel tried again.

Essentially ignoring him completely, the women locked eyes on Adelle and continued on as though Miguel wasn't there.

"Oh, honey," the brunette said, grabbing a towel from the counter. "You look like you need a little help here." She passed by me and held the towel to Adelle's cheek, wiping gently at the powder on her face. "Your skin is as beautiful as ever, sweetheart," the woman cooed condescendingly. "But I'm not sure if you're quite blended here with your powder."

The blond behind her roared with laughter, joining in on the joke.

Adelle's hand jumped to her face, grabbing the towel away.

"It's just a little flour from the, um, donuts," Adelle said, clearing her throat and standing up straighter.

Come on, Adelle. Pull it together.

"Oh, yeah, we heard about those. You're launching a donut line at the parade? That's so exciting," the blond said, baring her teeth in a smile. "Tell us more about these cute donuts. Aren't you so glad we took over on the parade, so you have more time to focus on your little donuts?"

I didn't need to hear anymore. These were the witches from the Junior League that were giving Adelle so much trouble, Kim Lakes and Brandy Morgan.

"I'm not sure if you've met my sister, Kelly," Adelle said, standing up from her chair finally. "Kelly, this is Kim Lakes," she said, motioning to the brunette. "And Brandi Morgan," she waved her hand over to the blond.

I reached out to shake both of their hands, which they barely touched before their eyes slid back to my sister. Clearly, they were not here for me.

"Do you do home parties?" Kim asked. "I would be happy to

host a home party for you to help launch your business. Us business owners have to help each other out, right?"

"Oh, what kind of business do you have, Kim?" Adelle asked weakly.

I cringed. As out of it as I was navigating the world of mean girls and alpha women, even I knew Adelle had just walked into some kind of trap.

"Oh, sorry," Kim laughed a fake light laugh. She flipped her long, glossy locks with one hand and set her hand on her hip with the other. Brandy watched her with a glow in her eye. I imagined that they'd practiced their lines at home and were now at the peak of their performance. "My husband has a business, I mean. I can't take any credit. We're fortunate enough he does so well I don't have to work. That way I can stay home with the kids full time. And thank God because I can't imagine having to work! I'm so busy with the kids. And they're so young. They need you every second. I can't imagine letting someone else raise my kids. I'm just not that kind of mom. I couldn't be selfish that way, you know?"

"Who's watching them right now?" I interjected, wondering how she was out and about in the middle of the day if her kids were "so young" and needed her constant attention.

Adelle shot me a warning look. Kim ignored me as though I were nothing and babbled on, but Brandi had felt the hit. She turned and stared openly at me and my audacity to not worship her idol, Kim, The Great Selfless Stay-at-Home Mom.

"So, we thought you would want to know that the parade details are going really well," Kim said, switching topics. "The Junior League is going to be represented by over fifty of our members who will be handing out giveaways. You helped build the core of this group back in your heyday. We really appreciate all the groundwork you did for those that came after your time. We only hope we could be half as good as you were when you were their leader."

Adelle brushed at her face and nodded her head. I'm sure the passive aggressive way Kim was telling Adelle she was old and needed to step aside was not lost on her. I was waiting for Adelle to snap back, praying for it really. The shaky, self-conscious Adelle in front of me was not the super mom and trend setter I was used to.

"All Sweets Network confirmed! They're excited to meet you, Adelle!" Nikki yelled out, pumping her fist in the air and making a grand entrance into the kitchen from her small office.

"What?" Adelle and I asked in unison, looking first at Nikki and then at each other.

"They heard about your donut launch and the possible reality show and they're interested!" Nikki smiled. "Oh, hi, ladies. You realize you're in the presence of a future star. Adelle is being shopped around at some major networks. The agents and producers just love her."

Kim and Brandi were finally knocked off of the high-horse they rode in on. It was my turn to stare at them and wait for their reaction. It was hard to keep from laughing as I watched them flounder and look to each other for direction. This was clearly not written in their script.

"Kim and Brandi, have you met Kelly?" Nikki asked.

Both ladies forced glossy tight smiles and nodded their heads.

"I won't keep you long. We're busy, busy, busy getting Adelle camera ready, and I know you've come to pick up your uniforms."

"Our uniforms?" Brandi sneered, finally speaking. Although it was slight, from the angle I was standing, I was able to catch Kim elbow Brandi.

"Yes, didn't you know? I'm asking the heads of the Junior League Club to march at the front of the parade with the toy soldier puppets. We thought it would be great if there was a human element this year. All Sweets Network would love it, and it would really put Junior League in the spotlight, just as it should be, right girls?" Nikki smiled, flashing them a brilliant glow.

"Well, don't you think we should be back with our girls, I mean, the other ladies in Junior League?" Brandi balked.

"Oh, no, they'll be okay. All of the leaders of the various organizations are going to be wearing the costumes and representing. You wouldn't want to be cut out of that, would you? I mean, you are the president and the vice-president now, aren't you? Their fearless leaders?" Nikki asked, smiling and openly taunting them.

"Of course," Kim, the brunette said, smiling with effort. I could almost see the injected Botox breaking down underneath the caked on make-up.

"So, with the All Sweets Network coming, you'll want to tell all of your family and friends. Just think, you could be featured on national television. They are one of the largest cooking networks going right now. It's going to be so fun," Nikki said, way too enthusiastically. Being in charge of the parade, Nikki was using her authority to try and humiliate these girls. They knew it, she knew it, but they were playing the game.

Nikki reached back into the office and pulled out two toy soldier costumes, complete with red and white jackets, white pants, and tall black hats.

My face crumpled in laughter, which I tried unsuccessfully to disguise as a coughing bit.

"Now, if you would be so kind as to complete the outfit with tall black boots, I'm sure you have those, everyone does, and red cheeks, that would be great. You're going to look great," Nikki smiled.

Kim and Brandi reluctantly reached their hands out and took the costumes.

"I know they're a little over the top, but for All Sweets Network, you pull out all the stops, right?" Nikki said, shooting them a thumbs-up. "If you think you have it bad, I'm going to be in a full donut costume. Can you imagine? Ha!"

We all chuckled lightly at Nikki's lead.

"Well, we better go and let you get ready. See you at the parade," Kim said, shooting us a fake, tense-looking smile, before turning and pulling Brandi with her out the door.

"All Sweets Network is really coming?" I heard Brandi whisper to her on the way out with a note of excitement.

"Shut up," Kim breathed curtly, clearly not wanting to add any level of enthusiasm to Adelle's success.

"Bye, ladies! Thanks again!" Nikki sang out cheerfully.

When they were gone, Nikki, Adelle, and I stared at each other for a few silent seconds.

Finally, Adelle spoke up.

"Are you really wearing a full donut costume?" she asked.

"God, no," Nikki said, turning to head back to her office.

Chapter 38

I left the store shortly after Kim and Brandi made their exit. It was obvious that Adelle and Nikki needed to be alone with all they had going on. Nikki hadn't even asked me about my engagement dinner once all the parade planning talk started, which was so out of character for her. That told me how stressed she was; launching Adelle's business had to be priority, and I felt like I was only getting in the way. When I'd asked how I could help, Adelle looked at me with tired eyes and said, "Please go check on Mom and Dad. They're okay, but I've spent so little time with them over the last two days."

On the way over to Adelle's, my cell phone rang. Diane Nosely. This woman would just not let up.

"Not until Diane Nosely gets the story!" I sang sarcastically, pointing a finger in the air.

Climbing up the stairs to Adelle's home, I wrapped my arms around myself, trying to warm my body. The snow had stopped, but yesterday's storm had pulled the temperatures into the mid-thirties. Again, I worried about the parade.

When I'd asked Nikki if the story about All Sweets Network coming to the parade was real, she'd shrugged and said, "Sort of." I didn't push her any further. I'd learned never to doubt the great and powerful Nikki. That woman always had something up her sleeve. If she promised to make Adelle's business launch a success and get a lot of attention, whether it be through All Sweets Network or some other media venue, she was going to come through. It wasn't the success I was worried about, it was the stress. Was Adelle going to be able to handle it? Nikki seemed to be able to do it, run the successful business and keep herself together. This was going to be a new challenge for Adelle.

"Well, where have you been? We've been missing you, my dear," Dad said, whipping open the door and pulling me into a gigantic hug. If he knew about my failed attempt at getting engaged last night, he wasn't going to bring it up. Something told me that he did know though by the way he was overcompensating with the dramatic hug.

"Hi, Dad," I said, wrapping my arms around him in return.

"Hi, honey," Mom said quietly from behind him.

Uh oh. From the way she slumped over, a bit deflated, my guess was she was taking such good care of Dad that she wasn't focusing enough on herself. Caretaker burnout.

"Hi, Mom," I said, peeking over my dad's shoulder. "Everything okay?"

Mom stood up a little straighter and smiled back at me. "Of course. I'm just a little tired."

"Are the kids here?" I asked, already feeling a bit of anger growing inside of me. I was right; Adelle was dumping everything on my parents, which at this point meant Mom.

"Just Craig is here. He's upstairs. We're interviewing a new babysitter this morning. He wanted to show her his room," Mom said, pointing up to the top floor of the house.

"Oh," I said, instantly feeling bad that I was about to crucify Adelle. At least she was trying to get more help. "What's wrong then?"

"What do you mean?" Mom sang, sounding a little bit too happy.

"You just look a little tired," I said.

"I'm okay. We're worried about you girls," she said, shrugging her shoulders.

"Okay, I'm going to go on my walk now. I'll let you girls catch up," Dad said, releasing me and sliding out the front door.

"Dad, you're going on a walk in this cold?" I protested, wanting to pull him back in.

"Will you leave me alone? Everyone stop treating me like a baby!" Dad called back half joking but half serious. He was already down the steps and zooming down the front walk before I could respond.

"Geez, what is with him?" I turned and asked Mom, closing the door and feeling a little scratched by Dad's quick flip. One minute he'd seemed happy to see me and the next he was telling me to butt out.

"The doctor said this would happen. They get crabby when they start feeling better," Mom said, slumping her shoulders again.

"But do you think he should be going out in this cold? It's pretty chilly out there, and his body is probably not used to it anymore," I said.

"Yeah, good luck stopping him," Mom said, turning her back to me to head into the kitchen. "Come on, let's get a cup of coffee. I want to talk to you."

Mom fired up Adelle's fancy coffee machine with expert care. I could tell she'd had some practice.

"We've made up our minds, we're moving back," Mom said.

"Are you sure?" I asked, feeling a bit shocked by the news.

Mom nodded her head and plodded on with her coffee preparation.

"Yes," was all she said.

"But what about the beach? You love Miami," I said, not wanting to say too much. If they were coming back, so many issues would be solved. The worry of who would take care of them if something worse were to happen to Dad would be over. They would be around all of us. It was a good thing. But, what if they had twenty more years of good health and their dream of living on the beach was squashed too early?

Suddenly, Mom stopped what she was doing, leaned onto the counter and put her head down on it. Her back shook and convulsed in a weird rhythmic way.

"Mom, what is it?" I begged, my eyes filling with tears. To see Mom cry like this was like a knife to the gut. My mind raced at rapid speeds, assuming horrible things. Something was wrong, really wrong. I ticked off a couple possibilities in my head. She was sick, Adelle had a life-threatening disease, and Dad needed a heart transplant.

"Tony," Mom finally sobbed.

"Tony, the doorman?" I asked, understanding immediately.

Mom nodded and wiped at her eyes, allowing me to put my arms around her and hold her tight. She kept quiet and laid her head on my shoulder. It wasn't a surprise to see Mom upset by the news about Tony. In fact, I was a little relieved to see her opening up and expressing her grief.

"I'm sorry, Mom," I said. "You guys were close?"

Mom nodded her head.

"He was such a nice man," she managed.

"His death makes me want to leave that place. I don't feel safe there anymore. Who would want to kill Tony? Miami is too violent for me now."

"Chicago is not much better. Not that I want to discourage you from coming back home. I'm just worried," I said.

"I'm worried about us there, I'm worried about us here," she said, expressing exactly what I was feeling.

We were both dancing around the hard truths and assumptions. At least, I thought we were. I wanted to ask if she thought Tony's death might have something to do with me and the jail break at Steve's prison, but didn't want to say it aloud.

"Well, and then there's Adelle and Mike. I'm just worried about them. This is such a stressful time in their marriage. How can I not be here to support them?" she asked.

"Let's sit down," I suggested, releasing her and grabbing the cups of coffee.

Mom reached for a paper towel and wiped at her eyes before following me to the kitchen table.

"What do you think, Kelly? Do you think they are in trouble?" Mom nudged.

"What do you mean?" I asked, selecting ignorance as a way to buy time.

Mom simply stared back at me, her eyes suddenly razor sharp and digging into my soul. I wanted so badly to get up from the table and get the heck out of Adelle's kitchen. The inquisition was about to begin, and I was caught on the wrong side of it.

"If they lose their father, these kids will fall to pieces," Mom said with conviction.

"Mom, what exactly are you talking about?" I said, not willing and not really able to show any of my cards.

"Kelly, do you know something about Mike that I don't?" she asked.

"Do you?" I asked, using my next tactic, deflection.

Mom stared back at me for a few silent seconds. I refused to fold, not wanting to give Mike up unless I had to. And I didn't have to. I liked Mike. Or did I? How well did I really know him? Mom's persistence was making me question a lot. I'd been willing to buy Mike's story that he didn't know what he was getting into when he'd agreed to keep the safety deposit box for Steve, but now I was confused. Seeing Mom, who as far as I was concerned was the sharpest knife in the drawer, so shaky made me want to think more on my decision. Or at least hold off on making a decision.

"Mom, if you know something about Mike, you have to tell me

right now," I said. "No more games. What are you dancing around?"

"I'm not dancing around anything," Mom snapped back. "I'm worried about Mike and Adelle's marriage and their kids."

"Then why are you coming at me like this?" I asked, remaining calm despite the fire in her eyes. This was so typical Mom. I'd been in this position so many times in life. Things were tough for Adelle, so Mom would get mad at all of the rest of us because we weren't helping or pitching in on making things better for Adelle. But the thing that Mom was refusing to see was that we were all trying to help Adelle. Nikki was supporting her with the business, I was trying my best to be a support for Adelle, AND I was even meeting her husband in secret to try and figure out how to best hide his secrets. We were all trying so much to help Adelle in our own little ways that it was starting to make me feel crazed.

Instead of replying, Mom put her head down on the table and started sobbing again.

Chapter 39

I left Adelle's house that afternoon swirling in a daze of confusion, guilt, and utter disgust. It was crazy what you did for people you loved, or what you considered doing. My normally steady moral compass was being rocked.

My cell phone rang in my pocket, pulling me back to the here and now. I shook my head and looked down at the screen. Nikki.

"Hello?" I said, into the receiver.

"Kelly, I feel horrible that I didn't ask about your dinner last night," she said.

"Oh, well, it didn't exactly turn out as it was supposed to," I said.

"You didn't ask Jack to marry you?" Nikki questioned.

"No, it didn't feel right. I'll tell you more later. The timing was just off," I lied, not wanting to get into the details.

"I'm sure it will be great once it is the right moment. You'll know. Hey, I'm so sorry to ask you this, but are you busy today?" she asked, sounding a little hairy.

"Not really. What's up?" I asked, unable to tell my sister, the one who dropped her life whenever I needed her, that I was too busy for whatever she needed.

"It's just, well, things aren't going good here at the shop. Adelle's having a little, teensy weensy bit of a meltdown over the parade and the launch tomorrow," she said.

I pictured Nikki huddled in her miniature back office, whispering into the phone so that Adelle wouldn't be able to hear.

"What kind of a meltdown?" I asked, slipping my key into the front door of Jack's condo. Our condo. It was still hard to keep that straight.

"She, well, there are some issues with the food truck we rented for tomorrow's parade. It's kind of," Nikki cut off. By the way her description ended so abruptly, I figured that Adelle had just walked in.

"You need me to come over?" I asked, already making changes to my "to do" list for the day. I had one vital errand that just had to be done.

"Yes, and bring clothes that you don't mind getting dirty. Or maybe never seeing again," Nikki said. "Okay, gotta run."

"Wait," I said into the phone. Too late. She'd already hung up.

I disconnected and immediately started punching a text into my phone.

Have to run an errand. Will be over after. What did you get us into this time??!!

Nikki responded with a brief and elusive:

Great!

I couldn't help but laugh a little. As bad as it sounded, I knew everything was going to be okay for Adelle's new business venture. If Nikki was involved, if she had faith in it, it was going to be a success. That's just how things were when you had Nikki involved.

"Now we gotta figure you out, Mike," I said aloud, heading to the bedroom to search for the envelope he'd given to me at Big Rock Library.

* * * * *

Twenty minutes later, I walked through the front door of the bank right off of Third Street where he'd opened the safety deposit box. My hands were sweating so much that the handle of the door actually slipped out of my grasp three times before I was able to pull it open.

All of that snooping and guessing about where in California Steve had his safety deposit box, and low and behold, it was right here under my nose the whole time. Just a few short blocks from Chocolate Love.

"You can do this," I breathed quietly to myself. It wasn't like Steve was going to be here. Gripping the envelope in my hand, it felt like he was going to pop out at any second and shout, "Boo!" His ghost was definitely here. I still couldn't believe Mike had hid this from me for so many years. Mike had partnered with the Devil. He knew it and he hid it.

"May I help you?" A personal banker asked me from behind a desk across the room.

There was no one else in the bank right now but me. I hated but also appreciated that fact at the same time. All eyes were on me, but there would also be fewer witnesses to my meltdown should I find something really horrific. I closed my eyes, allowing that fear to sink in for the first time.

What exactly was I going to find? Steve had sent a woman to kill me and my sister for the key I held in my hand. What was worth killing for? Mike seemed terrified of the whole thing. He wanted that envelope out of his possession as soon as possible when we'd met at Big Rock Library. What could this be?

"Ma'am?" the woman probed, a little softer this time.

I took in the woman sitting at her desk, her hands splayed out on the table, leaning forward. Her sandy blond hair was falling forward, and her blouse had opened slightly, exposing a tad too much cleavage for this formal setting.

"Sorry," I said, shaking my head to get back in focus. "I would like to get access to my safety deposit box, please?"

"Of course," she said, smiling and sounding a little bit relieved.

My mysterious silence was probably a bit scary in this setting. I considered making light by saying something like, "Don't worry. I'm not a lunatic here to rob the bank," but reconsidered, worrying it might backfire. The goal was to do this thing as under the radar as possible. I was working on a hunch and wanted to play it out.

She stood up and wobbled over to me, a pregnant belly leading the way. That explained the excessive cleavage. By the way her walking was so labored, she looked as though she was well past her due date. This poor woman really needed to be at home with her feet up, waiting for her big day.

"You're expecting?" I asked uncharacteristically, allowing my excitement for her to show in my smile. My mother had taught us to never comment on a woman's pregnancy unless they brought it up first, lest you risk offending them. But in this case, it seemed obnoxiously rude not to do so. She was clearly going to be a mom sooner rather than later.

"Next week," she said. "Trying to work up until the due date so that I have more time at home with the little guy."

Suddenly, I felt terrible making this woman stand on her feet and take part in my little experiment. I wanted her seated and comfortable again as soon as possible.

"Congratulations. That is wonderful. I won't keep you on your feet long," I said.

"Oh, no worries. It actually feels a bit nice to be up and about. I've been slumped in that chair all day. They treat me like an invalid. Not that I mind. Things could be much worse. What box number are you?"

"Huh?" I said, baffled by her words.

"Your number on your safety deposit box? Oh, and I need your ID," she said, rummaging through a drawer. She turned and smiled brightly while I ravaged through the envelope I'd walked in with. Surely it would be marked somewhere on the package Mike gave me.

Sure enough, the key Mike passed on was accompanied by a little red envelope with the number 241 marked on it.

"Here you go," I said, unsure if I was supposed to tell her that I was actually in possession of two keys. I was still a little unsure on why or how I'd stumbled upon my key. Was that what Steve intended? I was hoping the contents of the box would tell me more.

"Okay, we'll just sign your name right here," she said, pulling out a small file with the names Michael Stefano as the primary account holder and then mine on it as the secondary. As soon as I saw that, things started to fall into place. "My name is Colette, by the way."

"Nice to meet you," I said, signing off on the form and trying my best to keep from choking when I saw my signature a couple of times above where I was signing. How was that possible?

"Oh, I see your last name has changed since you opened this?" she said, checking the ID briefly and comparing the signatures and the photocopy of my ID.

"Yes, I dropped the hyphen for business purposes," I said, breezing over the full story.

"Got it," she said, handing back my ID.

"It's been so long since I was last here. Can I check the form again?" I asked casually before she put it back.

"Yes, of course," she said.

"We're considering closing the box today to be honest. We just don't use it like we thought we would," I said, doing my best to remain blasé about the whole thing.

"Well, of course you're free to do so, but you'll need to both be present," she said helpfully. "We can set up a time for you to do that today if you like."

"Oh, you'll need Mike's live signature as well to close?" I asked.

"Yes," said Collette. "You need to both be present."

"It's so funny," I laughed. "I just can't remember coming in with Mike on this date," I said, pointing to the sheet. It's amazing what the mind can forget, isn't it?"

"Well, not to worry. You're not going crazy. See, right here. It says Mike opened the account first and later you both came in on this date to add you on. Remember that?" Collette asked.

"Oh, of course," I lied. "How silly of me. Too much on my plate."

My eyes focused in on the date she was pointing to. The December before Steve was arrested, apparently I, or someone posing as me, had come in with Mike to add me onto the account.

"Okay, so we time stamp that and here we go," Colette said, leading me down a hallway toward the back of the bank.

"As you remember we'll enter the vault together and find the box that corresponds to your number," she went on, walking me through a large steel door that looked very intimidating.

"Now I just need your key again and then I put my key in and here we go," she said, placing the two keys into a box on a wall separated into hundreds of individual boxes, some larger than the rest. My mind raced, thinking about not only what could be in mine, but what all of these other boxes held. What did people feel the need to secure so tightly in a bank? I ran through my own items of value and was ashamed to think I really didn't have much. Maybe just some of the jewelry Mom had passed on from Grandma. I guess that deemed valuable enough to have its own box.

"Here you go," Colette said, pulling out a long rectangular box that seemed to just keep coming and coming.

"Thanks," I said, accepting it into my outstretched arms.

Now what?

Was I supposed to just walk out the door with it? Open it in front of her? I really didn't know what to do. Was the second key the one that actually opened this box? Taking a quick peek at the box, I could tell there wasn't another place to insert a key. There was just a simple latch that needed to be pushed for the box to open.

"The rooms are right over there," Colette reminded me, her head tipped a bit to the side. Apparently it wasn't protocol to open the boxes right in front of her.

"Oh, yes, great," I said, allowing her to lead me out of the room with all the boxes. "Was just double checking that the latch would work."

"I'll just be a few minutes," I said, entering the teeny-tiny room she'd unlocked for me. It consisted of a small table and one chair. The room was sterile and reminded me of a miniature police interrogation room. When the door closed behind me, I took a couple of seconds to look for hidden mirrors or cameras. Nothing. Although I was clearly alone, it felt like I was being watched, which was insane. This room was smaller than a closet. And surely, installing a camera in here would be illegal. Right?

I knew who was watching me. Steve. His ghost was here standing over me asking, "What are you going to do, huh?"

"Well, it depends on what's in the box now, doesn't it, Steve?" I said aloud to his imaginary form.

I released a heavy sigh, and put both hands on the box. It was time. Time to see what was in this bad boy. What led a psychotic woman to come after me last summer for the key that opened this mysterious box? It had better be good. This box was causing a lot of stress, not only for me, but my extended family.

"Do it," I whispered to myself. "Do it."

Taking a deep breath through my nose, I flipped the little clasp and opened the box. When I took in the contents, I stopped breathing and my eyes filled with tears.

Chapter 40

Reaching my trembling hands into the box, I let out a quiet sob and picked up the little bundles. How could he? This? This was what it was all about?

I placed the small bundles of cash on the desk and put my head down on it, my eyes blinded by tears. My body was shaking so bad, I struggled to keep the loud sobs that wanted to escape inside. I didn't want anyone to hear me and come knocking on the door. No one was to witness this low.

My mind raced to the moment Dad let go of my hand at the altar and proudly gave me over to Steve at our church wedding. Dad's quiet confidence solidified mine. We'd been so happy. And now, the pathetic stacks of cash in front of me were proof how little I was worth in Steve's mind. He just wanted me out of his life for good so that he could move on. Having me dead would mean he didn't have to worry anymore.

Wiping at my eyes, I breathed in and out, determined to pull myself together. I couldn't stay in here much longer without drawing attention. Who knew how much time had passed already.

"You scumbag," I muttered, pulling a Kleenex from my purse and wiping at my face. The IVF treatments, the debt, the affair, the attempted murder, the trial, the attempt on my life and the life of my sister, and now this. Hiding money and suckering my brother-in-law into doing it?

"How much could this possibly be? Not much," I estimated,

grabbing the two small stacks and unabashedly talking to myself now. All of a sudden, I was beyond caring. What did I care what Colette thought of me? I was the crazy lady in the closet counting money. So what?

Counting feverishly, I was able to come up with a number.

Eighteen thousand dollars.

Eighteen. Thousand. Dollars. Steve threw away his life, my life, our life all for that? Eighteen thousand dollars was nothing to sneeze at. I couldn't come up with that much if I tried right now. Every dollar I made came in and went right back out to paying off the debt I'd acquired from my failed IVF treatments. But still, eighteen thousand dollars seemed like such an inconsequential amount of money in relevance to the giant mess it had caused.

I glanced back into the box, feeling that I may have missed something. Surely, there would be bigger stacks of money hiding in there. Diamonds? Proof of espionage? Something that would explain the great risk and horrendous things Steve had done.

Squinting, I was able to see that there was something still in the box stuffed into the very back of the rectangle. I picked the box up and shook it until it fell onto my lap.

Alarmed, I jumped in my seat, brushing it off my lap, my hands fluttering in a panic. The miniature, fluorescent pink stuffed animal hit the wall and landed on the floor, eyes on me.

"Remember me?" It seemed to laugh up at me.

"Oh, I remember you," I said, picking it up slowly and holding it up to get a closer look at it. "What are you doing here?"

"So you know it's a girl and you know the due date," I laughed, placing the dish of homemade spaghetti I'd been slaving over all day in front of Steve. I'd assumed that my sudden need to nest surely must mean I was pregnant.

"Yes, I do," Steve said, reaching out and grabbing my hand. "Third time's a charm, right?" he cooed, smiling up at me from the

table.

"Let's hope so, Steve. These treatments cost an arm and a leg. I just don't think . . ." I said. Before I could continue, Steve cut me off.

"Baby, don't talk about the money. It's bad luck. Just come here," he said, pulling me into his lap. "I'm sure this time it worked. So much so, that I bought you this."

Steve pulled a tiny, fluorescent pink bear from his pocket and placed it on the table. It smiled up at me. It seemed to offer everything I needed so badly. Hope. A purpose. A justification for the money we'd been doling out on the treatments. That little smile was there just in the nick of time to remind me that everything was going to be okay. A little hand would soon be grabbing for this bear, and Steve and I would be happy parents.

"Let's set a place for her," Steve laughed, putting his arms around me and snuggling me closer.

"For the bear?" I laughed.

"No silly, for our baby girl," Steve said, kissing me and helping me forget the anxiety that seemed to find a permanent home in the pit of my stomach.

Holding the pink bear now, I felt sickened by this memory.

"Steve," I said aloud, at a loss for words. Should I curse his name? Hold the bear in the air and swear vengeance for all of the trouble he'd cost me? Make an oath to erase him completely from my life? That would be great, but I felt so powerless to take that kind of control. He was popping back into my life every chance he could get.

Curling my hand around the bear, I turned back to the table to look at the money. If I were smart, I'd gather the money, deposit it directly into my account and use it to pay off a big chunk of the debt that Steve had left me in. Now that would be vengeance.

"Take the donut," I heard Tony laugh somewhere in my mind,

remembering our conversation in Miami when he'd talked about his retirement from the police force. He'd been drowning and needed a life donut, so he'd taken the retirement package and the job that was supposed to be less stressful. Sometimes you just needed the help. Needed to make the decision that would make your life better. Easier. Save you from being pulled under.

Still, was it the right thing?

"Oh, hell," I said, exhaling.

I threw the bear into my purse and made a decision. All at once, I knew what to do with the money, the bear, everything.

Back in my car, I pulled out my cell phone and dialed Mike's number.

"Hello?" he said, answering on the first ring.

"Mike, is this a good time to talk?" I asked.

"Sure. Do you want to meet?" he asked. "Or over the phone?"

"I've made a decision on the safety deposit box. I'm going to go check out what's in there. You don't have to go. I would actually prefer you stay out of this now. For your safety, I mean."

"Kelly, I appreciate that, but that's impossible. I'm the only one on the box. They're not just going to let you just walk in there and have access to it just because you have a key," he said, confirming my hunch.

"So, you never went in and put me on the box?" I asked.

"No. You would have had to go in with me in person. I haven't stepped foot in that bank since the day I opened the account for Steve," he said.

"Hmm," I said simply. "Okay, well, that changes things. Let's get through the parade and then revisit this. Sound good?" I asked, flipping the ID I'd brought with me into the bank over in my hand and examining it.

"Okay. Are you sure?" Mike asked.

"Yep," I said, nodding my head and holding the ID up to my

eyes to examine it closer.

"I'm so sorry about this, Kelly. All of it. It's such a mess," Mike said.

"I know you are, Mike. I know."

* * * * *

"Just breathe, Adelle. Breathe," I said, pouring her a glass of water.

"This is a disaster. Everyone is going to be laughing at me," she said, scrubbing pans in the sink at Chocolate Love.

We were closing in on two in the morning, and Adelle, Miguel, Nikki, and I were still frantically working in the shop, trying to get things ready for tomorrow's parade.

"Adelle, you're overreacting," Nikki insisted, lining up product on her baking sheets and sticking them in the oven.

We were frantically baking Nikki's products because we'd put off her stuff, so we could get Adelle's launch in order. So far, the signage had turned out wrong, and the company that she'd ordered the rental food truck from had sent the wrong truck.

Adelle had repeated over and over for at least an hour, "No deep fryers! How do you make donuts on the truck without deep fryers?"

We were able to get a new truck ordered, but it wouldn't be here till six in the morning, which at this point, looked as though we'd still be awake to see.

"Okay, this is the last batch and then we are out of here. Miguel, you should leave right now. This is nuts," Nikki said, trying to shoo off her most devoted and loved employee. He'd insisted on staying after hours to help get things rectified.

"I'm just going to stay here and wait for the truck," Adelle insisted.

"Oh no, you're not. You need to get some sleep, Adelle. You don't want to look like the Bride of Frankenstein for your big day.

I'll stay here," Nikki said.

"No, no, no," I said, putting my foot down. "You're pregnant, Nikki. This is too much for the baby. I will stay here. The apartment is still set up upstairs. I'll just go up there and grab a few hours of sleep and then be here for the truck."

Adelle and Nikki both stopped working and looked at me. From the resignation on their faces, I could tell that it made the most sense.

"Yes, that's what is happening. You guys go get some sleep. You could get a good six hours in. When you come back, I'll head home to Jack's place and get more sleep. This is all going to work out," I said, turning back to my job of frosting cupcakes. I was topping cupcakes with vanilla buttercream in Nikki's signature swirl and then dropping little candy Christmas trees on the very top. We were estimated to sell over five hundred of these at the parade. And if the All Sweets Network was coming, as Nikki had promised, they needed to be perfect.

"But what if the truck is wrong?" Adelle moaned.

"They promised us an all-white truck that we could smack the magnet of your logo on with deep fryers. If they get this wrong this time," Nikki said, growling.

"I will watch for the color of the truck and make them walk me through the deep fryer. If they get it wrong, I will get someone's head on a stick. I promise. Just go home and get some rest. Tomorrow is your big day," I said.

"Okay, fine, I'm leaving. Will you text me at six if everything is okay? And text me if it's not okay," Adelle said, looking like she was about to fall over with fatigue. Her tall form swayed back and forth before reaching out for a chair to slump down in.

"Honestly, Nikki, I don't know how you've done this for all of these years. It just takes so much work," Adelle said.

"It's a lot in the beginning. I won't lie. But once you've got yourself established, things will slow down a bit, I promise."

While they spoke, I continued to pop trees on and swirl the cupcakes as best I could. For some reason, I wasn't feeling fatigued. Probably the resolution I'd come to earlier at the bank had helped ease some of my stress. Now I just had to carry through with my plan. That could all be done later. Right now, I needed to concentrate on helping my sisters out of a jam.

"Seriously, you guys scoot. I'm all good here."

While Nikki and Adelle were bundling up to leave, Adelle turned back to me with a strange look and said something that made my stomach drop.

"Hey, Kelly," she said, scrunching her eyebrows over her red-tinged eyes. "Have they caught Franklin Ford yet?"

Chapter 41

At five-thirty that morning, the front doorbell to Chocolate Love rang, waking me from a dead sleep. I'd finished decorating the last of the desserts in the kitchen around three and crawled upstairs to my old apartment above the store to catch a nap before the truck arrived. It took a while for it to register that the bell I was hearing was someone trying to get my attention, not a part of the dream/nightmare I was having. In the dream, I was running on a treadmill, trying to escape a large donut that was rolling behind me in a continuous loop on its own treadmill. Even in dream state, my mind registered the irony of the donut chasing me, when really we were prisoners of our own loops. Neither one of us were going to get anywhere. Why weren't either of us simply jumping off the treadmills? In the dream, the sound of the bell was the treadmill registering that I'd just completed another mile.

Finally popping my eyes open, I rubbed at them and winced at the crick in my neck from sleeping funny. Normally, I slept on a pile of pillows, but in the apartment, only one remained from my time here. I'd folded it up as best I could for more support, but my body wasn't fooled. It knew this wasn't where I normally laid my head.

Ding Dong.

The bell sounded again downstairs, and all at once I was awake. I couldn't miss them. Adelle would be so upset if I slept through the delivery of her food truck. Today would be a disaster without it.

"Coming!" I yelled, bolting up from the bed and pulling my hair back with a rubber band. I made quick work of slipping into my ballet flats I'd left on the floor next to the bed.

"Please let this be okay, please let this be okay," I repeated to myself, running down the stairs.

Without a glance through the window, I disabled the alarm system, and threw open the inner door, marching out the walkway to open the door leading to outside. At first glance, I couldn't see anything because it was still dark out, but my skin started to tingle with worry. Sure enough, when I unbolted the second door leading to the outside, my fears were confirmed.

No one.

The porch was empty and the streets looked deserted. The wind blew rustling leaves down the street and a few cars drove quietly past, but for the most part, the town was still fast asleep.

The air was noticeably warmer than what it had been over the last couple of days, leaving me feeling hopeful for tonight's festivities and Adelle's moment. All the snow that had fallen in the last storm had completely disappeared, which would be great for the parade and the launch. The launch that wouldn't happen if the truck didn't show.

Or had it been here and I'd missed it because I'd overslept?

Feeling terrible, I turned back inside and let the door shut behind me.

Now what?

I didn't know how to get a hold of the company, and I didn't want to go running to Adelle or Nikki to get the phone number. In my rush to get them out the door last night, I'd forgotten to get that information. They were supposed to be sleeping and getting their rest for the day. I was supposed to be taking care of this part. I'd promised I would. The plan was that I was going to have the luxury of sleeping in all day while they were working like mad putting the finishing touches together.

I had to figure this out.

As I started back into the store, something crumpled under my feet. Assuming it to be a leaf that had blown in, I was surprised to see it was coming from something much larger. I knelt down and grabbed the piece of paper from under my shoe. Someone must have left it in the door.

I opened it, hoping that the food truck company had left their information. Perhaps I could call them right back and tell them to return as fast as possible.

The words were typed in a large black font and said:

Revenge is best served cold and sweet. Watch for a taste-coming soon.

"What?" I said, turning it over and examining it closer. If this was some kind of advertisement, it was terrible. There were no graphics, nothing enticing about it. It did have my attention though.

Then it struck me. Was this left for me? As a threat of some sort? If it was, it wasn't very well spelled out. And if it was for me, how did they know I had spent the night here?

Looking behind me to make sure the door was locked, I reached out with my hand and pulled on the door once to check. Then I turned and moved quickly into the store, locking the second door.

Should I call Jack?

No, too early. Too dramatic.

Call Nikki?

No, she was supposed to be sleeping.

The food truck company. That was where my attention needed to be. What if this was some kind of weird advertisement/calling card for their company they'd left? That was it. It talked about revenge being served sweet and a tasting. It just had to be about this food truck; some kind of twisted way of promoting their trucks. I had to find their number, and I knew exactly where to locate the info. Nikki's office.

Cutting through the store, my attention was pulled over to the coffee cups hanging on the wall. Yes! That was exactly what I needed. Coffee would make me think clearly and be less scatterbrained when I spoke to someone. I'd become a pro now at Nikki's machine. It would only take me a quick second.

Pushing a few buttons, I had a warm, steaming cup on its way. Smiling, I put my hands on the counter and let out a sigh of relief. Everything was going to be okay. Adelle was going to launch her super successful business, silence her mean girl critics, and secure the finances for her family. Nikki was about to have a baby, and I was going to get married, eventually, once Jack was really legally divorced.

I cupped the mug with two hands and breathed in the heavenly smell.

But what if it took Jack years to complete the divorce? What if we had to go hunt Callie down? Or worse yet, what if she came to hunt us down?

In a flash, the mug was down on the ground, shattered into a million pieces, hot coffee spraying up onto my legs.

"Revenge is best served cold," I heard my own voice saying. Of course, that was it. She'd been watching us. Watching me. She was here to get revenge because Jack had divorced her. She knew we were planning to get married, and she was here to stop it.

Laughing nervously, I shook my head, trying to pull myself together.

"Relax, Kelly," I said to myself. That thought was insane. Jack couldn't even find her. She was off the grid.

"I need more sleep. I'm going crazy," I mumbled, bending down to wipe up the mess I'd made.

After a few minutes, I had the floor all cleaned up and the cup of coffee I'd been craving. The only thing I allowed my mind to settle on was the truck. That was the only thing that mattered right now. I'd promised Adelle I would handle this and that was what I needed to do. Enough of my own insecurities and worries, today was about Adelle.

Leafing through Nikki's desk, I found what I was looking for immediately. The business card from the company I heard them choose yesterday for the new truck was sitting right on top of Nikki's desk, next to the phone.

A gentleman answered on the first ring.

"Hello, Food Truck for Hire. Can I help you?" he said, sounding very awake for this early in the morning.

"Yes, I'm expecting one of your trucks this morning. I think I may have missed you. Can you tell me if you've sent a truck yet to Chocolate Love?"

"Give me a second, let me check," he said.

I flipped on the under the counter light above Nikki's desk top, illuminating her neatly organized and efficient little office. Squinting down at the business card, I wondered how big this company was that they'd chosen to lease a truck from. Was this a call center? What company had people answering this early in the morning? I was glad they did.

"Yes, they are scheduled to be at your store any minute," he said.

As if on cue, a knock sounded at the back door.

"Oh, thank God, I think they're here. Thank you. Oh, and this truck has a deep fryer, right?" I asked, trying to do my due diligence.

"Yes. We're even sending a few of our employees out to help with the frying. Nikki told us we can feature our logo on the truck for the show. It's not every day we get to be featured on All Sweets Network. This is a great opportunity for us. We want to make sure it goes well."

I rolled my eyes thinking about Nikki and her promise of All Sweets Network. God help her if they didn't come.

"Oh, good," was all I could say.

"Is this Adelle? Good luck today. We're very excited for you," he said. "My name is Ken. I'm one of the owners. I would be there myself, but we have an event out of state today."

"I'm actually the other sister, Kelly," I said.

"Oh, how nice, a family that works together. I can relate. I work with my three brothers," he said.

I heard the sound of someone descending the back steps outside, which immediately made me nervous. I didn't want them to leave.

"Ken, I'm sorry, but I have to let you go. I don't want to keep your employee waiting."

"Oh, sure, that should be Immanuel making the delivery of the truck. He'll set you up. Call if you need anything," he said, disconnecting.

I hung up and made my way quickly over to the back door, feeling pressured to catch Immanuel before he walked around to the front door.

"Wait, don't go," I said, flinging open the back door.

No one.

Just as I started to step out of the door, my eye registered a large, dark mass I was about to step on. I caught myself with my two hands on the doorframe and jumped back with a shiver. I'd nearly stepped right on the large, grotesque, dead rat left at the foot of the door. Its long, pink tail curled out over the mat that read "Welcome" in black letters. I could see the two front teeth of the rat protruding out of its mouth.

I flew back, threw the door shut and bolted it closed. I put my hands over my mouth and finally released a gut wrenching scream before racing back to the phone.

Chapter 42

"No, Kelly, you're not listening to me. That's impossible," he said, speaking clearly and calmly into the phone. "I was going to call you this morning, but I wanted to wait until it got a little later. I didn't realize you would be up so early or I would have called."

The sound of a knock on the back door froze my trembling body.

"He's back. Please, you have to send someone over right now. Franklin Ford is here for me. Steve sent him. I know he did. Detective Pavlik, you have to get someone here, NOW," I screamed.

"Kelly, you're not listening to me. That is impossible. Franklin Ford was caught in the middle of the night last night. He was near the Canadian border. He wasn't anywhere near you. This had nothing to do with you."

"There is someone knocking on the back door right now. They're leaving threatening messages and rats. Please, you have to send someone over. They're going to kill me."

"Kelly?" I heard a man's voice call out from the other side of the door.

"Did you hear that, Detective? See! I told you. Now send someone," I screamed into the phone.

"Kelly, this is Immanuel from Food Trucks for Hire. You just talked to my boss, Ken? I'm not going to hurt you," I heard the man on the other side of the door say.

My eyes slammed shut in embarrassment, realizing I'd been

yelling so loud he'd certainly heard my panicked request for police.

"Ugh," I grunted.

"Kelly, I'll send someone right away if you're scared. I just want you to know that you don't have to worry about Franklin Ford. That's all over now. We have double and triple checked this for you. Steve is safely locked up in prison. You are in the clear."

"Mmmhmm," was all I could manage, trying to figure out how to get my bright red cheeks to cool before answering the door.

"You're getting threatening notes?" Detective Pavlik asked.

"I'm not sure. Can I call you back?" I managed to squeak out. "I just realized that the person knocking on the door is from the food truck company my sister hired."

"But what about the rat? Do you still want me to come check it out?" Pavlik asked kindly.

"No, no, I'm good. Thank you so much for telling me about Franklin Ford. I think that situation has made me paranoid. I'll be better now. Let me call you back, okay?" I said, sniffing and trying my best to compose myself.

"I'll see you at the parade tonight," Pavlik said. "I'll make sure to find you."

"Great," I said, before hanging up the phone and taking a deep breath.

"I'm coming," I called out.

Glancing for the first time in the small mirror Nikki had hanging in her office, my reaction was to gasp. If insane woman was what I was going for, I'd nailed it. My hair had somehow managed to come out of my ponytail holder and was blasting out in all directions in a mountain of frizz. The make-up I'd decided not to wash off last night when I dozed off was smudged on my face, and the clothes I'd slept in were wrinkled and in disarray.

Licking my finger, I wiped at the smudged mascara and flattened my hair down with both hands. Giving up, I turned to the door, thinking my only option to save face here was to act normal, regardless of how I looked.

Just as a precaution, I peeked out the window next to the door, making sure that Detective Pavlik had been right. This stranger was not Franklin Ford posing as Immanuel.

Sure enough, the man outside looked nothing like the mug shot I'd seen countless times on television. Immanuel appeared to be a good twenty years younger than the hard criminal that had been haunting the evening news for the last two weeks.

"Hello," the man waved enthusiastically at the window.

Unlocking the door, I held my breath.

Instead of greeting him, I cringed and looked down at his shoes, keeping one eye protectively shut.

"If you're looking for the mouse, I got rid of it," he said. "It's safe now."

"You saw it, too?" I asked quietly, relieved that I wasn't going mad.

Immanuel simply stared at me, his eyebrows raised in question. I guess it was a weird thing to ask.

"You're scared of mice?" he asked politely. "It's okay, my sister is as well. She's terrified. Though I don't know if she's ever called the police over one. That's a first," he smiled, obviously trying to make light of the conversation I was now sure he'd overheard.

"I thought that maybe someone had left it here on purpose," I said, a little defensively.

"Oh, probably just a cat," he said. His eyebrows moved up again and his head tilted to the side. "Or are you being serious? You think someone is trying to threaten you or something?"

I stood there deciphering what to say. Instead of coming up with something, my eyes moved to the truck parked on the street behind him.

"Where did you put the mouse?" I asked, avoiding his question.

"I disposed of it in your dumpster. Don't worry, I used gloves and sealed it in bags. We're trained on how to handle this kind of stuff. As gross as it is, it's really not that uncommon in the food business. The mice are drawn to the smells. They're always a threat to the business."

"My sister has never told me about any problems with mice. The timing of this was," I stopped, saying more than I wanted or planned. "Never mind, thank you for taking care of that. Please come in," I said, directing Immanuel into the store.

"Would you like some coffee? Oh, and before I forget, did you, by chance, leave a flyer by the front door?" I asked.

* * * * *

By three that afternoon, I was waking up in my own bed, feeling better and rather foolish for the scene I'd caused that morning. As promised, I'd finally sent a text to Nikki and Adelle once I'd confirmed that the truck was as it should be and everything was in working order. By then, the news about Franklin Ford had made national headlines, and my phone was buzzing every few seconds as updates started pouring in.

Apparently, Franklin had been taken in rather peacefully after surrendering to the police. All had ended without much drama despite the weeks and weeks of work for hundreds of officers, not to mention the media. Thus far, Franklin had made no reference to Steve, or any other prisoner for that matter. Diane Nosely had been wrong. There was no connection. Ha! I don't know what made me happier-the fact that I appeared to be free and clear of a connection to this case, or the fact that Diane had been wrong.

Tony's death still hung over me like a dark cloud, but at least now I could cut Franklin Ford out of my theories. Perhaps it really was just a random shooting.

The strange note this morning, the knock on the door, and the rat, still remained a mystery. Adelle did have an excellent theory though. She thought her two biggest haters, Kim and Brandi from Junior League, were behind it. Nikki dismissed that theory though, saying even they would not stoop so low.

Adelle silenced her by saying, "You'd be surprised what mean girls in power are capable of. I should know."

Nikki and I both kept silent on that, possibly both sharing the same thought-we didn't want to know.

So, by three, feeling safe and secure in Jack's big, fluffy bed, I rolled over, turned off the alarm and went back to bed in the king sized haven I had to myself since Jack was at work. I wasn't due back to the parade until four and had every intention of getting as much sleep as I could. Tonight was Adelle's big night and things were shaping up to be quite the adventure. As long as I could keep calm and keep the focus on Adelle, I had a feeling she was going to be a smashing success. No more escaped inmates on the loose, no crazy reporters sneaking around the store, and hopefully no ex-spouses on the prowl. Just a nice night with All Sweets Network and Adelle's rented food truck shooting out delicious treats.

Just as I was snuggling in under the blankets, my phone beeped. It was a text from Adelle.

Things are all coming together here. I finally feel like the launch is going to be okay. Guess who showed up and is filming the inside of the store?! ALL SWEETS NETWORK! Thanks so much for all of your help today, Kelly. I don't know what I would do without you.

Seeing that text made me sit up straight in bed. I'd almost forgotten the unfinished business of the safety deposit box. I'd made up my mind. I wasn't going to let a few thousand dollars ruin my sister's family, especially when she was about to fulfill her dream of launching her own business.

I'd made a decision. I needed to get rid of that money. All of it. Then, close the account with Mike.

But what to do with the money? What if the money was stolen, or worse, counterfeit? What if by donating that money, it flagged a government agency and brought it to light? No, I couldn't take that risk. I had to be smart about all of this. I needed to clean up the mess entirely. I needed help, but couldn't risk telling any family members. They might not agree with my decision, and there was no way I was going to budge. The only way to do this was by myself. They needed to be kept "clean." They were already too close to the situation.

There was one way around all of this. It would take some humiliation on my part, but this way, it could all end. I could bring all of this to an end.

Yes, there was definitely a way.

I punched a few buttons on my phone. After two rings, a familiar voice answered on the other line.

"Well, Ms. Clark, I can't tell you how nice it is to see your name pop up on my screen. Long time, no talk. How are you?" a friendly voice asked on the other end.

"Hi, William, how are you?" I asked.

"I'm well. I've been meaning to reach out to you. I caught the story about the prison break. Wasn't that the same prison your ex-husband is being held at?"

"Yes," I said simply.

"You're okay?"

"Of course."

"I was happy to hear that they caught the two men on the run finally."

"Yes, me, too," I said.

"Is everything okay? You sound kind of funny. I'm here if you want to talk about something," William said.

The kindness in his voice brought me right back to a few months ago when Nikki and I helped William solve the mysterious death of his twin brother, Brian, here in Geneva. William had dropped everything in California to personally take on his brother's case. He'd begged us to help him and after much cajoling on Nikki's part, I'd acquiesced. With a little luck and Nikki's natural sleuthing abilities, we were able to bring his murderer to justice. William had struck up a friendship with us, albeit a rather flirty one. Harmless though. We'd stayed in touch from time to time, and now he was the first person I thought of when my plan came together on what to do about the safety deposit box. Jack would hate that I was doing this, but it was for his own good that he be kept in the dark.

"William, I need your help," I said, reluctantly. It was never easy asking this of someone.

"Anything," he said, completely devoid of any flirtation that had been there a moment before. He must have sensed the level of seriousness in my request.

"Good," I said, then dove into my crazy whirlwind of a plan.

Chapter 43

An hour later, I approached Chocolate Love with a sense of glee and excitement. The air smelled of donuts, roasted nuts, and cinnamon. Crowds of people were already filling the streets in anticipation of the parade. The temperature was nearing fifty, a sharp contrast to a few days ago. Adelle had somehow landed a gorgeous day for her launch, making me think that the odds were greatly in her favor for pulling this off.

Five gigantic toy soldiers stood in front of Chocolate Love. These must have been a last minute decision because Nikki had never included them in the past years for the annual parade. I was sure that the fact that All Sweets Network was coming had upped the ante on pretty much everything. Nikki and Adelle were pulling out all the stops.

"Kelly!" I heard Adelle squeal from the top steps of Chocolate Love. At first, the frantic pitch to her voice scared me. It made me worry that some other strange prank had occurred while I was off in dream land. Had another dead rat appeared?

The second I made eye contact with her though, I knew the squeal was in response to her excitement, not stress.

"Did you see the truck?" she asked.

Her demeanor was so non-Adelle like; at least not the stressed out Adelle we'd had over the last couple of weeks. She looked the way she did when we were little kids and were about to do something exciting like go on vacation or check out what Santa had left us under the tree.

Turning my head, I looked back over my shoulder to take in the truck. I'd been so distracted by the toy soldiers that I'd almost completely missed the truck. On the front, the truck read, "Adelle's Pastries" in cursive. The bright red logo she'd agonized over had finally turned out perfect, at least in my eyes, and from the look on her face, she was happy with it as well.

Adelle was at my side in a flash.

"What do you think?" she asked. "Isn't it perfect?"

"I love it," I said, turning to hug her. "How does it stay on there?"

"It's magnetic. A giant magnet. When and if I get my own truck, I can just transfer it. Nikki knows someone who makes them."

"Are you happy with the truck?" I asked.

"It's awesome! So much better than the first company we hired. Come see. They even sent workers, so I don't have to worry about making them myself. I can do more of the interaction with the crowd and the interviews for All Sweets Network. Kelly, you're not going to believe this. We got a call today from The Best Donut Challenge, the reality cooking show. They heard about my company and they want me to be on it. Can you believe it?" Adelle jumped up and down in delight. She reminded me so much of Nikki right now.

"Wow," I said, unable to resist absorbing her energy.

"Come on, come on, let's go see inside the truck," she said, pulling me by the arm.

"Immanuel, you're still here?" I asked, feeling bad. He'd been here since before six this morning. Three more people buzzed around him in the surprisingly immaculate but miniscule truck. It looked so much bigger from the outside.

"Yes, I'm still here. No worries. Your sisters have fed me enough coffee and sugar to keep me going for another twenty-four hours. How are you, Kelly?"

"I'm good, I got some more sleep. But you must be exhausted," I laughed.

"Oh, don't worry about me. We're just thrilled to be a part of this. The All Sweets Network has already gotten a ton of footage of the truck and even interviewed me for the show. We're going to be featured on their special about Christmas traditions and businesses in the Chicago suburbs. My boss is thrilled. He's going to try and stop by later to thank you in person if he wraps up his job in time."

"Yes, we're going to be part of an hour long special about the parades and lighting ceremonies. I'm just so glad we've been building this parade up over the last few years. We've gained quite the reputation. We're scheduled to have almost two thousand people here tonight," Nikki bragged. She appeared out of nowhere and had the same glow as Adelle. It gave me confidence that everything was going to go smoothly.

"Nikki, how did you manage to pull this off with All Sweets Network? You never told me about your connections there," I said.

"I've been trying to get them out here for years. I guess we just finally built up enough momentum to get their attention," she said humbly.

Knowing Nikki, there was probably more to the story. Bottom line, Nikki got the job done and she really wanted the attention for Adelle.

"So, I notice they're all wearing Adelle's shirts in here. I feel torn. Whose shirt do I wear tonight? Chocolate Love or Adelle's?" I laughed.

"We're keeping my employees in Chocolate Love gear if they're in the store, but out here, we've printed a boatload of Adelle's shirts. Tonight is about her," Nikki said.

"Are you sure, Nikki?" Adelle said. "This is a huge advertising opportunity for Chocolate Love and Bean in Love. You'll be missing out if everyone is walking around in shirts with my name on it."

"I'm positive. I have the storefront everyday screaming my name. This is your chance to make a big splash."

"Thank you, Nikki," Adelle said, grinning and moving in for a hug.

Nikki accepted a hug from Adelle cheerfully. For years I'd watched these two be at odds with each other. Once they got in a fight over a Barbie doll that ended so poorly I thought the house would implode. Now there was finally peace.

"Oh, Kelly, before I forget, someone left something for you." Immanuel passed me a sealed white envelope as Nikki and Adelle turned to leave.

I frowned, wondering what this could possibly be. It reminded me of the note Mike had left on my car asking me to meet him at Big Rock Library.

"Someone dropped this off?" I asked.

Nikki and Adelle were already stepping out of the truck babbling away about All Sweets Network. Something about the best television angle to shoot the truck and the store.

"Yeah, some kid dropped it off," he said.

"Really?" I asked, ripping open the seal. "A young kid?"

"Maybe ten?"

The paper inside was folded in three, just like the flyer I'd found under the door this morning. The first thing that registered was the fact that the writing was also typed, just as the note this morning.

Life isn't the same when your family is destroyed. Enjoy yours while you still can.

The paper shook in my hands. My heart beat faster as I slowly folded the paper back up and stuck it into the envelope. What the hell was happening here?

"Immanuel? Can you tell me more about the kid?" I managed.

"Are you okay? Is something wrong?" Immanuel asked,

probably picking up on the fact that I was spiraling into a panic.

"Was it a girl or boy? Are you sure it wasn't a woman?" I asked, thinking about the two women that Adelle had been sure had left the notes. Would they have sent one of their kids? Why would they come after me right now? This made no sense. Why were they threatening my well-being just because they were jealous that Adelle was launching her own business? No, that angle was wrong. This was someone else.

"It was a young boy, sandy blond hair. It's the boy that works at the store," Immanuel said quickly. "He had on an Adelle's shirt. Stands about this tall," he said, placing his hand up near his chest.

"Works in the store?" I questioned. What young boy did Nikki have working in the store?

All of a sudden it clicked. Frank, Adelle's oldest son. Was he sending me some kind of secret message? Why?

Adelle and Nikki stood on the steps leading out of the truck. They jabbered away, oblivious to my internal turmoil.

"Kelly, come on. We want to show you the giveaways we put together. Wait, what's wrong?" Nikki asked, regarding me with a raised eyebrow. Her eyes fell to the envelope in my hand.

Working hard to readjust my face, I folded the envelope and stuck it in the back pocket of my jeans.

"Nothing, just a note from Jack. He left it for me when he swung by earlier."

"He was here already? Why didn't he stop in and say hello?" she asked.

I shrugged my shoulders, watching Adelle closely for some kind of sign that she knew what was going on. Nothing. Just that same look of pure glee and excitement she'd been carrying since everything started coming together. My guess was she had no idea about the envelope or the notes. So, why was her son involved? Could Mike have asked Frank to deliver it? That didn't make any sense. Mike had told me himself a few days ago that he wanted to turn himself in.

"Are the kids here, Adelle?" I asked, trying to sound casual and motioning for us to start walking toward Chocolate Love.

"We kept Craig home with a sitter. It's too much. But Frank and Cindy are here. They're so excited. Come on. Let's go inside. They're dying to see you," she said, leading the way.

Walking past the toy soldiers, I chuckled a bit and nudged Nikki.

"What in the world possessed you to get those?" I laughed.

"Hey, it's All Sweets Network. I wanted to pull out all the stops so that they would come back next year."

"They're kind of freaky. They're not going to come to life are they?" I teased, glancing up at one of the wooden soldiers standing at least twenty feet high in the courtyard in front of the store. I had to admit, they were a nice touch, extremely festive and eye-catching, yet for some reason a bit intimidating. Perhaps it was just my fear of inanimate dolls. The creepy notes had also put me on edge. My imagination was running wild.

"Let's hope not," Nikki laughed. "I'm not paying for any extra effects like that. But that's a great idea for next year."

"No!" I laughed.

The buzz inside the store was like walking into a bee hive. Workers inside the store were coming in and out of the back kitchens, loading the shelves with goodies, and passing out tee-shirts for others that had come to march in the parade or volunteer. The store was already so crowded with customers and workers that we were barely able to walk.

"Wow, this place is packed," I said, feeling in my back pocket for the envelope. "Where are Mom and Dad and the kids?" I asked as nonchalant as I could.

"They're all upstairs in the apartment. Mike's up there with them," Adelle said.

"Okay, I'm just going to run up and say hello," I said, heading in the direction of the staircase leading to the second floor.

"Alright, I'm heading to the kitchen. I just remembered one small detail we may have forgotten. Do you want a coffee, Kelly?" Nikki asked.

"Oh, you know it," I said, always in the mood for a caffeine burst.

"Okay, I'll send one up. If anyone wants one upstairs, text me. I'll send them up with someone in a few minutes," she said, folding her body into the sea of people. She smiled and greeted loyal customers and friends. Adelle followed her and suddenly I was standing alone on the staircase.

I watched them go and felt a pit in my stomach begin to form. What were these stupid notes? It was Mike's style to do something like this, considering he'd done exactly this when he wanted to speak to me at Big Rock Library. But why would he threaten me through secret letters now? Why, when he'd been the one to bring the truth to light and offer to turn himself in? It just made no sense.

Turning, I bolted up the staircase to my old apartment.

Knocking lightly to give everyone a heads up, I pushed the door open and was greeted by a warm scene. Mom and Dad had chairs set up facing the front window and were watching the festivities forming below. They looked warm and cozy here on their little perch overlooking the town of Geneva. For a brief second, I imagined a future where they lived back in town, surrounded by grandchildren and family, perhaps even living here in the apartment above Chocolate Love during their golden years. They'd be right amongst the hustle and bustle of the store and under the constant watchful eye of Nikki and Adelle as they worked in the store. It could be perfect, except for the stairs. That might be a deal breaker.

"Aunt Kelly!" Cindy said, jumping down from the chair and bolting in my direction. "Are you going to watch the parade from up here, too?"

"I'm not sure, but I think so. I just have to see where your mommy needs me," I said, wrapping her into my arms.

Frank came up to me with a huge smile on his face. He bear hugged me and pointed down at his shirt.

"Look! I got to wear the shirt for Mom's new company. And she said I get to help make the donuts and pass them out!" he said, his voice bellowing proudly.

Mom and Dad sat in their chairs watching us with big smiles on their faces. With the announcement that Franklin Ford had been caught, they were visibly more relaxed and at ease. Mom's usual underlying look of worry remained, but she seemed just a bit more relaxed. Almost as though she'd had a glass of wine and was able to chill out a bit.

"Hey, Kelly," Mike called from the kitchen. He was prepping some kind of platter with treats and drinks for the parade. "Looks like things are going well down there. Thanks so much for helping Adelle out with the truck this morning. She's so much happier with this new truck. Did you see the logo? So much better."

I watched Mike closely, trying to read some register of guilt or regret for sending me those horrible little threats. Either I didn't know him as well as I'd thought, and he was a really good actor, or he had nothing to do with them. I wasn't able to pick up anything other than excitement.

I let the kids pull me around, showing me this and that until they settled down a bit. When I saw my window, I took it.

"Mike, can I show you something in the back bedroom? I think a window is stuck," I said.

"Of course," he said, standing up from the chair he'd plopped down in once the snacks were served.

My father continued to watch out the windows, but Mom turned and gave me a funny look. Her mouth fell down slightly in a scowl, and once again, that look of anxiety crossed her face. I flashed her a smile, which she quickly returned, covering up anything that I'd just seen a moment before.

We turned and headed into the bedroom just off the living room. I slanted the door so that it would close as much as possible without having to actually be shut. I didn't want to make it look obvious that I wanted to get a private moment with Mike.

"You don't have to do this, Mike," I whispered.

"What?" he asked, raising an eyebrow.

"I figured out a way. We're not going to go through with it," I said. "I'm not destroying your family over this. You can stop sending me the notes."

"Notes?" he said, widening his eyes. "What notes? You mean the one I left you on the car?

"I know you sent Frank to give me a note this afternoon. Mike, I know what you are putting at risk by turning yourself in, and I'm telling you, we can end this by doing it a different way."

I reached behind me and started to unfold the envelope I'd tucked in my back pocket.

"We can still do the right thing, but not necessarily the way we discussed it. I think that way is just, well, dumb, considering all the extenuating circumstances."

The sheet was now open and in my trembling hands.

Mike reached down and mouthed the words on the sheet slowly.

He shook his head and looked up at me.

"Kelly, what is this?" he questioned.

All at once I knew with utmost certainty that I'd gone down the wrong path and pursued the wrong suspect. Mike had not sent the notes.

Chapter 44

"I don't really know," I mumbled, feeling foolish and scared at the same time.

"Hey, guys," Jack said, peeking his head into the doorway. Something must have registered on my face because his smile fell immediately. My hand holding the note dropped to my side a little too quickly.

"Am I interrupting something?" Jack asked, staying in the doorway.

"Nope, not at all. I was just sharing some last minute instructions from Adelle about the food truck," I said, trying to cover the strain I was feeling at the moment. I had this weird sensation that I was sitting on a bomb that was about to explode, trying to buy time. If I could just keep it from exploding for a few more hours, everything would be okay. It just needed to be contained until Adelle's launch was over.

"Anything I should know?" Jack asked, stepping further into the room. I noticed for the first time that he was wearing a shirt that read, "Adelle's."

"Nope, we've got it covered," I said sharply, making our meeting even more suspicious looking.

"Okay," Jack said slowly. "I'll just go sit with your parents for a bit."

"I think I've got it, Kelly. I'll join you, Jack," Mike said, clearly trying to keep this awkward situation from getting more uncomfortable. Jack turned to go and Mike began to follow. I wondered if Jack would confront Mike and Adelle tonight about telling me about Callie. This would not be the right time to do it. I hoped Jack would be able to sense that.

Before Mike left, he turned and said closely to my face, "Are we in danger here, Kelly?"

I shook my head no, mainly because I didn't know what else to do.

"Are you in danger?" Mike asked, refining his question.

"I don't know," I said truthfully.

"Show Jack that note. He needs to see it," he said. "Jack is probably the only one with a clear head on his shoulder at the moment. The rest of us are too distracted. We'll talk more about my situation later. I'm determined to do the right thing, Kelly. I've been working around this for years and I'm done. I don't want Steve to have something over my head anymore."

Mike turned quickly and left me alone in the bedroom, more confused than ever.

I stood in the room gathering my thoughts, trying to buy some time to put on the proper cheery face. I couldn't let them see what was happening inside of me right now. The right thing to do would be to call Detective Pavlik immediately and tell him what was happening. Face this head on. I was receiving threatening notes.

It couldn't possibly be Adelle's son, Frank, behind all of this. I needed to ask him in an off-hand casual way what was happening, but I didn't want it to be in front of anyone.

While I was trying to figure out how to do this, I noticed for the first time Mom's purse sitting atop the bed I used to sleep on when I lived here. A white envelope sticking out of her suede bag caught my attention. No. It couldn't be possible.

Without a moment's hesitation, I pulled the envelope from her bag. The first thing I noticed was that it was unopened.

I contemplated ripping it open right then and there. If this was what I thought it was, Mom was still in blissful naiveté. I could protect her. It would be a major violation of her privacy, but at this point, I didn't care. Something was happening.

"Are you going to join us?" Jack said, peeking his head back into the room.

Swiftly and efficiently, I turned my back, keeping the envelope hidden behind me.

"Yes, of course," I said, shooting him a radiant smile.

"Kelly, are you okay?" Jack asked, coming through the doorway and walking up to be close to me. I dropped the envelope on the bed behind me and moved closer to him to keep him distracted. "You're acting very funny today. Did you get enough sleep?"

"Probably not," I said, accepting the easy excuse he'd laid out for me. "Too much coffee and too little sleep. And I'm a bit nervous for Adelle. This is all so exciting."

"Where are you stationed tonight?" he asked, pulling me closer to him and resting his forehead on mine.

"I think Nikki wants me in the parade. How about you?" I asked, breathing in the comforting smell of Jack.

"Wherever you are," he said. "Tonight is going to be great."

I smiled up at him and noticed for the first time that he had an extra glint in his eye.

"Because today was great," he said, widening his smile.

"What do you mean?" I asked, raising an eyebrow.

I hadn't seen Jack all day. We'd been like passing ships. He had meetings, and I'd pretty much slept the day away.

"I had a meeting today with my attorney. I think we're finally going to get my divorce resolved. Everything will be wrapped up so that we," he said, leaning in to kiss me quick.

"Can get," another kiss.

"Married," he said, cupping my face in his hands and kissing me again.

Though the news was thrilling, I was too distracted by the envelope behind me on the bed to fully appreciate it. My reaction was probably not what Jack was seeking.

"Wow, that's great," I said, smiling and kissing him back.

"Wow, that's great?" Jack said, imitating my blasé reaction. I didn't mean for it to be, but even I knew my enthusiasm level was rather pathetic.

"I'm thrilled, Jack. I'm sorry. I'm just very distracted," I said, releasing a breath and trying my best to be present with him in the moment.

"What happened? What changed?" I asked.

"I'll tell you more about it later, but the bottom line is my attorney in London really came through," he said, smoothing my cheek with his thumb.

"How?" I asked.

Jack tipped his head to the side and gave a little smirk.

"We were able to locate Callie through a top notch private detective my attorney knows. We finally found her at some crazy hippie compound she lives at now. That's why we couldn't find her. She goes by the name Flower now, if you can believe it. Anyway, we by-passed her attorney and contacted her directly," Jack said.

"What? Why would you do that?" I questioned.

"Because it all came down to the fact that Callie, or rather, Flower, had not signed a piece of paper that we all mistakenly thought she had. That was all that was left to complete the deal. So, we asked her to do it, and she said yes. It should be wrapped up by the end of the week," he said. "She said she's changed," Jack said, rolling his eyes. "She told me she was happy to hear from me and was glad I called her directly rather than alert her snake of an attorney of her whereabouts. I guess she still owes him some money and she," Jack put his fingers up in the air to make quotes. "no longer uses traditional communist money, as she calls it. She lives off the land now."

This just seemed way too easy to me.

"But, she's a stalker? She's your stalker. Are you two even allowed to speak?"

"Well, she can't contact me directly. But the way the Order of Protection is drawn up, I can contact her. Kelly, I can't believe I'm saying this, but she sounds as though she has moved on with her life. And, I've saved the best for last. She has a mutual interest in getting everything dissolved. Can you believe she told me she's getting married?" Jack said, releasing me slightly and looking over my shoulder.

I worried that he spotted the envelope and was going to ask about it. But instead, his eyes remained a bit glazed over and he said, "I feel really bad for this next guy, but I guess it's really not my problem anymore, right?"

"Right," I said, watching him closely. I'd never met Callie. Never saw the two of them together. Never witnessed firsthand any of her infamous stalking incidents, but in my opinion, this was all too easy. How could a person go from the intense, neurotic behavior that a stalker demonstrates to, "Never mind, I'm getting married again and I'll leave you alone and let you go forever." This just didn't feel right.

My phone beeped in my back pocket alerting me to a text.

"One second," I said, reaching for my phone. It read:

Get down here immediately. We have a problem.

"Jack, I have to go. Nikki needs me downstairs. Can we talk more later?"

"Kelly, we're still on, right?" Jack asked suddenly, raising a teasing eyebrow and tilting his head at me. "Me, you, a ring, a dress, an altar?"

"Jack, you couldn't get rid of me now if you tried," I said, pulling him close to me to plant a kiss on him. I pulled away abruptly looking up at his face and laughing. "Wait, that's not the right thing to say to someone who has had a stalker, is it?" I laughed, trying to make light of the whole situation. This was great news, but I couldn't focus on it right now.

"Ha ha," Jack said sarcastically, reaching down to kiss me again. When he pulled away, he turned and bounced to the door, appearing light and breezy.

Was it possible? Really? All he had been through with Callie and now it was just over? I half thought of calling him back into the room to show him the letter, but dismissed the idea. Later. There would be time later. As soon as the parade was over, I was going to lay this on him, and we were heading to the police.

Reaching back and grabbing the envelope from the bed, I quickly left the room and headed to the door.

"I'll be right back. Nikki needs me downstairs." I glanced down at my watch noting that the time was going quickly. The parade was due to start in thirty minutes and through the apartment windows, I could see the streets were filling up quickly with tons of people.

My eyes met Mom's, the only one who turned to watch me go. Everyone else was too distracted by the scene developing outside. There was no way she could have known that I took the envelope. It was now safely tucked into my back pocket, hidden from her watchful eyes.

I waved to her and turned to leave the room before she could question me. From the way her eyes squinted at me, I could tell she knew something was up. She was ready to pounce with questions I didn't have answers for. Later. We'd deal with it all later.

Halfway down the stairs, I stopped. This was probably going to be my only private moment for the next couple of hours. I reached in my back pocket and pulled out the envelope. Ripping it open, I pulled an identical piece of paper from the one that had been left for me. Even the font was the same. The only thing that was different was the message.

Watching your family be humiliated and fall apart is like having your soul burn to pieces. Can you imagine what that would feel like?

Chapter 45

"What the hell?" I whispered, staring down at the note.

"What the hell, indeed," Nikki said, standing at the base of the stairs, grasping onto the arm rail for support. For the first time in a long time, she looked like an overwhelmed, tired pregnant person. "Did you spot them from the window?"

"Who?" I asked, folding the paper up quickly and stuffing it in my back pocket. If I could have eaten it, I would have, but I needed the paper for later, as evidence.

"I knew they would pull something, but this is beyond."

I smiled weakly, trying to appear as though I knew what she was talking about.

"What's going on? What was that paper?" Nikki asked, picking up quickly on my inability to focus on her and probably the freaked out look in my eye.

"Another bill," I said quickly. "I'll tell you about it later. I can't believe they're still trying to make me pay," I said, throwing out my best disgruntled sigh.

"So, you didn't see them?" Nikki asked, distracted enough to not investigate my story.

"Who?" I asked, genuinely confused.

Nikki stood up straight and motioned me to come with her. I followed, my eyes scanning the crowd that had filled the store, wondering if my mysterious note dropper was here.

Nikki greeted guests as she made her way through the crowd to the front door. I could hear little murmurs and heightened talk about "All Sweets Network" and "Adelle's Pastries." Apparently, they were a hit. Nikki and Adelle's marketing plans had worked. The town was abuzz with excitement.

"Look," Nikki said, pointing out to the crowd once we'd reached the front porch of Chocolate Love.

I tried to follow where Nikki was pointing. The street was absolutely bursting with people at this point. Children squealed with joy, holding tightly onto their parents' hands, pointing up at the soldiers. The sound of Christmas music blasted from speakers in front of the store, and the parade floats and participants were lining up on Third Street, getting ready to go. I was happy to see that the majority of people were holding donuts or shoveling them in their mouths and smiling. The smell of the fried dough made it a picture perfect scene. As the sky darkened around us, it felt like a scene right out of a Norman Rockwell painting.

"What? It all looks great," I said. What could possibly be upsetting her in this picture perfect scene she had helped create? What more could Nikki ask for?

"Really? You don't see them?" Nikki said again, sarcasm filling her voice. "The two luscious ladies who stick out like a sore thumb."

I sucked air in when my searching eyes finally fell upon what Nikki was directing me to.

"No, they didn't" I croaked out.

Adelle's mean girls, Kim Lakes and Brandi Morgan, stood on the front lawn just off to the side of the donut truck, smiling and waving at people like they were being presented as contestants in a beauty pageant. They were wearing the toy soldier costumes Nikki had asked them to, but they looked nothing like what she had passed onto them. The legs were cut into short shorts that barely covered their butt cheeks, and the jackets were cut so low, I could see cleavage from where I was standing. They had made sparkly sashes that read, "President" and "Vice President." They wore them across their chest proudly and waved to people.

"Aren't they cold?" I questioned, my mind immediately jumping to that.

"No worries. It's all falling into my master plan. Mayor Grant has final approval over all floats and participants. The second he lays eyes on them, they're out of here. He'll kick them out. And there's no time for them to offer to change. This is going to really upset him. They're new in town. They don't know his reputation for being conservative. Remember when he made the cheerleaders wear pants under their skirts? That was nothing compared to this," she said, smiling.

"Was this your plan the whole time?" I asked, not that surprised.

"Kind of. Like I said, I was expecting something, but this is just too easy. I just hope he doesn't kick out the whole Junior League. That would not be in my plan. I like those ladies. If they're smart though, the moment they hear about what Kim and Brandi pulled and what they risked, they'll kick them out of the club for good. In fact, I'm going to talk to some of the ladies I know well in the club and push for that. This is ridiculous," Nikki said.

"Where is Adelle? Has she seen this yet?"

Nikki pointed a finger to a bright light on the other side of the donut truck. Adelle was standing with her back to the truck under a boatload of lights with a camera pointed at her.

"She's being interviewed by All Sweets Network. Oh no, look at the angle of the camera. Do you think it's picking up the hussies? Come on, we have to move them," she said, making a beeline for the girls.

I ran after her, doing my best to keep my mind on the matter at hand. It was hard to not be distracted by the note in my back pocket.

"Hi, ladies," Nikki said, completely disguising any negativity.

"Hi, Nikki!" Kim and Brandi sang in unison, all bubbles and

light.

"So, you ladies look amazing," Nikki said, without even a hint of sarcasm.

"We thought we would just spice things up a bit. Hope that's okay, Nikki," Kim cooed, flashing Nikki a brilliant smile. I imagined what she really wanted to say was something along the lines of, "You can't tell me what to do, Nikki. See!"

"Oh, of course," Nikki said.

"Hope it's okay we cut off the legs," Brandi spoke up. "It's sexier and flashier this way."

"I agree," Nikki said, shaking her head up and down.

"We didn't want to get into this in front of Adelle, Nikki, but we really need to spice things up at Junior League. Our numbers are way down. The fire is really gone from the club. People are leaving in droves," Kim said in a fake, sympathetic way.

They're probably leaving in droves because of people like you, I thought.

"We thought we'd use the parade as an opportunity to attract new blood. You know, young, hip blood. People who have the energy to do things for the community," Kim smiled, flashing her whitened teeth at Nikki.

Not old people like my sister, was what she was implying. Adelle was not that old. She was in her mid-thirties. Why were these witches digging in on that so much? Get a clue.

"Do they have to have a certain cup size to be admitted?" I mumbled, unable to hold back.

Nikki nudged me.

"Plus, in these outfits, it helps to promote my husband's business," Kim said.

"And what business is that again?" Nikki asked.

"Oh, you don't know? He's the owner of Muscle," she said proudly, referring to a nationwide chain of gyms that seemed to be everywhere.

"Oh, that's right," Nikki said.

Kim looked a little annoyed that Nikki didn't remember this, but moved on.

"So, they see the hot bodies that we're sporting, and they know we're sculpted to perfection at Muscle," she laughed.

And probably at your plastic surgeon's office based on the looks of those humongous breasts.

I just couldn't see how these ladies could be behind the threatening notes that were being left for me today. They seemed just too, well, vapid and shallow. The notes that I'd received had a deeper feeling of revenge. And the thought of these two princesses coming near a rat and leaving it at my back door was not likely.

"You look great! I'm sure you'll attract a lot of new recruits today," Nikki clapped. "All you need to do is go sign in at the desk over there with Mayor Grant. He'll give you your raffle number as well. All participants in the parade are going to be eligible for a big spa package."

"Really?" the ladies asked in unison.

It was the first genuine, non-rehearsed reaction I'd seen from them all day. This was the first time I'd heard this news. Something told me Nikki was embellishing a bit to guarantee Kim and Brandi would head over to the table.

At that moment, Frank appeared next to me, and I had other things to worry about. I leaned down and pulled the envelope from my back pocket.

"Aunt Kelly, Dad sent me out here to see how things were going and to see if you needed help. He said something about steering the cameras away from those women," Frank said, giving the hussies a once over. He seemed genuinely confused by their get-ups, but not that interested.

"And Mom said I could have another donut," he said, pointing to the food truck. I got the feeling he wanted me to help him initiate his donut retrieval.

"Frank, did you leave me this note earlier?" I asked, trying to sound as casual as possible.

Nikki babbled on about the spa package behind me. I ignored them and watched Frank closely. My questions didn't strike a nerve at all. He met my eyes, no problem and said, "Oh yeah. Some lady left it at the truck for you. She asked me to give it to you. And one for Grandma."

Some lady?

"Someone you knew?" I asked, looking around. The lights from the television crew were abruptly turned off and Adelle was shaking someone's hand. Her interview must have been wrapping up. The crew started to head in our direction, which would mean they would probably spot the hussies very soon.

"What did she look like?" I asked, feeling a morsel of fear.

At that same moment, I spotted Diane Nosely being wheeled up the sidewalk in the direction of Chocolate Love. She had a camera crew walking along behind her and was barking out orders and pointing her finger. When she spotted me, she waved, as though we were old friends reconnecting after a long time apart.

"Was she in a wheelchair, by any chance?" I asked.

"No, she's right over there," Frank said, pointing a little finger in the direction of the food truck.

BOOM!

Before I could look, a loud explosive sound obliterated the joyful buzz in the air. The sound of glass breaking instinctively made me shut my eyes and scream. When I reopened my eyes, it registered that Frank was tight to my chest, clinging on for dear life.

There was screaming all around me and smoke everywhere, like I'd stepped into Armageddon. The sound of Nikki screaming got me back into focus quickly.

"Kelly, what happened? Kelly!" I heard Nikki yelling through the smoke. Frank was in my arms, not making a sound. I was with it enough to register that somehow we were still standing in an upright position. I patted Frank all over his body searching for blood or limbs out of place but felt nothing other than a normal child's body shaking in fear beneath my hands. I pulled his head close to mine with both hands and said, "Frank, you're okay. We're going to be okay," I said, trying my best to sound comforting.

"What happened?" he sounded terrified, but not in pain. "Where's Mom?"

"Kelly," Nikki screamed, grabbing onto my back. She was standing as well, which I took to be a good sign.

"We're okay. You're okay?" I asked, keeping my grip on Frank, but reaching for Nikki.

"Was that a bomb?" I asked.

"I don't know, but I can't see anything. Where's Adelle? Can you see her?" Nikki cried, uncharacteristically panicked sounding.

I did my best to squint, desperately trying to spot my sister. The smoke kept me from seeing very far. I saw people roaming around, dazed and screaming. There was so much screaming.

"The truck!" Nikki yelled out. "The food truck is on fire!"

Chapter 46

People were running in all directions, and smoke was pouring out of the truck at a rapid speed. Even through the smoke, I could tell that the front windows had been blown out. Nikki, Frank, and I huddled together, watching. It was Frank that broke our huddle first as he ran for the truck.

"Mom!" he screamed.

"Wait," I screamed out in haste as I released Nikki and took off in the direction of Frank.

"Kelly, Adelle's not in the truck, remember?" Nikki yelled at me. She grabbed onto my shirt and was running behind me. "She was being interviewed outside of the truck."

"Frank!" I screamed out in a panic as I watched him disappear into the sea of people that filled the space between me and the food truck.

I was distracted by the sound of glass breaking and another explosion this time coming from the direction of Chocolate Love.

The explosion momentarily halted Frank in his tracks. I took that moment to grab him by the shoulders and pull him to me.

"She's not in the truck, Frank," I yelled at him. "Stay with me. We'll find her."

People were knocking into us as they ran out of and away from the food truck, desperate to escape the smoke that kept pouring out. I worried about Nikki getting knocked down and injuring the baby. In this moment of mania, manners ceased to exist. Fear seemed to eliminate all rules of society, the most important to me being, don't knock over a pregnant lady.

"Look out," Kim Lakes yelled, as she pushed Nikki out of the way with brute strength. If this were any other moment, I would make light of the fact that maybe Muscle really was doing the job. Apparently Kim had enough muscle to knock Nikki into Frank, which sent him straight down to the ground.

"Hey," I said, pushing Brandi, who followed closely behind Kim. My shove barely registered with Brandi. She pressed on toward the street to get away from the explosion, kicking a dog in her way.

Nikki's fingers raked down my back as she grabbed for me.

"Oh no!" she screamed.

I braced myself for another explosion, pulling Frank up from the ground.

"It's Chocolate Love! Kelly, look!" Nikki yelled.

The smoke from the initial blast in the truck was waning a bit, and I was able to see what Nikki was pointing to. The store was starting to glow a sickly orange/pink.

"It's on fire! Look at the front window," she screamed.

Right at that moment, Adelle slammed into us.

"The store!" she screamed right in my face. "They're all upstairs!"

"Nikki, get Frank as far away from here as possible," Adelle barked. Frank had grabbed onto her the second she appeared. She disentangled him from her arms and shoved him at Nikki.

"Go across the street and call 911. Now! Now!" Adelle yelled like a wild banshee.

"Mom and Dad!" Nikki whimpered, pointing up to the apartment window. Even through the smoke, I could make out their frames plastered to the windows looking out.

Adelle turned Nikki quickly in the direction of the street and screamed in her ear, "Go! Now!"

Adelle grabbed my hand and we ran in the direction of the store, fighting through the crowd of people that was streaming out in a mad panic. Adults had children slung over their shoulders in a fireman hold and others assisted elderly customers who looked around frantically from side to side. The fire appeared to be maintained on the first floor, but by the way the light was growing, my fear was it was moving fast. My family probably didn't even realize the danger they were in. If I had to guess, I bet Jack and Mike probably told my parents, as well as Cindy, to stay put while they ran down to look for us when they heard the first explosion.

The crowd of people leaving Chocolate Love blocked us from being able to get in, regardless of how much we both screamed for people to get out of our way.

"Move! Move!" Adelle kept yelling.

"There are people upstairs!" I tried yelling in vain. It was useless. Everyone was in a panic, trying to get as far away from the shop and the truck. Who could blame them? The town was scattered in desperate search of their loved ones and family members. It was dark now and the screaming and smoke were just adding to the confusion. This was a disaster. I didn't even want to think about how many people were hurt tonight.

"We have to go to the back," Adelle said, latching onto my hand so hard I could feel her finger nails digging into my skin.

Somehow we made it to the back door and ran into Miguel standing at the stairs, directing people out to safety.

"We got them all out, I think," Miguel yelled to us at the bottom of the stairs. "This is the last of them."

"Miguel, the kids. Mom and Dad, they're upstairs," Adelle screamed.

Miguel didn't hesitate. He turned and disappeared into the store.

"Lookout!" Adelle screamed at the last two employees coming

out the back door.

We ran in and were immediately hit by a blast of smoke. The sound of sirens filled the air, giving me hope that we would have help soon. But would it be soon enough? We pressed on into the store. Dad's weak heart. Surely by now they would have registered that something was wrong. They'd be able to smell the smoke. I fought to keep from sobbing at the thought of Mom and Dad huddled together upstairs with Cindy, not knowing what to do. I hoped that Jack and Mike had stayed with them, but that would mean their lives were at risk. I didn't know what to pray for.

Adelle covered her mouth and nose with her shirt and directed me to do the same. The store was ablaze now, but that didn't seem to faze Adelle. She ran through the kitchen toward the front door to get to the staircase

Miguel ran into her on his return from the front of the store.

"We can't go through that way. The fire is completely blocking the staircase," he yelled through his shirt.

"No! No, we have to. We have to get them out!" she screamed back at him. All of us were coughing now, and the smoke was building so quick it was getting tough to see.

"No, we won't make it. We'll get them out the window," he said, pushing her.

"No!" Adelle insisted. "That will take too long. It won't work. We have to get them."

She pushed past him and forced herself forward.

"Adelle!" I screamed, as I watched her helplessly disappear into the smoke.

"Don't, Kelly, it's too risky." Miguel yelled at me, pushing me backwards to the back door.

Before I could protest, two hands latched onto my back and pulled me from behind back down the hallway. I struggled to break free, but in an instant, more hands were on me, overpowering me.

"No," I yelled out, coughing and fighting.

The next thing I knew I was outside of the building, upside down over someone's shoulders. I was able to lift my head to see the sight of a large ladder reaching up to my old bedroom window of Chocolate Love. I saw Mom and Dad making their way slowly down the ladder, assisted by men in large spacesuit looking outfits. My body shook in a fit of coughing that I couldn't seem to control.

"Down," I coughed out, trying to pump my fist into the back of the large spacesuit wearing man carrying me further and further away from Chocolate Love.

He did not respond to me, but continued at a hurried pace away from the building. My body spasmed again in coughs, but I managed to look up and see Cindy getting passed out the window by Jack. What about Adelle?

"Down," I banged again, trying to demand a release so I could go back and pull Adelle out. The thought of her running into the black smoke gave me a shiver of fear. Both of my sisters were just too brave for their own good. What if Adelle didn't make it out of this one? I couldn't, and didn't, want to think of a life without them.

"Ma'am, stop fighting. You're only making this harder," the fireman barked at me.

I wanted to explain that Adelle had run back in. What if no one else knew that? What if Miguel was unable to tell them? They had to know.

Suddenly I was being placed in a big, white truck of some sort where people buzzed around me like bees. Something large was placed over my face and the relief was instant.

"Ma'am, we're going to give you some oxygen," I heard a man's voice say kindly. He was seated very close to me. So much so, that I could count the number of freckles on his face. I coughed again, and started to try and tell him about Adelle. He nodded at me as though he were listening, but made no attempt to rectify the situation. Frustrated, I started to pull the mask off and get up, determined to go back on my own.

The movement sent me into another coughing spasm that stopped me in my tracks.

"Just sit back down. They'll get everyone out. My name is Nathan. I'm going to help you out today," he said, holding me down firmly on the bed and attaching something to my arm.

"They know what they're doing. They'll get everyone out. Trust me, I've been doing this for a long time. I've seen a lot of fires and they always get them out," Nathan said again kindly.

Yeah, but do they get them out alive? I wanted to ask.

Little lines around his eyes registered as I watched him closely, giving me comfort. Perhaps he had been doing this a long time. At first glance, his freckles had me thinking he was a young kid.

Probably in response to the river of tears that started to flow down my face, he stopped the busy work of lining wires this way and that and looked me square in the eye.

"You inhaled too much smoke. In a few minutes, you'll be feeling much better. Just keep coughing it out and taking in the oxygen. Everything is going to be okay. We got here very early. We were on alert because of the parade. Everyone is going to be okay," he soothed, his voice calm and professional.

My whole life was in that store. My sister, my parents, my niece, my brother-in-law, and my Jack. And here I sat, helpless and strapped to a gurney.

"Kelly!" I heard Nikki yelling from somewhere outside.

My head popped up, and my eyes searched widely around for her. The excitement brought up another round of intense coughing, leaving me gasping for air. Nathan pushed me forcibly this time back onto the stretcher and did something to the mask covering my face. Unable to move, I simply lifted my right arm and moved it frantically to attract Nikki's attention.

Nikki's form appeared by the back door. Without asking permission, she was pushing her way inside, snapping at the two other paramedics that were trying to stop her.

"That's my sister, get out of the way," she said, nudging them out of the way with her elbows.

They both looked at me, and I nodded my head frantically for them to let her in.

"You're okay," Nikki said, racing like a demon toward me. "I was so scared," she said, pulling at me and bursting into tears. As happy as I was to see her, my spasms hurt so bad I couldn't hug her. My body shook and my chest felt like it would burst.

"Just calm down, Kelly. You have to try and calm down," Nathan said, his voice much deeper than it was a few moments ago.

"Ma'am, give her a second," Nathan barked at Nikki.

Nikki moved away and sat across from me, silenced by Nathan's orders.

I stared up at the ceiling and fought to calm down. I wouldn't get any answers if I coughed myself to death. I needed to let the oxygen do its work. Finally after what felt like an eternity, my hands pulled at the mask.

"What's wrong? What?" Nikki asked, coming close to me.

I pulled my hand up to the huge mask to pull it off, so I could speak better.

"Adelle?" I coughed out. I pointed my finger up in the air to signal the upstairs floor of Chocolate Love. I didn't have the strength to start rattling off all the names of our family that was stuck in the fire. I coughed and coughed, watching her with frantic eyes for an answer.

Nikki burst into tears again and pulled my hand into hers. "Everyone," she managed through tears. "They got everyone. They're all okay," she said, sobbing, but smiling. Blessed relief pulsed through my blood, giving my body exactly what it needed to recover. I started to cry happy tears, interrupting the flow of oxygen and sending me into another coughing fit.

"Okay, you have to wait outside now, please," Nathan said kindly but firmly to Nikki.

She immediately released my hand and shouted back to me on her way out, "Adelle is being treated for smoke inhalation as well, but they got her out right after you. She's okay."

Finally, the oxygen took full effect, and my lungs stopped the spasms. Although I had a million more questions, the main one was answered. I laid my head back down on the gurney and let my body relax finally.

"See, Kelly," Nathan smiled down at me. "I told you they'd get everybody out."

I smiled up at him, allowing tears of gratitude to run down my face.

Chapter 47

Thirty minutes later, I sat wrapped in a blanket on the edge of an ambulance parked just off Third Street to the side of Chocolate Love, watching as the firemen overhauled what was left of the store. The building was still standing, but the dark cavernous opening that was once the first floor of Chocolate Love revealed the mass destruction caused by the fire. All of the glass from the beautiful front windows was now being raked up on the front lawn by the firemen who worked tirelessly to clean up the mess. The sound of wood splintering and dry wall falling filled the air as the firemen used their axes and chainsaws to knock out loose debris, while ensuring fire wasn't smoldering beneath. Nikki's store was now a ruined soggy mess. I couldn't imagine how it could possibly be recovered. The whole thing would probably have to be torn down.

Jack sat on one side of me, his arm wrapped around my shoulders. Nikki was on the other side, releasing heavy sighs every few minutes.

"Well, thank God for insurance," she said glumly, rubbing at her belly in slow, rhythmic motions.

"I just can't believe it," Jack said. "What could have caused this?"

Nikki shook her head and I remained silent, scared to say what I was thinking.

"What I can't get over is why the truck is not that damaged? Wasn't the initial explosion in the truck?" Nikki asked. "We were standing right there, right Kelly? Am I crazy or was there a huge explosion in the truck? Look at it," Nikki said, pointing to the food truck still parked on Third Street in front of the store.

"It sure seemed like it," I said, happy to have found my voice again. My lungs had fully recovered, and I felt back to my old self.

There had been a lot of movement in and out of the food truck by the police and fire department, but little was being said. My eyes searched constantly for Detective Pavlik, knowing he would give us the story.

"I saw someone take something out of it, right after Adelle left. They carried it out in some sort of bag," Jack said, pointing in the direction of the truck.

Adelle had been sent to the hospital for observation because she was in a little worse shape than me, having been exposed to more smoke. I wasn't that worried about her, considering all reports about her condition were coming back very positive.

Mike had gone with her to the hospital. Mom, Dad, and the kids had been sent home to be cleaned, changed and probably locked away until this was all settled. Knowing Adelle, she would put those kids on lockdown for a while.

"But there were no flames in the truck. Maybe it was a diversion," Jack suggested, sounding grave.

"Piper from the kitchen swears someone threw something on fire through the front window of the store," Nikki said, finally revealing what I'd assumed. Someone did this on purpose. I gulped, swallowing hard. "The police aren't saying anything though. They're very quiet. Something is up."

My head hurt, thinking of the notes I'd been getting. The note Mom got that I took from her purse.

"I didn't tell you guys something earlier," I said quietly.

"Kelly, Nikki, here you are," Detective Pavlik said, coming around the ambulance.

"Oh, are we glad to see you," Nikki said, standing up to hug him. He unabashedly engulfed her in a hug and held out his hand to hold mine.

"You girls okay?" he asked, releasing Nikki and stepping closer to me to put his arm around my shoulder. We both nodded our heads in unison.

"What a scare. What do you think happened here today?" he asked, sitting down on the truck next to me.

"You tell us," Jack spoke up. "This was insane. One minute the food truck is exploding and then suddenly the store goes up in flames. Did someone purposefully do this to us?"

"Well, technically, the food truck didn't explode. Someone threw a couple of smoke bombs and maybe a flash bomb into it. Thank God, no one was hurt. That was pretty risky, but a great distraction, if that's what they wanted," he said, standing up. "You girls well enough for me to show you something?"

We all jumped down from the truck, anxious to get to the bottom of what happened.

"Come with me to the front yard. I'll show you what we think happened to the food truck."

"What's a flash bomb?" I asked, more confused than ever. We walked as a group toward the front of Chocolate Love. By this time, it was completely dark outside, and the majority of people had gone home. There were a lot of curious stragglers standing by watching the clean-up, but for the most part the grounds were filled with only first-responders. By some miracle, the only people that were hurt in tonight's madness were me and Adelle. The rest of the crowd had scattered fast enough that they'd escaped any injury. Thank God.

"Look. Over there," I broke off, distracted by a shrouded figure standing behind a tree near the front of the store. Alerted by my attention, the figure turned and made a bee-line away from the store.

"What, Kelly?" Nikki asked, halting in her tracks.

It was really more the cape that I recognized first, not the person. It was too dark to see their face, whoever it was. The hood on the cape bloused out in a way I'd seen before. And just like that, the figure was quickly escaping my line of vision.

"It's the cape in the video. The one that shot Tony," I said, bolting in the direction of the cape.

"What?" I heard Nikki yell out.

I continued in full sprint in the direction of the caped figure that was quickly retreating into the shadows. If they got away, all of this would remain unsolved, and we would be open for further attacks.

My feet pumped as fast as they could and my breathing, although labored, remained steadfast. My determination to unmask the person who tried to destroy my entire family led the way.

Jack ran next to me, eventually bypassing me with his long legs and catching up with the cape. In a flash, Jack's long arms were able to successfully reach out and spin the shoulders of the caped culprit around to face me. Instantly I knew why the pace was so slow. The cape hid the body of an old woman. A wrinkled, angry face glared at me with such intense hatred, I ground to a halt and recoiled backwards.

"Come on, let's dance, Kelly!" Bernadette called out to me from across the floor. "You married my son tonight. You've made me so happy," she smiled at me. Her left arm swung out quickly to the side in a jerking motion. "This is the best day of my life," she said warmly, hugging me close to her.

I allowed her to embrace me, happy that everything had turned out so well with the wedding festivities after months of stressful preparations and details.

I knew I'd seen that arm jerking movement before. It was my ex-mother-in-law. She killed Tony. My mind had registered something familiar about the way her arm jerked to pull the gun on Tony. Now it all made sense.

"You never deserved my son!" Steve's mother, Bernadette, screamed at me. Her voice was weak but filled with devilish fury. I could tell by the way her eyes lit up and the sarcastic smile twisted on her face; she'd been waiting for this moment for a long time. Her haggard appearance, wrinkled skin, and hunched over body made her look thirty years older than my mother, who I knew to be her same age. She reminded me of an old, cursed witch from one of my books as a child.

"What?" was all I could manage, shocked by the reveal.

She didn't struggle to break free of Jack's grip. She seemed content to face me with her hatred and own what she had done.

"You destroyed us. All of us, when you sent my Stevie to jail. Do you have any idea? Do you know what suffering you've caused us?" she screamed out into the air, clawing at her chest dramatically.

Nikki, Detective Pavlik, and a number of police officers joined in around us, which was great because Bernadette appeared to be in full confession mode.

"Yes, I set the fires. I wanted you all to burn. Burn in shame for what you did to our family," Bernadette screeched, pointing her bony finger at me.

No, no, no. She had it all wrong. Her son was the one that cheated on me. Her son was the one that tried to kill his pregnant mistress. How was I in the wrong? This woman had it twisted.

"She was behind all of this. She couldn't live with the shame of her husband cheating on her, so she set him up for murder," I heard Bernadette snarl in court. I refused to look at her and register the accusations that were coming out of her mouth. They were so outlandish that I couldn't bear to look. Had Steve really sold her that story? Was she that stubborn in her love for her child that she would actually buy this? Was her superiority complex that great that she thought a child born from her blood would never be capable of doing what he had done?

My breath caught at the flashback of my days in court when Steve was on trial for murder. She still believed the lie. She still thought the whole thing was my fault.

I shook my head vehemently, looking her straight in the eye this time.

"Do you even know what happened to us? To my husband? Do you even care?" she yelled out at me. "Stevie's dad never worked again since the day his son went to jail. We lost our health, our business, our home," she rambled on, even when two police officers took hold of her from Jack and slowly started to escort her away. She allowed them to take her, but continued her rant, twisting her body quickly and dramatically, so that she could face me head on to yell, "You ruined us!" she screamed.

Nikki walked up behind me and put her arm around me.

"Wait!" I yelled, motioning for the police officers to stop pulling her away.

"Did you kill Tony?" I demanded, determined to take full advantage of her obvious need for confession.

"Who?" she asked, stopping in her tracks and scrunching her mouth up in a snarl.

"The guard. Did you kill the guard in Florida? In my parent's building?"

"Do you know how many years I've been waiting for an opportunity like that? When that Ford fool broke out of Stevie's jail, I had my chance. Everyone was distracted looking for him and wondering if he was connected to you somehow. That reporter even hunted me down and told me her theories about Stevie getting married again and wanting you dead. None of that was true. But she told me where you were. And I thought if I killed you, they might say it was Franklin Ford, not me."

The officers let her ramble on, probably seeing this was the window for a full confession.

"So I decided it was my time to go after you and your parents in their Miami castle in the sky. Only you weren't there. The guard informed me of that when I tried to get in. I lied and said we were scheduled to meet. When he started asking questions, I shot him. I didn't want him to be able to identify me. But you know what, now I don't care."

"But Franklin Ford is in jail now. You wouldn't have been able to pin it on him if you exploded all of us tonight," I yelled, finding a hole in her story.

"I don't care anymore," Bernadette shrieked at the top of her lungs. "Don't you see!" she bellowed like a witch burning at the stake.

I gulped, not surprised by her cruelty but still a bit shocked at her ability to kill someone like that in cold blood. And her aim, for that matter. How was Steve's mom such a good shot?

"Don't look at me like that, Kelly. My Stevie is a good boy. This," she said, waving her hands in the direction of the ruins of Chocolate Love, "is all because of what you did. I wish they would have all died," she snarled at me, hatred pouring from her mouth. "I wish you never stepped foot into my son's life. You've caused so much suffering. You deserve to hurt. You are a manipulative, destructive devil."

"Alright, that's enough," Nikki's voice cut in. "Let's get one thing straight. You did this, you crazy witch. You and your entitled son are going to rot in hell. And I have to thank you for tonight. Now you'll both be in jail and the world will be a better place," she said, stepping in front of me.

"Now, get crazy out of here," Nikki said, motioning with her thumb for the police to take her away.

Bernadette let out a soul sucking howl of despair. With great difficulty, she was dragged away and shoved into a police car. I watched for just a second, and then finally turned away. It was too much to bear, watching my ex-mother-in-law, the one that cooked Thanksgiving dinner at my house, helped us move into our apartment, and nursed me back to health when I came down with chicken pox in California. How was it possible that the wild animal being twisted into a police car was the same person?

It was too much. I hid my head into the crook of Nikki's shoulder and cried.

"It's okay. It's all over now," Nikki said, holding me close.

Chapter 48

"We're all set, Ms. Clark. Please follow me," the guard said, buzzing me in through one of many barred entranceways.

I looked behind me again, still shocked at my decision to come alone. No Nikki. No Jack. Just me. The flight had been long but peaceful, and the hours allowed me extra time to go over and over what I planned to say. All it would take was less than three minutes. A few sentences and the presentation of proof. That was it. I wouldn't allow anymore.

The sterile hallways here scared me more than anything. Every white brick seemed to verify the theory I'd had over the last three years, almost four, that Steve had been imprisoned here. There was nothing to look at, nothing to do here. There wasn't even color on the walls. The only thing to look at was the past and the future. Present was a white, blank canvas for these inmates.

My mind naturally ran to my future. At least, what my anticipation of the future was. It was all based on occurrences in my very near past.

In the past week, Nikki, in true Nikki form, had bulldozed the old building of Chocolate Love, with her father-in-law's permission of course, considering he was the one that had gifted her the store after he retired. She was working on plans to rebuild in the spring. When she'd heard that the building was not salvageable, she had taken Bob's hand, looked at her husband and asked, "Want to rebuild? We could just keep Bean in Love going?"

I'd been in the room with them and was not surprised one bit when he merely nodded his head and Nikki rolled out a piece of paper on the table, detailing her plans for the future Chocolate Love.

"You've been working on this?" I'd guessed.

"For years," she smiled, though there was no mistaking the light tears in her eyes. "It's hard to say goodbye to that old girl, but this will be fabulous."

"I know it will," I'd said, reaching across the table for her hand. I had no problem allowing my tears of pride to fall on my face. Nikki's positive spirit was going to once again, be proven as unbreakable. She was what I aspired to be someday.

"And now we can rebuild the kitchens so that Adelle doesn't need to outsource. We can accommodate her production as well," Nikki beamed. "Oh, and most important of all! Better accommodations for Mom and Dad's first floor, private suite for when they move back to Geneva," she said, referencing their recent decision to put their Miami condo on the market.

Adelle was more determined than ever to make Adelle's Pastries a hit. That horrible night of the fire had brought tons of media coverage to both Nikki and Adelle's businesses. And you know what they say, all press is good press. The media had taken tons of interest in my sisters and their determination to rebuild after that horrific night. They were even in talks with All Sweets Network to star in a reality series, highlighting their adventures in the dessert and coffee businesses. My sisters were excited, and ironically, happier than I'd seen them in years, considering their place of business had just been knocked to smithereens.

Mike and I had closed the safety deposit box account together a few days after the fire. He didn't agree with my insistence on handling the contents on my own, but when I brought him to the bank and showed him the card that tracked the visits of the account owners, his face had turned ghost white. Once we were behind the door in the little closet room, I shared what I thought Steve had done. After Mike had been suckered into opening the account, Steve had come in posing as Mike to get some woman, posing as me, on the account. That was why a woman was coming after me and the key. After she had the key, she would have the ability to go in and take from the box again, posing as me once again. There were still a lot of unanswered questions. Why didn't Steve just leave a key with that woman, whoever had opened the account? Was that particular woman even alive still? That thought scared me. How evil was Steve? And why didn't he just send her to Mike to get the key? It was still a mystery to me.

I showed Mike the empty box and told him that I'd taken care of what was in it and what was in it was not enough to put his family in jeopardy. They'd already been through enough, and he'd already carried too much over these past years.

"Trust me, Mike. It's over. You've been through enough. What was there is now gone. You know I would go to the police if I thought it had to be that way. Your family has been through enough," I'd said quietly, looking him straight in the eye.

"You sure, Kelly?" Mike had asked, his blood shot eyes, meeting mine.

I'd nodded my head slowly.

"You're going to be okay?" he'd whispered.

"It's already done, Mike," I'd said.

Mike had just leaned forward, hugged me in the little closet room and whispered, "I'm so sorry. Please accept my sincere apology for getting involved with Steve."

"I will if you'll accept my apology as well. I never should have let him into this family," I'd said, knowing that things would be different between us now. We had a dirty secret to keep, which would be hard. But some secrets, though hard to hang on to, were best kept hidden. This was one skeleton I was going to be happy to leave in the closet.

The sound of a camera going off alerted me to the present. I looked around me, trying to spot where the sound had come from.

"Oh, don't worry, Ms. Clark. They're just testing out the cameras in that room for the new identification tags."

"Oh," I said. "I thought someone took my picture."

"Oh, no way. No cameras or media in here. We never allow any of that nonsense here," the guard said over his back.

His mention of the word media made me think of Diane Nosely. She'd escaped the night of the fire unharmed, but her reputation was currently taking a beating. Steve's mother, Bernadette, sticking to her history of seeking out a scapegoat, had fingered Diane Nosley as the one behind pushing her to plan the attacks. She claimed Diane had contacted her after Franklin Ford's escape and put the idea in her head about Steve motivating Franklin Ford to attack me. She even claimed Diane gave her the idea of the bomb she used to distract everyone from the fire she started in Chocolate Love. Diane had supposedly egged her on to stop anymore "misrepresentation of the family name," which seemed hilarious to me. The family name had been destroyed the second Steve had been caught. Coming after me wasn't going to save anything. If anything, it would just make it all worse.

The other thing that happened was that the cameras from the local media had caught some unflattering reactions by Diane once the fire was in full blaze. Apparently, Diane had screamed at her camera man to, "Get them burning! Try and get a shot of them burning! Darn it! They're getting out!" She'd screamed this all from her wheelchair while my family had attempted to exit out the window of Chocolate Love.

A camera man from a competing network that she'd worked with in the past and had treated poorly chose to turn his camera away from the fire and onto Diane. He'd been all too delighted to expose her for the person she was, even if it did mean missing the big story. His angle also picked up Kim and Brandi, the mean girls from Junior League, knocking people down and then nearly running over three kids when they'd tried to squeal away in their car. When the upstanding members of Junior League saw this video, they had no choice but to finally impeach Kim and Brandi. Apparently, the word was they had just had "too much" of their antics and were looking for a reason to rid themselves of these jokesters. Although Adelle was offered the role, she'd turned it down to concentrate on her new business, but recommended a friend that she trusted to be the right person for the job. By all accounts, the Junior League was once again back on track.

As for Diane Nosely, once her obnoxious behavior at the fire scene aired, she went into a very unDiane-like hiatus from the spotlight and had not been seen since. There was still a question as to whether she would be charged as an accomplice to the fire. My guess was probably not, knowing Bernadette's reputation for fingering the wrong person.

"Okay, take a seat here. Give me just a minute," the guard said, stepping out of the room.

I sat down on a small plastic chair, a wall of glass in front of me and a small, black phone hanging on the wall next to me. Another small closet room.

In order to deal with my anxiety, I pulled out the two pieces of paper I'd brought with me. I wanted them ready, so I could make this quick and then leave. Eye contact wasn't even necessary.

Looking at the pieces of paper reminded me of the one Jack and I were waiting for back in Geneva.

"Still hasn't sent it back?" I'd asked Jack over dinner a few nights ago, referring to the sheet Callie was supposed to have signed and sent back to us immediately, so that we could get married. It would also mean, of course, that she could also get married to her unsuspecting new gentleman.

Jack had merely nodded his head no and looked down at his untouched plate.

"She will," I'd said. "Let's eat," I'd nudged, wanting him to enjoy the dinner he'd worked so hard on.

Somewhere on the other side of the glass, a door opened and the sound of chains rattling drew me back to the present.

As much as I had planned this out in my head to simply present my evidence then leave without making eye contact, I was unable to tear my eyes away from the sight in front of me. Steve, the man I once knew as my husband, stood before me, a shadow of who he used to be. His skin had turned a sickly yellow, and his eyes moved wildly around the room until they settled on me. He had suffered a significant weight loss, making the skin on his face sag beneath his cheekbones. His once full head of hair was now buzzed tight to his head, revealing his receding hairline. The thought of him once disguising himself as my brother-in-law, Mike, seemed impossible now. He looked like a cancer patient, fighting for his life.

My anxiety faded quickly, and as much as I hated to admit it, there was a part of me that felt sorry for him right out of the gate. He was clearly suffering. He was paying for his sins. Didn't they feed him here?

He plopped down on the chair seated on the other side of the glass and looked at me, his eyes wild with confusion and something else. It was hard to tell what.

Steve grabbed for the phone and stuck his chin up, motioning me to pick up the one on my side of the glass. The way he did it made me come back into focus. It was like he thought I would just do what he wanted immediately after not seeing him for almost four years. No way. He may have been able to pull that before, but that girl was gone. This new Kelly Clark wasn't going to be bossed around by the likes of him.

Instead of picking up the phone, I reached down and stuck a piece of paper up to the glass. I allowed a few silent moments to pass before picking up the phone. Steve squinted at the sheet in confusion.

"This is a receipt for the safety deposit box. We closed the account," I said, into the phone that I'd finally picked up.

Steve took his eyes off the sheet and watched me. After a moment, I removed the piece of paper from the glass.

"And this is a receipt for a donation to the American Heart Association for eighteen thousand dollars," I said, slapping the form onto the glass window for him to see.

Steve squinted his eyes again and read the form. I didn't know what I was expecting, but the look on his face wasn't it. He looked up at me expectantly, as though he was waiting for me to present more.

I didn't have anything else.

"It's over, Steve. The money is gone. You have to leave me alone now. Leave us alone. I have nothing else that you want," I said, doing my best to sound threatening and scary.

"Kelly," Steve said weakly into the phone, his voice barely a whisper. "I would never hurt you," he said in a sad pathetic voice.

His comment struck me harder than any threatening thing he could have said. It caught me completely off guard.

Just as I was about to hang up the phone, Steve put his hand to the glass and yelled,

"Wait!"

Shocked, I stood with the phone still to my ear, watching the guard approach him, ready to pounce. I didn't know what to do.

Steve sat back down, quickly tucking his hands back down on the table.

"It wasn't me, Kelly. You know it wasn't. Look at me. You know me. I'm innocent."

I shook my head, and closed my eyes, ready for this to be over. This wasn't what I expected. Anger and hostility would have been easier to deal with, not this pathetic, sad, delusional whimpering.

I wasn't buying it, and I think he could tell because he changed direction.

"My mother set me up. You see now how crazy she is," he said into the phone. "I figured it all out while I was in here."

My mouth gaped open, wondering if he'd gotten word yet what happened to Bernadette. He must have. It was all over the news. He was going to throw her under the bus now?

"She was behind the whole thing," Steve snarled, getting a little more aggressive. His teeth bared, I saw that they had at least remained intact. Perhaps things weren't as bad as I initially thought. In fact, as his anger built a bit, he began to look more like himself. His face reddened with color and his shoulders squared back.

"When I get out of here, I'm going to prove it. And you can help me, Kelly. You've got the proof. I still love you, Kelly. We can be together again," he said, trying to sound suave and loving. He touched the glass softly this time, as though he were caressing my face.

I recoiled back and hung up the phone quickly, standing up to leave.

"I'm ready to go," I said, to the guard stationed on my side of the glass. This was a mistake. What I'd shown him wasn't enough. He wasn't satisfied. I'd missed something. I was sure of that now. I still had something he wanted. I could tell by the way he was attempting to sweet talk me in his sick and twisted way.

"Wait! Don't go," Steve said, banging on the glass with a fist, still holding the phone. When his guard grabbed him from behind, he started screaming words I couldn't make out. I turned one last time to look at him and saw Steve completely unhinged. From what I could tell, it looked as though he was yelling my name repeatedly.

Spittle flew from his mouth and he struggled until a sea of guards filled the room. I turned, unable to watch them roughhouse him into submission.

"Get me out of here," I implored, desperate to put this scene behind me. It felt like I'd only made things worse. This had been a huge mistake.

My mind raced to my decision to burn the money. His money. I'd taken on eighteen thousand dollars of new debt that my friend William had graciously loaned me, just to make sure I'd donated clean money to charity and now it seemed dumb. The money hadn't bothered Steve in the slightest. What else could he want from me? Maybe I was wrong the whole time about the key. Maybe it was something else?

I walked quickly down the sterile hall, anxious to drive away from this horrible mad house and get back to Geneva.

The apartment was burned down now. If it was something left in the apartment above Chocolate Love, it was gone now. The first thing I would do when I got home would be to rip apart all of my things at Jack's and search for whatever it was Steve was after.

It certainly wasn't the box. I'd emptied the box. There was nothing left. The money was all that was there.

But wait.

There was something else in the box. The pink teddy bear.

"You've got the proof," Steve had said.

The proof of what? We caught you red-handed, attempting to kill your mistress and your unborn child.

"Proof of what?" I said to myself aloud, more confused than ever but sure of one thing.

It wasn't over.

Becky's Cinnamon Chip Scones

Yield: 18 small scones prep time: 20 min. cook time: 10-12 minutes

Ingredients:

> 3 cups flour
> ½ cup sugar
> 1 ½ Tablespoons baking powder
> ¾ teaspoon salt
> Fillers: 1/2 cup of cinnamon chips (can also use berries, chocolate chips, raisins, etc.)
> 2 cups heavy whipping cream (need a little extra for brushing)

Optional: brush lightly with extra whipping cream and sprinkle with coarse sugar before baking

Directions:
1. Preheat oven to 425 degrees Fahrenheit. Adjust baking rack to middle-low position. Line a baking sheet with parchment paper or use a baking stone (preferred method).
2. In a large bowl, whisk the flour, sugar, baking powder and salt. Stir in cinnamon chips.
3. Add the 2 cups heavy whipping cream to the dry mixture and mix with spatula until combined.
4. Flour a work surface and separate dough into 3 equal balls. Press each dough ball into a disc and cut into 6 equal

wedges. Use a pastry brush and brush lightly with cream and sprinkle with coarse sugar. Separate the scones and line them on the baking stone with a little space in between each one.

5. Bake 10-12 minutes or until lightly golden on top and cooked through.

Dear Reader,

I hope you've enjoyed *Take the Donut.* I'd appreciate your review on all of my books! Please visit my Amazon author page: https://www.amazon.com/Annie-Hansen/e/B00CXSUTCQ. Feel free to stop by my website (http://kellyclarkmystery.com) to learn about Kelly's latest adventures and where to find me for book signings. Thanks so much!

Annie Hansen

Acknowledgements

Thank you to my husband, Brent Hansen, my partner in all things.

Thank you to my mom, Gail McCarter, for always reviewing the first draft.

Thank you to my editor, Carrie Reitz. I really enjoyed working with you.

Thank you to my graphic designer, Cristen Leifheit, for all of your artistic work on the series.

Thank you, James McCarter (Uncle Jim), Retired Cook County State's Attorney, for your help with the criminal aspect of the series.

Thank you, Julie Oleszek, my writing friend and motivator. Without our author meetings, I would lose focus.

Thank you, Becky Wit, for your yummy Cinnamon Chip Scones recipe.

And a special thank you to Wheaton Fire Department-Tower 38-Gold shift, and my friend, Lieutenant Chris Hunecke, for allowing me to spend the day at the department to help come up with ideas for this book.

About the Author

Annie Hansen is a partner with Hansen Search Group, a staffing firm she co-founded with her husband and business partner, Brent Hansen in 2001. Annie is the author of The Kelly Clark Mystery Series and can be reached through her website: http://kellyclarkmystery.com. She lives with her family in the western suburbs of Chicago.

Made in United States
North Haven, CT
29 March 2024

50671958R00204